W9-BBZ-778

A TOM DOHERTY ASSOCIATES BOOK / NEW YORK

AN ANTI-LOVE STORY

GARY S. KADET

D/s

Copyright © 2000 by Gary S. Kadet

This book is printed on acid-free paper.

A Forge Book
Published by Tom Doherty Associates, LLC
175 Fifth Avenue
New York, NY 10010

www.tor.com

Forge® is a registered trademark of
Tom Doherty Associates, LLC.

Design by Jane Adele Regina
Title art by Peter Lutjen

Library of Congress Cataloging-in-Publication Data

Kadet, Gary S.
    D/s . an anti-love story / Gary S. Kadet —1st ed.
    p. cm.
    "A Tom Doherty Associates book."
    ISBN 0-312-84884-6 (acid-free paper)
    1. Sexual dominance and submission—Fiction.
    I. Title.

    PS3561.A353 D7 2000
    813'.6—dc21   00-026463

First Edition: June 2000

Printed in the United States of America

0 9 8 7 6 5 4 3 2 1

For the Davis women: Henrietta, Lorraine and Leigh.

ACKNOWLEDGMENTS

The author wishes to express here his profound gratitude to the following, without whose help *D/s* simply would never have come about: Karla Zounek, my visionary editor and "the most efficient woman in publishing"; Jon Land, for all his various efforts on my behalf; Marc Songini, crime maven and boy sleuth; Linda Marrow, for her exceptional savvy and guidance; Phil Reed, for his input and kindness; the *Boston Book Review* for its invaluable faith and support; Jan Brown, for putting up with me; Lois Johnson, for a myriad of tasks; the late Dan MacMillan for the unspoken and the unspeakable; Jack Powers, unsung bohemian poet, reluctant professional saint and my first encouragement; and Alexander Alarid, longtime sybarite and friend.

If you were queen of pleasure,
And I were king of pain,
We'd hunt down love together,
Pluck out his flying-feather,
And teach his feet a measure,
And find his mouth a rein;
If you were queen of pleasure,
And I were king of pain.

—A Match, ALGERNON CHARLES SWINBURNE

PROLOGUE

So, you think it's about whips and chains.

Handcuffs, leg-irons, posture-bars, gags and bits? Someone spread-eagled on the rack, tensed for the kiss of the cat—the long, smooth impact of an Australian bullwhip after it snaps clean in the air to make a tremor in the ears? You think it's about masters and mistresses cinched and pinched by fearsome fetishwear of leather, grommets, buckles, corsets, chaps, polished PVC or miraculously shiny latex glistening as if wet?

You think it's about sex—and you privately find some appeal in it and publicly revile it to save your skin? All right, so you're not kinky. Fine.

I am.

I admit it, though I know it has no pride or power in itself. I used to think it had that, but I was mistaken.

That wasn't the sex. It was the thing that scares everyone into the next room and makes them spend all their life savings on something slightly less reliable than playing the market.

It wasn't the S&M, the B&D, the rough wonder of the puissant sex I had coat my skin and surround my body, enter it up through the center and split it down the spine. It wasn't every elegantly inexcusable dildo and toy of the whole phenomenon I have taken so close to the wild heart of my own life called Dominance and Submission—or simply "D/s." No, it was the same old thing, no matter how you shake your head, no matter how you disapprove of a twist like me.

It was the love.

It was the love that intruded on my tattered life, ruined my fragile heart, broke the spirit everyone thought was inured to breakage. I believed it too. But of course my life and my mind have both since gone beyond belief.

As love destroyed me, so D/s reclaimed me. As belief unmoored me, so cynicism anchored me in some safe and foreign harbor. To the life that moves forward in success like the shark in the ocean, safety is death. To the life that stands still to live for its own sake in a small niche, safety is another hour, another day of the life nearly lost.

I live like that now.

You wonder how I keep it all together? This complex life of mine?

Balance the D/s sublimity with the business of expected "vanilla" sublimation? It's simpler than you ever considered: I do it because I have no hope, no love; and because my dreams are all dark, spindly things, I live them out fully now and suffer no separation from reality, no driven dichotomy—integrity at last. I take my reality straight, no chaser of fantasy, no mix of aspirations, no yearning sweetness or hopeful bitters in my sleep like liquor or dry waking time.

I sleep empty and live fully. I live in safety, my weakness and wounds protected by good sense, by the conservative estimate, the retirement plan, the career track, the vested friendship, the tax-deferred affinity.

And I am, like so many, so dead and buried in this life of mine.

Dead without an afterlife, dead without a prayer.

It's a better plot than some in the graveyard and not so good as others. But, like any journey that ends in death, there is a chronicle, a log of sorts, not faithfully kept, as faith was so often broken, but ardently remembered, visited so often like the ghost of my own dead life. This is the tale it tells, the sheer story that lies silently struggling in decay beneath this granite-gray, heavy headstone I carry with me to work and back.

Let me tell you how I died and perhaps by the end my soul will be free. Let me tell you about the pain. Let me tell you about the pain, and about love, the destroyer.

Let me tell you about how D/s turned the world back upon its axis to make me see again with fresh eyes before death blinded me forever.

Let me tell you before I undress, but for my shoes, and climb up to the stirrups on the chains of the suspension rack, reach for the fur-lined cuffs and open myself before you like a gift—so that I may have the chance to live again and welcome love, the destroyer, to bite at my skin.

I suppose you don't want to know anything about me, but I promise it will make the story better. Maybe you'll find some point of personal identification in my little history—something to admire, maybe understand or examine with pity.

You say you have no use for pity, but pity is an under-rated emotion. I'll take it, if it's real. I'll take any real feeling now, even that. And there is an ethic in pity, even when it's just a *pro forma* social construct designed to hide the routine hate, greed, terror, am bition and contempt for its object. If there is a god, this is where he lives before he visits the tele-temples, the stately monuments to suffering deadened with comfort, or changes his sex and direction to give the techno-pagans their minimal due. God lives in pity, true or false, and every object of pity is blessed because every corruption and gluttonous crime on this earth is committed first and foremost with them in mind, at their expense and in their name.

The meek shall inherit the earth— and submission will rule it, just as strength will eventually, inevitably be overcome by weakness.

You think I am exalting my position as a *submissive?*

I don't have the detachment to say. Let my story tell you.

Let it tell me too. Let it tell—*just before my skin listens to your whip.*

ONE

It started the way most disasters do—with a long, slow, potent convergence of scattered natural forces upon a single weakness that causes a collapse to reveal another and yet another until everything shifts, breaks down, falls apart. In my case, as in most modern disasters, it started with a meeting.

I was a freelance writer, a journalist, I suppose, but no one at *The Miltown Register* would have called you that if that's what you did—*freelance*. If you wrote for these elitists from the outside, you were a generic *writer*, bar-coded and shelved until needed to fill a hole in the layout. Fortunately, such servility from afar suited my diffident personality, my distrust of enforced operation within groups governed by secret personal pecking orders and bathroom vendettas, as well as my towering distaste for the industrial barnyard effect of most modern offices. In fact, from time to time on those rare occasions when I would set foot in the anonymous physical plant of the *Register*, I would get the feeling from looking at the average staffer, clacking doggedly away at his dumb terminal walled off in his little stall, that a maintenance man would come by and connect metal-ended hoses to his genitals and brain like a milking machine to the teats of a cow and routinely pump him dry.

In my little fantasy, however—for reasons that will be made clear later on—women were exempt from this treatment. They just minded their own business and went on typing.

So, I had a nice life. It's true that I had no renown, even within the little tidepool community of Miltown proper, a puddle stocked almost exclusively by bigger fish than me, but things were far from hard. Since freelancing and remote-control servitude suited me well, my assignments from the dailies and weeklies and insubstantial tabloids dwindled down persistently to a single contract with the *Reg-*

isterer. It was one of the benefits of a hidden office skirmish and petty personal politicking that usually falls to a big fish rather than to one of the plankton like me.

A position in the *Life-Arts* section became available with the death of some ancient, overdone, very local critic more concerned with affiliate PBS-TV appearances and the onset of Alzheimer's than with anything else. While the staffer who had been banging out said critic's weekly column "Round the Towne" with covert blessings from above in addition to his other work was rewarded for his discreet service with an editorship. He had effectively jumped a rung on the evolutionary ladder of features staff life. Naturally, the fighting over the vacant columnar slot within the section was so bitter and severe that the newly anointed editor decided that the fairest and best solution was to piss everyone off equally rather than to show favoritism. The slot went to a capable, well-used, outside freelancer who could be counted on to show a low profile—me.

Two years later and the battle lines of unforgiving hatred and resentment around my little slot were *still* drawn in the creative, spirited, arts-oriented and life-affirming atmosphere of the *Life-Arts* section. I made it a point to drop in every now and again just to watch them all trying to hide the wildly seething anger that hissed behind their taut, clipped, decorous demeanors and to indulge my little fantasy.

Unfortunately, there were drawbacks to owing your professional existence to the initial swaggering error of a rookie editor. First, he refused to get rid of the moldy "Round the Towne" title for the column. Second, because of the first, readers persisted in the belief that my doddering predecessor was still finding willing ambitious ghosts to help him churn out columns vastly inferior to mine, despite the fact that he was dead and my name was there (albeit in tiny type) in the by-line. The managing editor himself, that once-national news figure making a whistle stop at our paper on his stupendous career downslide, kept referring to me by my dead predecessor's name— and apparently no one ever thought enough of me at the paper to even make a joke out of it.

I was the house anonymity.

So, it was inevitable that the rookie editor would, after a suitable period of mourning and retrenchment, try to stir up the habitual fear of a shake-up in the section and cancel out his first mistake all at once by boldly and shrewdly making another.

People are forever moving backward, remaking and reshaping what they have done. And even an editor has considerable trouble resisting that ceaselessly destructive tendency to *edit*.

He phoned me and set a lunch meeting—something friendly and informal, he said, to talk over some ideas and possible directions for the column. No big deal.

I had no qualms at all, as I hung up from our breezy, humorously ironic conversation, that I was in nothing but trouble.

My live-in girlfriend of seven years picked out a jacket, shirt and tie for me to wear to this meeting called for by my invisible benefactor-turned-nemesis. She helped me with the knot, presented me with a breakfast of bananas on toast with coffee and lovingly gave me a lift to the commuter rail train station, cautioning me all the while to watch my behavior. "Don't come across as an instigator," she said. "Just say 'yes' to whatever they want and keep your column. It's good money." We then fell back to the standard discussion of our much-put-off marriage. As usual, this soured my stomach, because I wound up having to swallow the fact that a large, looming doubt that lived far better than I did in the shadows of my inner history prevented our moving together in that direction. I had no answer for her, yet I loved her. Bitterly.

I gave in as I always did: against all doubt while marshaling every ounce of ambiguity contained in the phrase "I'll try."

It wasn't enough, but it got me on the train.

I skimmed a book of literary short stories, all of which seemed to be about suppressed homosexuality, the apathy and entropy of post-industrial middle-class suburban home life—and the muddle-headed insistence of all concerned to travel an intended path to well-being that led inexorably to the oblivion that concluded each piece. Only we savvy readers could see it, silent, helpless Cassandras watching disaster befall these stodgy, persistently bland character-ciphers who were too busy finding solace in "small, good things" to admit what was happening. Clichés of quiet desperation, I thought, closing the book, watching the trees and the telephone poles march by against an empty blue sky as the train hit the boonies. I then added, somewhat cagily and aloud with eyes closed, "My readers."

I entered the citadel—actually a rehabbed cannery with the aspect of a blockhouse and the quaint, epic charm of Hitler's bunker—informed the dowager receptionist of my presence and was immediately set upon by jackals seeking dead flesh.

"Duck your head and feint left," greeted blue-leatherette–clad layout designer Sue Horoschow, swiftly waddling by on platforms.

"I heard about your meeting," said "Edge" Tatty, senior arts writer in his frayed brown suit with the black elbow patches. He had earned the name "Edge" not because of his fondness for covering interior design, *feng-shui* and the art of flower arranging, but from where he firmly set his colleagues' teeth. "A word of advice then: get 'em young, treat 'em rough, tell 'em nothin'!"

He was positively boisterous with false glee.

"What? *Editors?*" I queried as straight man.

"Yes—if you can. It certainly works with *interns.*"

"I was worried. I thought for a moment you were going to say 'girlfriends.' "

"That," he sniffed, "would be out of character."

Too tense for any more pointless repartee, I let this opportunity pass. "What have you heard?"

"Why, you're next up in the food chain, Perry. Time to get involved in the struggle for survival against hungry predators. You're about due, you know, and Happy Boy must be served—his *lunch.*" He puffed the "ch" of "lunch" out of his mouth like a thick smoke ring.

Happy Boy was my benefactor/nemesis, the wunderkind *Life-Arts* editor who was showing absolutely no talent for the cut-throat intrigue necessary to land him a yet higher position in the editorial pecking order. Rumor had it, in fact, that he had "Petered out"—reached his greatest level of incompetence, maxed out hierarchically speaking and might any day now be shuffled off to his own honorific "critic-at-large" column with *Life-Arts* restructured out from under him should he continue to play the part of philosopher-king on bad acid.

"You look *shook*, Per," Edge said in a wheezy monotone, placing

a grubby hand on my shoulder. "Listen," he muttered *sotto voce*, his
breath tickling my ear, "try to enjoy yourself at your meeting. And
if you want to press Happy Boy's buttons, just call him the Lifer-
Arts editor, or something, *okay?*" Edge winked and withdrew. "I got
to fly."

He was being coy. He knew I knew that Happy Boy had
punched out another editor who had accepted a job in a better market
at his farewell dinner for having made that crack. Everybody knew
this, of course, but our dear readers. "Later, Edge," I said.

"Join us for martinis and lies at one at The Roisterer, if you
can't get better therapy elsewhere."

I considered it, and reread the "Happy" version of my "Round
the Towne" column for that week until the fat finger of the mutilator
of my work poked my shoulder.

"Good to see you, Patetick. It's been awhile."

I lifted my head to stare straight into Happy Boy's boiled-shirted
gut, then stood and shook his plump, clammy hand. He wasn't wearing a jacket, his tie was loose and he was too tanned to have gotten
that way lying on a beach. He towered over me, a sneer on his
generous lips and a dewy, feminine look in his long-lashed eyes.

"It's been too long, Crane." I damn near said "Happy Boy."

We small-talked down cramped corridors defined by cubicle di-
viders until we hit a conference room flagged as vacant. I was amazed
by his walk—despite the hefty, college athlete's build undermined
by stress-food and expense account dinners, he had the cool, delicate
sashay of a runway model as he minced down the hallways ahead of
me, clearly eager to bring me to our destination. He showed me in,
and I recognized one of the junior copy editors sitting at the table.
I was hungry, but I knew, despite our phone conversation of the day
before, that the only lunch would be me.

"Take a seat," Happy Boy ordered.

I shrugged and sat.

"Where shall we eat?" I asked sweetly. "Or shall we order in?"
To my delight, Happy Boy's lips twisted into a mocking pucker and
his eyes narrowed. His protégé smirked nervously.

"This *isn't* a lunch meeting," Happy Boy said with exaggerated
grimness.

"This is about your copy," said Happy Boy's protégé hopefully. He had a name, Steve or something, but let's just refer to him by the chief characteristic that our little confab brought out in him: Eager Stooge. "You've been turning in bad copy," he announced, boldly letting his eyes meet mine.

"Bad enough so that I've had to rewrite it," Happy Boy knelled rather than chimed. "And I'm not here to do *rewrites!*"

"Libelous," said Eager Stooge, crossing his arms over his narrow chest that was inadequately padded by an argyle sweater. "We're *exposed.*"

It was bad. I had been ambushed, and Happy Boy was standing over me, making threatening gestures like a schoolyard bully. I was sure he wanted me to react so that we could get into it physically and then he could win by sheer bulk, with the only witness in the room sitting squarely and none-too–securely in his voluminous pocket.

I smiled and sat back in my chair, fearful as hell. "Libel? I don't see how that could be when this is a column, not a straight news spot."

"But I say it *is* a straight news spot." Both of Happy Boy's fat fists quaked the table when he slammed them down at once just inches in front of me.

I squelched all trembling as my blood sugar dropped below life-support. "But it's set out as an omnibus review—snippets of events delivered in brief, snappy phrases and single sentence 'graphs," I said. "The title *implies* it."

"That's not how anyone sees it but you," said Eager Stooge, hugging his sweater if not himself. "Your editorializations have got to stop, one way or another."

"*Implies* it?" Happy Boy growled. "*Implies?*" Both palms raised up and smacked down against the edge of the table, thick fingers grasping it, knuckles whitening like grubs before my eyes as Happy Boy began to snort with little breaths through his nostrils like a steer directly in my face. I resisted blinking. "This is a *news*paper, Patetick. Nobody gets anywhere around here by *implying* anything."

I stifled an urge to correct that thought and answered the assault calmly, still sitting back apparently unmoved, blood sugar and cognitive ability both plummeting into the noontime abyss. "Gee—I thought I was improving on the old column, which seemed largely to fabricate its content, never confirming quotes or even checking sources whenever it bothered to include anything newsy at all, instead of just a series of bluenose opinions. Or *editorializations,* if you like."

"I *wrote* that column, you little fuck," Happy Boy sneered, his lips unnervingly close to mine, "and I don't have to say I did it better than you, because everybody here knows anything I do is better than you. I've been a gallery artist, a critic, a playwright, *and* a fast-track editor. I am way beyond that column now. I know more about it than you do and you will do it my way or say good-bye. I can get any intern to do that column better than you and for *free.*"

Eager Stooge was unprepared for this tack. I could see that he had a list of my alleged stylistic errors of commission to neatly read off, but the methodology of his patron left him no room for safe initiative. All he could do was act as a one-man cheering squad to his boss' one-man home football team and hope to stay out of the line of scrimmage.

"*Every*body at the copy desk knows it's true," Eager Stooge oozed, then winced slightly as if it were a given that Happy Boy's wrath might come down upon him too.

"Why *not* get an intern to do it then, and save the paper some money?" I asked equably, trying to ignore the little flecks that flew out of Happy Boy's nose and mouth as he continued breathing in my face. "Oh yes," I corrected myself, "but you're not here to do rewrites." I rolled away to safety backwards in my chair.

Happy Boy straightened up, composed himself and made a show of holding his temper. "I want you to do it right so that I don't have to touch it. I want *A-wire* copy from you, straight local news and nothing else. No more *libel.*"

"Opinion isn't libel in a column, Crane." I turned to the Stooge. "You at the copy desk—how long have you been at it? You look new. Maybe you didn't know it was a column?" He grabbed for his list.

"You aren't well-known enough to be a columnist!" Happy Boy spat, literally. "Steve, on the other hand, is an excellent copy editor."

His face exploded into a brief smile, he shot a curt nod at Eager Stooge, then resumed his target fix on me.

"I am a very experienced copy editor," Eager Stooge sang airily.

"It is *not* a column," Happy Boy raged, balling his fists tight and getting too close to me again.

I sighed heavily with the condescension of a well-trained slave who has a better sense of his place in the scheme of things than his masters do. "You know I'll do it any way you want, Crane. Just tell me how you want it, *specifically*. Maybe you'd like to discuss it outside? You look . . . uncomfortable in this stuffy room."

As I said this, I had the fleeting thought that it might be fun to take a crack at kicking Happy Boy's considerable ass. He was bigger, sure, but fat and out of shape. I was smaller, quicker and very much *in* shape. And he had all that body fat to lug around, while I had only nervous muscle. I made two calm fists of my own hands to make the implication plain while he paced the room. Now, however, he just wasn't buying.

Happy Boy kicked the base of the table once so hard it made Eager Stooge involuntarily gulp. "You know what I want: boring textbook *news*. No style, no opinion, no creative writing, just an enumeration of local events! Can you do that or not, Patetick?"

"It's not rocket science," the Stooge risked saying.

I wanted to say, "Not even rocket science is rocket science," but that would have meant open acknowledgment of the importance of the Stooge. I stood instead, smiling and obedient. "Certainly. I can and I will. But I write the way I write, Crane—we all have a style. I have mine and you have yours. I can't get rid of who I am for this column, but I'll do my best to accommodate you." Vomiting would have been nice, but that would have required my having stomach contents, which I was, of course, fresh out of by then.

Happy Boy looked practiced daggers at me, nearly betraying a full-lipped smile when I opened the door. Eager Stooge's shaky posture caved flaccidly into his sweater.

"Change who you are or say good-bye," Happy Boy offered me with dead cheer.

"Good-bye, Crane," I responded by way of acceptance.

I dizzily negotiated the corridors, making my way toward Metro

News Editor Habanero Bahamian's desk, feeling as though I were an idle shopper at a wholesale warehouse outlet journalist superstore, passing cubicle after cubicle of desperately typing or phone-schmoozing reporters. Miraculously, Bahamian was off the phone and his dumb terminal was moaning the theme from *Jeopardy* like some electronic dirge to human accomplishment.

"Hey, Hab," I said.

"What's up, buddy," he replied in a nonquestioning tone, not bothering to look up at me from his first round of the game, as a dulcet voice mail message played in the background fielding an out-raged call from one of the usual lunatics screaming about typos and movie times.

"Listen," I said, "could you make a big deal of appearing to have a discussion with me in which you were both openly positive and extremely interested?"

"Sure, buddy," he drawled with soft wonder in his voice, still not bothering to look up from the game. "I can act with the best of them—I did some extra work once." His eyebrows arched. "How come?"

"Well," I said clearing my throat, "it would be nice if the people around here still thought I had a job while I took the time to go out and find one."

I turned my head and waved solicitously to Happy Boy, who was standing and watching me (the Eager Stooge nowhere in sight) on the opposite end of the tens of thousands of square feet of maze-like space that had been set aside for news.

MY SUCCESS AT AN END, I OBVIOUSLY HAD TIME TO KILL. I SPLURGED on a cab back to the center of Miltown and walked around gazing at the shops, putting off the dreaded call to my girlfriend that would officially mark the death of my column.

And it *was* dead.

Happy Boy and I both knew I would write the next one *my* way, his man at the copy desk would complain strategically, it wouldn't run and that would fulfill the terms of my boilerplate contract enough for him to end it. On the off-chance that I was weak and cowardly enough to actually write it the way he wanted it, it simply wouldn't be *able* to run—sort of like entering a greyhound in a sulky race—and the same predictable events would ensue.

Another phase of my life at an end.

Was I blue? Was I in a funk?

No, I simply ducked the whole thing. I had made a space in the perfect little limbo that followed where nothing evil could happen to me until I stepped back into my life and started living it again. I stepped out for the afternoon and idly walked into a little shop with black curtains whose display window was framed in a lanyard of cheap black bullwhips and whose miniature mannequins, posed gaily on leather and rubber sex devices, could only be described as B&D Barbies and Kens. The sign above this window said "Cruel & Unusual."

This is in fact the exact point where I stepped out of my little limbo only to miss my own life by a mile. I went somewhere else. I wish I could say I knew then that my whole world had been permanently set back upon its axis, that I felt the planet shift, but, truth to be told, I simply regarded it as another secret guilty pleasure whose substance was smoke.

Spiked collars, some in chrome, some in leather, some in latex, some with locks thin as a dog's or thick enough to affect a full-grown man's posture covered a wall. There were motorcycle jackets on rack after rack—studded, painted with skulls, spiked, knotted, braided, laced, hardly made for riding—ornate zippered chaps, multitressed whips I naively thought were cat o' nine tails, scanty female sexwear outlining empty places for breasts and vulvae, chained harnesses, thigh-high laced boots, shiny PVC stiletto-heeled shoes impossible to walk in, weird metal constructs with leather cuffs I could only presume were bought and employed by rock and roller types with a highly developed personal sense of Dadaism—in a word, too much stock in too little space and all of it kinky.

I was cool, though, nonchalant and unaffected for once by the throbbing drone and angry crashing chords of the nearly atonal industrial music loudly pumping out from the miniremote speakers set in each corner of the ceiling. I looked down into the glass case, expecting to see rings, earrings, nose rings and studs—the usual frou-frou of the twenty-somethings trying to shock the world and show defiance while working office jobs or angling loans for graduate school—and saw instead *clamps*, big and small D- and O-rings of chrome, sometimes a telescoping progression of them, and *weights* suspended by chains from clamps and clips. There was a snarl of handcuffs and ankle cuffs surrounding heavy carbon-steel shackles. "My, my," I thought. "What fun for the sick-o masochists, those inscrutable pervs who enjoy pain and injury enough to let some equally psychopathic hornbug get his or her giggles by producing squeals of torment and tears of agony using this junk." If there had been a suggestion box hung on the wall, I'd have inserted a slip suggesting a name change of the store to "Serial-Killers 'R' Us"— aim straight for your market, I always say, or bent, as was more apt in this case.

If you had told me then that I happened to *be* one of the sicko masochists looking to have all those things used on me, considering my mood and state of mind at the time, I'd have broken your nose.

I was touched—a hand took mine, cold and smooth. I looked up and saw skin, *further* up and then a face. It was a lanky, pallid young woman—a Generation X student type—handling the counter and register. She was nude but for a black patent leather thong, black vinyl boots that jetted up towards her crotch and a bikini top made of chain mail whose gaps revealed much tantalizingly innocent flesh. Her lips were brushed glossy black, her fine-lined eyes were wide and bright, bruised with mascara, somewhat hazel with a rusty shock of agate running through the iris of each, and her dyed black hair was cropped in the once again fashionable Lulu Brooks or Bettie Page straight-banged crypto-ancient Egyptian 'do.

"Welcome to Cruel And Unusual," she said, releasing my hand. "What's your pleasure? Adult toys, fetish fashion or fantasy foot-wear?"

"Just browsing," I managed to say without staring too closely at all that pale, firm, smooth skin.

"Well, if you need any help, feel free to ask me. I'm Chlamydia. Meanwhile, go right ahead and gawk till you *shop!*"

"*Chlamydia?* Isn't that a sexually transmitted disease?"

"Oh, tra-la," she said with a foppish wave of her hand. "Some have been known to say that about me, but it's just an ugly rumor." She minced off with a practiced manner, ducking behind a door decorated by two pin-studded masks of tragedy that looked like something out of a horror movie, presumably for a cigarette. Either she had a feeling that I simply didn't have it together enough to shoplift or there were cameras. I bet on the latter.

Other customers came and went, as Chlamydia slinked forth from the door to wait on them—usually sniggering students asking about handcuffs on a dare or mumbling mustached men in business suits testing their hesitant fantasies out on the willing and brash Chlamydia in the guise of legitimate customer queries. Meanwhile, I tried on biker jackets and ran my hands through the unfamiliar soft leather tresses of the innocent-looking whips. I examined the improbable rubber suits and hosed masks, and tentatively stepped into a harness—merely to further an homage to absurdity, I assure you— and stepped out just as quickly.

She looked at me with detached interest, her slick lips frozen into a practiced pucker, as she leaned on the glass counter snapping her fingers to the thrash-metal band playing on the sound system that it seemed impossible for anyone to keep time with.

I realized that I might have overstayed my welcome. After all, I had no intention of actually *buying* anything. My girlfriend wouldn't permit it—even if I could convince her that the item of kink in question was free (frivolous expense in light of our impending marriage being strictly taboo), she would have had me committed or at the very least sent in for observation. There was no room in her world for this sort of sophisticated sexual whimsey, no matter how experimental.

I made motions to go, but left slowly.

Chlamydia touched me from behind the glass case and spun me around. "Here you go, *slaveboy*. Take this and maybe I'll see you at the club."

"Slaveboy?" I began to sweat.

"That's right." She pushed me away playfully from the counter with amused viciousness. "I can always tell. Here." She held up a handbill that showed some clip art of an obvious dominatrix in shiny boots and corset, holding a buggy-whip, pasted into the center ring of a circus and made to look as if she were whipping a centaur. "Come to the Carn-Evil of Despair at Ubu Roi this Friday," she ordered, reading off the copy from the handbill and pronouncing *Roi* like the Roy in either Orbison or Rogers. I surmised all the club's other patrons did the same.

I took the handbill, mumbling some excuse I couldn't get through like one of her previous businessman clients.

Chlamydia put her hands on her hips. "*I* see. Still in the closet, but not *entirely* vanilla. Well, then, do you have a computer?"

"Live and die by it," I managed to enunciate. I felt a bead of sweat trickle down the back of my neck.

"Mistress Athena runs the Dreams-Come-True BBS—an electronic bulletin board service with an Internet gateway. Go log on from your home PC and meet the folks that hang out at the club—safe, anonymous and from the privacy of your own living room. Get a little cybersex kink in your life, if you can't venture out for some."

I fumblingly pocketed the piece of paper, looked at her unflinchingly and said, "I, uh—"

"I said do *it!*" Chlamydia snapped and glared at me hard.

"All right," I said, clearing my throat as I saw her expression unchanged. "It might be fun. Sure. Why not?"

"Then leave!" Her unique eyes narrowed. "Now."

Having trouble speaking, much less arguing, I complied and walked out to the electronic meow of a cat triggered by the door into the now seemingly kaleidoscopic colors of the day and the peculiarly harsh wind. I thought I heard faint laughter behind me, but I ignored it.

I stopped at a pay phone and broke the news to my girlfriend, Ms. Right, about my column. She told me to come home, a catch in her voice. I told her it would be all right. I told myself, too, after I hung up, again and again with every step.

I caught a bus home from the Miltown theater district at a Plexiglas kiosk a block or so from Ubu Roi's street address, unfolded the handbill and stared at it fixedly until my stop.

TWO

Amazing how a deliberate knowledge of doing wrong, a chosen practice of it, eliminates all the guilt, grief and mourning sins promote like a dose of Ex-Lax. And the clarity of purpose you feel is directly proportionate to the cloudy-mindedness necessary to carry it out. Something like the urge to shut your eyes before taking a lethal shot and feeling the kick of the gun.

I have no intention of hanging my head in shame while recanting my life to you as a warning, so that you can tread some safe narrow footpath leading to whichever suburban death-plot you've so shrewdly chosen. I won't confirm your caution with my reckless life, warn you, vicariously straiten and chasten you.

Instead, let me take you to the club.

Skin-head kids with headsets and plastic IDs hung from neck-lanyards carded me at the door at the mud-brown concrete facade of Ubu Roi. I was just your average lurker in my all-cotton eclipse of black, with deferential head-gestures. Another nervous tourist.

There it was: dim, expansive and grim, but too loud and crowded to be depressing—exciting perhaps in a negative sense, so I had all my feelers out, prepared for a full-on assault. It was the kind of club known in the industry as "a toilet." But, considering its scope, it could have passed for a full-scale trough-urinal. It was blacklit, cold, suffused with a dry-ice fog of second-hand smoke. Transvestites sashayed about with mixed aplomb on fuck-me pumps, not stopping to check the murky mirrors mincing through the cloverleaf setup of rooms.

I knew no one, and yet I was confident of making crucial meetings soon.

I ordered a drink—special of the night: an "Impaler"—and nipped at it in the darkest quadrant of the club biding my time.

After all—I had planned the betrayal of my girl with skill and care.

While she slept dead on the couch through what once were our evenings of intimacy, I made my electronic connection with the dinky, closed-end local BBS where the hard-core perverts all logged on under revealing—often disgusting and ludicrous—pseudonyms. Handles, to keep to the broadcast argot of the on-line culture of the cyberlife, to identify a preferred practice or repressed yearning that flew in the face of the ordinariness that the terms were devised and intended to conceal.

In their aberration they seemed vulgar and common, these handles, trumpeting the sort of doings that were considered seamy and repugnant even during the protracted death rattle of the last sexual revolution, when even homely men and women could count on getting laid several times in a lifetime from several different people. Homosexuality was one thing, even the more grotesque end of it made up of plumose, heroic linebacker drag queens, but you can bet there was never any piss-drinkers' pride parade ever heard of in my quarter but in some of the sicker jokes my cronies and I made to help us weather college.

But there he (or she) was, in "Open Teleconference," the only lively region of the otherwise-diluted version of your average Internet service: Piss-Drinker, spouting misspelled, chatty badinage with all the other colon-punctuated entries in what was the scrolling version of a cacophonously bad one-act play written by a Dada group bent on boring their audience with sexuality. The saving grace was that you could type along with all the other authors, adding your own tart monologue, baneful soliloquy, snappy commentary or Socratic interrogatory to the melee. You could, with instant gratification, with the added rush of feeling as brave as only e-mail can make you, posture and strike attitudes along with Bootlicker, LadyPain, MooseCock, CyberSub, LisaTV, Assboy, EliotTS, Toilet Slave, CramDown and, moderator and sysop of this nightly virtual gathering, Mistress Athena. You could whisper, command instant lewd actions described on the screen as if a line of narrative or even spirit away another identity for some "hotchat"—which was really just phone sex once removed—cheaper, though much harder on the wrists, especially as passions would build, distracting busy digits from keys.

You could do all of this, and receive e-mail to boot, all in a little cyberplace called Dreams-Come-True. I joined right away and hardly logged off at all for a solid week. Ms. Right snored away like a congested infant, most likely of the type she dreamed of having, looking sweet and vulnerable while I ignored her, hotchatting away with whoever came down the electronic pike, trying it on for size, looking into the places I had long ago secured with ethical sophistication and locked away, broaching practices and scenarios, touching the images of partners in sexual tastes and titillations I had long since given up on.

Of course, while I clicked away, hoping for the right moment for my skill at one-handed typing to come into play, she ignored me. Always frightened over a buck from the day she first went into business for herself as the publisher of *Alpha Waves; the East Coast's Largest Newsletter of Metaphysics and Meditative Arts*. That this rag of cliquish, largely self-aggrandizing "advertorials" made any money at all was a tribute to the relentless compulsiveness that drove our relationship into the coma of denial.

No use complaining. As all electronic media have alerted me time and again, love is cheap, though somewhat less so than life itself. Anyone can be killed for any reason, but a good romance is hard to find, so hold on to it and, should that union of intimate sensitivities die, forget about it. It happens to everybody and everybody gets used to it. If you have to kill for it, go for it —as long as it's the right person. If you have to betray for it, do so—as long as it's the right person. So, for that first week of cyber-luxuriance as Ms. Right slept, I ejaculated into the night, sometimes with one hand.

Ms. Right encouraged me to go out on Friday night—have a drink, see the boys. She needed to sleep and was far too agitated for happiness in crowds even just with me among them.

Sleeping with me had become risky. There was the chance I might violate the cocoon she spun from sheets, blankets and arms. I was an intrusion into her retreat from her fears—but I was also the emotional bulwark and linchpin that kept the daytime fears away.

She was coupled up and settled with me, Mr. Right, in the kind of relationship where she could dreamily and productively plan our marriage. She had made her decision and was willing to stick with it—despite my considerable shortcomings as husband and father material.

We slept apart. That way I could type into the computer, and she could snuggle to the tune of the TV in the sanctity of her blanket carapace on the loveseat.

She was so vulnerable, sleeping there on her custom-embroidered loveseat huddled in blankets in her flannel pajamas like a child, breathing hope while I just about drooled it while greeting the scripted posturings and constructs of all the on-line players in the scene. On that first Friday night she was the world's sweetest little girl bundled up in her fabled place on her loveseat, a romantic video rental popped into the player, ethereal and cozy while I, dressed from head to foot in black, pulling on my first black leather jacket, kissed her on the cheek and left her in favor of the Carn-Evil of Despair at Ubu Roi.

My eyes and mind lingered on the promise of the young, wriggling women in their PVC dancing outfits and Bettie Page haircuts, on the promise of an unspecific fullfilment beginning with sex and going far beyond sex. I was daydreaming, watching the dancing girls glisten.

Out of nowhere, my "Impaler" jaggedly impaled me through the groin. I hopped up from the stool and started sopping at the crotch of my jeans with a handful of available cocktail napkins before the thick-looking man in the overcoat next to me could apologize for having emptied the plastic cup into my lap.

He didn't and I gave him a look.

He looked back, unfazed.

I nodded.

"You want something?" he asked thinly.

"You spilled my drink," I said.

"Get off on it?"

"Despite the fact I got it in the groin, no."

"Some do, you know."

"Really," I queried, determining now that I was suffering an exchange with a moron—the first, no doubt, of many. "You're telling me there are people who get off by having sickly sweet whiskey cocktails with too much damn grenadine spilled on them?"

"Among other things," said the man glumly.

"I'm shocked."

"Probably not," he added with a wave of one ham-hand into the fickle light that defined the edge of the bar. "You look like one of them."

"Them?"

"That's right." He stank from a drugstore cigar that he was no longer smoking, from sweat and from rye. His chin was covered with a brush of gray stubble threatening to become a patchwork beard. His hair was a salt and pepper cowlick that hinted at having once been black. He had a gut that was developing a life and personality of its own beneath his checked shirt and polyester rust colored tie. "The pain-people," he said, "the twisters, whatever they go by nowadays. The perverts. They like to call themselves that now. It wasn't always that way, though."

I decided, as I usually did working in a field involved with citations of fact, that the truth was always the most confusing information that you could give somebody. "No. I'm not one of them. But I would like to be."

He gulped his rye with difficulty, tucked his chin and pointed with a grimace on his lips to the far corner of the room where there was a bar by the dance floor. "Go sit over there then—don't waste your time with me over here. *There's* where you want to be."

"Not that I doubt you, or anything, but why would I want to sit over there anymore than I'd want to sit over here?"

He killed the rye and gestured curtly for the blonde dye-job bartender in his leather Viking suit and helmet to pour him another. "Because—" he was cut off by an incipient wheeze. "Because that's where Athena sits. And you want to get to know Athena."

I was gone. I didn't have to tell my moron that he'd out-thought me.

He knew.

A fresh-faced boy hopped and capered about in the one unpopulated corner of the ancient wood flooring which was so thick with layers of urethane it could barely reflect flashing light. The boy's hair was without color and he looked as if he suffered from some form of genetically dull albinism. Dancers cleared away from the gamboling figure: blonde, wan, raw-skinned and easily the best dancer in the place, outdoing all the bad music with turns and athletics that created a sustained blur of vitality and lust. Of course he was a she— the boy she wanted to be just wasn't pretty enough to have the balance tipped away from butch in favor of the feminine. In a word, she was too boyish to be a boy.

I sat down next to the towering parody hybrid of some comic-book black widow and the camp commercial movie icon Elvira, narrowly preventing fright-wig jheri curls from slapping me in the eyes. With bony features and harsh, lanky angles that seemed to punch out into the atmosphere, a wide chest threatening to cave-in at a moment's notice, elbows and knees—however waxed and polished— that suggested ditch-digging rather than salon-basking, Athena was as masculine as the dancer was feminine. If the bopping androgyny on the floor suffered from excess in being too boyish to be a boy, then Athena suffered from a similar deficit: She was simply too manly to be a woman.

He was a bad pass.

I didn't care. Athena, for the time being, despite whatever efforts were being made to unseat him from the papier-maché throne on the club stage contemplated by players who felt themselves more worthy to sit there, in effect ran the scene. And the scene was where I wanted to be, even though the desire was masked and camouflaged to seem to be something else—even to myself.

I had every intention of entering this scene, playing it, then making my exit after the inevitable dead-end such life explorations always posited for me. Studying theater arts in school had taught me the necessarily bitter fact of life that, if you wanted to act, you had better quickly find a way of going to bed with the director—in whatever sense you might find most distasteful, if not in the literal.

As usual, my tack was to start at the top and work my way down.

Athena looked down on me blandly, as if I were just another

soon-to-be rejected suitor. He was holding what looked like a shot glass of Vermont maple syrup, which he tossed down his throat, then suspended in front of his nose by his thumb and forefinger, lapping at its rim daintily once or twice with the tip of his tongue. His eyes were a penetrating blue, his face craggy and marred from abuses I could only guess at, ruddy with the luster of a tanning booth.

He clearly noticed me noticing him as well as the obvious gaffe that I had dared ensconce myself on the stool next to his—a spot annexed to his own and identified as such by certain unmistakable hallmarks of the Athena personality: a pack of Virgina Slim Menthol 100s, Vampire Vermillion lipstick, an imitation art deco make-up compact, a black lace spiderweb scarf and a riding crop with a two-inch wide leather loop flattened and creased at the end which I thought little of at the time.

"Ye-e-e-s?" he drawled.

I introduced myself as Propertius, the anonymous broadcast handle I took as a condition of opening an account on the Dreams-Come-True BBS (before I learned that such sobriquets as TitFucker and ReamMe were more the main in this virtual world).

"Propertius!"

He was openly delighted, flashing glossy black, inch-and-a-half long press-on nails as he pressed palms together prayerfully beneath his chin. Suddenly, the black talons rested on my shoulder. Before I could order another "Impaler" from the Morticia behind the bar, the seven-foot (in six-inch heels) Goddess of Wisdom manqué was coaxing me off my stool and began dragging me about the club by the scruff of the neck, distressing my all-cotton, cable-knit sweater. His patter, while acting on my behalf as social director of this nether world, had nothing to do with either dreams or unsatisfied impulses. It was all business: the usual intention for global market domination that gushed freely from a would-be entrepreneur yet to fully experience his first blush of success.

I was patient and charming. I was busily ogling the young women in their vinyl, leather and latex outfits, showing as much skin as the civil code permitted, with cleavage and buttocks teasing and bragging in my mind far more loudly than Athena. I was a sleepwalker, barely able to match all the names to the faces as he ticked them off as he pointed them out in action on the floor, at the bar or cruising for a mistress with sad eyes and tentative shamble.

I could hardly contain my excitement along with my disappointment at seeing how few of the broadcast handles from Dreams-Come-True resembled in any way their self-described appearances and attitudes.

Margaux, the most vocal, outrageous mistress in the rolling script cyber-reality of the BBS, was a diminutive, plain librarian with pinched expression, bad skin and asymmetrical features—covered in tight, powdery latex with a red spiked hood that made her look a comical, somewhat vulnerable Statue of Liberty.

Bambi weighed three hundred pounds.

MooseCook shouldn't have been taken off life-support so soon, and looked ready to head back to his hospital bed at any moment, the plastic tube connecting both nostrils much the same way the single silver chain connected both his pierced nipples.

LadyPain looked as if she suffered from more than she inflicted. Though young, she had developed some sort of kyphotic hunch to her posture along with the face and disposition of a dowager aunt. Mouth and teeth were precise and rodentine as she gave me a curt greeting before moving along toward the next room, two flabby, thick shirtless men in leather pants following her on their knees, leashed in tandem.

The pretty women were rock-video voluptuous, but fell apart at the hips. The men had dashing profiles and lacked teeth, or hair, or sported guts that overhung jodhpurs and leather pants. It was a panoply of flesh and flaws, the unbeautiful unashamed in their most sexual dress—or black and covering like mine to connote the danger and taboo, the unanimous cultural ascription of evil to sexual practices that at that point were specifically unknown to me but were attractive nonetheless: the dry, undrunk wine of my fantasies, seen clearly without embarrassment, never tasted nor allowed to confer that final loss of control that the world I had always known so precisely reviled.

This was a different world that I had stepped into. Now that I had, could I ever step out?

"You!" shouted a pretty housewife in a jet-black leather cat-suit, latex boots laced with stays all the way up each leg to the tender vertex of her upper inner thighs, the Miltown accent thick in her voice even with just this one word, "Prop-er-tius! Here—*now!*"

Athena flitted away—he had to walk delicately on those unstable fuck-me heels—escorted by some frog-like factotum of club management. But, before flitting, he, casually and with the scrunched-up expression of a disgruntled toddler, pushed me with all seven feet of leverage directly into the ample bosom of the beckoning housewife. The housewife pushed me in turn back upon impact, making me a sort of darkly awkward shuttlecock.

As I was falling backward, she grabbed the front of my sweater, stretching it hopelessly out of shape, I remember thinking at the time, while flirting with the morass of the club floor. Her hands slipped under that and the equally black turtleneck, caressing my chest, raking my pectorals with nails that were decidedly not press ons.

"So, this is little Prop," she said. "Don't you recognize me? Don't I live up to my description? Aren't I as I said I was?" She rough-kissed me, her fingers locked tight behind my head, and bit my bottom lip.

"Virtuosity," I sputtered, meaning no comment on her performance, but taking a stab at her name. "You're *Virtuosity.*"

We had hotchatted a bit during the previous marathon week of my BUSing on the little electronic cul-de-sac of the Dreams-Come-True system. I may have persuaded her that I was a bit more advanced in S&M or B&D practices than I in fact was. But I didn't think this was the time to admit to it.

The slap of her hand turned my head around.

"That's right. Don't forget it." She spun me around. "Not bad," she said, mussed my hair then spun me again. "No, I think it might do. It might just do at that." She pinched my stomach hunting flab and found none.

A salesman in a suit and tie passed us wearing a neatly typeset, white Bristol-board sign hung around his neck that read, "I am Mistress Lucretia's sissy slut slaveboy."

A sign worn on his back tied with a black sash around his middle read: "Beat me hard! (But only if you know how.)"

A human greeting card for the D&S scene.

A wizened dominatrix about 4'6" tall and quite svelte in red leather lounged on a nearby bench against the wall and allowed a fat man in shorts, sandals and wide-buckled body harness to lick her vinyl, lolling relaxed in the filth and detritus of the floor.

"Have you taken an AIDS test yet?"

"Well, no. I hadn't planned on it—" I was about to explain I had been monogamous for nearly a decade, and before that had practiced safe sex that passed purely as birth-control measures in those few carnal lapses that actually met with fulfillment.

"Get one then. I like to make sure all my pets come without bugs."

She was certainly attractive, but in no way associated with the exotic viciousness and supermodel-as-prostitute affection that the usual dominatrices, professional and not, strove for with predictable failure. She was a ripe matron, likely with children, obviously from the hinterlands, the boonies, the kind that organized bake sales for the church, headed the block-beautification project, prided herself on little household amenities like a Jacuzzi, treasured her own glass menagerie with the happy surprise of its having an actual literary reference and considered the hour or so trip downtown as a treat.

Her cleavage was generous and enticingly arrayed by the taut cut of the catsuit. Those motherly breasts could have been down to her knees for all I knew. But even with that possibility and her just a-wee-bit-too-zaftig hips, I was spellbound by the words and the message that was nearly strangled by that drab, rural accent.

A chill rode my spine the way I rode a rollercoaster as a child.

"I might want to do more with that ass than whip it," she honked.

A tape of distorted organ music replaced the techno and this mistress nonchalantly grabbed my cock and balls all at once through the fabric of my jeans and lifted. I became mildly uncomfortable and blushed in the fast-moving shadows, but wasn't in much pain. She wasn't squeezing, she was just sizing me up and demonstrating that she could in fact squeeze. She gave me a minor dose of tension in her hand to drive home the point.

"What a relief you aren't one of those short-dicked little subbies always puppydogging around here. Did you do what I asked you to do?"

It occurred to me that she might have taken one or two of our frenzied, whispery typing sessions a bit too seriously. "What was that?" Her hand on my cock and balls had almost become comfortable enough for me to forget about. In retrospect, I think it made me feel secure. Probably too secure.

Virtuosity sent me to my knees with one hand on my shoulder and the other engulfing my groin. I cried out. "I asked you to tie this cock up for me and bring it to me so I could lead it around on a leash. But you didn't do that for me, did you?"

She knelt a bit to maintain her grip, I winced and struggled for an answer, seeing flashes in the darkness. "No—I didn't."

"But you will next time."

She rose to her feet. I stayed down.

"I will next time."

I noticed some rumpled lech with auburn hair in a nonfetishistic brown tweed suit drooling over Virtuosity's shoulder, looking for all the world like the newly rolled-out WASP revisionist version of Groucho Marx. I looked up and Virtuosity kicked my knee playfully with the toe of her boot. She kissed the ridiculous face of the deracinated Groucho passionately over her shoulder, leaning back slightly into its owner while making little slopping noises. "My husband," she said, catching her breath, "Merv. You remember we talked about him."

"Oh, yes," I lied. "I remember."

"That's a good little Prop. Isn't he, Merv?"

"Oh, Propertius. That's him? Very good, dear," Merv said inattentively as he nibbled at her trapezius.

"He hasn't learned to dress yet, though," she sighed. "We'll have to fix that."

"I'll take care of it." Someone was behind me. A woman.

I felt a sharp pain in the small of my back—unenjoyable, just as most of the pain I had felt all my life had been. Any exceptional pain of even the bittersweet kind was far from my mind at that moment. I had been kicked again, and by a boot with a much sharper toe.

Why was I even there? Pain had never appealed to me before, why should it now? Here I was getting kicked around on a filthy floor by a good-looking woman slobbering all over her mess of a husband. I knew I was nothing like that Pillsbury Dough Boy in his home-made harness lying in club grunge greedily licking at some crone's boot. I wasn't anything like that. In fact, I was getting just about ready to bag it.

I could close my eyes and instead of the sparks and phosphenes of unwanted pain, I could see Ms. Right snoring peacefully on her gilded, imported loveseat. I felt an even more painful wave of love wash out all my other pains.

"He's mine for right now, Vee," said the young woman's voice behind me without much challenge in it. She sounded almost laconic.

"Oh, shoo-ah," Virtuosity said dismissively, steadying herself on Merv. "Go ahead and take 'im. I was just playin' anyway." She crouched to give me a peck on the cheek then moved on using her husband for support.

"Stand up and turn around!" shouted the woman behind me. She took a fistful of my poor abused sweater to help speed me on my way and I turned with an effort toward recovering my center of gravity.

She was a stunning sight—naked again but for chainmail and she wore little enough of that. Her boots were lethal, coming up in points beyond her hips on each side, made of seamless PVC and glinting with black danger. She drew my face hard to hers. Nose, nipples and eyebrows all were pierced. "It's me," she hissed—"Chlamydia."

I learned with that hiss that her tongue also was pierced, its thick metallic bead flickering at me in uncertain light.

She dragged me—again by the sweater!—to a comfortable spot on a bench against the wall, in which she sat, shoving me down at her feet. I spent the rest of the evening there, quietly watching the amateur sexual histrionics performed by bored students and would-be regional theater actors clumsily and without flourish, adorned with catch-as-catch-can props and tattered club set-pieces in a state of uncritical beatitude.

Though in my mind's eye I had escaped her, I wondered what my girl—and she was my girl, the one who truly loved me and put up with me—lying asleep back at home on the loveseat so vulnerable and angelic would say if she saw me now.

And then Chlamydia grabbed my longish hair, pulling my head between her thighs, and spoke harshly with hot breath directly into my ear: "That *bitch* was talking to you about something she had in mind for your cock. I want to hear everything about it, and I want to hear about it right now!"

I was there until closing.

THREE

My life goes by from that night on in little vignettes, episodes like falling needles that glint and disappear and haunt my flesh. I can lie in darkness or distract myself in daylight, but the exactness of each incident (so blindingly clear) jolts me to a new, unwanted awareness like one of those lost and fallen needles found with a bare foot, a lolling hand, an idle finger. Oh, how I earned and slaved for each of those moments, strove for and connived to bring forth the vivid freshness of a risky double life into the stale domesticity of the life I led with my unintended.

Unintended. That was my joke with Dwight DeSeigneur, the elder statesman of the local old-time press who actually knew and used to drink with the columnist that I in my short undistinguished stint replaced upon his death. We joked a lot, Dwight and I, but at this stage only by phone, as he was, by then, dying in minor degrees from major cancer—a by-product of the cigarettes he denied having ever smoked which he smoked incessantly. And even in this early phase of his long decline, he didn't want to be seen as anything less than the vital personification of trumped-up machismo he wrote about so sententiously in his antique *Register* column "Man Among Men."

So, he would call me, his unlikely declassé freelance friend and associate, from the lowest level of his triplex townhouse at the top of Breed's Hill in the very hub of Miltown, old money thicker than savored puffs of smoke in his voice as he bragged to me—just guy-to-guy—about his deflowering of one debutante after another back when white dinner jackets and garden parties punctuated by furtive, strapless-gown–clad sex on the divan and red carnations were far from rare.

He loved that concept, "deflowered."

"Fucking *defoliated*," I can hear him cackle now through suppressed coughing.

"Great days for sex," I said, circling job offers in the *Register* where Dwight's column, "Man Among Men" ran on and on. Bad as it was—or good as it could be—at least old Dwight did his own writing, which was bad for me, as I needed a gig. "No AIDS, no possibility of a tryst ever really mutating into a marriageable romance—"

"You're right about that, kid," he said. "Not in our set, anyway. You did what you were supposed to then: you stayed married to whoever was right for you, had your hanky panky with someone who wasn't and sent the kids off to boarding school—a sort of collectivist Skinner box to benefit the parents, keep relationships stable."

"There's a lot to be said, Dwight, for seeing your kids only on holidays."

"You talk like you have some."

"I don't—that's how I know."

I waited out the coughing jag.

"You're due for some then, aren't you? You and your unintended."

"You mean the Red Menace?" Another term for Ms. Right, a fair-complected redhead with green eyes.

"If we had common law status here in Arcadia, you'd be barefoot and pregnant by now."

"You mean she would."

Dwight cough-laughed. "Not if she gets her way, I don't."

"Unemployed writers without private income make dubious marriage prospects."

"Don't worry, kiddo, she'll reform you and have you pulling down commissions in an insurance office before you can say *corpus luteum*."

"Really?" I said, jotting down the names of former editors, sipping coffee in my mismatched pajamas and worn red plaid robe, sitting cross-legged on the carpet in my room. "Do you have any intention of reforming me by throwing some work my way?"

Dwight was grave. "There's no reforming guys like you in that department. You're positively unregenerate. Being in the same category of professional disadvantage, I can only say I'm lucky to have my little column and a hard-working third wife."

"It's a mystery to me why they still run it when all you do is write up how you spend time with your son Duke in a style cribbed from Hemingway's *In Our Time* and explain haltingly why things are not as good as they once were." I really didn't begrudge him this—it was a nice thing to leave his son, a happy arrangement where he could work at home and be close to the subject of his work. It was, of course, more than luck that a dying man was paid to publish a personal legacy in columnar installments in the biggest daily in the market. Dwight DeSeigneur was the Monmouth of Miltown, always to the left of the throne where the principals with all the riches and control would stingily throw him select chunky crumbs from the cakes at their table. He was a poor relation, a cousin twice removed, an in-law with good credentials and not much else. "Close—but no cigar launch," was his occasional tagline when famous cronies routinely published a book, had scandalous affairs with sex goddesses, were profiled on television, obtained the deference he lusted for, went yachting.

"Why does our frilly little rag run my junk, you want to know, you jaded cynic? Because it's brilliantly written and deals with all the forgotten manly virtues, not least of which are the ineffable ties between father and son. Of course, if I were a cynic like you, I'd say it was because they no longer bothered to notice me, even though I also happen to wear ineffable ties."

"Well, it's probably those bowties that do you in, Dwight." I bit my tongue about the cigarette he was no doubt sucking back slowly, keeping the smoke welled up in his throat before allowing it to drift up and hang there in a gout between his lips and nose, flung back in his lambskin office chair in the delight of another moment stolen back from responsibility and care.

"Habits kill more than chances, I've heard it said," Dwight rumbled phlegmatically. "Which is precisely your problem, Perry. It's the reason you won't get any work in this button-down town."

"The fact that I lack ineffable ties?"

"No, the fact that you simply refuse to go un-noticed."

I had to laugh and he had to cough.

"Now," he said, "pay strict attention. Did I ever tell you about the lioness position? It's my favorite, you know. My first, best experience with it was with the Weyerhauser heiress when we met up in Monty Clift's sister's swimming pool. You remember her, don't you? She was the one I told you about who got away with murder? Well, she was in with a very fast crowd even before she cut off her boyfriend's *schlong* and high-tailed it off to Las Vegas with the bloody souvenir in her handbag." Dwight loved Yiddishisms like *schlong*— they proved he had more than just a passing familiarity with New York City, however bound up in the sticks of Miltown he might have been. Dwight hummed with the pure savor of the story. "He died of shock, you know, the boyfriend, and she did six months for illegal possession of a penis in her purse, being temporarily insane and permanently rich, which even then was no shock at all. In those days, however, there was a much better understanding and appreciation of class and its proper role in events. Now we have Lorena Bobbitt, which is no class at all."

"John Wayne Bobbitt survived," I said.

"Really?" I could actually see one of his red eyebrows dusted with white arching as he spoke—the picture in my mind drawn perfectly by his tone of voice. "I thought he was dead. He certainly looked dead the last time I saw him on one of those afternoon talk shows   hardly even reanimated for all the miracles of modern surgery the health care system focussed on his prick."

"He says it works better now."

"It would have to. But they say he has the movie footage now to prove it." Dwight never said "film," it was always "movie." He steadfastly refuses to watch films, only movies.

"You rented it while the chief organizer was off for a meeting with the Junior League of Breed's Hill."

"That's right, bucko, me and the good pastor of the Church of John the Evangelist."

"An evaluation of sin?"

"Not even on our list of one stars. The pastor and I were in agreement: you couldn't even see the stitches."

And that was how it went then: he would tell me his and I would tell him mine—except I had none yet to tell. Or at least nothing that could compare with his rich rondelets and ostentatious assignations held under porticos, cupolas and Monets with all the prissy grim Republican dowagers of the future. But the S&M was brimming on my tongue and he would hear about, I swore, as soon as I made it happen, as soon as I cheated on the love of my life with the girl of my dreams, whoever she would be on any given night. I wanted to explain about how, in losing my column, I lost my footing and had fallen into a new realm where even Dwight DeSeigneur's most ardent cardinal sin was a drop in the bucket that brimmed with my own planned perfidy.

It never happened that way.

I still talk to Dwight as much as I ever did—now that he's gone. Things are pretty much the same between us. We argue, call one another stupid, and bitch and moan and curse each other out just as before. Of course, only one of us means it now.

Even over the phone the gruff voice boomed: "She took that crouched position I was telling you about," I can still hear him say, "just like a lioness. But I was the one tearing the prey apart. And when I *shtupped* her, we left a large wet spot on the otherwise dry velvet upholstery of the divan."

Vignettes.

Like Ms. Right coming home full of the hatred of her day transferred to me, screaming, where the apartment was a mess, disorder reigned and I was at fault. Like when we cuddled and exchanged our longing in front of the timeless flickering tube on the couch, made up again from the last uncounted argument. Like when we fooled around and teased in private those in the world who would destroy us. Like when we kissed and lived in a place peopled by no one else, a little sovereign state headed for turmoil.

Vignettes.

Like the afternoon of my first cock-ring.

Milt Pecksniffian, gay rake, adventurer and leather-sex dabbler with a dungeon in the basement of his building across from the washer and dryer—who wasn't one of those self-sensitive queens (just on the lookout for one)—was leaving town, leaving the *Register* and leaving behind a long line of querulous lovers, some of whom were not slated to survive the winter. And though his last test was a resounding negative, he needed to distance himself from what he referred to as "the disease pool."

Adding to his itch to flee was the fact that, despite his disease-free status, he had a case of candida in his mouth that just wouldn't go away.

I ran into him in the herbal remedies section of the Miltown Food Co-op comparing the prices on little dropper bottles of tincture of echinacea.

"Boosts your immune system," he drawled, looking boyish in his forties with his gapped tooth smile and his marine-style brush-cut hairdo.

We traded our usual double entendres, all of which would likely fall flatter on the page than they did in the open air when we spoke. He flirted with me, I made allusions to the S&M that I was beginning to grow comfortable with and see in a new light.

It was like having a secret power I could turn on and off at will: a way of stepping beyond the usual into an elite understanding. It was the usual sought-after American rush: a snobbery one could wield like some new, untried weapon.

He patted my ass and I let him.

Rather than my flinching, Milt jumped when I smiled.

"Rough trade," he breathed.

"I like it rough," I said, and then explained myself before he closed in.

"Too bad," he said. "If anybody could turn you now, I bet I could."

He regaled me with the details, the psychological manipulation — or mindfuck—of his last scene, which required the use of a bullwhip. At my initial grimace, he stopped me right then and there, holding up his hands and insisting, to my relief, that few did. Then he went into some detail about the construction and use of his dungeon and offered to show it to me.

It was the most natural thing in the world for me to accept. I had known Milt for quite some time, a competent newsman, good with the local political scene and bitchy as all hell through subtext about infighting. He had a tough outer aspect which was completely cultivated, down to the tailored all-purpose motorcycle jacket that was his trademark. What lurked beneath, however, was a garden-variety obssessive-compulsive personality replete with all attendant issues of adolescent nerdiness—albeit a very gay and a very horny one.

A little silver man clung desperately to one of his multiply pierced ears with his arms and legs hugging the edge, glinting in frustrated sunlight.

I suspended my grocery shopping and helped Milt carry his back to the tridecker in Nelson Court, Somerset, the student and young-strugglers' enclave that edged on more tony Trinity, where ancient, famous Trinity University and all its classes of hangers-on, associates, faculty and attenuated servants spun their collective wheels furiously within the few choice blocks of money and prominence in Stuart Square.

I related to him the beginnings of my entry into leather.

His lover, Maurice, a thin, snitty type, shirtless in beltless black leather pants worn white at the knees and at the behind with a well-defined ribcage protruding from beneath golden-brown lamp-tanned skin, met us at the door and helped with the bags. He seemed to have just gotten up.

Milt's apartment was the entire first floor of the old house, Edwardian by way of textile mill, lit in mid-day by bruised fluorescent circlets set in twelve foot ceilings, each laid bare and intermittently flickering. It was one of those cheap deals on the edge of tenement row that clusters of near moneyless students or drop-out fringe cultists would pool their meager assets to rent under one name in order to set up a squalid hive with nooks aplenty for crashing. Milt's place was just such a squalid hive, but was shared solely by Maurice and him, evidence of crashing guests and late-staying party guests notwithstanding.

As we walked from the foyer through the sitting and dining rooms long since adjusted from their original purpose, I got the sense of visiting a crime scene, perhaps a crack house after the execution of a search warrant or a multiple murder. Milt indicated a room closed off with French doors, with boxes in it piled high. He explained that this was where he composed amateur cantatas for the

Greek Orthodox Church, which he somehow did not find inconsistent with the gay leather life and casual D/s in the basement.

Maurice sauntered in, both belly and ribs sticking out, his beltless pants threatening a dive to floor, holding up some straps of leather connected together by nickel-plated snaps and O-rings. "Moving sale!" he sang.

"Yeah," said Milt. "Maurice's old cock harness. You interested?" He pronounced Maurice "Morris."

"Cock harness?" I had no idea what it was, much less how I was supposed to get it on, but I was suave and blasé. "Is it big enough?"

Milt made a grab at my groin, which I dodged. "I don't know," he said. "Is it?"

I backed away, failing to contain my nervousness completely.

"I was talking about the harness."

"I wasn't," said Milt and Maurice guffawed.

He handed the tangle of leather straps, snaps and rings to me and let it dangle in front of my eyes before I took it. My body language suggested I was afraid to draw near, so I reached for it as if he were about to snatch it away from my grip.

Milt released it into my palm. I could feel his sweat in the leather strap as I grabbed it. "Geez," he said, "don't be so uptight. Don't you have a sense of humor?"

"I do, I do," I said, experimenting with different angles of attack for somehow getting into the tangle of leather and metal, the end in mind being both to eventually attract and blend in with the accepted gang of perverts at Ubu Roi.

"Then take your hand away from your crotch, for Christ's sake! Because, this being a cock harness, we're going to have to use that as the point of anchor. Mo, get the baby oil?"

"Sure thing," Maurice said, hiking up his pants from the waist.

"Baby oil," I repeated dully. "Why do we need baby oil? You're going to lube me for some reason and I don't even know how much this thing costs or even if it's the right thing."

"If you want to do more than just hang out with the S&M crowd, you're going to have to wear more than just the usual black— or less. To put it simply: if you want to be in with the fetish people, you're going to have to be in some fetish. Mo! Don't just stand there—get that motherfucking baby oil!"

"Sir-yes-sir!" mocked Maurice, scampering to the bathroom then making a show of his search amid the well-distributed debris of moving.

Fetish.

I kept thinking in anthropological terms. Some tribal item of totemic magical properties, some incantatory routine centering about an object of spiritual contact and content, something out of Frazier's *Golden Bough* or Roheim's *Twilight of the Gods.* Fetish wasn't a cock harness, was it?

"Tell your boyfriend it's thirty bucks," keened Maurice from the garbage-bag-dampened echo of the bathroom. A cloud of plaster dust hovered near the door.

"For a bunch of straps and snaps?" I queried. Ms. Right had inculcated a sense of poverty in herself as well as me where frugality to the last penny was our only defense against living like students— her private horror.

Being a writer, I was used to scraping by and tended to live cheaply even with money in the bank, but to her I was extravagant. She had gotten me used to carrying so little cash I would have to resort to checks and credit cards, which accounted for every penny spent.

"I'll take a check," Maurice said pertly, tossing a half-full jumbo store-brand bottle of baby oil underhand to Milt's swift one-armed overhand catch.

"Don't be chintzy," said Milt, snapping up the back.

"Looks lousy," Maurice yawned, heading for the kitchen.

"It does when you put it on over relaxed-fit jeans and a flannel shirt—it goes over *skin*, Mo."

"You think I don't know that? I've worn it enough." Maurice added something that went unheard due to a clatter of pots and pans that indicated either further packing or cooking.

"Not near enough as I can see," grunted Milt through his teeth.

"Does this mean you don't think it would work?" I was feeling disappointed in this elder statesman of perversion who ridiculed and took lightly my own exploration of his already established realm. Of course, I must have been somewhat ridiculous then, bunched up and trussed in leather and denim, a worn nickel-plated O-ring straining piteously at my crotch.

"Just let me get these groceries into the kitchen before Maurice either causes an explosion with his cooking or tears the place apart and packs it all in a trunk, forcing us to depend upon McDonald's for sustenance before we blow this godforsaken burg."

He carried the bags into the kitchen while I negotiated my pacing about the obstructed sitting room (it wasn't quite a den, and bore no likeness to a dining room), fingering the sewn and folded leather of my projected harness and running fingers over the slightly tarnished snaps, feeling no excited stirrings at all save a casual admiration for the painstakingly outlandish symmetry in the cartoon artwork of Tom of Finland adorning every wall in framed and blown-up glory —a man who, say what you will, always knew what he had in mind.

"How does it feel, the harness?"

"Sort of hard to tell the way I'm wearing it."

"My sentiments exactly. Want to go down to the dungeon and see my ex?"

"Your ex?"

"That's right. In the dungeon."

"Your ex is there?"

"That's what I said, chief." He left the room, walking through a cascade of plaster dust, disappeared and shouted, "C'mon, will ya!"

I followed with zero apprehension and complete confidence in the normality of the situation, having long since given up my struggle to sustain any objective mental vantage point that would have provided me the illusion of having a detached and outside view. I thought perhaps Milt's ex, doing god-knows-what in the basement that passed for a sexual torture chamber, might help me get a better fit with this harness.

In a far corner of the basement I could see a jarringly incongruous bright spot, under an angrily buzzing fluorescent fixture, decorated by worn sofas with plain, ancient coverings, one busted straight-backed chair and a coffee table with mismatched legs, on which was stacked hundreds of out-of-date wrinkled and water-stained issues of *Time*. Indeed, there was a washer-dryer combination situated against a patch of dull yellow color against the rock-like concrete wall in dull and dusty avocado splendor.

The dungeon was directly across from it.

It was more a cave than a dungeon—an ancient side room off the main space whose ruined cement walls trickled grim tears of condensation from uninsulated pipes and large scattered damp spots whose origins I didn't want to know. I could see shadows and damage from where junction boxes and circuit breakers must have been moved and sealed to prevent the moisture from shorting them out.

In the feculent expanse of the basement's main chamber, you could barely stand, and I walked behind Milt, wary of inhaling the dank mossy smell as we entered the dungeon. He flicked on a red light bulb from a naked fixture whose wiring was protected by dull segmented aluminum tubing. I was able to stand up straight in some comfort, and when my eyes adjusted what I saw surprised me, not through any sense of horror or shock, but through a sense of order. The room was pleasant in its way, with smooth walls painted glossy black, a sideboard of a kind covered with crêped leather riveted to the wood and upon which lay sparkling clean implements, which are all more than familiar to me now but which I could hardly identify then.

There were whips hanging from a pegged rack on the wall, including a long, thickly braided shot-loaded blacksnake bullwhip. I absently picked up one of a matched set of nipple clamps and, not knowing what they were, toyed with them.

"You like the clinging claw?" asked Milt

"The what?"

"Clinging claw. Isn't that what it looks like?"

I lifted the little gew-gaw close to my eyes in the palm of my hand. It looked like a tiny kitchen whisk broken open at the ends with a little ring of rubber that slid up and down at the base. I tried sliding it and the open end squeezed shut, giving a claw-like effect.

"What's it for?"

"Your nipples," Milt said with mild exasperation. "Wanna try it on and see if it fits?"

I let the spidery little implement fall back to its place at the table.

"Like my dungeon?"

"I do. It's very neat." That was no lie—it was by far the neatest room in the house, down to the little collection of CDs discreetly housed in black lacquered shelving in a corner on the floor convenient to a little black boom-box whose infinitesimal black metal-housed speakers were almost completely concealed in opposite corners of the ceiling. A full-length mirror on the wall even created the illusion of greater space, if not light. "So, where's your ex?"

"Right behind you."

I pivoted quickly on my left heel, half expecting to be jumped from behind, and instead came face to face with his "ex"—a wooden X-cross positioned on an outsized easel frame outfitted with cuffs, straps and stirrups for the heels. There were screw points to adjust the positioning of these for height. It didn't faze me at all that a man was supposed to be strapped or tied to this crude wooden device and tortured or used as his master saw fit—but the thought of this master being dryly sarcastic and overly conscientious city beat correspondent Milt Pecksniffian did. I tried not to laugh.

"St. Andrews' cross," said Milt. "Like it?"

"It's divine."

"Spreads you out, makes you available. Tons of fun."

"I bet," I said, having no idea nor wishing to develop one, assuming this wooden structure facilitated the kind of gay exchanges in which I had no interest. I was so overwhelmed by the nonchalant treatment of a sexual taboo that was peculiarly yet compellingly attractive to me, my exploitive nature apparently failed me when I was presented with anything but a direct opportunity. I was hungry, tempted and tantalized, yet too cautious to take my fill.

But I wouldn't leave the table, so ultimately I was to be served . . . or to serve.

"Well," he sighed dejectedly, "think about it for later then."

"There *is* always later." I began to wonder if any of the items on the table would be included in Milt and Maurice's moving sale. "So," I gestured toward the leather-crêpe table, "about all these things—"

Milt cut me off. "Are you *kidding?* None of this is for sale. It's all going with me and Maurice to Wyoming, where all the cowpokes go. Hopefully, we'll get to use some this stuff on a few of them without our having to actually go around cowpoking."

"Hopefully," I echoed.

"So, let's get you into your harness the right way. Strip, will ya?"

"Why?"

"Because I'm asking you to!" he shouted in a huff.

I stood stark still and gave him my patented look of ironic incredulity.

Milt backpedaled. "You can't tell anything trying to put a cock harness over gladrags like that. So take off your clothes and let me adjust it. Geez."

I shrugged, unsnapped the harness and quickly stripped to his grudging approval.

Of course, I had known exactly why he wanted me undressed all along and simply had wanted to give Milt as much of a hard time as he liked to give others whenever their particular peccadilloes came into play. I knew this just as firmly and surely as I knew that in no way should I have been doing what I was doing, but that I was going to do it anyway.

I stood naked in the vermillion half-light before him. Beads of sweat sparkled on Milt's smooth shaved upper lip. "Been working out, I see."

"A trait shared by unemployed writers and convicts alike."

"Whatever," he said, holding up the harness. "Now," he breathed. "Let's do this *right.*"

He had reconnected all the snaps and left one entire side open and held the harness up so that I could step into it from the left. It was as if I were being fitted for this cock harness by a professional tailor. Milt's hands darted about, skilfully making adjustments, tugging, snapping, fastening, repositioning. Finally, when he stepped away from me and turned me about so that I could look directly into the full-length mirror, it no longer looked ridiculous. In fact, it looked pretty good, flattering my build and proportions just right, giving the illusion that I was just a bit too big for the cross-straps which in turn gave the impression of restraining my flesh.

Milt's breathing was somewhat labored. "Looks good," he said.

"Really?" I asked, beginning to feel a bit excited and, perversely, like the young ingenue and former cheerleader being fitted for and trying on for size for the very first time her very first gown for her very first coming-out party.

"Really," he said. "*Damn* good. But we're not done yet. Now, we have to get you into the cock ring."

Pouting, I looked down at the strap that dangled from a thong in the back between my legs with a smallish nickel-plated O-ring at its end. "You mean this?" I played with it.

"Yes." Milt knelt down with the baby oil. "I don't usually do this— especially on my knees —but being that you're clueless, you're going to need some help to lessen the risk of injury." He squirted my cock and balls liberally with the baby oil and distributed it with his hands. I yelped with the combined sensations of cold and outrage.

"Hey!" shouted Milt. "You have to be shown!" He cleared his voice and adopted a didactic tone. "First, you make sure the baby oil is well distributed. This will help you slip through the ring without hitting any sticking points and will also prevent any chafing after it's on. Chafing hurts like a bastard, ya know, but you never notice it—or suffer from it—until you take it off."

He grabbed my sensitive flesh with firm assurance, not stopping either to caress or explore. He was all business. First, he positioned the ring, then he tugged my left testicle slowly through it by the stretchable skin of the scrotum, not letting up on his pull in the slightest at my first dulcet grunt of discomfort. Then, he grasped the retracted neck of my cock tight and fed it through the ring, briskly tugging the scrotum of the right testicle, forcing it to move forward through the tiny bit of space that remained between my cock and the ring.

Milt fastened a final snap at the bottom, and with the burning vibration of that last click, I stiffened and he stepped back.

"There we are," he said, "belted in nice and tight. How does it feel now? Take a good look in the mirror and tell me."

For some reason, nude yet bedizened in constrictive leather straps and gleaming rings, I looked even better than before. I felt a rush, a sensation of heat and excitation play across my skin. And then I noticed it: I was totally erect and gleaming from the baby oil. I looked fit for a leather-dungeon photo spread in a gay stroke book, a parody icon. In fact, in a sense I *was* in a gay stroke book: Milt's. I was tempted to ask him where the cameras were hidden, but I restrained myself, without even a smirk at the double entendre I was living out.

I was erect, but felt absolutely no attraction for this prissy, fastidious local political reporter with his affectations of butchness in the homemade dungeon where, for some portion of a few rare days, he could pretend to having some type of mastery.

"Getting *hot*, I see," commented Milt.

"Not because of you," I said, feeling in reality a bit of a chill, but somehow unable to get rid of my erection. I whirled my finger about it. "I think it's the *thing*."

Milt removed his shirt, looking for all the world now like an eleven-year old boy fresh from summer camp with his bristly close-cropped hair, and his ruddy, sun-lamp–tanned and smooth hairless chest that clung stubbornly to its original store of baby fat.

"It's *your* thing," he drawled. "I know it isn't because of me," he added with exasperation exaggerated so obviously that I would discount it. "It's because of the fetish."

"I'm hot for the fetish."

Milt scratched his brush-cut head, rubbed his brow. "Sort of. It's an object of power, ya know. It plays into whatever hierarchy of fantasies and mental imagery that gets you off when you think about dominance—or in your case, *submission*."

"You think I'm submissive."

"'Course! What else *would* you be? Just look at yourself in the cock harness and in the ring. I don't think any self-respecting top would be caught *dead* in that ring. This is what you hinted around about isn't it?—it's the stuff you came for, items of or relating to bottoming."

What was surprising was that I didn't mock the fetish I was dressed in, bathed in the stagy, red, ruinous reflection of the dressing mirror. Mockery with an absurd pose fancifully struck was my standard method of distancing myself from circumstances whose intensity and seriousness carried consequences I was unwilling to fully embrace. As it was, Master Milt was mockery enough for us both, coming off as perhaps the Carlos Castaneda of the profane or even as the dead-wrong Don Juan when it was plain that the right one would have been needed to lure me further.

I heard a muted rumbling and Milt gave the door a violent kick shut. He eyed me with a squint of frustration, taking plain notice that I was erect through the ring with priapan indifference. He could see I was worried about other things.

"What the hell was that?"

"Awww—somebody just *had* to go and start a load of laundry right now."

"Good thinking. I'm going to buy this, you know."

"I know," Milt said, fondling the bullwhip from its peg on the wall rack. "I have a better harness, you know, one a bit more involved, a little more showy. You could borrow it for your debut for club watchamacallit, if you want."

"Ubu Roi," I said. "That would be great. By the time they recover from seeing me in that one, I'll be in this one." I looked down. "But maybe not so . . . outgoing." Milt shifted gears.

"So do you want to check out my ex? See what it's like?"

"I told you: I'm not into men."

"Yeah, I know, but you're into the fetish. And don't tell me this dungeon doesn't excite you!"

I didn't want to admit it. It was cheap, jerry-rigged, homemade, crude—but it *did* excite me. The fetish I wore excited me. The subterfuge of this entire visit excited me. The fact that I was possessed of an urgent erection that acted entirely independent of me and without a woman to focus it on excited me.

"Oh—just step into the cross, for Christ's sake!"

I obliged, completely unaroused by Milt but as erect as I had ever been in even my most sexually irrepressible days at school. He strapped in my wrists so that they stretched my arms as high as they would go with strict care, then cross-strapped my midriff and buckled my legs in securely. I was just noticing how he did this with seeming tenderness, when—abruptly—he changed the angle at which the cross rested to one more extreme and I almost swallowed my tongue. When I recovered I saw Milt fingering the long bullwhip that he had grabbed off the wall.

"Going to whip me now?" I asked in a dead serious tone, realizing without relief that there was hardly enough room for him to use such an implement. I was guessing that Milt was no gaucho with it, to be sure, and that for him it was all just a part of the mindfuck of a reluctant nerd.

"I thought of that—but no." Milt rubbed his hands, turned toward the sideboard and picked up the baby oil. He squirted some on his hands until they shone lubriciously in the half-light. "No, boy," he said *sotto voce*, a husky affectation in his voice. "I'm going to make you come."

With that, he roughly grasped my swollen cock—which, perhaps due to the ring, didn't feel half as bad as I expected—then expertly held, pumped, massaged and tickled it with his slick fingers and palms. I struggled, squirmed, resisted, grew even harder, burned with mild shame and humiliation as I suffered the knowledge that *Milt Pecksniffian* of all people had been able to take possession of my cock against my will and do with it exactly as he pleased. Milt Pecksniffian!—the guy who openly and seriously petitioned for a more manly motif in the city room lounge at the *Register* and for a ban against pink toilet paper in the men's room. I had to laugh, but I *could* not laugh.

All I could do was come.

What's worse, all I could do was come with a stertorous involuntary grunt, getting it all over Milt's bare UV-roasted chest, which he stuck out at me to make sure it happened that way. He used me again and again the same way. I was surprised at how easy it was to stay erect and how irrelevant it was that another man was directly involved in my orgasm.

I had gotten off on my lack of control.

Milt's bare chest glistened with my semen and, at one point, he took his finger, stuck it into the thickest coating of the stuff and tasted it, smacking his lips, crooning, "Hmmm. Not bad, not bad at all. But you've *got* to lay off the coffee—makes it taste a little too much on the bitter side."

Before my equilibrium returned, I was unstrapped. Milt helped me down from the cross, then out of the cock harness—what a relief!—(at the same time making sure that I didn't fall over) and, as if nothing had happened, we were back to gossiping about office politics at the *Register* as we made our way back upstairs without either incident or irony, making not a single reference to our little scene in the basement dungeon—*my first!* We were cool and unruffled, as if he had only taken me down to the basement to show me his washer/dryer, the sole evidence of any transgression against god and man being the slight, persistent odor of baby oil.

After writing Maurice a check, I stuck the cock harness at the bottom of a bag of books I agreed to take home with me to help with the move and to smuggle past the vigilant scrutiny of Ms. Right.

It was late when I got home, but Ms. Right was uncharacteristically understanding and glad to see me. She threw her arms around me hungrily, full of affection and need for affection. Her breath was hot and sweet. She said she had missed me, noticing the overstuffed shopping bag of books that I had dragged into the house. She fussed over me, served me dinner and didn't even raise the not-unjustified complaint that I was bringing yet more books into the house to take up space and collect dust—I could see the enormous effort it took! She was attentive and gazed at me with doe eyes full of innocent love as I greedily ate the meal she had prepared, one of my very favorites.

I had forgotten all about the kink, my basement orgasms, content to move with the rhythm of the affections of Ms. Right.

Afterward, we lay entwined on the loveseat and kissed, the television blaring nebulously but somehow pleasantly in the background. Her breathing was like the delicate, vulnerable sigh of a small child. At that moment, I knew I loved her terribly and was profoundly grateful to god for that fact, which seemed not at all inconsistent with what I had done just a few hours earlier. It all seemed to fit. I held her and put everything I had into it. I closed my eyes tight and saw everything then as I do now.

Vignettes.

They play before me now, over and over again, running in a loop as they caper grimly in some sadness-mocking *danse macabre*.

I see them now as they run still in my mind's eye, indifferent to truth and falsehood, indifferent to pleasure and pain, all just cruelly composed of what they are, of what I had made them.

And I know the vignettes will kill me.

Just as I know in the same way the vignettes will never let me rest.

Vignettes.

Then as now, they drove me. Then as now, I juxtaposed them, stunned and attracted to their heightening contrast. Then as now, I went to collect them as a child collects bright images on cards, flashy toys.

Then, I placed them together, earned them and lived in them back and forth. Playing over them with eyes, mind and heart, I went from one to the other—

Until the day came when I found I could never go back.

FOUR

Summer hit hard out of the murk and indecisive mists and driz-
zle that characterize what passes as spring here in Miltown and its
environs. The summer was every bit as resolved as the spring was
ambiguous. Ms. Right had happily settled upon our marriage, with
its promise of an instant baby, and I had struck my deal with the
devil, knowingly, cannily and with a loving acceptance of corruption
that I was positive I could make work in my life as easily as others
made their average moral hypocrisies fit the convenience of their
jobs, ambitions and the embracing of whatever impracticable set of
moral ethics had been predetermined for them.

Ms. Right and I were in accordance, as were the devil and I.

We were all three of us in agreement as we optimistically flew
apart in different directions and I was split like an atom yet fixed in
place by whatever force it is that keeps molecules from spraying off
into the relief of spatial oblivion.

I doubt the devil did any more in tempting me than Ms. Right
did. In fact, Ms. Right's temptations were the more insidious and
harder to resist: she dangled my place in society as a work-a-daddy
and newly beleaguered familial patriarch before me like some poisonous reward. Here was my chance to make a bid for a corner of
social acceptance and unquestioned approval—a more unanimous in-
demnification of manhood than the loss of virginity and the next
milestone short of impotence. I could, however, with my deal in
place, have my parenthood and my kink as well, so long as I was
energetically clever and unregenerate enough in my moral elasticity.

Before I had known it, I had booked a stay with Ms. Right at
some southern family resort where her extended family was conven-
ing to celebrate not only our engagement, but the renewal of her

parents' wedding vows as well. Ms. Right was beside herself with joy.

Before I had known it, in the harsh light and cool nights of the newness of summer, I had modeled—with great success at Ubu Roi—Milt Pecksniffian's fanciest cock harness.

Before I had known it, one foot was planted squarely in one world and one was dug in just as hard in the other. All it would take was a significant movement of the earth to pull me over to either side.

And that's exactly what happened.

It was the usual Friday night—it's always those moments that change our lives so irrevocably that seem the most usual—and I was on the phone with Bootlicker, my newfound cohort in D/s club excursions. Bootlicker was a sensitive, sad-eyed unemployed computer theorist named Mossman, dapper to a fault, whom I otherwise took to be impoverished until I later realized that he was just cheap. Nevertheless, he was that figure with the physique of a puff pastry in shorts, sandals and home-tooled torso harness (minus the all-important cock-ring!) who lolled amid the filth and debris on the Ubu Roi floor licking and adoring whatever feminine set of boots would have him.

Bootlicker shared my sense of snobbery, repugnance and driven fascination about the scene and could express it on a higher level than the usual parroting of clichés or malapropish struggle to capture a significant thought that was all too fleeting. I introduced Bootlicker, or Mossman, to Ms. Right in his threadbare tweeds and trifocals and she thought him cute, a sort of teddy-bear companion for me—nice, polite, meek, and why wouldn't I associate with more like him? Oh, I would, I *would*.

Boot and I had arranged to meet by the ATM, as usual. That way, his half-finished state of undress and guilty winces enhanced under the anxiety of getting there wouldn't alarm the already suspicious sensibility of Ms. Right.

I didn't lie to Ms. Right about where I was going, though she was relieved I was going in such company as Mossman's—after all, he was so skeptical, ironical and unbeautiful. What could he *really* know about this kinky club set of—to her mind—passé suburban swinger holdovers from the 70s? He had also managed to collect a number of discount passes to Ubu Roi. So much the better to Ms. Right's mind. I was both chaperoned *and* discounted, exactly the way she preferred to have me so as to ignore me.

I was safe.

Boot and I met at the ATM—in warm rain, bondage gear and other contingent accessories packed in a discreet gym bag in my case, and in Boot's in an ancient GI knapsack. He was late, as usual, doddering down the main drag of Divinity Street in his claptrap of a car that was always on the verge of breaking down. From where I stood on the street corner, I could see Ms. Right waving happily as a shadow on the shade of the living-room window of our second-story apartment. I tried not to look back as Boot honked the clownish-sounding horn of his mongrel Asiatic jalopy to get my attention.

I hardly noticed it was raining at all.

The bouncers—shaven-headed Goth-boy twenty-somethings with black painted lips in preparation for the new dark ages tricked out in black fatigues, overt headsets and a self-consciously unanimous drugged-out look—recognized both Boot and me for who we were immediately at the head of the line and admitted us without checking for proper dress (no "streets" or "sneaks" allowed on Fetish Fridays) or IDs to prove our age, which would have been done otherwise, no matter how much at least one of us appeared to be a significantly elder statesman.

We were regulars—if anything on Friday night at Ubu Roi could ever be considered regular.

We would get there early, somewhere between eight and nine, brave the cold, dark empty smokiness past shambling willowy Goths in black caftans and nervous middle-aged mustachioed tourists fidgeting with their undrunk drinks on the prowl for women yet to come. Peals of Athena's screeching, late in the set up for her stage routine—as always—would penetrate our skulls, while nameless techno's industrial throb would blast us as we hoped to adjust, heading for the basement, the coat check and our changing ritual.

There, in the seamy stalls of the men's room drenched and slicked with unspeakable moisture (even at this early hour), Boot and

I would clamber into our respective harnesses, swapping street-clothes coverage for scenewear. While boot tinkered and fussed with his home-tooled rig, I snapped straps and fiddled with the cock-ring, oiling up to prevent chafing around the scrotum and perineum, doing a delicate dance on a plastic bag in which my scene-gear had been packed within my black canvas gig bag. Then, having thus far successfully avoided the permeation of my white athletic socks with the urine and slops of the befouled tile bathroom floor, I would teeter from foot to foot, sliding just enough with one heel balanced in fluid uncertainty on the flattened plastic bag to make my heart infrequently leap as I pulled on the pointed-toe flat-black cowboy boots.

Next came the chaps, a zipper and lace-up affair worn without pants, framing my naked buttocks whose cheeks were cleaved by a leather g-string—a tempting target for any dominant, man or woman, cruising for such objects of play. Then, having managed to drape, fold and place all my street clothes at various anchor points in the stall, over the toilet paper roll, on the back of the toilet, over the metal door or even hung from the handle, I would proceed to fold it all methodically, placing it piece by piece as flat as possible into the gig bag, carefully toilet-tissuing off the plastic bag for the five minutes after last call that would bring me back down here again to reverse the procedure.

I would emerge from the stall amid the pissing leatherboys, the vulgar frat tourists in their backwards hip-hop baseball caps, the one or two transvestites and their unconcerned girlfriends either tightening corset lacing or consulting on mascara and lipgloss, and primp myself against the mirror above the filthy flooded sinks as unconcerned as one who lived there. One of the many tall and hirsute Evangelines of the club would more often than not help me buckle my submissive's collar from behind as I accessorized with a chainmail biceps strap and brushed my dark overgrowth of wild hair. I chatted with the incoming vanillas, stage performers, leatherboys with guts puffed up with more exaggeration than the shoulders of their elaborate biker jackets as if this sordid, violated men's room were just another room in my home.

And in a sense it was.

Ubu Roi had by then become my second home. Dangerous, unrepentant, filled with the low-end, law-breaking excesses of hipness, laced with the continual threat of whatever the current drug of choice, frivolous violence, sexual risk, deviance and defiance in the face of imminent disease and all its servile naysayers—nevertheless the dank, spacious, cigarette-tarred dance club had become, under the aegis of Mistress Athena and her Friday nights, my refuge. I derived no small titillation from the fact of just how much at ease I was at the club and how accepted I was on Fetish Fridays in my Propertius incarnation by all variety of disreputables: bikers, strippers, pro-doms, drugged-out dropped-out Goths, club pros, would-be club pros, would-be vampire children and certified public accountants frustrated enough with the swingers scene to come all dressed in the priciest fetish (and therefore the most incongruously ridiculous) to score themselves a piece of kinky ass—which would amount to someone just like them, if not their ex's themselves, down to the wildly expensive and equally mismatched fetish dress.

I got to know all the players at the club, especially those who tried to make a living off the scene through the clubs and the selling of helpful little devices, bits of gear—cuffs, restraints, floggers and whatnot—and they knew me, but not as anything more than a newly dedicated player in search of play.

Or, as every other avowedly submissive male eyeing every scantily clad stripper wannabe or neophyte pro-domme no doubt was, one in search of a mistress.

This was sniffed out quickly, as my sudden onrush into their element was, despite my continual presence on the Dreams-Come-True BBS, considered somewhat of a threat, as all new incursions were in this realm of paranoia and brutal lust. The unanimous policy of behavior within the nearly atomistically fragmented kinky hetero sex scene was uncritical acceptance of new entries into it, or "newbies." The actual fact lurking beneath each and every welcoming smile was unbridled suspicion and, in the case of partners in the several "open" play relationships and couples in search of other couples or singles, rampant, venomous, almost purely territorial jealousy.

There was such a desperate breathlessness to this gaggle of sensual hypocrisy that its effect was to make me giddy, uninhibited and ready for anything. I felt released in the unashamed yet furtive interplay of venal sin with a vast magnitude of apparent sexual corruption.

Or, more particularly—my largely bare ass stuck out for all to see, my bared and well-worked–out chest adorned by the cock harness as well as a threateningly scanty male pouch g-string to drive home the point: I was ready for play.

But hadn't I already played, with all my recent experiences tucked under the belt-straps of my harness? Not at all. But for that minor interlude with Milt Pecksniffian—who had since been pursuing me urgently by phone (and who wound up instead forming a bitchy afternoon alliance with Ms. Right, discussing at length the measure and amplitude of my flaws), I had played no S&M scene and had only the dimmest conception of what this play was.

I entered Ubu Roi each Friday night with zestful will to find out.

I added all my accessories in the oblong, grimy men's room mirror as I usually did on this ordinary Friday night, to the tune of some Angelique, Evangeline, or Ruby commenting on the status of my primping while Mossman—Boot—and I traded *bon mots* about what to expect from the floor that night.

"So, what is it tonight?" I asked, adding pancake makeup to hide a shadow of stubble on my face.

"You should know what it is from what Friday it is," he said with smug humor.

"Well I don't," I said, rezippering the zipper of my chaps' left inseam, checking for the bulge of my wallet in the boot.

"Perv-*o*," said Boot.

"Another slave auction?"

"I believe," he said, worrying at the overly stressed stomach straps of his homemade rig, "that *that* would be the standard stage attraction to get a good gathering of the tribes interested."

"Anything else?"

"Rainbow night."

"So?"

"Last week's Bettie Page bucks are good this week—as are the week's before. Could be some high bidding wars."

"And?" I yawned, squaring away my gig bag to leave at the coatcheck.

"Presided over by Magdalene the Royal Pain, Contessa the Undressa and your own object of perfidy, Chlamydia Perfidia."

"Why do they feel the need to provide stage entertainment for a clubful of ardent fetishists and S&M players looking to meet one another or recruit suitable vanillas for unspeakable acts?"

"Aren't we entertainment enough?" Boot shrugged, spreading his palms apart like a borscht-belt comic. The answer to his counter-question hung in the air so obviously, we both laughed, creating more of a din amid the wet echoes of the men's room. "Let's go trippin'," he added with a crisp nod, one of our terms for cruising or "surfing" the club for the lovelies likely to abuse us both in the manner to which we had yet to become accustomed.

"Surf's up," I said, and we began at the beginning where all the potential mistresses stripped: coatcheck.

Before I could survey any quality or value of charm among the uneven influx of women shedding jackets and coats to reveal what was very often past the legal limit of exhibited skin, Bootlicker was already writhing on the concrete floor in an uncaring orgy of indiscriminate footwork. This behavior was purely reflexive, as it was a tubby crew of novices with frizzy dye-jobs full of semishocked giggles who were the night's first object of Boot's pedal peregrinations. I noted this in the time it took me to recover from Boot's slithering display of audacity underfoot, which was also having the effect of making the disgruntled pimply Goth's thankless job of tracking all the coats and gear on the other side of the counter all the harder. He shouted witless comments at the wriggling academic on the cold concrete floor as the logjam of club-goers impatient to shed their evening layers—necessary here in Miltown even in summer—grumblingly accumulated. It set my teeth on edge. I reminded myself how common it was in the scene—at least in this tide-pool community chapter of it—for one pervert to absolutely loathe and revile another's perversion. It was okay to beat them up, as long as you didn't pee on them, or something absurd like that. A mindfuck good enough to seem nonconsensual but which palpably was not, was—in a word that should have been taboo itself within the scene—taboo.

Amid the Goth's obsessive Monty Python references, I let Boot do his recruiting and made my usual strut about the club, an obvious cruise not precisely for women—all those sought-after mistresses, dominatrices or tops encased in the sexiest fetish whose bodies held the least years and whose minds held even less experience. Admittedly, these self-styled lynxes and vixens were often fun and receptive and could be topped from the bottom, coaxed to experiment to satisfy any hard-won, profoundly experienced, dearly nurtured perversion on a whim—often the more socially reprehensible the better (from their standpoint)—but I was in search of something more encompassing, something out of my control, something that might overwhelm me, hold me within it without losing me at all. I was looking for a scene, any scene, that could suck me in and build around me. I was looking for further entry into this world of such disunity and disagreement as to its content and meaning, and so much unanimity as to the fundamental satisfaction it held more firmly than a promise that could not be granted fully anywhere else. I wanted the roleplay that would strip away the civility from its players, excise all mannered refinement and promote some unspoken intensity, a transcendent religiosity founded in lust, violence and a shared emphasis on flesh and the mortification of flesh.

In my perverse way, I wanted to be saved through corruption then go home at the end of the night and cuddle steeped in love against the formerly dormantly and now solely reproductively sexual Ms. Right, as innocent as a baby.

What I didn't know was that someone else in the building crowd was watching me—someone who would destroy me forever. Someone who would damn me forever to live with myself as I could never have been and yearned to be. But I had been far too successfully seduced into action to think, to consider—to even want to know.

No, I wanted the bitchy blonde mistress by the back bar swatting away at some gray and paunchy cardigan-wearing payee with the momentous cleavage and the bee-stung lips to take me up by the scruff of the neck and do with me what she would. I made my way over to her corner, the leather loop of my leash firmly gripped between my teeth.

I was stopped by a hulking figure with silver hair, one of those extra-large, pug-nosed rural denizens who usually wind up as contractors working on the houses of the Trinity yuppies or as mobile bully boys for the state police with a score to settle—usually against the Miltown yuppies. He was wearing the full uniform of a state police officer, down to the jodhpurs, jet-black handcuffs and holstered sidearm. Balanced in his left hand was a thickly menacing double-handled black riot stick, which he holstered when I stopped at the tip of his right jackboot.

His face was boyish, despite the silver hair, lined features and vascular spiderwebbing about the nose. He went for my center harness ring—as they all seemed to—and bent his face to meet mine.

"My name is Mount," he said.

"Mountie?" The din of the club was nothing short of distorting at this point.

"No—Mount. Like the horse." He patted his groin. "Officer Mount to you."

I nodded. I had handled this sort of pass before—and a peculiar sort of flirtatious diplomacy was called for to bring about extrication from it without backlash. "Yes, Officer? Are you arresting me, or do I get off with a warning this time?"

"A warning this time, I should think," he said in a voice somehow eerily redolent of Bullwinkle the Moose.

"Well then—I'll just have to consider it a lucky opportunity to reflect on what I might have missed in narrowly avoiding a trip back to headquarters." I coyly spun about, wriggling free of his hand on the center ring of my cock harness.

"You are not exactly an unknown quantity around here, Propertius," he said in a haughty tone with an irritating emphasis on the broad 'a,' "and far and away the most beautiful *domme* in this entire establishment would like you to sub for her and you'd be an absolute fool not to do it."

I felt a stirring at his indirect tugging of my cock-ring from the center strap timed with what he said.

This was a new one—as if any dominatrix worth a second look had to send even an apparent master to alert and secure a potential slave when the merest distracted crook of her little finger would have done just as well at a cost of far less effort. But, like all the submissive

men in the place on semipermanent cruise control in search of a
mistress, I was acutely attuned to the barest hint of attention that in
any way seemed to originate from a potential object of my lustful
need. Perhaps it was even the butch blonde dom beating ever so
nonchalantly on the flanks of her overtly ornamental gray-flannel
man kneeling rigid there at the back bar like a horse on the floor.

As I said before, I was ready for anything.

"Who is it?" I asked. "Where is she? I certainly don't want to
be a fool—unless, of course, Mistress decrees it."

"Oh, but you *are* a fool," said Mount. "So, in order to educate
you, I'm afraid you're going to have to guess."

The head games—even within a scene—lose their allure rather
quickly when they a become a transparent device for someone else's
nonsexual gratification at your sexual expense, so I shrugged with
disinterest, still half-eyeing the butch blonde. "Since I have nothing
to go on, I have no real need to guess. It could be anyone. If I luck
out, I'll find her. If I don't, I'll still luck out, because, if you know
anything about me, you know I always do." I wagged my ass playfully at him to stop him in his tracks and make my getaway.

Puckering his lips, Mount put a thudding, comradely hand on
my bare shoulder. "But you'll be missing out—and besides, you're
not listening: I *said* she's the most attractive domme in the place."

"That's a highly subjective clue—"

"But it's all you've got," he interrupted with mock drama. "Take
it or be left behind." Then, with his affectedly boyish grin he swag-
gered off, convincing a clique of uninitiated vanillas as he left that
he was an actual on-duty state police officer instead of a just another
uniform fetishist with a charge account at the local law enforcement
supply shop. I took it that he loved doing this, being that he did it
so quickly and effortlessly, showboating about with a blustering guffaw and a booming voice I realized could be tracked from any point
in the club—not that I would want to. The women—tourist secre-
taries with moussed and marcelled hair and little cocktail dresses with
bangled accessories appropriate for any other club but this—were
aroused by Mount's performance, feeling up his riot stick and admiring the handcuffs before he slapped them about the wrists of the

willowiest one and dragged her off into the front room and out of my line of sight.

The beat of the techno increased and I went off to flirt with the blonde, who played with my harness in wrenching yanks, intermittently beating her accessory man on the floor as the dejected Mossman watched with interest. When the flirtation ended, I sidled up next to Athena in his perch to pay my respects and get the lowdown on what had been happening in what I then imagined to be the full-time scene while I had been spinning my wheels with Ms. Right and the vagaries of job hunting and freelance journalism during the earlier part of the week.

It was after I got a rundown of a week's worth of professional scenes—all of which made my skin crawl—and a record of hustling pro-dom attentions for a range of services from desperate submissives (including car washing and shiatsu massage) that Athena hit me up for the auction.

"We're doing a scene auction tonight," said Athena, his sustained falsetto cracking a tad as he dragged on his ultrathin cigarillo and sipped his Southern Comfort. He was blonde tonight in a rubber tunic and black lace pinafore. He flipped through a bunch of index cards checking off names on a yellow legal pad and I couldn't help but notice his fingernails—each one sparkled in a different color with a little agonized face on it. Vain to a fault, Athena noticed my noticing and spread his fingers before me to be admired. "Slave Murray the K did these for me," he said proudly. "Ain't they cool?"

"Cool. What kind of scene auction?"

"Both sub and dom—it's not just the person, but the scene they're into that goes up for bid. We match the doers to what they either want to do or have done. So, Propertius, just tell me what scene you're into and *do the do*."

I suffered lockjaw.

What *did* I want to do? I knew I wanted submissive play—but what was play? Ceremonial violence followed by rough sex? And could I put that on a card and perform it in a club? Maybe, but not here in Miltown. Bondage? Here—without sex—that would be nothing short of annoying. Foot worship? Massaging, kissing and licking feminine feet? Though its traditional symbolism of sexual submission was on point, the act itself for me was not. That was Boot's bailliwick. Body worship, however, I had it in my mind then at the time, would simply be the same sort of attention but performed on a grander scale. Certainly stageworthy. I opted for that.

Athena sprayed Southern Comfort with an assault salvo of laughter. "You can't do that here, little Prop! Don't you realize that? They'd positively shut us down. We have one or two cops here mixing in just waiting to make arrests for lewd and lascivious behavior."

It hit me like abruptly stepping on a nail that Athena was right: there was no reason for there not to be at least one undercover vice cop in such a well attended, exceedingly public S&M club event. "There's plenty of lewd and lascivious stuff happening every Friday here right out on the floor, but there haven't been any arrests since I started coming here."

Athena pouted and lit another cigarillo.

The heroin cadaver bartender with the fire-engine–red fright wig of hair and the 60's go-go tunic mini hanging off her dilapidated body listlessly asked Athena about his next Southern Comfort. Athena tentatively laid a bill on his cocktail napkin, tonguing the rim of his glass stiffly, which was empty but for a thin coating of the syrupy drink. He smacked his lips close to my eyes and breathed cigarillo-tainted breath in my face.

"What'll you have, honey? Your usual?" Her overbite dominated her face as surely as heroin had claimed her skin. I deduced that the energy she displayed in keeping up with the steady stream of bar orders was as artificial as the lassitude that lurked behind it.

"Of course. Akasha—I'll have a Marlon mixture but—"

"I know, I know," she said, her long body slumped as always, waving her arm dismissively, "hold the urine." It was our little joke. Marlon was a kinky gay leather boy in his late thirties whose passionate fetishes focused on muscle, piss, shit, spit and anal play. He liked his boys as steroidal as he was and his girls—when he had them—to be incongruously demure little flowers of near-Gibson–Girl femininity, the hint of Evelyn Nesbitt-ish naughtiness notwithstanding. Marlon had been stacking everything from dianabol to bo-lasterone for years and was, for a short while—unattended to by any of the bodybuilding slicks who could deal with the occasional discrete gay competitor but not a sharp-tongued leather boy in latex trunks with nipple rings who wore STP performance auto lube in his slicked back DA—*Mr. Miltown.* Sometimes when Askasha mixed his drink—cranberry juice, vodka with a splash of seltzer—she'd discreetly piss into it for him as a favor.

Marlon got off on kissing everybody after refreshing himself in this way. We had become good friends regardless, and though I let him stroke my butt, we remained on a handshake basis.

"Southern Comfort and a Marlon mixture," Akasha said, setting down the drinks and Athena's change. "Hold the pee!" she added, shouting.

"The cops don't care as long as it's not onstage—the lewd and lascivious—and kept hidden in the dark corners, beneath the vending tables, when we have them, and in the lavatory stalls before club security rudely interrupts. They don't care about the beatings as long as everybody's happy—the last thing they want is to have to deal with the paperwork in the arrest of some insurance salesman for consensual assault and battery with the state pressing the charges."

"Not that they wouldn't if they had to." I sipped my Marlon and made a face.

"Don't be paranoid," Athena said. I didn't know if he was referring to my drink or my remark.

I drank up anyway, reminding myself that it was only Marlon and besides, at least I knew him. Ah—how easily one does slide into perfidy. Athena scribbled furiously on a card and checked me off on the yellow pad.

"You're all set," he said standing, or should I say telescoping up to his full seven feet of vinyl boot-aided height.

"Set for what?" I asked, downing the rest of the Marlon nervously.

He bent and kissed me on the forehead. "I put you down as a 'dom's choice' entry."

I bit into the rim of my now empty plastic cup.

"Oh now don't get tense," Athena said, his voice descending two octaves. "This is a club setting—what can they do? Give you an enema right here in the goddamn center of Ubu Roi?"

I had to admit—he had solved my problem in a businesslike fashion. "And I can quit anytime."

"Even before the half hour they're entitled to is up. There's always club security to back you up. Of course, should that happen, you may not be doing any scenes for a long, long time—at least in this scene."

"I can always safe," I said questioningly. To safe was the slang for an agreed upon "safeword" chosen by the submissive so that such fun exclaimations as "no more," "don't," and the ever popular "help" could be used to heighten intensity rather than put a stop to it.

"Safe away," said Athena adjusting his falsetto. "Later, Prop— I got to mambo."

Marlon came up behind me and lifted me up in both arms like a child. "Well if it isn't little Prop—and what are we drinking tonight, Prop?"

He was wearing his usual biker jacket, dully shining armless latex one-piece top, latex pants and seven-league boots all arrayed with skulls, chains, spikes and a miniature rubber replica of dog feces pinned to the lapel of the jacket where he could occasionally lick it. "You can't buy me a drink if both your hands are full, Marlon," I said.

"True—and I also can't shake your hand." He puckered his lips to plant a kiss on mine and I responded with a quick twist at the hips, managing to jump down from his arms to the club floor, narrowly avoiding the outsized buttock of some squat dominatrix busy having her high heels tongue-polished by some nearly toothless codger on the ground. Marlon gracefully grabbed me and pressed his large, hard body against mine, spit on my cheek and licked it off all so quickly I didn't have a moment to remonstrate, let alone sputter. "Would you mind terribly if I sucked your cock, Propertius? We could do it downstairs in the little girl's room. It might be fun!"

"It might be." I touched my cheek where he licked me and found it smooth and dry. "What would your wife say?"

"Who? Ned? Oh, he hates you anyway—so what. Let's go," he

said with offhand glee. "I can go kick open a stall, toss some bitch out on her ear and then you can come all over my face. Such a deal!" He grabbed my crotch. "Oh, you really don't just stuff a gym sock in that g-string, do you?"

"All me," I said. "But I don't think we can do that, as Ned is standing about four paces behind you with a very pissy look on his face. Not only that, Marlon, but I know where you've been."

"Well, I would think that would be extra incentive to go down with me, wouldn't *you?*"

"After possibly the third Marlon mixture, it would be. But I'm only on my second now. And I have some business to attend to. I have to go solve a riddle."

"A riddle," he repeated, totally unfazed by my standard demur, peeling off small bills from a Michigan roll he carried to impress any available twinkie boys who generally circled about cash like vultures, and handed me my drink. "If you answer it, do you get a prize?" He mouthed: "I gave my love a cherry. . . ."

"I'm hoping to," I said.

"Well, if it isn't a sexual prize, don't bother with it. Hey, did you know these taste better if you have Akasha piss into it a little bit? I'll bet she does so much heroin it probably makes you a little high in the bargain."

"I've heard. But it isn't really my thing, so I'll have to take your word for it."

"Well," Marlon said thoughtfully, "I could always spit in yours for you, if you want— to give you the flavor of things, so to speak."

"It's just not for me," I said, not entirely sure I could prevent him if he really wanted to.

"Okay." He shrugged happily and collected a wad of Bettie Page bucks from Akasha in passing. "As long as you have fun, that's the main thing. Maybe I'll buy you and suck your cock anyway—Athena told me you'd be auctioned off tonight."

I laughed. "I'd better start collecting my own Bettie Page bucks to save me from the likes of you."

"Okay-see-you," said Marlon as a single word, turning his attentions toward a very effeminate boy named James dressed in a slickly shining spray-siliconed rubber shirt and spandex pants. There was a spike through his nose that gave the appearance of a sinister vaudeville mustache.

I went off to solve the riddle—and to cruise. I noticed as an afterthought that I was totally erect and poking out of my PVC g-string. I stuffed myself back in and proceeded to hunt for the mystery mistress hoping that, by the end of the night, with the help of the small bottle of baby oil I brought with me in my bag, that the painful evidence of persistent cock-ring chafing would be minimal.

The prevailing rumor in S&M is that nobody drinks, as it muddies the clear waters of intense sensation, makes the whiphand less assured—but here, in Miltown, *everybody* drinks, straight and kinky alike and I proved to be no exception. Downing a few more Marlons, I wound up recumbent on a couch stretched across two older but comely mistresses, one blonde and tanned with freckles transected by lines, the other brunette with a smoothly cultivated alabaster pallor. The blonde wore a standard latex minidress with leggings and the brunette was corseted, her thighs laced tightly in crotch-high boots, and buckles and studs scraped against me from her amply soft and well-filled décolletage. These night-and-day twins scratched and teased and bit at my skin, reveling in my availability every bit as much I reveled in their attentions. The brunette, whose name was Auntie Maim, chewed and licked and sucked at my ear as she whispered: "Do you know who I am?"

"Auntie Maim." I winced and wriggled, having long ago lost the humor of her sweetly perverse cookie-cut *nom-de-guerre*.

She slapped my face. "No silly, I'm the puzzle you couldn't solve."

I got up too quickly and saw white lights play against my field of vision. The blonde—one of the many Shebas of the club—bit into and licked my trapezius as I tried to focus. "You're the one?" I rubbed my wounded shoulder as Sheba grinned demurely, raking my left scapula with transparently lacquered nails.

"That's right, darling." She struck a pose. "That's me—the most attractive *domme* in the place." She tittered girlishly, almost nervously.

Mount came bounding by. "Ah," he bellowed. "I knew he'd

figure it out. You were right, Auntie Maim, he was certainly bright enough. Now get him on his knees and beat him."

I wanted to acquaint Mount with his riot stick from the bottom up—but he was so oblivious to the roiling sea of lust and self-interest that surrounded him, I figured, "Why bother? He's bound to drown himself soon enough." And I had other matters to attend to, not least of which was maintaining the ability to walk upright.

I tried undertaking this, but Auntie Maim tugged up on the center ring of my harness with surprising roughness and I fell back down to the couch off balance, twisting directly into Sheba's chest— which was totally exposed but for little strips of electrical tape over the nipples—face first. "*Do* try not to smother, there, darling. Mother has plans for you." Sheba held my head in place with both hands, making it difficult to leave on literally more than one front.

"All good little boys have to learn how to suck," she said. Sheba had me remove the tape with my mouth and so I did as Mount looked on with what can only be described as goofy beatitude.

They lured me from the soiled red divan into the main room where Athena was screeching the exhortation to spend money at the tourists and regulars to keep her night alive. Sheba playfully smacked my naked behind while Auntie gaily clasped a leash onto the O-ring of my Christmas-tree spiked collar. I didn't have to be dragged, although Auntie enjoyed the aspect of keeping the leash as short as possible while jerking me off my center of balance with abrupt and jagged tugs that led me to the stage.

"And now," Athena burst forth from the stage with popping reverb, his respiratory system threatening to heave up from the mic' with each and every syllable, "our own Propertius will demonstrate how a good little slutboy takes his punishment in the capable hands of Mistress Auntie Maim!" Now, every self-styled female dominant, or femdom, prefixed her special nomenclature with the title "Mistress," whether she wanted to or not, whether she was styled Goddess, Lady, Madame or Auntie. "Mistress" was how the public remaking of herself was remade. So, Mistress Auntie Maim bade me to get down on my knees with a sharp jolt of the leash, while she primly and daintily curtsied. Sheba bowed out, beckoned back by her husband to whatever display of tricks and toys meant to impress whatever group of tourists he had dragged to Ubu Roi that night that he had in mind for her.

Auntie Maim, however, would not shrink from what I had not known then was to be her first public spanking—in fact, it was to be her first public scene of any kind—I was too far gone to notice, too entranced by the fact that it was to be, for whatever the limits of sham and showmanship the club imposed, my very first scene.

It was not a revelation at first. When it began, my sense of it was similar to the slipping on of a leather winter glove—snug, comfortable, initially cool but rapidly warming. She started out with her bare hand on my bare buttocks, exposed by tight studded leather chaps and skimpy PVC and Spandex g-string. Her hand was relaxed and stayed concave to the shape of the object that it smacked. Auntie did not forget the all important smoothings and caresses of her gloved hands across my shocked and sensitized flesh to vary the sensation and give some counterpoint to her punishing impact.

She sat on a bench, the center spotlight trained on us such that any vision of the audience—most of whom ignored us anyway—was obliterated. I lay across her lap, compromised by my cock-ring. My flaccid member, finding itself unable to get rigid, lodged squarely between her more rigid thigh and the nickel-plated steel of the ring—the rock and the hard place. She switched to the hairbrush.

It hurt.

My mind screamed that this wasn't fun anymore: time to quit.

"Stop squirming," Auntie ordered through a smile that threatened to become a grimace, her teeth gleaming frostily like white sequins toward the audience.

"Beat him good," hollered a hip-hop boy holding a beer with his team cap worn backwards, his shorts and tee-shirt the requisite two sizes too big.

"Spank his ass," some drunken harridan in a cowgirl outfit screeched, falling off her stool and into the arms of the nearest beer-gutted brute who would have her. You might ask how I could see this from my vantage point of watching her knee and the floor amid the bleaching wash of light from the center spot. I didn't have to. I could hear it as my pain mounted. I had seen it all before on my hunt for this moment, in my quest for the secret it yielded: the pain.

And I wanted to reject the pain—was this *it?* Where was the sex? Where was that gratification that caused me to trample the heart of Ms. Right after I tossed it aside in the gutter in my all-consuming effort to chase down the dream? Certainly I was being touched, attended to, even focused upon by a beautiful, authoritative, severe mistress of the type that once peopled my adolescent fantasies before I put them away like the insubstantial toys they were.

Or were supposed to be.

As it turned out, they put me away instead. Apparently such toys were not to be treated lightly, as I was learning just then. I wanted to be finished with them, but they were never quite finished with me. They wanted to be played with, and play with me they would in order to renew my interest in this desperate reciprocity. So there I was, lying across a beautiful—albeit hippy—mistress' lap getting the stuffing beaten out of my ass while my poor cock was at her indifferent mercy.

I was not hard, I was hurt.

The pain got worse; what was I, crazy?

Auntie Maim stepped up the blows and I groaned and winced to the desultory jeers and cheering of the sparse crowd on the floor. The fun had ended long ago, it seemed. Now I just had to find some way to get through this onslaught against my prone and reddening buttocks. She had switched to some sort of wooden paddle and was hefting as much of her torso into her arm as she could—throwing her center of gravity into it.

"Auntie's been shopping," she said brightly, holding me tight against her thighs as I squirmed.

The blows were bad and stung thunderously, causing me to make all manner of involuntary noises that went unnoticed. I complained about my cock and she spread her thighs just a bit, allowing me a measure of relief there, the cadence of her strokes hardly suffering at all from this minor distraction.

"That's right—beat his ass!" Athena exploded into the microphone, the sensitive insides of the speakers no doubt tearing somewhat at the receipt of her plosive "b" and with her thick and heavy broadcast breathing. "How many of *you* are going to bid on Propertius the Slutboy to spank his bubble butt as part of the Dreams-Come-True Scene Auction?! Remember, if you want to bid on that butt, you're going to need the bucks—*Bettie Page* bucks, to be precise—a murderous crackle came after the "p" in Page followed by a buzzing—"we don't take no stinking greenbacks here and we don't take no VISA-Mastercard neither! The only way to get the bucks is at the bar from the lovely Akasha and all her hot and sexy staff. The more drinks you get, the more you can bid on scene-play just like this one. So c'mon—put in some drink orders already!"

To set a good example, Athena downed her So-Co and returned to her favorite spot at Akasha's bar for another.

Auntie let up and began the caressing and smoothing; this time it seemed as if she really enjoyed it. Then it hit me—not Auntie's paddle but instead some sort of warm interior golden glow, one of those ineffable, inexplicable moments of elation when the illusory balance of life in its order is restored to frightening credibility and the resolution of even the most drastic questions seems imminent. The closest thing to it (I have it on good authority, mind you—not that *I* would ever do such a thing myself) must be the way heroin spreads its poisonous warmth through the bloodstream to get you off with the calamitous assurances of a fool's paradise regained, complete and unabridged.

Then the pain came again, this time with simultaneous double blows from Auntie's outstretched palms.

She was letting me have it as good as she could give, but by this time the secret had dawned on me. Endorphins notwithstanding, all I had to do was what I had done my entire life:

Eat the pain.

I had been on the receiving end all my life, fair or not, meant for me or not, beneficial or not. And I had been given riches of pain, dividends, interest, *superannuities* of pain—I was a goddamn *potentate* of pain. As they say, the rich just get richer and so it was with the pain. Because I had been given so much by the vagaries of life, I could take the pain and make it mine. I could own the pain, control the pain, work and shape the pain with my bare life and do with it what I would as it in turn did me.

I could literally make the pain a pleasure—something I once emphatically could live without that now I no longer wanted to.

I smiled a soft, secret smile, braced against the stony thighs of her lap and heaved a sigh before continuing the involuntary noises that the use of a small bamboo rod across my upper thighs (a cane, I found out later) evoked.

It was a simple concept and one that all at once moved me to a different plane of sexuality, if sexuality was now involved at this point at all: I had mastered the pain by allowing someone else to master me. I had taken the pain and kept it by giving myself over to someone to keep me for as long as I could hold it.

At the end, I got off very quietly and elegantly in Auntie Maim's lap, moistening one leg the merest bit.

As always, life being a desperately far cry from romance novels (which sometimes touch upon such matters as part of a repertoire of standard fantasies), the auction of slaves, masters and mistresses was a disappointment, the highest bidding as usual going either to some female pro-stripper ringer supplied on the quiet by the club, the best looking seminude woman in the joint, or the trash-babe with the biggest and best-looking boob job. Luckily, I was bought by a consortium of women headed by Chlamydia, who had become my somewhat distant scene standby and champion—a guardian demon of sorts who looked after my worst interests. So, after having been bought for a staggering amount of Bettie Page bucks—for a man anyway—I capered around on stage and gave my new coterie pony rides back and forth, as that was their chosen scene, much to the gratitude of my beleaguered and now quite flushed buttocks.

I had the feeling just then that something strange and all-consuming was happening to me—as I smirked nervously, shivering slightly as though cold, running the women around in a clamor onstage to catcalls and applause—but contrary to my newfound conviction at the time, I had absolutely no idea what it was.

What I know now was that someone in the audience was watching me, absorbing every detail of what I was sure was a throwaway moment of cavalier exhibitionism, patiently waiting for me to be replaced onstage before discreetly leaving the club.

Looking out at the audience, I could almost tell for certain that there was someone out there whose eyes and mind were fixated very specifically and intensely on me. It wasn't vanity, it was apprehension that brought me to this vague realization. I thought of my first contact at the club, the older guy with the cigar. In fact, I was sure I smelled him, his thick sebum scent vaguely covered up by the drugstore cologne, the mossy, half-rotted odor of his chewed cigar end before Chlamydia twisted my nipple pinched between two knuckles and I screamed out in pain and she tightened her grip—till I laughed.

FIVE

We had already left each other, Ms. Right and I, so to help us get over this fact we stuck close together.

We preserved all the intimacies that define and comprise a relationship but the most essential two: sex and hope.

We cuddled and muddled and kept house while living lives furtively apart, coexisting slyly in the small enclosed space of our apartment. This was just fine with Ms. Right. After all, our engagement was to be announced in barely a month at the renewal of her parents' wedding vows in the full flush and forum of her assembled family. She pursued with hesitant joy and a great deal of nervous energy a prim, potpourri-infused life that was diametrically opposed to mine.

And I did the same.

One day, there was a breakdown in the kitchen.

When was I going to break up with her? she asked. When was I going to stop leading her on?

I wasn't, I said. We were going through with her plan—I had made up my mind. Actually, she knew exactly what it was that she wanted. It was fixed in her vision with all the centered balance and irony of a born-again church snake handler. She was no fool—she knew we had problems. The words escaped her lips in a torrent of hot and ruddy tears: couples counseling.

Would I do it?

What *wouldn't* I do?

I realized at that moment, I was capable of anything. I was capable of staying with her and I was capable of leaving. I was capable of delving deeper and going further with the demimonde of kinky sex and S&M while sustaining, even exalting in a nearly sexless, unerotic conventional marriage all designed to pursue the ubiquitous dead-end adult pastime of baby farming.

If I was capable of all that, why wouldn't I be capable of thrashing out my deteriorating relationship with the love of my life in some arid, neutral HMO office, with some smug, overcertified, underexperienced psycho-prattler who cavalierly reduced the very elements of my soul to a series of autonomic responses and sanctioned trade journal trends. I wondered how they might work the psychopharmacology of improving the dynamics of our relationship—maybe whip a little Prozac, Zoloft or some other sort of happy-making serotonin-style cocktail on us. Mixed up, shaken up, stirred, dry-cleaned and reunited in under twenty visits!

Regardless, I was relieved that her health plan still carried the prescription rider, because drugs were the only concrete, validating solution that the would-be shamans of armchair anthropology and middling social science could come up with to solve the convoluted moral dilemma of the human heart. Perhaps the drugs would calm at least one of us down.

The dominance of hard science over soft was plain.

So the breakdown in the kitchen became a—what's the therapeutic buzzword for it?—a break*through*.

But a breakthrough into what? I wondered, sprawled on the vacant off-white of the kitchen linoleum, her body neatly fitted into the contours of my own as she wept with infantile relief on my shoulder.

A breakthrough into what? I wondered, standing out in the street on Divinity Ave. In the hot sun waiting to be picked up by Auntie Maim and Mount, late for my rendezvous due to the emotive antics of Ms. Right, and eager to see where the afternoon's pool party and get-together would lead.

They never showed. I went home to find Ms. Right on the phone with Auntie. I would have some explaining to do.

"Don't worry, dear boy," Auntie said. "She doesn't know who I am—not that she doesn't know who you are as well."

"Wonderful. And what about this afternoon?"

"You'll have to provide your own coverage for that. However—"she dropped the receiver abruptly and I could hear the guffawing, cartoonish, vitiated boom that was unmistakably Mount's in the background, married to Auntie's musical cooing as they both fell into a muffled struggling in which the sole comprehensible word "behave," spoken by Auntie, could be heard. Auntie must have slapped him, I surmised, as she regained control of the phone all too quickly. "How*ever,*" she repeated, "we're going now and we'll see you there shortly. Don't be late! Or Auntie will be unhappy. You *don't* want to see Auntie unhappy."

Auntie was laying it on a little thick, as she always did. The cruel attitude she struck lacked the force of conviction. She would practice her menacing glare and glower at me, but all the while curling up just beneath the surface was the hint of a smirk, which took very little effort to coax into something more full-blown and obvious. Her eyes lacked resolve. They wanted to wander; and a wandering, inconstant eye can hardly stare a recalcitrant slave into shamed submission.

"How am I going to get there? I thought you were coming to pick me up?"

The myth of ownership bore repeating: "Remember who owns *who,* dearie. You'll just have to—oh, hold on—" I could hear Mount's muted bluster negotiating with Auntie's high sharp chirps until the crackling of another grab for the receiver brought me back to attention—Ms. Right listening intently all the while to my end of the conversation, fighting hard to restrain her outward mannerisms, all of which would scream out silently her nervous desire to know.

After a telephonic *chunk* I heard a voice.

"Here's what we'll do," Auntie said, the desire to please in her voice far more genuine than the desire to punish. You just meet us here at Mountie's little apartment and we'll go together in his car."

Mount tackled her with his considerable bulk on the bed (I guessed) and our conversation ended. I made for the door, but Ms. Right's hurt expression and moist green eyes stopped me at the door more effectively than her standing in the way ever would have. She smiled a weak, unconvincing smile. "This picnic is a literary thing, right?"

"Right," I said, not wholly lying. "Do you want to come? Because if you do, we have to leave now, otherwise . . ."

"No, I don't want to go—all that book talk is too heady and I'll get sleepy."

"As you've said, you've met all the types before."

"I have to work on the magazine."

"And I have to work on getting work. You know this is how you get the gigs, by finding out they exist through the strict network of informality."

I was getting anxious—time was passing.

"I know what you say," she pouted, "but I don't know how you do what you do."

I told the truth: "Neither do I. But I have to go."

She gave her left shoulder a single shrug so high it almost hit her ear—a mannerism I thought she had given up years ago—and then she threw herself up against me and hugged me close for all she was worth, like a toddler so full of the unrestricted impulse to love that she couldn't let go of its object until both sated and distracted.

"I have to go," I said. "I love you."

"I love you," she repeated somberly.

I stepped out the door and down our winding steps, nailing yet another plank solidly and squarely into the structure of my life that was to become my coffin.

The 88 Divinity bus to Trinity was so late I sought out a taxi, which only made me later. To complicate things, Mount's house was a number on Chestnut Street, of which there were two that ran together at the border of the town with two separate sets of addresses. Naturally my Creole-speaking cabbie picked the most wrong—and furthest-flung—address first. By the time I got there all that greeted me at the door was a tart note:

"If you see fit to join us, or find yourself in any way able, prepare for a good, strict whipping at poolside while Mount observes and directs—he hates to wait for anything, let alone for *my* toys.

—AM"

Luckily, I had asked the cabbie to wait, fearing (with good reason) that they would have left without me. I felt like I was on some sort of scavenger hunt for abuse and disparagement as we pulled away from the broken curb for the next tortuous leg of the journey.

One depleted wallet later, having back tracked a few times to second guess painstakingly confused directions, we pulled up in front of an expensively nondescript split-level house accented with garish tinted glass, razor-sharp corners, an obtrusive gable that was really more a rhombus and a high pine fence backed by a redundant hedge in the verdant, hilly heart of the Coventry suburbs. There was no way to see into the yard, but as the cab jerked and sputtered off leaving me penniless and stranded amid the green rolling hills and milky smooth streets of the land of the grossly well-heeled, I could hear giggling and jabbering just ahead—the kind that's unmistakably adult but refers consistently to childhood. As I began to negotiate some way in, Auntie Maim and Mount pulled up together in a gaudy sunburst-orange *Scilia* sports car (which I found out later was leased). They emerged carrying plastic shopping bags jam-packed with picnic miscellany. Mount, with a face minutely slashed and ruined by shaving under what I could only guess was either *delirium tremens* or the Parkinsonian symptoms of some unidentified psychotropic medication, made for me to let me have it. I looked as contrite as possible before he reached me. Auntie Maim was a bit too wobbly to get there first, let alone intervene.

The sun was oppressive. I was almost grateful for Mount's hulking shadow.

I set forth the mis-steps of my journey in modest terms, parenthetically counting myself to blame at every possible point, and Mount soon slumped into his usual negligent posture, relieved to hear I was afforded no pleasure at the expense of his patience. Auntie oozed perfunctory sympathy, promised me a ride back when the time came and snapped her lacquer-nailed fingers for me to come take the bags.

Auntie made it plain that I had beaten them there, even in my lateness, because Mount didn't know where the hell he was going.

We went in through a high garden gate made of halved logs with the bark still on them. It was a far from rustic scene that revealed itself to me when we came to the end of the flagstoned side path by the monolithic house.

The spacious yard was dominated, but by no means swallowed, by a kidney-shaped swimming pool on whose edges lolled an exaltation of nude S&M players, all of whom were overweight, at least ten years older than me, and who sported (like outré leisure suits) lined discolored skin that was either tanned like nonfetish leather, sallow or pallid, erratically carbuncled by miscellaneous moles. It was like a backyard gathering of naturists gearing up to start either a colony or co-op or organize an outing to some private beach where they could display their paucity of physical gifts to one another—instead of a gathering of staunchly heterosexual fisting, flogging fetishists. Not a single trapping of S&M was in sight.

The only thing to distinguish them at all from the geeky clubbishness of the pagan new-age nudists was *the attitude.*

The attitude was complex: looks, fitness, attractiveness, didn't matter; personal sophistication, didn't matter. The way of all flesh was death and decay. The secret to overcoming this was to transcend the needs of the flesh with those of the mind and psyche—to use the body's own protections against pain as providers of joy. The new mortification of the flesh—the safe religion of libido without sex, of sex without union, of union without fealty. It was a zealous new heresy as full of self-mutilation and excoriation as early Catholicism.

The attitude was simple: jovial acceptance accompanied by gleeful, supportive approbation in the face of perversion—with the undercurrent of a death threat ready to meet the slightest infraction against the perceived group.

The problem was, though, that the group had yet to define itself; hence the absence of Athena and the presence of certain others.

Mossman was there, waiting in his cutoffs and sandals, brooding over some Boolean nuance of social sexual politics that I blissfully ignored as a rule. He explained to me that our sole purpose for being there was to serve.

Auntie ordered me to strip down—either nude or into something scanty enough to be appropriately decorative for this outing. I opted for the latter, as total nudity had been somewhat devalued by its poolside participants. Mossman, or Boot, followed suit.

I settled my effects into the poolhouse, dodging a giant, senile poodle named Shlomo, and changed into my slavewear for the afternoon. This consisted of a spiked collar, chainmail armband worn above the right biceps (to flag submissive), a PVC g-string fastened at the hips with small patches of Velcro and nothing else. The plainly submissive O-ring on the collar made a charming jingling when I ran up and down two flights of outer-deck stairs fetching trays of pigs-in-blankets, Swedish meatballs, rumaki and other needful treats.

Capering in the pool like a spastic seacow was the doyenne known only as Muffy, whose husband Herod was some sort of shady divorce attorney with a discreet practice in Coketown with only a P.O. Box for an address. He wore a big, glittering Hebraic symbol for life on a gaudy chain about his ample neck. He seemed like the sort of jolly, good-natured fat man that you go miles out of your way to make sure you do not cross. Easily dwarfing Mount was Deprav-o, an antique hippie technocrat from the early hot tub days of the seventies who stood almost seven feet tall with a gut and flanks that could only be described as Dionysian. He looked like a nude, sun-parched, dilapidated version of the Spirit of Christmas Present from Dickens' *A Christmas Carol*.

The gnome-like, self-important self-published author and mail-order pornographer Tutor was there.

Originally from Texas with a self-amputated accent, his name was actually Warner Cousins, failed fifth-rate academic (associate professor of freshman and remedial English), freshly fired from some local junior college equivalent (they don't use the adjective "junior" anymore—perhaps they should be called "collegettes"?). Cousins' well-planned sobriquet of Tutor derived not only from the special outside interest he had once shown in his students—rumored to have cost him his last professional job—but from the very special niche in the Miltown scene that he had managed, with the exhaustive help and financing of his newest submissive "O" (who in a literal geometric sense resembled her name more than her literary namesake) to carve out: that of continuing education *newbie-hawk*.

Having little else to attract female playmates, and with the physical charms of a Colonel Sanders gone to seed, Cousins took the high road by appointing himself to a position of authority (as no one else would do it for him) with endless, noisy bragging and distorted resumé quoting all of which sounded as if it were spoken directly from

his intestines, bypassing trachea, epiglottis and vocal chords altogether. His discreet way of hitting on all useful newbies was to use
their own curiosity about the scene as the sexual lure, exactly the
same way more mainstream sexual harassers do, but clad instead in
leather and couched firmly in the exotic-seeming cult terminology of
D/s.

Under the guise of educating these "pupils," after using their
own bodies for the instruction dummies, he would summarily screw
them, then recruit them into his political camp.

When they later caught on and rebelled, he would slander them
to whatever following remained.

I was learning that, even in this realm, politics was a compulsion
more irresistible than kinky sex. It nearly went without saying that
the two went hand-in-hand.

Cousins was just one of a number of tireless (and apparently
lifeless) self-promoting high-profile types within the scene who intended, since they could run nothing else in their lives, to run it
instead.

Naturally, he and Athena were mortal enemies.

In fact, there were so many mortal enemies within the scene I
was beginning to lose count. The *attitude* seemed to result from this.
To any outsider, it looked like the friendliest, most mild and non-
threatening group imaginable—just like a visit to *someone else's* office.
All the internecine backbiting was hidden and remote. Until you
worked there.

"O," perhaps one of only three archaeologists employed by the
City of Miltown to fend off militant preservationists—and who still
managed to sustain some kind of life outside the scene—had made
the shrewd move of coming out publicly by labeling herself Cousins'
submissive. It was her foremost scene identity, and she wore it as an
electronic placard on Internet newsgroups and even on such local
closed-end BBS's as Dreams-Come-True. She had no need to *top
from the bottom*—the frequent means by which female submissives
saw to their own satisfaction by manipulating their insecure masters'
fragile macho posturings (to which Cousins was no exception)—as
this might call some of his trumped-up mystique into more obvious
question. What she did instead was to run Cousins the way a watch-

ful mother runs a spoiled toddler: with a heavy edge of superior psychology and the ultimate iron-fisted control of the all-important *sweets*.

"O" lay across her gleeful master's lap, limp, naked and wet, causing him to squirm perceptibly as his knees buckled.

Amapola was there, her white suit for the moment discarded. She favored dressing in white to emphasize her childish, virginal quality while pushing fifty with a form, physique, skin tone and personal demeanor that itself favored the Australian cane toad. Amapola had just started up the Ties 'R' Us BBS to compete with Dreams-Come-True. She tee-heed at me in some grotesque parody of demureness when I emerged from the pool house, then resumed innocently discussing the necessary demise of the conniving, paranoid bitch who ran Fetish Fridays at Ubu Roi.

Tutor nodded with the grim maculation of his face that passed for a smile.

I emerged from the poolhouse amid these personages at a brisk clip followed by the drooling Shlomo, just as Muffy and Deprav-o got frisky in the center of the pool, mingling on all too grand a scale like two mooning manatees. Auntie indicated the kitchen with a theatrical clap of her hands, her tone of voice and imperious gesturing heavily redolent of opera, which she had long since made plain to me was the centerpiece of her inner life from which all other such refinements flowed—even those as tepid as the practice of beating on men's backs and buttocks for fun and profit. Mossman and I took her command wordlessly, in our best approximations of what good, servile submissives would do—which we were emphatically not—and scaled the half-finished outer-deck steps to furnish food again and again, ever mindful of the fact that the burgeoning corpulence of the elder scene die-hards must at all times be fed.

Couples showed up as Boot and I served officiously. I scurried about granting individual requests for ice or for any specialty items that might be missing from the plate-laden table, which was being picked clean almost as fast as we could keep it stocked. Boot massaged all denuded feminine feet with moisturizer, whether they invited him to or not, *pied*-crawling arduously across the grass. I jingled about bringing drinks, taking absurd requests in order to be kept in motion so as to provide a further dimension of entertainment for the newcomers and so Auntie could regale them with such comments as, "Isn't he scrumptious?" and "Every self-respecting dom should have one—except for you, Tutor, dear," to which Tutor grunted tastefully, ever the reluctant homophobe.

As I ran my submissive show-pony steeplechase, lending a Ganymede-like effect to the affair, I couldn't help but discern the none-too-subtle crossconspiratorial subtext festering beneath the banal chattering of Tutor and Amapola—to which my own Auntie Maim and her Bullwinkle the Mount contributed their excruciating naïveté—while Amapola's silent fright-dyke factotum Nightbird nodded ominously with prominently disfigured teeth, resembling more a weathered woodchuck gotten up in black janitorial togs than anything remotely avian.

I shuddered with relief that we were all at least spared her nudity.

Cousins—which meant largely "O," as she ran him—and Amapola (who persistently referred to herself somewhat nauseatingly as "that pretty little poppy"—with the demeanor and complexion of bad heroin, she forgot to add—were apparently making an incipient bid to take the scene away from Athena. Not that he really owned it—he was just the first to provide a local public forum for it as well as an actual *club* setting for play, however scant it may have been. Of course, owning the only board and presiding over the only night would tend to give the impression that he owned the scene and he would never deny it. It didn't matter. The desperate jumble of newbie nonentities in their urgent struggle to affect some more glamorous identity than their positions in the Miltown job bank ever would have permitted had caused them to fixate on the monumentally tall and monumentally bad transvestite Athena as their leader, for good or for ill.

And where there was a leader, there was unrest and discontent from those who would lead, even in the scene.

Cousins needed to be thought of as a leader to justify his own sad affectations and Amapola needed to control *something* to better establish the fact that she existed at all, a fact that was admittedly in question.

"O" needed to control Cousins, which of course meant continually addressing the matter of what items of the moment could be correctly identified as being her precious toddler's "sweets."

So, there they were, making their first foray to carve up the scene.

Let them.

They had all been so badly carved up by their straight lives that this evolution of a kinky community seemed to them to be their second chance.

They didn't know they had no chance.

No doubt other similar self-styled handles on either Dreams-Come-True or the fledgling Ties 'R' Us were doing the same—every third player was a conspirator. The sex seemed secondary to a sense of potential prominence and esteem among the defiantly shamefaced practitioners of D/s sexplay. Anybody could be a big fish in a pond so small that even the lowliest newbie could quickly be on a first-name basis with even the most celebrated figures of the New York scene simply by showing up. The pond was easy to be big in—the boat was easy to rock. If you couldn't do one, you could at least do the other.

It was all D/s and it was all the same.

Just as Miltown and environs resisted the basic fact of D/s in workaday commerce and behind the inviolate suburbanite scrim of hearth and home—let alone in some dissonant community predicated on exalting that basic fact—so it resisted the equally basic fact of group formation. Cliques, cronies, coteries and cabals, yes. But a group that was large enough and whose atoms could act in concert long enough to be led—or *dominated*—as a political force to be exploited, coerced and bullied into usefulness as such groups usually are? The history of Miltown was clear on the matter—even to the most cursory viewer of PBS programming routinely lionizing those who had managed to do so in the past:

It took a fuck of a lot of money.

More money than even Muffy and Herod had, and they could buy and sell the rest of the players in the scene put together.

Even here in the sunlight, delivering drinks barefoot and mostly naked across the grass while playfully picking up slaps on the ass, the scene was already beginning to seem like some downsized state office for grants administration—full of frustrated artists, pseudo-intellectuals, groupies and conniving functionaries. All of them seedy and dead-ended in civil-servile comfort, all them vain in their own arcane definitions of bureaucratic procedure that would never allow anything to be done unless—almost impossible in Miltown's roiling sea of pettifoggery—it somehow reflected well on them.

So, the safe, the trendy, and the mediocre won the day—and the grant.

As it was in art so it was in life.

Money.

The scene lacked for money.

Oh, but like most of those spending more and more time in the grudging dimension of consensual, mutually acknowledged heterosexual perversion, I had begun no longer to lack for *play*. I didn't bother to determine whether this had anything to do with the lack of money.

My eyes went elsewhere.

I noticed a fairly attractive women—I was tempted to say girl—she had that yearning unconcern of youth along with skin which, under the circumstances, could only be described as a lovely *tabula rasa*. She wore only a backless leather one-piece bathing suit designed, of course, never to be submerged in water of any kind, much less the bluish chlorinated soup of the pool. She was short and stacked, compact with thick legs set in a sort of bulldog stance. Her face was a pert little girl's—a darkish Pippi Longstocking peppered with freckles and framed by pigtails. She was looking me over with a leer of practiced wickedness.

Shlomo licked at my ankle.

I ran my course about the yard with drinks, but she put herself in my path, blocked my progress, upset my tray. Glasses fell to the grass and I ignored them.

She sucked her finger thoughtfully, then slowly removed it from her mouth. "I bet you know you're easily the best-looking man here."

"Not saying very much," I said, recovering my balance along with the tray.

As she eyed me, settling into her posture so that her hips favored my direction, I noticed LadyPain, with her kyphotic posture and her face frozen in a permanent gnaw like some traumatized hedgehog, proudly displaying her porcine mate Floyd's shaved, bound, beringed penis by stretching open his Bermudas to all interested onlookers by a yellow bowl of potato salad on the picnic table. Floyd preened, potato salad dappling his face. Meanwhile, Mount displaced gallons and gouts of water from the Jacuzzi as Auntie Maim lolled all over him along with some swing couple making their public scene debut on what was apparently familiar ground.

Clouds of pot smoke filled the air, a ritual holdover from the days before AIDS and the reclosenting of weird sex. The pot was a *post mortem*—a pining, pallid elegy for a decadence no longer fashionable.

I heard fresh whip cracks and turned to spy the homely joy of Allie beating on some young thing while his old thing, the loving, bespectacled Hedda, looked on with hungry approbation. It was obvious to me from just one indifferent glance that this might have been an interesting story—but I snapped my head forward and set my gaze directly ahead.

I was more interested in the obstacle before me than in the story behind me.

She grabbed the ring of my collar—no bold move, as I was patently available and said, "Tell me, pretty boy, whose little toy are you?"

Not to be cliché, she then grabbed a pec and squeezed it like a peach for firmness and freshness. "Mmm," she vamped, "it feels as good as it looks."

Our attention was caught by the giggling Auntie in the Jacuzzi. "I'm hers," I lied by way of fact.

"Lucky Auntie."

So she knew Auntie's name—but before I could continue her back was turned and she was off.

"Where are you going?"

She turned and shrugged her incongruously thick shoulders, walking backward. "Well—you're owned, aren't you?"

"Not really," I started to explain.

"It doesn't matter. You're very pretty, but I'm just not in the scene. I thinks it's fun to hang out in—I like the look of it sometimes, the edginess, but I don't get off on S and M."

"D/s."

"That too."

"Care to play anyway?" I knew the answer, but sometimes directness presses a reversal.

"Yes," she said in concert with a sigh. She smirked at my surprise, then added, "But not your game."

"Then what about your game?"

She raked her nails across my chest, leaving reddened trails.

"Sensitive, aren't we?"

I nodded slavishly, not wanting to undo her tenuous acceptance of a scene.

"Well," she said, pausing her tongue on her finger tip, "I like long walks."

"Sounds like the headline of a desperate personals ad—unless it's some kind of death march," I said.

"Well, I'm a composer who works as a bike messenger, pedaling everyday all across town. What's a little walk compared with that?'

"I don't drive, so I walk everywhere anyway."

She wrenched my collar ring to test its solidity and focus my attention, then jerked me back harshly with a violent release—the usual newbie's way of yanking my chain. They are always so delighted with the literalness of it.

"Good," she said. "I like your idea about a death march. A death's-*head* march, perhaps—a long, slow dirge. There's a tonic possibility that exists somewhere in there."

"Maybe some screaming?"

"I would need a chorus of that, maybe some moaning and a few little contrapuntal dog-yips. But I'm not much on vocals."

"I am."

"Really? We'll have to see about that," she said and walked off with unexpected briskness, eyeing me overtly over her shoulder as she did, her lips in a little pout.

Auntie, nude, sloshed and high on commemorative pot, came up beside me and grabbed me by the elbow. "Come on now," she said pushing me forward, "and stop your struggling. It's time to give

Master Mountie his poundie of flesh—of course in your case, I don't think you could afford to lose that much. "She patted my abs. "He wants me to give you what-for for having been tardy. And Mountie is getting bored and needs to be pleased." With that, she directed me to grab the rim of the above-ground Jacuzzi and thrust my buttocks up in the air. Then, without any sort of warm up or readying of the target in question, she began flailing at my raised flanks with one of LadyPain's green suede floggers till the red welts came bubbling up from my skin like fat blisters which—thank god—they did very easily. So much so Auntie was shocked enough to stop several times while I mocked submission with my eyes aimed slavishly toward the grass and with the rigor of my posture.

Stealing crowd glances, I noticed Floyd's mouth lolling open, slack with potato salad, his gut flopping forward as his earrings dangled in the breeze like wind chimes while he paid me occasional notice. LadyPain cheered Auntie on with sarcastically insincere taunts about her submissive deserving the worst. Tristana hurried over bearing her heavy petticoats lightly and betraying girlish frills beneath gingham, her hair dyed jet-black beneath a red bonnet, her eyes less feminine than sage beneath rimless, rectangular grannyglasses.

LadyPain nodded approvingly as Auntie got into the swing with the whip, wisely laying the leather tresses to me lightly in order to account for an aim that might otherwise have sent me to hospital with kidney damage. Knowing this to be so, and no doubt resolving to correct her later, LadyPain tightened her perpetual rodentine smirk.

Mount guffawed and clapped, bobbing limp and unattended in the roiling foam of the Jacuzzi, now its sole occupant. He seemed to be either furtively or desultorily playing with himself. The crowd was attentive to us, yet ignored us as much as possible, intrigued at these new personalities while routinely unimpressed by the less than expert display of what was apparently the same old thing. And I hadn't even removed my PVC briefs while everyone else was, as Auntie would say in her persistent anglophilia, "starkers." Herod finally put a stop to things by informing Auntie that we were just too close to the picnic table, which was making it problematic for some of the less svelte guests to belly up to the buffet while at the same time detracting from whatever trenchant conversation might be had by those who had plainly gathered by the potato salad for the sole purpose of watching us.

LadyPain began explaining flogging technique to the addled Auntie, tentatively at first as I began to step away, then the further she could see that I was from Auntie, the more fervent her lecture became, the more urgent her detailed instructions. She was cultivating her, and as I was a new male submissive and intimately connected with this smart new doyenne of the scene to be, LadyPain made me instantly as an obstacle to whatever her plans were. It was a truism droned again and again as both complaint and indictment; there were simply too many submissive men in the scene—but dominant women, possibly bisexual in the bargain, well, they were of premium value. Should one actually prove attractive, that was when the players for power circled about them like carrion eaters who would be predators, making their moves, using their S&M sex proclivities desperately for far more humdrum pursuits.

One attractive dominant female was worth twenty attractive male submissives in the unforgiving economy of the scene.

I didn't mind. Auntie was plainly not a player, but the commodity that she turned out to be allowed me entrée into the play I sought or thought I did.

No, I never thought I did. I just followed it out like some dumb hunger, willing to hash out the emotional or ethical consequences after I was well slaked and sated and could afford such platonic luxuries. I went looking for my composer.

Muffy intervened. She waved her hands and proceeded to gush with a manner that was reminiscent of a plump docent at an art museum. I tried imagining her wearing clothes, to take some of the sting out of her performance.

"Excuse me! Everybody pay attention now, for I have a real treat for you!" This barely made any impact on the slopping noises at all, but the already stilted and diffident conversation wilted and died, though Deprav-o's ham-handed fisting of a young Trinity College undergraduate on a picnic-table bench in the furthest corner of the yard went unimpeded, as did the attendant squeaks and squeals.

I listened intently and could almost hear the smacking and sucking of the lubricated surgical glove between the girl's lusty moans. I just about missed Muffy's portentous announcement.

"Excuse me! Excuse me! If you will all join us in the breezeway, The Miltown scene's very own poet-laureate Tutor and his lovely submissive "O" have consented to give us all a spanking demonstration for tops and bottoms alike. Personally, I feel we could all use a little touch-up on our technique? Yes? Why don't you join us for finger sandwiches, hors d'oeuvres and wine served by our two wait-slut submissives, Bootlicker and Propertius!"

There were neither finger sandwiches nor hors d'oeuvres waiting in the Breezeway.

Mossman had the same thought and bolted up so fast from a pump-chewing scene that he managed to kick himself in the face with the object of his adoration.

We brought trays down from the kitchen piled with whatever miscellany we thought would fit the bill, balancing bottles of anything we could grab off the wine rack on the way out under our arms and set them out just as the nude convocation of corporal-punishment enthusiasts sat flaccid asses down on couches, rugs and throw pillows. Tutor centered himself on the largest couch while consort, submissive and benefactor "O" batted her eyes and daintily positioned herself next to the gnome-like curmudgeon, who at that moment resembled one of the lesser demons in a Gustave Doré print from Dante's *Inferno*. She plumped herself down, flopping breasts and meaty thighs propelling her forward into Tutor's lap. He grimaced as she splayed herself across his thighs.

Suppressing a groan, he began.

At first, it was just a bunch of pointless thank-yous and self-serving acknowledgments to would-be scene conspirators.

I sat Indian-style in the front row, my ears assailed by munching, smacking and sipping (as if of hot soup through chipped teeth, instead of wine), turned my head and wound up staring straight into the ursine elbow of Deprav-o, which nearly hid from view, but not quite, the brownish-pink nipple of the undergraduate muffin he only moments ago had been fisting. It poked forward and up toward the fustian, elfin-bearded former associate professor of remedial English with pert insouciance. She smiled at me softly from one side of her mouth, shifting her eyes my way—a flirt, a tease, a challenge to my submission. Would I be able to top her? Could I switch for a lissome bit of otherwise-conventional undergraduate tail?

That would be a fool's game, of course, the point of which would be to provoke Deprav-o or some other to exert his claim all the more harshly, earning her added punishment for the indiscreet overture— a new take on the old jealousy game. A *scene* take.

Perversion was truly taking hold of me. I began imagining her in a pink cardigan sweater carrying her books to class.

Mossman achieved the bifurcated feat of serving wine on a silver-plated tray of hastily defrosted canapés to pudgy fingers while sucking equally pudgy (and not altogether exclusively) female toes. Inadvertently or not, Mossman was doing me a favor by taking the onus of ornamental servitude from me so that I could—incredibly— *not* ogle the resilient body parts of the fisted young miss by Deprav-o, but instead attend the wisdom of the nutty professor.

The flatulent grunt that passed for Tutor's speaking voice grabbed my attention.

"*Now*, when you spank your submissive, you're going to want to focus your activity on this area of the buttocks here—the nerve endings are spread further apart here, so feel free to slap away, developing a pattern like this."

"O" lowed like a cow, shook like jelly, began to sweat perceptibly.

Tutor smoothed the entire surface area of "O" 's copious ass to the sloppy murmuring of the room. "Remember to caress the buttocks intermittently as you spank to vary sensation. And remember: at *no* time do you ever give your submissive more pain than he or she can take. And," he spanked away freely, "this is established before you start. Now, as her body begins to recognize the shock you are inflicting on it, endorphins are released into the brain, her blood flow and metabolic rate increase—she is getting warmed up!"

His voice cracked at the word "up," his square-john horn-rimmed glasses beginning to fog.

"I like to use nipple clamps at this point," he said," producing the standard nickel plated white rubber tipped tweezer-handled items connected by a chain that, when tugged on, would cause them to grip the nipples just a bit tighter.

I thought he'd be better off using ice tongs, considering the size of the target.

The clamps were affixed and "O" kicked her legs, moaning with some calculated exaggeration, making sure all the while not to struggle enough to dislodge herself from the lap and grasp of the love of her life. It looked like Tutor was straining to keep a handle on things enough as it was. The fleshy audience was hushed with rapt and breathy attention.

His raspy grunt, like that of some greedy animal feeding, asserted itself. "This diffuses the effect instead of keeping it localized. Then, if you and your sub have discussed it, you can torque it up a bit." He began slapping with smacks and a scowling concentration that caused some to wince. My lissome fist-ette smiled broadly with mischievous delight.

Looking at the faces of the quiet, largely late-middle-aged audience, it occurred to me that what I was taking for riveted attention was something else altogether: respectful boredom. It was similar to a church service where the congregation, though needful of communion with other believers, had heard it all before, a place where the crochety minister had long ago ceased to do anything but preach to the choir.

Feeling grateful for my newness and inexperience, I listened closely along with my fist-ette, wishing at the same time that Tutor would have his adenoids removed. He slipped a fluffy mitt on his hand. "Then we give her a little pleasure in counterpoint to the pain, keeping her nerve endings sensate, then we balance her on the lap and go forward with a double-handed slapping."

He used both hands in unison, one for each buttock, and "O" whimpered uncontrollably.

"You can pyramid the intensity," he said between breaths slapping. "Then at the finish, ice is nice." He stopped, smiling delightedly with his own wit, poured out some of the ice from his drink and rubbed it over "O" 's bright pink butt cheeks. She tried to purr like a kitten but managed only to emit a bleat. "Feathers, nerve wheels, ice—they're all good for inspiring the nerve endings to sit up and take notice." He suddenly raised his left hand, which now sported a jet black leather glove. He spread his gloved hand out flat and held it sideways so what we could all see clearly against the sunlit window behind him little prickly spikes sticking out viciously from his fingers and palm. "This is Dracula's Gauntlet," he announced gravely. "Manufactured especially for me. Very sharp, very lethal." He glared in my direction. "Under no circumstances do you spank with this. Instead, you caress the contours of your sub's butt— just like this."

"O" produced an unholy whine that made Deprav-o jump up cataclysmically from where he sat. My fist-ette's hair was being stroked in his lap until he grabbed and pulled.

Tutor beamed. He was being impish and lighthearted, which in no way came easy to him. "That ought to make those little nerve endings rear up on their hind legs and beg for mercy."

That was my cue. Nervous laughter and the dislodging of "O" from Tutor's lap prompted me to begin removing empty trays and the detritus of half-eaten food, wadded napkins and discarded plastic cups to legitimize my way out. Tutor's acolytes assembled around him as I made good my escape, admiring both "O" 's brightened butt and Dracula's Gauntlet. He was so busy taking orders for gauntlets on a clipboard, he almost had no time to overpraise himself with a blow-by-blow account of what he had just done to those who had just witnessed it—*almost.*

A bit more serving, and dusk approached along with mosquitoes and the smoky tang of mesquite-flavored charcoal briquettes. The crackling of porch-suspended bug zappers was constant. The verdant moistness of the lush shrubbery and imported tree saturation of the yards and streets of the Coventry suburbs brought on a chill as the light of the late summer afternoon dimmed as if on a rheostat in the fingers of a geriatric. I shivered, mosquitoes already beginning to raise welts on my exposed flesh. I suddenly got warm—knowing hands were rubbing my chest and a thickish set of legs had become entwined with mine.

It was her—my untried dominatrix yet-to-be and bike-messengering gamine of self-proclaimed perverse dilettantism. It was easy to yield to her advance. In fact, as I warmed to the attentive and focused probing and touching, I melted into her embrace for enough of a sustained moment for Auntie to intervene. The precise coldness in her tone indicated the jealousy of possession, not of ardor.

"Don't you think it's time you *changed,* dear? You'll catch your *death.*"

I made my way to the poolhouse and Auntie walked alongside me, her spongy pink nipples brushing my elbows as she gesticulated with flitting arms. "You know, she's really nothing to look at when she shucks her clothes—not your type at all," she insisted. "You know I *know* what you need."

Going in to change, offering her entry first—knowing all too keenly that that inadvertent brush with her nipples was our very first intimate contact of skin—I said without anger: "If you know what I need, why don't you give it to me?"

"You're involved," she said protecting herself with the towel, not dressing as I did so hurriedly. "I can't get that close to anyone who's involved."

"You're involved too—but I don't see that preventing you from having use of submissive men, doing threesomes with goofy out there and lolling in the hot tub oh-so-glandularly with the newbie swingers."

"Yes, but he's in love with me."

"It looks it," I said adjusting my shirt.

"And you love what's-her-name."

I winced at the comparison. "I do. I love her. I don't want to lose her. But you have to understand: I'm in the scene now. She won't give me what I need, so I'm in the scene to find people like you to give me what I need, while presumably taking what you need. Call it refined erotic reciprocity, if you want. Call it corrupt lust or just plain infidelity, I don't care. I'm not looking for love in all the wrong places, I'm looking for scenes where they're rumored to be, in the *right* places. I'm looking for *scenes.* It's my need. But you won't give me what I need and thus far nobody else will either. So, I have to go out and find it and take it the moment it's offered. And I'm not going to give up that moment before I find it."

"And likely not even then," she mumbled.

I went over to her. She had let the towel drop and her luminescent, still-mascaraed eyes were dewy with insincerity and their long lashes flickered. No tears fell.

"I need the play. Are we playing?"

"You're in love. I can't. It's not right."

I adjusted my shirt and carefully combed my hair, which was growing out now, to avoid kinks, using the mirror beneath the orange-colored forty-watt bulb. I squinted to see. "Love is the problem," I said. "It's the enemy of play. And you know what I am."

"A player," she said, her voice dripping with a bitterness of years as she modeled her body in the strained light, making little fetching poses. She was a bit pear-shaped, but her skin was delightful, her aspect vulnerable and girlish, her posture wounded.

"No," I said as she dressed, ignoring me. "*I'm a player in the scene*—not far enough in it, but going further. There is no way I'm going to let even scene play itself stop me from playing. Your Catholicism notwithstanding"—and Auntie was even more Catholic in her way than Lady Marchmain was in *Brideshead Revisited* (her favorite book)—"in the scene, the workplace or on the street this much is true: Submissive does not mean *schmuck*."

She shrugged her shirtwaist on as I made for the door and the darkness.

"Be careful dear—there's more than pain in the scene that can hurt you."

"How promising," I said and let the screen door slam.

My pursuer was there with her blue bike, going for the tomboy look, waiting for me in a tank top, cut-off jeans and sneakers with white tube socks. She looked like she came fresh from summer camp.

"I'm going now," I called to the poolhouse. "Care to walk me?' Auntie emerged.

"Mistress," I hailed her officiously as a matter of protocol. "If it's all right, I'm going to escort—" I realized I didn't know her name.

She looked at me and said, correctively, "Bee."

"I'm going to escort—"

"You're going to *walk*," said Bee.

"I'm going to walk Bee home."

"Yes. I can see that you are. Well, that's all right." Her speech was clipped and her eyes moved sharply to follow Mount, who was receiving fellatio unceremoniously from some eager *hausfrau* mercifully tented in an orchid-patterned muumuu. She bit her lip. "You have my permission. Ta-ta." She marched off.

Bee was going my way, back to Trinity, a seven-mile hike. Of course I agreed to walk the entire way with her.

She was an exotic, one of those unsettled types with a crazy quilt of accomplishments and activities that were all apparently for naught, for she was with me, tied to the moment with me, the unemployed hack who lacked all that flibbertigibbet pizzazz, earthbound and walking with me before her next great leap. She was a composer, educated at one of the slightly less ancient sister institutions to Trinity University. She had just come back from New Zealand after a stint in Madagascar, paid for by some mysterious source other than her parents that I could not gently wring from her. An inheritance, a secret loan from granny, the fruits of a dope deal, who knew? While attempting to get into the Trinity University Medical School, she was writing a symphony to complete her masters at Cornish Conservatory, working nights too as a bouncer in a dyke bar.

All this range and no S&M. I supposed I was yet another piece in the purposely rich and varied mosaic that was her life.

I wondered what it was that grouted all the broken pieces together.

I told my own modest story and gave her the bits about D/s that she needed.

It all shocked and appalled her, which was evident in the easy manner with which she listened to everything with staid calm, like a psychotherapist affecting a deliberate demeanor. She dryly noted that there was a lot of that going on when she was an undergraduate and she thought of it at the time as a cliché holdover from the largely-defunct so-called "sexual revolution."

My knees were bothering me by the time we made it to Divinity Commons, right near the school for Judaic studies in the very heart of the Trinity University campus, which I usually avoided crossing because of unpleasant memories. Bee insisted we do so anyway. As I was matching her undergraduate anecdotes with one of my own, something forgettable which contained no component of D/s whatever, she pushed me to the grass of the common with surprising strength and timing.

She was on top of me and pushed me back down before I could make complete sense of it. I gave a token struggle.

Bee chuckled and licked her lips. "You could get out of this if you wanted to, but you don't want to." She had her hands up my shirt, pinching my nipples, which was uncomfortable at first but before I could flinch away, as if the result of some newly reflexive habit earned through training, I felt a rush of pleasure which I immediately recognized as the endorphins coming to the rescue.

She took her thick index finger and stuck it in her mouth. She sucked it with her eyes closed, miming a familiar routine. She removed the finger and poked me stiffly in the chest with it.

With the puckish grin of a tomboy about to play doctor for the first time, she announced in my ear, "I'm really oral."

"That's nice," I said, my heart racing.

She tore at my pants and before I could squirm, I was in her hand, limp and shrunken with cold. Her palm pressed against my chest. I was off balance and as I tried to right myself, her superior leverage and weight pushed me down. She was unexpectedly strong. This time she had me for real and conveyed to me by the heated nuances of her body a thrill of absolute control. She had taken to this experiment, recognized it and was determined to press her advantage.

I blushed with arousal.

Blood rushed through me, cold and shrunken no more.

She turned about with sudden force and planted her haunches on my shoulders, lowering the crotch of her cut-off jeans to my mouth. I could taste the denim, feel the muscles of her thighs—her quadriceps—hard up against my ears.

Then there was a burning wet tickling down below that started slow but soon increased in speed. I struggled to avoid it, but couldn't.

Bee turned about again and pried my mouth open to deliver a rough kiss. She whispered into my sensitive ear canal loudly and with heat, "You're going to give it up for me or I'm going to bite it off. Do you know why I have the name Bee?" She grabbed my hair and gave my scalp a vicious wrench.

"Because bees sting?" I asked.

"Oh, this Bee does sting," she agreed. "But sometimes I might like to take *your* stinger if I have to. Do you know what *piquerism* is?"

I did, but I hoped it meant something less direct than its usual meaning, worrying admittedly about the state of my skin.

"You like to bite?"

I was forced down to the moist grass by way of reply. She sat down on my head again and resumed the slick and heated tickling until I grew rigid, taut, urgent, the blood-engorged muscle and vascularity yearning to split the sensitive skin now stretched so very thin. She knew the exact place to lick, and so must have known all along and all too well the anatomy of the circumcised penis. Bee anticipated every contour and subtle place of sensation with skilled fingers, sensuous mouth, flickering teeth and tongue. Then she slowly narrowed her approach to my cock, which was so turgid and thick with need that she now almost literally owned and controlled the heart that palpitated though it wildly, desperately.

The little recessed arrow-shaped indention on the underside of the glans was her point of attack. She licked it pointedly and with insistent focus until the tip of her tongue was a white-hot poker burning with pinpoint precision against my most sensitive flesh. I vocalized uncontrollably, not quite screaming or moaning, not quite grunting or wailing.

I cried, but she smothered the sound with the "V" of her crotch.

My mind wandered with the distant distraction that helplessness brings toward some wispy thought or vision of how I once trod these Commons as an adolescent with nothing but perhaps the slightest hint of flirtation ever thrown my way by any of the coeds from the now defunct Bunting College (all schools having long since been merged into one megalithic "multiversity"). Being neither theater-arts charmer, moneyed sybarite hipster, nor football-squad stud, I had no memories of any sexual adventure or romance whatever with which to decorate my unwanted view of this lawn whenever I passed it.

Not anymore.

I was ripped back to the moment by harsh sensation. I was as hard as I had ever been and Bee knew it, claiming my cock with wicked timing, working it more quickly and expertly than a teenage boy works a joystick at his favorite video game. She controlled my every motion from that point on, manipulating me now solely through the skin and nerve endings of my cock. I became her helpless psychoneural marionette, her penis puppet, her toy. Her jeans were soaked, as likely from the helpless mouth without as from the sweat and lubricity of her arousal within.

She rubbed the edges of her teeth in precise rhythm against the most sensitive nether place, skirting the purpled and assertive rim of the head of my cock.

I got ready to blow my guts.

"Succulent," I heard her whisper.

Then she bit me there on the desperately engorged head so hard I lost my breath.

The air had been driven from lungs.

I began to choke.

My world spun hard to the left then crashed. I clawed out wildly with my hands and pulled up divots of grass. My body struggled for movement, but was put down in spark-infused blackness.

I bucked, my wailing successfully smothered by the saturated crotch of her cut-off jeans. Bee shifted her weight to keep me still, but I thrashed nonetheless.

The pain made my dark vision red.

I glimpsed her face, her chin and lips glistening with the soft glaze of my ejaculate.

She worked me with fingertips lubricated by saliva and come until I was stretched out straight. She had me firmly in two strong hands, indicated to me that her grip could go to vice-like in a moment's notice.

Her teeth brought down a storm of sensation upon me, prickling every region of my skin.

She licked me tenderly in that certain place, steadily, once, twice.

My body rumbled, my back arched.

I lifted her with me.

I shot, but this time it went nowhere. She had by then taken me in completely and sucked it all down, holding me firmly in her mouth, laving the tender underside of my cock now with the flat of her tongue and milking me rhythmically with the back of her throat.

It wasn't long before the burning tickle of her nibbling began again and I saw my frustrated undergraduate days slowly diminish into nothingness on the very same grass where they once held terrible sway.

As I lay there trembling in sweat, she repositioned herself atop me and casually forced me to bite the nipple of one her generous breasts hard enough to crush my head against it. She wanted aggravated sensation and she wanted it now. Her nipple was large and she used her hands to make my jaw bite down. I did the other without her help and she engulfed my face with them both. Unexpectedly, she drove my hand down into her jeans and motioned my lax finger to play on her slicked clitoris.

"How many more times can you go?" Bee demanded, loud in my ear.

She jaggedly pulled my face to hers.

"As many times as you need," I said shakily and without certitude.

"Good boy," she breathed. "Right answer."

SIX

I arrived home about an hour later readied with explanations, justifications, counterarguments and charges, but when I made my way upstairs through the French doors that led to the our den to give this full accounting, I found Ms Right fast asleep on her gold brocade loveseat, breathing as sweetly and evenly as the newborn she so deeply craved, oblivious to me, the TV or anything but the dream she dreamed. Waking her would have been pointless, perhaps cruel, and I was glad to avoid a fight. I kissed her unresponsive cheek, adjusted her blanket, turned off whatever video she had rented— most likely a romantic comedy (she doted on them, as they were so reassuringly unlifelike)—and held my crotch by thoughtless incident, with a fond spasm of momentary sense memory.

I could still feel it.

The burning tickle of Bee's nibbling fresh and urgent, watching the ghosts of my frustrated undergraduate days slowly diminish.

I opened my eyes, now conscious of her breathing and the time.

It was way past midnight, but did I go to our resplendent king-size bed in the vacant bedroom and call it a night? Oh no. I went straight to the computer and logged on to the BBS to see if any of the D/s crowd were on. And of course they were. It hardly seemed funny to me or the least bit questionable (but perhaps should have at the time) that by now I knew who all of them were.

I started typing my late-night hellos, unconcerned.

You are in the Main public Room!
Type "LIST" to see a list of available Rooms.
———————

MooseCock, "O", and DicksyChick are here with you.
Just enter "?" if you need any assistance.

:***

Hello.

—message sent—

DicksyChick has just goosed you in the you-know-where . . .

MooseCock is yawning.

From "O" (whispered): You seemed to have fun this afternoon. Any interesting developments with Muffy's friend,
who you left with?

***

She bit my cock.

—message sent privately to "O"—

From "O" (whispered): Sounds like an evening. Not too
hard, I hope.

From DicksyChick (whispered): Suck my cock, slaveboy.

***

Just hard enough.

—message sent privately to "O"—

Eat my shorts.

—message sent privately to DicksyChick—

Run and hide—Muffy's coming out to play!

Muffy has arrived!

From Muffy: Hey kinky people!

***

Re-hi, Muffy.

—message sent—

From MooseCock: Re's, Muff.

From "O" <to Muffy>: Great pool party, Muffy!

MooseCock missed the pool party and is weeping bitterly.

Muffy is spanking Propertius until his bottom is nice and
pink.

Muffy is spanking Propertius until his bottom is nice and
pink.

Muffy is spanking Propertius until his bottom is nice and
pink.

From Muffy <To You> I just thought you deserved that. You
liked it, didn't you?

***

Thank you.

—message directed to Muffy—

From Muffy <To You>: Anytime, bad boy.

x

Exit

You are about to log off the Dreams-Come-True BBS. Press (y) to terminate your connection, (n) to return to the TOP menu, or (1) to re-log.

y

***

Black balloons at the food court—that's what I was looking for. It had been all over Dreams-Come-True, the Monday ASB "munch." ASB was not an association, but one of the better-known Usenet newsgroups of electronic ASCII or other types of encoded, encrypted or anonymized (then through Finland!) postings. It stood for alt.sex.bondage—a message forum for grandiose posturing, inflated pontificating, dubious philosophies, unaccountable moralizing and exchanges of hot club dates. ASB: where formerly hidden perverts were now able to express themselves far beyond their normal capabilities, to be read, repudiated, lauded, despised then dispensed with by hundreds of thousands of lurkers like me.

A lurker never posted. After wading through all the speculative ethical cant and shameless self-aggrandizement—emboldened by electronic anonymity and safe remove—what was there to say?

You scanned, you skipped, you deleted, you lurked and moved on, hoping to find something worth finding.

I composed notes in my head, forcefully and eloquently deflating the grandiloquent hype artists who took a purity of perversion and contorted it into the tooth-rotting taffy of their own fractional agendas with opining posts of deadening pedantry. Of course after each tart missive reached its scathing conclusion, there was no point in writing a response at all. It would add to the din and out me as the type of player I had no interest in being. As target, rallying point or even dismissed upstart—active newsgroup posting would have only served to dissipate my intensity of purpose and misidentify me as yet another political looking to push for social acceptance of the unacceptable; and the fact that it *was* unacceptable was precisely why such enthusiasts as myself sought it out—we wanted to be forced to accept that which we knew was bad for us, which we knew was considered to be morally wrong and in a way that would not irrevocably harm ourselves or those we loved.

In short, like everyone in the scene, we newsgroup lurkers wanted the impossible and were so devastated by the desire for it that, should it prove in fact to *be* impossible, we would then simply redefine social law, if not physical law itself to make it work.

As these notations fled my head like the little motes of desperation they were, I moved closer to the epicenter of practical S&M by meeting its die-hard practitioners, hangers-on and wannabes by the black balloons at the food court of the local mall.

And there they were—Deprav-o, Muffy, Tutor, Amapola—sitting in the sunken, railed-off area of the football-field-sized novelty fast-food atrium, crowding about tables in plain New England leisure dress, wearing anything neutral or nautical that smacked of faded prep schools that none of the players had attended. Auntie Maim, in an improbable frock of olive drab, was holding court with LadyPain, whose kyphotic back was made even more emphatic in its stoop by a fuschia turtleneck. Mount was there, flab spilling over his wide pewter belt buckle, laughing the laugh of a thousand cartoons no doubt archived on videocassette and watched again and again when he wasn't out looking for threesomes and making Auntie crazy. PennedDragon and MooseCock both greeted me as if we were old schoolfriends, as did EliotTS, looking primly nondescript in his hooped earrings, economical make-up, ruffled satin chemise and form-fitting pedal pushers.

I shambled into the hesitantly festive melee, and received a forceful if scarified handshake from the less-than-hearty, always wary Tutor. "Great turnout at this little get-together I organized," the snowy-haired pedant bragged nervously. "When you know how to communicate the event, your audience will come." There was no point in disputing, correcting, or even gently reminding him that this wasn't the case—he simply had made more crosspostings about it to the various related newsgroups than anyone else had done locally—and to do so would have been a mortal threat relegating me at once to his enemies list, which was exhaustive. I would wind up there eventually, but I wasn't quite ready yet. Instead, I took the opportunity to ask about Bee, who, despite the fact that she had so precisely and effectively bitten my cock, never confided in me what her apparently all-important political alignment within the scene actually was. I began to realize that my lack of alignment only increased my attractiveness within the scene. I knew this would be short-lived, but I intended to use it.

Tutor answered me with curt tactlessness and swiveled about to clasp hands elsewhere.

I was far from surprised to find that she had left town indefinitely to "rethink her goals" at her parents' house in Connecticut—I had had much too much of a good time with her for that not to have been the case. I shrugged. On to the next folly.

Athena of course wouldn't have been caught dead at this meeting in the food court of the Sidereal Mall. It wasn't a matter of style—no doubt he would have enjoyed having his lunch here in the normal course of things—but he would never directly associate with these bland computer fabulists, nerds and students in search of sexual definition (if not personal definition through sex), cliquish acceptance and a new and possibly sexually gratifying avenue for dungeons and dragons style role-playing games. Athena would never make that scene— unless it was an event tied to any one of the failing businesses that he, like most experienced players, was trying to *make* of the scene.

I was getting further away from the image and posturing, the flash of the club, further into the substance, the almost mundane actually—*the scene behind the scenes.*

I began to catch on to the fact that whatever virtues or defects had brought us to this sad pass had put our lives so much out of kilter that, out of the one hundred or so members of our scene, fifty perverts were trying to sell goods, services or even a piece of their own asses to the other fifty.

Cliques, atoms, ambition, greed. I was finding more of what I thought I had already known. I was becoming secure in what I found.

But, of course, the more I found, the more lost I became.

Carrying my tray of veggie jambalaya and mock crawfish étouffé from Cajun Savin's, I took a seat at the table nearest Auntie, but in a spot where I would be safe from the spittle-fallout of Mount's explosive guffaw. After I sat, and began to make sense of the mélange of food that lay somewhat unappealingly on my white styrofoam plate and orange tray, a diminutive, snub-nosed and funny-faced woman tapped me on the shoulder and sat down next to me. In the midst of a trembling arc meant to carry a forkful of Cajun miscellany to my mouth, the woman said to me in a child's voice: "That was you I saw you onstage at Ubu Roi, wasn't it?"

I admitted to having been spanked onstage and thanked her politely for noticing.

I liked the attention, but I was not attracted. She looked like some sort of spinster librarian, a throwback to an earlier day—but then, how progressive-looking was the rest of the motley crew of advanced freethinkers and staunch civil libertarians that made up our little scene? Not very. She was dressed in an ill-fitting black eighties-vintage power suit, smoky nylons, her mouse-brown hair tied back in some sort of quasi-bun. I asked her if she was some personality from Dreams-Come-True I had met under the local scene universal of a representative or, as was more often the case misrepresentative, handle.

"Oh, no," she said, her large brown eyes blinking nervously— or perhaps she was batting them? It didn't matter. I had lost interest. "I'm just on ASB—the newsgroup. It's not really interactive."

Another lurker, I thought.

I should have heard the slow, dumb strokes of the hammer nailing the lid shut, then and there—but I was deaf and drunken with hope and wonder.

"Total lack of repression!"

"What?" That came out of nowhere. Who was even thinking along those lines?

"Repression," she repeated, her large face aflame, a crooked sort of plastic surgery on her nose asserting itself. "You had no doubt— maybe just a bit of a nervous smile." She said it again: "Total lack of repression. You knew exactly what you wanted to do and you did it without hesitation. You were nervous, but you were having a blast. It was really great to see."

"Thanks. Good to hear I didn't look ridiculous up there."

"Not at all—you looked very . . . uh . . . natural?" She was fishing for something, in addition to me. It was time to wriggle off the hook. "I was having a bad day," I said. "I don't know why I got up there at all." My food began looking cold and dead there on the sparkling white of the styrofoam plate, and I decided against resurrecting it. The harsh, industrial, fluorescent cheesiness of the food court and the aroma of the overly salted, overly fatty food was making me both dizzy and nauseous. The laughter and sarcastic sexual innuendo–laced chatter of those around us began to blur in my ears.

"But you were having a good night. And it seemed what you wanted was happening to you right then and there onstage, in every way."

"Well," I pushed my tray aside. "Maybe not in *every* way, but I guess the public thing takes some getting used to."

"If not in every way then, then maybe soon. But, I wouldn't know about the public thing, myself. That was only my second night out in the scene—and both times were at the Roi."

"Forward motion is a positive thing," I bleated with divided attention, scanning our sector of the food court for something (or to be sadly more accurate, *someone*) I couldn't find.

She gave me a little twisted smirk. "That's the only direction for me," she said, with a deeply lined and furrowed brow, her eyebrows cartoonishly high over wide, flat eyes. Her skin looked gray, and the bad lighting gave her childish face a jowly look. "I don't go backward," she affirmed.

She was short enough for me to discreetly notice that her hair was thinning.

"I'm Propertius," I said, following the local etiquette of handle-only anonymity.

"Karenina."

"As in Anna?"

"No," she said. "Nothing to do with Tolstoy. Childhood nickname."

"What do you do?"

"In the scene? Oh, I'm sub."

"Me too," I said, feeling some relief that I was now no longer a viable candidate for her. "But I meant generally."

"Oh, for a living. I'm in real estate right now. Investments. You?"

"I'm a writer—or rather, I used to be one. Now, I don't know what I am."

"Really. Me too. I've been working on a book."

Oh god. Wasn't everyone?

"There's nothing one writer hates more than another."

"Did you just make that up on the spot?"

"Probably not, but I could have."

"Well I'm not getting paid for it, like you—*yet.*"

I shrugged. Her book would probably go over. Amateur, highly confessional accounts of deviant sexuality told from the feminine point of view always went over, no matter how dismal they were. I knew enough never to write one from the male's point of view— *ever.* Kiss of death.

"I was only paid when I worked for the *Register.* I did the " 'Round the Towne" column."

Her eyebrows went even higher. "Really? I thought that was— "

"Everybody does. I took it over for a couple of years— not that anyone in Miltown noticed."

"I'm not in Miltown, I'm in Swansea."

"Oh, well there, I'm a star."

We shared a laugh.

"Well, it was nice meeting you . . ."

"Propertius. Prop for short, like a plaything."

"Clever."

She shook my hand. I was surprised by the strength of her grip. Inexplicably, I began to warm to her.

Too late—she had fully processed my initial disinterest and frosted over.

"Maybe I'll see you at your next public outing."

"Maybe," she said and moved to the far end of the table.

MOSSMAN GAVE ME A RIDE HOME IN HIS BLOOD-RED ASIAN RUSTBUCKET which I imagined was a hybrid of several makes, not being recognizable as any one. We had a giddy, gossipy conversation about the underpinnings of the local scene, determining the significance of who was doing what to whom, setting our sights on various potential mistresses, who had proved to be *in absentia* at the munch, and generally airing the fine points of sexual submission as if it were a sport. I could see Ms. Right watching for me from the window. I had Mossman honk and I waved. She was already waving. When I went up and Mossman puttered off, she rushed into me hard and clung to me for life.

It was like embracing a large bird, she was so light, so fine and seemingly hollow-boned at that moment. We lay down on the bed together, breathing in one another's whispered air, discussing the fact that the next day would start our first round of couples counseling.

WE WERE NERVOUS AND JOCULAR AS WE WALKED TO TRINITY HEALTH from Ms. Right's powder blue *Trope*, a car she had inherited from her father's business as a write-off. This Trinity Health Center was a factory gutted and refurbished for—what was the phrase of currency then? Adaptive reuse. The square-footage rental on the new spaces had been so jacked up that the only tenant who could afford it was an HMO like Trinity Health which specialized in that volume-oriented, multi-triaged style of medical care that most resembled and was no doubt modeled along the same lines as a fast-food hamburger chain. We passed other businesses there as we checked in at the well-guarded check-in check point happily mislabeled "Information"—all the range of discount "rama's" laced with candy-colored neon clashing smartly against the ochre-aged brick of the still gloomy factory: "Spec-o-rama," "Orth-o-rama," "Pharm-a-rama." Spotless antique sign reproductions regaled us with outré hype of another age trumpeting defunct products.

We were told that these were new businesses opened by Trinity to "offer lower-priced adjuncts to care not covered by individual plans," then we were told where to go.

"Infernal medicine," I repeated and Ms. Right agreed, slipping my hand in hers.

They were late in calling us even though Ms. Right made it a point to be unnecessarily early. She read *people* and I read *Venus in*

Furs in the fluorescent lobby that connected several tunnels, each leading off into some medical specialty or other. Some townie dowd with cellophaned hair called her name and we were ushered back to an airless office with dark tinted windows Through which the sun burned dimly. There she was, archetype for her time, Dr. So-and-So, whose name was so nondescript as to match her character so that it had never even entered my memory. She was gray, smug, exuding the kind of tolerance that could only be mistaken for energetic indifference—and then she would correct you and overexplain herself, even though no mistake had been made. Her voice was the aural equivalent of flannel.

She wrote down the title of my book, intrigued by it, displaying some minor shame at not having read it when I remarked to her that it wasn't contemporary.

I explained to her about Von Sacher Masoch, and his impossible, lambent quest for his soul and psyche's satisfaction in S&M sex with the one true object of his romantic ardor—which we would so sapiently call obsession now. Her face opened like an aluminum storm door and she feigned a moment's interest before moving on to more urgent topics.

It was clear to Dr. So-And-So that we had no trouble communicating. We understood one another deeply, possessed vast affection for each other, had what she termed a "feel" for one another. Our long-time couples' interplay and faux spatting was humorous to her. We set down to the hard work of finding some way to move forward in our relationship without the sacrifice of that modern sacrosanctity, individuality. If it had been another time, I would have buried my secret. Now, I kept it and pursued it, and allowed it to be the one unmentioned thing that drove Ms. Right and me apart, as the three of us sat and repaired the minor fractures that hid the worsening irreparable breach that only I could mend, but did not want to, would not aggressively turn myself to do and instead submitted myself gratefully to all the possibilities of what could be.

My hope.

My need.

My punishment.

Our meeting was perfect, reasonable, a contemporary humoresque shot through with the incredible lightness of nonjudgmental therapy. We played games, we switched roles, we acted one another out, we made to-do lists of tasks that would plug the leaks in our sinking engagement. We left in agreement that nothing would happen—nothing major that is—and nothing did. We each had a list and mine of course began where hers ended.

And of course I knew it would never really begin at all.

We had lunch together afterward, a rare thing for us, since she had trouble parting with the money (in her economy, even my money was hers). She gazed at me with a love that was so patently beyond the carnal, it both frightened me and made me sad. How could I live up to it? How could I accept it at the cost set by the force of its personality. The answer was to hedge—but nobody hedges forever.

We may want to, we may strive to, but life itself never hedges. Either we do so in the wake of life, using its debris with an artful sleight-of-hand to cover up what was done or undone, or long after the chance has been lost.

I was somewhere in the middle then, hedging at my most desperate, clinging to her love but in some inexplicably dire need of sex of another kind that would recast the world in the truth of all its forces so that my life would possess it, rather than be possessed by it.

"I love you," I said. "I don't want to lose you."

Then she did something in a certain way that roughly touched my most tender places and went directly to the special nature of my shame: she cried.

Or wept, rather.

I was like a deer caught in the headlights, paralyzed with a fascinated dread of the oncoming collision. I shut my eyes and waited for the full impact to hit.

Line	Pervster	Location	Class	Baud	Sex	Flags	Mins
OF	Merkin	Sig Menu	PAID	9600	M		2
30	EliotTS	PERV-CURVE	PAID	38400	F		83
31	Monstress	Editor	PAID	38400	F		80
32	Big Fat Dick	BladeMaster	PAID	38400	F	B	3
33	Athena	Queen of the Damn'd	PAID	38400	M	S	77
35	Zorch	PERV-CURVE	PAID	38400	M		4
36	Emma Bovary	Menuing System	newbie	38400	F		27
37	Propertius	Menuing System	PAID	38400	M		9
38	Rubber-In Hood	Scrawl On The Wall	PAID	38400	M		1
39	Karenina	Menuing System	PAID	38400	F		1

Flags: B=Busy, C=Chat, S=Sysop
PAIDTOP (PAIDTOP)
Make your selection (T,H,O,S,E,O,F,V,R,A,P,C,G,J,D,B,? for help, or X to exit):
/p Karenina Hey thoro . . .
***
. . . Paging Karenina. . . .
***
. . . . Karenina is paging you from the Main Menu: Yes?. . . .
/p kar Nice seeing you at the munch . . .
. . . . Paging Karenina. . . .
. . . . Karenina is paging you from the Main Menu: Likewise. . . .
/p kar What do you think if our doing some sort of scene together?
. . . . Paging Karenina. . . .
. . . . Karenina is paging you from the Main Menu: I don't know. We're both submissives. . . .
/p kar It says in your reg that you're still exploring. Post-graduate work in dominance and submission?
. . . . Paging Karenina. . . .
. . . . Karenina is paging you from the Main Menu: LOL! Yes. . . . field work for my thesis!. . . .
/p kar Then you can't leave the dominant half unexamined. . . .
. . . . Paging Karenina. . . .
. . . . Karenina is paging you from the Main Menu: True. And although

all my fantasies are submissive, all my dreams are dominant. . . .
/p kar Let's talk about it at the next munch?
. . . . Paging Karenina. . . .
. . . . Karenina is paging you from the Main Menu: Okay. And mean-
while write me your fantasy and I'll see if it meshes with anything I
have a leaning towards. . . . E-mail it to me. . . .
/p kar See you at the munch . . .
. . . . Paging Karenina. . . .
. . . . Karenina is paging you from the Main Menu: Maybe. . . .
/p kar What does "LOL" mean?
. . . . Paging Karenina. . . .
. . . . Karenina is paging you from the Main Menu: Laughing out
loud. . . .
PAIDTOP (PAIDTOP)
Make your selection (T,H,O,S,E,Q,F,V,R,A,P,C,G,J,D,B,? for help, or X
to exit):
. . . . Karenina has received permission to log off of Dreams-Come-
True . . .
x
Exit
You are about to log off the Dreams-Come-True BBS. Press (y) to
terminate your connection, (n) to return to the TOP menu, or (1) to
re-log.
y
***

"Hey Hab."

"Hey buddy—what moves you to interrupt my private hell in the midst of deadline day? It's impossible to talk."

"It's always impossible to talk. How's life on the line?"

"Couldn't be better—the *Register* just got swallowed by the *Post,* and the parent conglomerate just gave everybody automatic bonuses. I guess they can afford to have us keep losing money for at least the next decade, so I'm set."

"Token downsizing?"

Senior arts editor Habanero Bahamian was obviously tickled. "Don't worry, Perry, if you were still here, you'd have been the first to go. I think the only columnist we have now who gets to stay home in his bathrobe and just phone it in is the former publisher."

"Peregrine?"

"Yeah, except he phones it in *transcontinentally*."

"I've always said that the best place to give local commentary was from somewhere else."

Bahamian chuckled—I could see him reflexively stroking his anemic ponytail. "Now *there's* a thought," he replied with the standard irony of practiced authority. "Good news anyway: They stopped running your column."

" 'Round the Towne? It was never mine, even when it had my by-line. . . ."

"Not so, great, caribou breath. The guy who took it over just couldn't sustain any interest in it."

"His or the readers?"

"Both, I'd have to say."

"They said that about me when I was doing it."

"Well, they might have been right, but they kept running it and paying you— the other guy let it die and went on to cartooning."

"Versatile. He obviously found his medium."

"Nah —his last one ran today. Nobody could figure it out. I think one of the news editors hated it enough to actually take a stand."

"Too cerebral."

"*Cerebral?*"

"They say that about unfunny jokes, don't they?"

"Hey buddy, you'd know that better than I would."

"Who took it over?" I could tell from the lag that I was losing him. Papers shuffled and an echoing voice shouted in the background like a kind of broadcast line interference. There was a ray of hope though as I could also detect the cheesy electronic harpsichord notes of the theme for *Jeopardy* in the background.

"Bet you can't guess. Tell you what, I'll help you. The answer is: a very unhappy *enfant terrible*."

"Then the question must be: "Who is Happy Boy!""

"You got it. Now that I've made *you* happy, can I go?"

"Not yet, I have something for you. A story query."

"Going for the daily double? Okay. Can you fax it?"

I laughed uproariously, drowning out Bahamian's own slight chuckle. "C'mon, Hab, I may be gone, but I'm not *dead.*"

"Okay—just testing. Shoot!"

"S&M—Miltown's kinky sex scene revealed?"

"This isn't the news desk, Perry. Any politicos involved?"

"We're talking feature."

"Club life?"

"Ubu Roi, and maybe a few others—some cybersex thrown in?"

"Oh, I like the cybersex angle. Can we take the high road?"

"You mean another indictment of social ills thing? Psychosexual perversion breaking up families, spreading AIDS, fomenting all the less interesting sins like lying, cheating on your taxes and everyday acts of middle-class larceny and embezzlement?"

"Don't forget violence toward women—always a crowd-pleaser."

"The O. J. effect! At the top of *the list!*"

"Well, in light of that, the powers that be and do nothing might just go for it with the usual attack here—you know, raised-eyebrow kind of thing, playing to the readers' love of the freakish while reassuring them that we think it's just as freakish as they do?"

"I have a better idea. Why not 'Miltown S&M: Perils of the New Safe Sex Hit Home.' The teaser: the *Register* goes underground to expose Miltown's Third Sexuality!"

I could hear Bahamian fling himself back in his chair to grapple with a thought and blow out a protracted sigh. I nearly heard his swivel chair creak amid mindfully dead air. "The alternative people will be pissed—they get touchy about being shown in anything less than a flattering light. They don't go for no strokes round here."

"The gays and lesbians do it even more than the hets and are more out about it. We'll make sure to put that in."

"But we're dealing primarily with the hets, right?"

"We know our audience."

He hummed a bar or two of some melody-less ditty. "I like it— it's an attack on something that isn't even established yet, but which takes the critical approach of treating it as if it were."

"Exactly." My coffee was cold, Ms. Right was screaming furiously at a late-paying sales client from her little room across the hall from mine, and it was getting close to the time for me to change out of my robe and pajamas, edging as it was on two o'clock."

"You're thinking five hundred words?"

"Fuck no! Fifteen hundred at least. We're talking arts cover."

"You want the *cover?* That could work. Hold on—let me get an okay."

I got the voices, the *Jeopardy* theme, the static in the background that passed as journalistic business—bless Bahamian for not having put me on interminable hold in the Classic Rock Tartarus of the phone system.

"We got it, buddy. Slated for the fourth. Gives you some weeks to do some digging. Can you get me pics?"

"The digging's mostly done. If you don't want your boys to take them, then I'll get a few for you myself."

"Remember: pretty Gen-X gals, semiclad, some gay beef boys in harnesses, happy grunge types, the leather and chains rock 'n' roll element."

"The very thing."

"Geez, buddy, no *wonder* you don't work here any more—your ideas are simply *too good.* It takes some jamoke like me to translate them so that the powers that be and do nothing *but* can let 'em go to type." His keyclicks were assertive and to the point. "You're on the schedule as of *now.* Good deal. By the way, did I tell you that with our new conglomerate parent came a new wave of new bosses?"

"There are always new bosses, Hub."

"A sad fact. So, listen, all my old outside stuff has to go through my newest boss to get clearance, which normally wouldn't be such great news for you and isn't— except that I managed to just get the okay directly from my new boss while you were holding. Bet you can't guess—"

"You've got to be fucking kidding!"

"Me? I haven't even *met* kidding. I can't wait to get his reaction at the next editorial meeting when he reviews the details of what he just signed off on—an S&M story written by *Perry Patetick!* It's too good! You know, there are *moments* when I actually enjoy what I do. Now, do me a favor, buddy?"

"Name it."

"Get the hell out of my face and let me get back on deadline."

PAIDTOP (PAIDTOP)
Make your selection (T,H,O,S,E,Q,F,V,R,A,P,C,G,J,D,B,? for help, or X
to exit):
. . . . Karenina is paging you from the Main Menu: That was so hot—I
lost my carrier!
/p kar What—my little e-mailing?
. . . . Paging Karenina. . . .
. . . . Karenina is paging you from the Main Menu: It wasn't so lit-
tle. . . .
/p kar What about it did you like?
. . . . Paging Karenina. . . .
. . . . Karenina is paging you from the Main Menu: Submission, pure
and not so simple.
/p kar I just have a need to be overwhelmed. . . .
. . . . Paging Karenina. . . .
. . . . Karenina is paging you from the Main Menu: That in itself could
be overwhelming. . . .
. . . . Karenina is paging you from the Main Menu: Like I said, I may
not be your physical type—but we could. . . .
Karenina is paging you from the Main Menu: try and see if I can do
some of the things you wrote about.
/p kar We could? When?
. . . . Paging Karenina. . . .
. . . . Karenina is paging you from the Main Menu: Hold on—the huz
is lurking about. He hates it when I get on-line.
/p kar The huz?
. . . . Paging Karenina. . . .
. . . . Karenina is paging you from the Main Menu: That's right—the
man I married.
/p kar Hysterical term—I can just imagine him hulking over you, trying to read the screen and your swatting him away.
. . . . Paging Karenina. . . .
. . . . Karenina is paging you from the Main Menu: LOL! Well, you're
right about the hulking part, but as for the reading, he's so slow in
that department he could stand behind me and squint at the screen
for hours before he got it.

/p kar Not the brightest bulb on the tree?

. . . . Paging Karenina. . . .

. . . . Karenina is paging you from the Main Menu: I think there's a short somewhere there—and when one bulb goes, the whole tree's out.

/p kar Sounds like he's out. . . .

. . . . Paging Karenina. . . .

. . . . Karenina is paging you from the Main Menu:: Unfortunately, no.

/p kar How'd you wind up with him?

. . . . Paging Karenina. . . .

. . . . Karenina is paging you from the Main Menu: Everybody asks me that. Hold on. . . .

Muffy has received permission to log on to Dreams Come True. . . .

Athena has received permission to log on to Dreams Come True. . . .

PAIDTOP (PAIDTOP)

Make your selection (T,II,O,S,F,Q,F,V,R,A,P,C,G,J,D,B,? for help, or X to exit):

. . . . Karenina is paging you from the Main Menu: That was a close one.

/p kar What if he finds out?

, , . . Paging Karenina. . . .

. . . . Karenina is paging you from the Main Menu: He can't. He already knows something's up with me, but doesn't want to get into it, the coward.

. . . Karenina is paging you from the Main Menu: He's yelling at the news, which gives him less time to yell at me.

/p kar Mine's snoring on the sofa with her mouth open. . . .

. . . . Paging Karenina. . . .

. . . . Karenina is paging you from the Main Menu: Charming.

/p kar Where do we go from here. . . . ?

. . . . Paging Karenina. . . .

. . . . Karenina is paging you from the Main Menu: Let's find out at the munch.

/p kar I'll be there.

. . . . Paging Karenina. . . .

***

. . . . Sorry! No user on the system has been found with the username "kar."

Karenina has received permission to log off of Dreams Come True.

. . .

SEVEN

It had become apparent that what was once the exotic, breathtakingly forbidden scene was now melding together with the familiar, workaday uncertainty of my professional life into an unsettling blend of happy confusion. What was once the guilty pleasure of logging onto the S&M board for a little foretaste of my next deliciously profane adventure had now become a necessity, but one no less charged with the hope and deliberate license that participation in an illicit, socially reprehensible underculture begets. Now that Happy Boy had unknowingly bought the S&M story from me, I was at least—perhaps in name only—working again. But Ms. Right was so delighted, she didn't raise the slightest criticism about my having wrangled biweekly unemployment insurance to underwrite my hours of exploratory indolence and secret infidelities.

It was fine with her as she went off to her little room to make the early-morning collection calls while I sat typing on the electronic BBS, not frittering my time away in a fruitless exercise of unrealized electronic flirting, but instead focusing my considerable analytic powers and well-honed journalistic craftsmanship on researching a story for a major local weekly. What I was doing was schmoozing with MooseCock, cavorting bawdily with The Thorn and sipping ersatz conversational coffee with Baron Land. I had moved beyond cybersex into a crystallized cybersocial sect—living the cyberlife in full by arriving at yet another layer of distance that came between me and my heart's desire while acting as if and believing that I had somehow come closer to it.

Then TechnoSlaver had to come into the chat room. Things up till then were fairly quiet—I had no further hot responses from Karenina, no exclusively perverse and politically galvanized play parties greeted me in e-mail from the log-in prompts and no salacious, delectably teasing, perpetually denying whispers came my way in teleconference (or the godawfully named and far too arch *Perv-Curve*, as it had come to be known). I was sipping my coffee, sitting in my plaid bathrobe wondering how long I could afford to tie up my one phone line, the other having been recently claimed by the newly home-working Ms. Right, before I would have to face reality and get back to some work of some kind. Then TechnoSlaver had to come into the chatroom.

When he did, through some of quirk of the Midwestern sense of decorum, TechnoSlaver managed to piss off everyone in the channel but me and did so unbeknownst to me, as all the poisonous back-and-forth was accomplished through the all-important whisper function and through a global numeric chat channel that would broadcast its messages to anyone who had the correct name of the channel and knew to input it after the proper global commands.

Bill, or TechnoSlaver had *had* it: he was leaving the scene.

You are in the Main public Room!
Type "LIST" to see a list of available Rooms.
———————

TechnoSlaver, The Thorn, Baron Land and Tutor are here with you.
Just enter "?" if you need any assistance. . . .
From TechnoSlaver (whispered): I'm serious. . . . I'm leaving.

***

Why?
—message sent privately to TechnoSlaver—
From TechnoSlaver (whispered): I don't want to be in some parking lot somewhere and get my head bashed in, for one.
From TechnoSlaver (whispered): For another, the defensive, territorial attitudes and poses everyone strikes here are just too much—I own him, he owns me, you didn't pay me the proper sign of respect, blah, blah, blah! Everyone pretends to be open when everything's closed. Then there's the gossip. Nothing anyone ever says is true, and it's always damaging.

Well, what you're saying is true. But who's going to bash your head in?
—message sent privately to TechnoSlaver—

* * *

Baron Land is skillfully performing oral sex on The Thorn.
TechnoSlaver has his whip at the ready—he is unsure as to why.
Propertius is twiddling his thumbs.
* * *

From Baron Land: Ouch
* * *

From The Thorn <To Baron Land>: Prickly, is it, dear?
From Tutor: I thought I pulled the last one out the last time I was there.
* * *

From TechnoSlaver: I didn't know you'd been to such exotic places, Tutor.
From Tutor: Unlike some us, I am in fact well-traveled.
From TechnoSlaver: Not in fantasy?
From Tutor: No. My reality might pass as fantasy for some, but it's more real than the floggers and dildoes I used on The Thorn last night.<g>
The Thorn is moaning softly.
—Tutor has left Perv-Curve—
From TechnoSlaver (whispered): Baron Land. He's making threats. Tutor, The Thorn—both bent out of shape.
Baron Land? That geriatric? Listen, just blow on him and he'll fold—as for The Thorn, she's short and frumpy, another one of these anthropomorphic rural dumptrucks with more attitude than sense. Are they telling you they matter some-how in the scene? You're being taking advantage of.
—message sent privately to TechnoSlaver—

* * *

From TechnoSlaver (whispered): How?
They know you don't know that the scene in Miltown is not

confined to those with an all-too-active fantasy life and a
less-than-varied playlife who spend all their free time on this
stupid, closed-ended BBS.
—message sent privately to TechnoSlaver—

***

From TechnoSlaver (whispered): I was beginning to think it
was. Tell me more. . . .

So I did. I convinced him to leave the stifling company of the
BBS and call me from the deep boondocks of Priory where his Wisconsin sensibility had landed him. I got his story. A refugee from
the American hinterlands, though he never viewed himself that way,
favoring the rusticated habits of hunting and the Scotch-Irish fra-
ternity of curling—throwing a stone across the ice, frantically sweep-
ing its path with brooms to smooth the way to dubious triumph and
to alcohol-soaked celebrations that followed. Perhaps the queer,
country-club cast of Midwestern rurality and clannishness of sport
held the key to D/s for Bill.

He certainly approached it as a sport, learning the language of
the less sports-oriented to communicate his experience with it and
more than zestful pursuit of it. Married and living Ms. Right's
dream for me with the love of his life, Bill furtively and with the
long-range planning protocols of the standard engineer trained at
Trinity Polytechnic had embarked on an overtly nonsexual campaign of pain and perversion whose avowed design would be complete only when his wife was somehow converted to an enamored
participation in the nonpenetrative sex acts Bill avidly compared to
sport. He insisted, despite the obsessive gleam in his eye that made
him breathless and dead quiet at the vision of a bound, stripped
woman in a cage.

If you saw Bill, you'd think he was a baby-faced, inexperienced,
slightly paunchy nerd—straitlaced, on the shy side with a turn of
speech that can only be described as a curt Republican twang filled
with thoughtful pauses used to process nonsense. If you saw me, you'd
head for the hills you would no doubt think that Bill had come from.

If you sat next to us together, you'd sit closer to Bill. And I would smile, knowing what he could do to you and what I could not.

It started for Bill when he was working his usual, compulsively late hours consulting at some forgotten conglomerate. He was seduced by a pretty (I take his word for this, despite more recent knowledge) executive who schooled him in all the basic ways of trading pain for pleasure without the addition of a standard across-the-desk, inside-the-cubicle office fuck. It was an eye-opener for Bill and he kept his eyes opened for it ever since, finding the right shops along his business-related travels, and in the shops the leaflets and literature, and in the leaflets and literature the clubs, the BBSs, the recurrent parties—and of course New York, and its D/s culture, encapsulated by its semiorganized, semiactivist party and workshop obsessed TES organization.

TES once stood for Til Eulenspiegel Society, an arch and pseudoscholarly reference to some mythic prankster celebrated in a nearly forgotten Offenbach opera of the same name. It was a small, heterosexual (but certainly a friendly fellow traveler to its larger gay and lesbian coevals), S&M support group when it was founded twenty-five or so years ago. Now called The Eulenspiegel Society, it had become party central for the studied players of the Manhattan scene, a positive magnet for ambitious die-hards and lifestylers from out of town, and, of course, another sad forum for those whose lives on most other fronts—particularly in the unforgiving city—were stalled and failing to thrive.

TES had semi-regular parties at the Vault and at Hellfire, both of which had swapped addresses and locations at least once, and at a sometime club enticingly named Paddles, which sometime around three or four on a Sunday morning would mutate into the all-gay meeting place and less-than-discreet sex club Boys Town. He had already been going to private parties on Long Island, combining them with business trips that would have dragged him to the vicinity nonetheless. Now it was time to try something a bit more centripetal, as he put it. Would I accompany him on his first run down to a TES party at the renowned vault in his new minivan? The midtown hotel suite was already booked on his corporate VISA, and he hardly knew

a soul worth going with. Hell yes, was my reply, figuring this never
to happen anyway. After all, why shouldn't I? I had done him the
enormous favor of convincing him to stay in the Miltown scene.
It was the least he could do.

BILL CAME BY IN HIS VAN TO PICK ME UP FOR UBU ROI THAT FRIDAY,
with still no word from Karenina. He was so late, Ms. Right begged
me not to go. I comforted her, but I didn't care. I had to go; my
heart at the moment was in nothing else but getting out the door
with my bag of accessories, the harness I wore beneath my sweatshirt
clutching importunately at my crotch while at the same time preventing me from even giving Ms. Right a farewell hug for fear of
discovery.

Her approval was hesitant, but she took one long, incisive look
at Bill and asked herself how I could get into any trouble with this
freckle-faced, aviator-bespectacled rotund son of the Midwest and
answered all at once with a grudging laugh. She asked Bill some
basic questions about himself with politely focused disinterest, joked
about setting my curfew and saw us down the narrow stairwell to
the door dressed in her sweetheart nightgown. She was going to go
to bed early to get a jump on the Saturday business.

She was knowingly letting me have my play on the line to reel
me in when I was spent—no dummy, Ms. Right.

She didn't know though that I had already broken the line.

She didn't know I was gone.

I changed in the back of the van on the way, decked out in my
bare-buttock-displaying chaps, O-ringed motorcycle boots, chainlink
armband, worn on the right to flag submissive. I looked lean, corrupt
and dangerous—like some thrash-metal band's video setpiece, like
just another gothic nine-inch nail. Bill was going to wear what he
wore: corduroys and a light, multicolored nylon windbreaker. While
I struggled into a codpiece that had no backstrap, leaving my butt
cleavage entirely up for grabs, Bill described his ambitions and aspirations, which centered around meeting a certain nymphette possessed of the qualities resembling the princess of a planet in a long
out-of-print series of science-fiction novels that he had taken to heart

as a teen. He gave a thorough technical discourse on how he would
extract her submission and then enforce her erotic surrender by slow
degrees—broken down to minutes and seconds, a geometry of pain
requiring fishing line, pulleys and carabiners—that ended only when
we hit the parking lot. There was an understanding between us,
processed again by one of Bill's ponderous silences.

We both got lost in it in different ways.

After the rigmarole of coatcheck, where I flirted with the coatcheck gothgirl and tipped her extra to care for my coverage and coat,
we took the stairs that led up from the clammy basement directly to
the main room of Ubu Roi, where the familiar faces amid the persistently dank, smoky threat of the club put me instantly at ease. I
was at home, and Athena was screaming. He was exhorting us to
drink as much as we could stand—hardly responsible or sanctioned
S&M behavior, but as he reminded us so refreshingly, we weren't
there to be good, but to have a good time. "Being bad is its own
good time!" he screeched.

Hear, hear!

Bill stood by smiling, taking in the usual Ubu Roi tableaux of
scantily clad collegiennes, his eyes glazing over subtly as he busily
plugged in images to the fixed and variable potentialities of his refined desires. Coming off as the most nerdly of tourists, I wondered
how the clueless writhing girls would react should they ever breach
that decency of Midwestern decorum and discover just how deep a
player Bill in fact was. Bill licked his lips, grinning at the girls on
the dance floor and their practiced, affected smoky looks. I could see
him think of how he could truly make them smolder.

Auntie was fuming about Mount's misdeeds again as he groped
a gaggle of female submissive wannabes, so she gave me away to
Athena as fodder for yet another godawful auction. Thankfully,
Chlamydia rescued me, briskly clasping the new leash she'd been
wanting to try on the O-ring of my spiked collar, striding nonchalantly away from the central cadre at the bar dressed as a gleaming
latex Catwoman. She held court with the mountainous jade who
owned Ubu Roi and kept it the moral and physical sinkhole it was,
the obese yet oddly hyperactive Mark Flange and his ermine-like,
pink-eyed goateed manager, Quinnie, who skirted Flange's periphery

whenever he could. I knelt on the floor, licking Chlamydia's jet black PVC boots, dulling their glassine sheen with my saliva as I painted them with long strokes of my tongue. Not that I enjoyed the flavor, or somehow achieved a direct sexual thrill in the adulation of a vinyl-clad calf. I knew she liked the image; I was her accessory.

It pegged me sharply as a submissive.

"Perky" would be the only way to describe Chlamydia's approach and response to Mark's old-school vulgarity, which was squarely of the "hey babe" type, with gold-plated neck chains. His was a turnip head with a helmet of close-cropped kinky hair that was no doubt the thinnest thing about him. She was pitching both Quinnie and Flange about performing onstage as one of the many attractions of Athena's Black Fridays, paid of course. I was learning from her dogged exhibitionism and affected cult intellectual references that she was yet another self-styled performance artist sucked into the scene even as she attempted to exploit its shock value.

I worried the lines would blur too quickly for her and like so many she would wind up a pro-dom in the service of some Faganesque pimp with a master's insecure swagger or a submissive's manipulative sycophancy. Nodding as if Chlamydia's every desire were a done deal and had been delivered upon last week, Flange used neutral-sounding sensitive speak such as "whatever you'll feel most comfortable with" and "you'll have all the space you need as you need it" while Chlamydia chirped and tittered her master—I should say *mistress*—plan. All at once Mark's hand shot out toward her smallish, though well-formed breast so beautifully framed in latex and Quinnie ran off, a scowl on his face as he verbally bitch-slapped the nearest available hulking gothboy on his security team into a less-than-feigned incredulity. I looked away and smelled a cigar, then felt rough fingers making their way through my hair, stroking my scalp.

I tried to ignore it as I did so many of the incidental attentions of men. My head was bowed in an affection of penance, my eyes cast down to strike that attitude, straining to look up, however cautiously. The thick fingers that played through my hair as Chlamydia and Flange followed their entirely separate—if not altogether opposite—agendas grabbed a substantial clump of my hair, wrenching up my head and neck. His face stared into mine, but he held the cigar away in his other hand, as if he had already figured that the smoke would bother me even in a club suffused with smoke.

"Found them, I see," he said.

"Found them."

"You look happy there on the floor—disgusting as it is."

"The floor?"

"That too."

"You're not into it," I stated as Chlamydia tugged idly on my leash pitching and sweat-selling Flange on absolutely nothing. Her cleavage, accented by the scoop-necked latex catsuit buffed to a high polish by yours truly, looked especially darling, beaded as it was with sweat. It was no mystery that the attention-deficit-disordered Mark Flange seemed drawn into my momentary mistress' patter and remained alighted on his stool without distraction but for the strategies that seemed to dance on his expression as he figured his angles while Chlamydia pitched.

"I'm not into anything."

"Just bad cigars."

"They're making a comeback."

"So's S&M."

"No. That will never make a comeback."

"Why not?"

He slapped my cheek like an uncle, straightened up from looking directly at me with his cloudy eyes then kicked me a little. He laughed when I jolted a bit and Chlamydia had to pull my leash taut to maintain appearances yet continue to fill Flange's wayward gaze.

"It never left even though it was never really here. It never *goes* anywhere. And neither do those in it. Unless . . ." He shrugged.

"Unless what?"

He grabbed himself and chuckled, shaking his head. "Unless they're dead."

Flange abruptly stepped over me, effectively ending both Chlamydia's conversation and mine.

I RUSHED OVER TO SEPARATE KARENINA FROM MOUNT AT THE FOOD court. Since she had billed herself openly as a submissive in the archaic BBS's registry of users, Karenina was fair game for his swinger's approach to S&M and as a means to play on Auntie's fears so that Mount could get what he wanted from her—whenever he decided what that was. She gazed at him with some disturbing degree of longing receptivity before turning her liquid hazel eyes toward me, her expression brightening with a rough-toothed smile that bespoke a kind of lurid fellowship. She liked what she saw when she saw me, and she knew I held the promise of being a coconspirator in her quest for play and her entrenchment in the scene. She had yet to realize that I wanted to get out of it what I could and then get out. She wanted to live there. I was another networked connection to her neighborhood of choice. I suppose that was the essential difference between us: she was a suburbanite and I was fighting—despite the efforts and cajolery of Ms. Right and the moving of my society away from my habits and predilections—to stay an urban bohemian.

But here I was, just as guilty as Karenina of trying to find the newest society of my life in the scene. But unlike Karenina, though I didn't understand it at the time, I wanted to do so as a means of scoring a scene. What she wanted was something more ethereal or poetic—her own notions of romance, fealty and perfect love perhaps alloyed to the steely, irredeemable fact of the scene.

There we were, sitting at one of the cheaply durable tables under the swirling, airy fluorescence of the junk atrium formed by the epicenter of the mall, discussing kinky sex, fetishism and all the aberrant practices of undisguised D/s while nibbling questionable indigestibles from the presumably low-fat Japanese-noodle bar situated just next to Shrimp-On-The-Barbie, whose female staff were all made up and wigged to look like the now-collectible doll.

In a mall, all cultural clichés were food of a kind.

And in a section of the food court marked by black balloons among the unsuitable, the low end, the decrepit and the vulgar, D/s was a banquet of possibility unfolding before the starving.

She arm wrestled me out of the blue and soundly (if not roundly) defeated me.

I can't quite say what passed between us then—it would sound

banal, all of our crossreferences of D/s discovery, the first time bondage made her respond, why I required some sort of female supremacy
in my life, consensual or not—and we both agreed the best fantasies
(unfortunately the experiences by their very nature could never
match them) were nonconsensual—even the time I tied my first girlfriend Terry to a radiator at her request and beat her senseless in
hopes she might try and do the same to me, something I lied about
to myself and others by calling a well-timed blip on the erotic screen,
but which had always stayed with me. We reveled in experiences
that comprised a continuum of stress, violence, oddity, perversion
and unapologetic sex for its own sake with the same calm center of
focus that two numismatic enthusiasts have when discussing treasured coins.

We were collectors of a kind, collectors of moments, savorers of
sex, relaters of pain, appreciaters of the aberrant. Images of chromium and nickel spikes danced in our heads, and like children we
cooed questioningly, "How shiny, how long, how sharp . . ."

She confessed that Tutor had been her first playmate in the
Miltown scene and I withdrew my hand.

"He's not so bad—harmless really as long as you don't tread
through the minefield of his insecurities and keep stroking that pathetic ego," she said, reaching for my hand, clasping it and crushing
it somewhat.

"Stroking might have as much effect there as in other forms of
impotency."

Anger flashed across her face, but she controlled it. "You have
a mean streak—ever thought of topping?"

"I'm not a switch."

"Neither am I. What makes you think we can play together, two
submissives?" She batted her eyes—was it nervousness or coyness
to offset her directness?"

"Just a hunch," I said. "And you said you wanted to explore *all*
the facets of D/s."

"It's true," she said, sipping green tea from her styrofoam cup.
"My fantasies may be submissive, but all my dreams are dominant."
She leaned toward me, again with that leer, that craftily innocent

expression of guilt-edged enthusiasm I had come to associate with all her unrealized D/s longings. "And when I saw you onstage, I said to myself, I said, 'Man—I'd like a piece of that.' "

A chill ran up my spine. She had no idea she had me, but I would never have admitted it. "Really?" I said.

"Really." She leered and clasped my hand with an exaggerated firmness I enjoyed.

She offered me a ride home from the mall, and at that point I hardly felt able to refuse any offer she could make, not that I had any better way of getting home without her back to the wilds of North Trinity. With her little Neiman-Marcus biker jacket she de-escalated down to level B of the mall's parking garage, dragging me along by my shirt and bantering skittishly all the way to the car, a dark blue Mercedes *station wagon.*

"A station wagon?" I hiccuped involuntarily.

"I like to ride in style," she said without irony and grinned her preposterous snaggle-toothed grin for effect. The car was a tasteless suburban grotesquerie—she must have known it. No, she didn't know it, holding that grin with an obvious pride in the thing's expense. Karenina disabled the alarm and unlocked the doors with a single key-press device on the Mercedes emblem of her key chain. She gunned the engine to a jerky start and we were off, speeding along Monument Ave., weaving through the loose tapestry of narrow traffic and playing intermittent games of chicken.

"Show it to me," she said, looking squarely at me, tailgating the Matsura in front of us. "I want to see it."

"See what?

"Your body—I want to see it."

"It's a little cold—you may remember we don't have spring in Miltown."

"Then your little nipples will stand out more—so do it!" She revved ahead and we shot across the Trinity Bridge inches away from sideswiping slower vehicles.

I removed my conventional nonbiker leather jacket, stripped off my sweatshirt and gave her the show.

"Good," she said absently, now seemingly more attentive to the road. "Your pants?"

"I need a bit more leg room to get them off," I deflected.

"There's plenty of leg room. Just wriggle them off the way you do at the club and give me what I want. You said you wanted to be submissive."

"I did."

"Then do it."

We stopped at a red light.

"What do we do when we have to stop?" I asked.

"We never have to stop," she lilted.

"I meant at a light."

"Then we can enjoy our edge-play even more."

"Edge-play."

"Afraid of being seen?"

"Aren't you?"

The lights changed and she grabbed my crotch at the same moment that she gunned the car. "I suppose . . . but I still want to see what I'll be playing with."

"Another time—I can see we're almost there."

I directed her to pull over by a heating-oil supplier off Divinity whose small lot was nevertheless ganged up with tanker trucks. On the opposite side of the street was an unusual item—a once upon a time generic family-run hardware store that in this, the age of the chains, was now a decided *rara avis* completely out of place even at the furthest ends of the shadow of the university in vaguely civilized North Trinity. I looked around furtively to see if anyone could see us from the street. The only activity was in the corner gas station whose broken blaring boom-box radio thundered blustering heavy-metal music of yesteryear. The greasemonkeys hung out blowing dope and shouting bully-boy epithets amongst themselves. They were oblivious to us. I shuddered once with the cold, my shirt still off.

There was a flash—I thought for a moment I had been shot.

I had.

"Just a camera," said Karenina. I forgot to tell you that I was a photographer—what I studied in school before I hit it big in real estate." She tossed it from hand to hand, leaving the shot to resolve my image on the dash.

She had mentioned it, but I wasn't going to argue. Who *knows* what I had told her up till then in the throes of all my reflexive scene-starved angling—and even if I remembered to be truthful (or at least limited in my exaggerations), I was lucky if at that moment I could keep anything straight. I was attempting to impose a fragile balance wherein I could both be led by possibility yet hold disaster in check without any loss of the potential qualities for which I was searching, on which I was dreaming and to which the bent of my entire life had become so unutterably attuned. Karenina pressed her hand to mine with an unsettlingly strong motion as I struggled to regulate my breathing.

It was the Polaroid. She passed me the results of the flash and I saw all at once a pale and cold boy-man suffering tentative joy without conviction apparent in the smile on his face. She snatched it away from me. "I hope to get more and better," she said absently, tucking the image away in her purse.

"You want me to pose for you?"

"I might want to *pose* you."

"I don't know about cameras."

"I do," she said, and flashed that uneven, jagged-toothed grin at me as if she believed it were the most charming of professional cover-girl smiles—and perhaps, as I remember it now, at that moment it might as well have been. In the oddity of her looks, the cool, swaggering manner that contradicted her small, ungainly frame, the growing focus of her interest in me, I saw a sort of chance for my life to be remade.

She was an avenue of escape, that was clear—but did that itself offer an escape clause? I jumped a little to see as I was leaving.

"Nervous?" she asked leaning out the passenger side of the Mercedes station wagon. Pivoting as I stood under the formerly empty white glow of the high-necked street light, I noticed something in the back of the car, a shape. I was even more startled by what I saw.

It was a toddler's car seat.

"You have a kid."

"Two," she said

I breathed a sigh of relief even as my pulse quickened.

"You have a life then—you're not just another of these incomplete personages who have nothing but some wreckage outside of the scene."

She grunted with amusement. "Well, it's not wrecked yet, but I'm working on it."

"You could say the same about me." I pointed through the trees. "See the light in the window just through the trees—that's my life, somewhere in there."

"Who's behind the light then?"

"My fiancée of seven years."

"Long courtship."

I indicated the car seat. "She wants what you have."

"And you don't?"

"I'm not ready."

"You may never be. It's very hard. I don't know how I do it, or even if I do it."

I leaned against the base of the street light by the dingy once-bright red and white oil trucks, watching the somewhat rustic mom-and-pop hardware store, out of place even on this more remote stretch of the urban avenue, out of the furthest corner of my eye. I had lost some of my own tension of control. I was giving way to the moment.

"And your husband isn't into it."

"Into what? The scene?"

"That was my take on what you said."

"He isn't."

"So divorce looms in the future."

"I hope not."

"But you're ardent about the scene."

She hopped out of the car and joined me against the streetlight, where I leaned, my head almost completely bowed. It was such that I could look directly into her rusted hazel eyes. She didn't blink.

"I will never stop exploring my erotic horizons."

"What will you do then—about the huz?"

"Play."

"Play," I repeated uncertainly as she reached up to grab my shoulders.

"Play for time," she whispered with an undertone of steel.

"I'm doing the same—playing for time," I said, knowing it was true.

"With your intended?"

I had to laugh. "I have a friend who calls her my *un*intended." I pointed my arm at an upward angle, shifting my body like a dangling scarecrow. "That light, that's all that's left."

"Play for time," she said again.

I pushed myself to stand up straight and shake away for a moment the ennui that was coming for me at the end of the night. "It's good we both have lives, lovers—"

"The huz," she said, screwing up her face.

"No danger of adhesion."

"Adhesion?"

"Getting stuck in the glue—emotionally."

"I wouldn't think so," she spoke through her wide smile, looking so funny and dog-like, so pugnacious and endearing. Her eyes were sad and had taken on a golden-toned hue under the metallic light.

"I'm relieved," she said, opening the driver's side and sliding her short and awkward-seeming body inside.

"Me too."

The window on the passenger's side of her navy-blue suburban monstrosity powered down.

"I'll see you soon I hope."

"You will."

"I mean it—think of a time for play."

"I want to play."

"We'll see about it."

Her eyes hit me hard and kept on hitting. I did not turn away. Her smile, like a Polaroid, took a moment to develop. "I know I will," I said. She hit the accelerator and gave me an almost-dismissive wave as she took a tight corner from the oil company lot with the sound of screeching wheels, which I had always up till then reserved in my mind's ear for *film noir* soundtracks.

I shambled toward the light in the window where I knew Ms. Right would be sleeping on her loveseat, embracing a pillow I imagined she dreamed was me. Of course, I was guiltless then, because I believed I was free, morally immune and beyond the man who once counted himself so wise as to understand the precise value of the intimate kiss, the fond embrace, the warm and yielding presence of a woman's need.

I was guiltless, then, free and clumsy, but so much darker than the shadows in which I hid.

I was a calm monster, a serial killer of love, quite willing to wear a mask of ordinariness, quite willing to do anything involving both strangers and those known to me, in a seedy, secret underworld where I was a recognized figure, a player.

A player in the scene.

That's what I was becoming—*a player in the scene*, achieving in life what had only been barely breathed about in art. I was heading toward the core of satisfaction and surrender, not hiding in the shadows, but befriending them and making them my own. In my mind I was remaking myself as a great adventurer in uncharted freedoms of perversion and truth.

Was this the revelation of a stalking monster set on the path of the first kill?

Was I remaking myself to be a great adventurer in the seething anomie of sensual, unforgiving flesh?

The summer night sighed about me as if itself some huge sexual entity (a reflection of myself, of course).

It was the shadows that called. It was the shadows I went skipping off to out of breath, heart pounding, lips sticky, exploding into hope, the darkness and home.

EIGHT

The truth that loomed between Ms. Right and me was now no longer just the scene, but rather a scene.

I *had* to have a scene with Karenina. It was simply next in the order of play.

Beyond humor, beyond whimsey, it was but the rigid dictate of the impulse itself, the *will* to D/s.

And, as was the protocol in such matters of profane D/s discretion, we were to meet for lunch to negotiate details.

So, while Ms. Right laid the groundwork to accomplish several or more print-run–related tasks on her way out to Chichester, I shucked my bathrobe early and dressed in an uncharacteristic sport jacket and tie—the one that splashed my old school's disgracefully overpriced crest all over it in a repeating pattern. It was one of the few ties I owned and that was because—so long ago that I still recall it only through the images of a drug-suffused haze—I had received it for free. I suppose wearing it now was my little way of dressing to impress. I almost called Dwight just for the pleasure of hearing him take me to task for having done so.

"You're wearing *the tie*," said Ms. Right, harried and bird-like in her nightgown.

"I have a lunch meeting with Bahamian about the piece."

"You mean the fat ugly kinky suburbanite piece for the *Register?* I didn't hear you set that up."

"You've been eavesdropping?" I feigned outrage but my heart palpitated. She knew.

"No—I just overhear you. I work across the hall from the flimsiest door. It doesn't matter that it's blocked. I hear you. I hear you move, I hear you speak. I hear you breathe. I can even hear your heart beat. You're nervous."

I looked at my tie. "A bit. I haven't worked in a while. I need this."

"I know." She put her palms to my face. "But tell me something: Have you fallen in love with someone else?"

I was being entirely truthful when I said: "No, I love no one but you."

It's just that love had suddenly become unimportant. I wanted something else, something better. Love of another kind, a romance so powerful it would destroy and then remake everything in a terrible, wonderful quantum blast. I wanted to become *life*, the destroyer of worlds, but instead I had become the J. Robert Oppenheimer of my own heart.

I was telling the truth, as she straightened my tie and rested her lips passionately on my cheek.

The phone rang: Bahamian.

She dangled the receiver for me to take, pouting.

"I thought you already talked to him."

I motioned for quiet and tried to get a fix on my editor's laconic queries and quick, breathless hits.

"Hey pal, what have we got on kinky Miltown?"

I shouldered the receiver in close enough to my face to bite it as I spoke. My lower lip pressed repeatedly up against it. "I'm lining some things up."

"Interviews, I hope."

"You hope correct."

"You know you made Happy Boy pop a vein."

"You're trying to make my day for a reason, aren't you?"

I cupped my hand over the receiver and spoke *sotto voce* to the fuming Ms. Right. "Happy Boy's having a stroke over my doing an S&M feature for the *Register*." I was angling for a little conspiratorial amusement. She would, as the love of my life, take my side.

As it happened, she produced some sort of fire-breathing whisper-scream at me so intense that it was almost certain Bahamian made it out: "Don't be an instigator! He'll kill it and we need the money. Can't you just be nice, even if he happens to be a flaming idiot?"

"But he also happens to be a flaming asshole. Do they get diplomacy too?"

She stamped her slippered foot. "When it comes to money, *they* get it too!"

Again I motioned for quiet, but she blew from the room calling me a son of a bitch loud and clear. I wanted to make it right, but I had an editor on the line.

"Buddy—I'm talking to dead air, aren't I?"

"Right here, Hab."

"I don't know if we're going with this thing."

"Jesus Christ, Hab—it's just a fucking story."

"They're *all* just fucking stories. That's the problem, baby. Nobody really cares, and the powers that be don't want to mess with Happy Boy—but Happy Boy wants to mess with *you.*"

"So let him."

"His way is to cut you a check and kill the piece."

"Feels like old times."

"It *is* old times. They're afraid of Happy Boy and Happy Boy's afraid of you. Should work out in your favor. If it weren't an absurd universe, it would."

"What if I made it serious journalism?"

I detected a sigh. "Then we would have a sudden death playoff."

"How many shots?"

"None from your end of the court, I'm afraid. Happy Boy's a gutsy guy—his way of dealing with you is not to. And you did pick one of those unfortunate stories that's just too interesting to ever really be considered news.

"What do we do if we keep it a feature?"

"Push the upbeat, positive, life-affirming lifestyles angle. Tone down the gory details. Make it bouncy—a feel-good piece about spanking your significant other in the privacy of your own bedroom kind of thing."

"That's really weak."

"I know. But in this business, weakness is its own kind of strength."

He could have been playing me. There was no telling. "Listen, Hab," I said as if having a moment of inspiration, "let him kill it. I'll write it the way I write it, do what you can with it. I still have his approval on an S&M piece he *re*hired me to write. I'll take that as the consolation prize."

Bahamian laughed. "The whole thing's a Sisyphean enterprise isn't it? That's why we have guys like you out on the front lines doing it. Nobody ever knows what to do with these things—too disturbing to be news, too compelling not to be some sort of feature, too damn sexy and violent to totally ignore. Like you, it just doesn't fit into our pigeonholing system. A word to the wise, buddy."

Yes, he was playing me. "I'll give it the full courage to be what you are spin."

"Beautiful, Ace. Now let me get off the damn phone so I can make my top of the hour deadline on this op-ed thing Happy Boy flung my way, okay?" His tone of exasperation was expert.

"Have a nice day," I tried reflexively to put in the gap between his last syllable and the hang-up, but missed.

There were little prickles on my forehead that itched. I wiped them away with the back of my hand. Sweat.

Something flew by my ear. A bug?

The smash against the wall woke me up. I turned my head and saw the darkened splotch on the wall where the water hit the dry plaster and paint and was sucked in. I felt a hard though incompetent punch delivered to my solar plexus.

"You were talking to *her*, weren't you?"

"Who's her?" I rubbed my chest with one hand as I straightened my tie with the other.

It would normally have been redundant to say that she was red-faced, but she was, a heart-stopping sight to see. "That bitch who's stealing my life away. You're not meeting with Bahamie-shmamie, or whoever he is, you're seeing her!"

"I am," I insisted, grabbing her close to me, trying to stave off the approaching crying jag. "Didn't you listen in—didn't you hear me fight the good fight for the story?"

"Bastards!" she sobbed and punched me again. "You're all bastards!"

"I know," I said. "It's what we do."

"Not what," she said, looking up at me wide-eyed as a marmoset, her eyes gleaming with frustrated tears. "Not what, but *who*."

I MET HER AT THE HERITAGE RESTAURANT, A TRINITY CIRCLE STAN-dard whose aspect could not have been more opposed to its name if it were immediately changed to Ye Olde Tory Watering Hole. From the batik cushions on the cherry-wood benches in the bar, to the Mayan-style tapestries and Sausalito crystal in the main dining room, it was in every way an elderly, high-ticket exemplar of the New Age. It served veal, of course, but with wheatgrass juice available in place of wine. Range of dress went from frayed khakis to Saville Row tailoring, so it caused no stir for Karenina to meet me at the little lectern of the maître d' wearing black jeans and a leather motorcycle jacket, steel O-ring snapped squarely into the right epaulet. My threadbare blue jeans and nonfetish black leather jacket worn gray were perceived almost as a status symbol by the maître d', who let us in ahead of fuming matrons wearing dresses like giant, floral pat-terned tea cozies. After all, I was wearing all that, a sport jacket, and the fatal old-school tie.

She grabbed one of my belt loops and dragged me over to a table she liked better than the one the maître d' had selected for us.

While this was going on, I noticed that the matrons huffily seated themselves in the same room not far from us, cackling like a gaggle of hens.

She grinned the grin that chills me up to the current moment, removed her sunglasses and recounted to me the essentials of her life. I listened at first, burning to tell her things I should have either offloaded in the more discreet, uncaring precincts of a therapist's office or a priest's confessional. Then, somewhere along the recapit-ulation of her complicated world view, I spilled—but not before receiving in full measure a taste of her life.

She had been excited by bondage since the age of three. Her first serious D/s play involving bondage and some spanking was in high school. In fact, high school was the absolute happiest time of her life, which I should have taken as some kind of warning, except that I was beyond such things just then. It was the hallmark of her life, and I could see how, from the tale of her misfortunes, this had contributed to her being a compulsive suburbanite joiner.

With boastful flair and sham nonchalance (a pretty trick in and of itself that she seemed to be waving before me for approval), she recounted that she was the cochair of her local chapter of the Junior League, chief organizer of her neighborhood's Block Beautification Program, and was business manager of her synagogue Beth Y'shua's annual rummage sale. For all that, she did not fit in with the white-bread stodgy ranks of the musty parochial enclave that surrounded her refurbished three-story house at the apex of Swansea Crest. She still rankled at the fact that she had been rejected with such subtle coldness by her local Methodist Church—a place that had existed long before the Tudors, Edwardians, and mock Federalist houses sprung up in the 20s to make Swansea an early modern Miltown suburb—even though she was Jewish. How dare they!

She didn't think that this being Jewish should bar her from the community of the Methodist faith. I shut my mouth on this front, lapsed Catholic that I was and am. I was sizing her up for play.

Her life had been a rocky ride: She had been deeply involved in the TV show *Star Trek* and in fact had lost her virginity to one of its supporting cast members. She had received honorable mention in one of the now out-of-print *Star Trek* convention nonfiction mass-market paperbacks.

To avoid the pain of rejection from the then love of her life, her fine arts professor at Miltown University, she married a coarse uneducated lower-echelon supervisor at the Miltown Division of Social Services, who she did not love and had little if anything in common with. She excused this as a function of youthful naïveté, explaining, "It was false advertising. When he drilled holes for eyebolts in the frame of our water bed then screwed them in, I thought he was the man for me." Once they were married, his interest in D/s fell off into an abyss of greed and anger at becoming junior partner in the pursuit of it, and a sense of towering insecurity at holding on to a position he knew he had scammed amid the thick of doctors, lawyers and privileged professionals who now surrounded him. He tried to become as much a joiner as Karenina was and, according to her, plainly failed.

Through a pooling of various crude mutual assets, the inflation of property and the deflation of social values during the 80s, Karenina and the huz made a fortune in real estate brokering the Edwardians, Tudors and mock Federalists to every status-hungry yuppie that came down the pike. She stated further that the fortune was hers, as "the huz," could not sell, was not bright, had no vision and was, when all was said and done, one of these do-nothing choke-artists bred from generations of Miltown malingerers who got state jobs, developed convenient health problems and "comped out," as she put it. I found out that this meant opting for an early retirement in order to dip even more heavily into the deeper end of the public entitlement pool from which retired state employees drew their disability checks.

Karenina and the huz did nothing after the real estate bust at the beginning of the last recession, which she had just barely been able to drag the greedy huz from the midst of a moment or two before their company—Elite Realty—went belly up. They coasted. He refused to work while she stayed home rearing children, indulging them in the fashionable way with every contemporary amenity as the cash reserves slowly drained away. If she could stay home, why couldn't he? If he had to work, so could she. Everything had to be equal, split down the middle, "even-Steven" he would say— even her motherhood. He had, when all was said and done, the malingerer's sense of progressive egalitarianism. He was a feminist in the sense of wanting to live off a woman he knew had a knack for making money. She collected rents, he went about trying to write a business plan for The Safety Club—the one-stop shop to protect yourself, your children and your home from intruders. After eight months, according to Karenina, he had yet to get past the first paragraph.

He rambled incoherently, angrily and ungrammatically on that single paragraph for months, smoldering with rage at whatever it was that had gotten away from him that he could not name. Karenina showed no remorse in telling me that her life with the huz had become suffused with the needs of two small children, a murderous siphoning of unreplenished assets and a sexless continuum of rage and resentment that itself had become integral to the irrefragable habit of their marriage. They slept apart, as sexless in their way as Ms. Right and I were in ours.

She felt the huz was responsible for her health problems—one of which was a herniated disk in her neck. She told me this was caused by her once having to admit he was right on one of the numberless occasions when he was not, just to keep the peace. At that precise moment, she felt her neck snap. Her other health problems remained opaque as her patter clearly shifted back to me.

She pressed me and, as I said, I spilled.

I confessed to kinky thoughts at the age of five, portrayed with relish and verve my first scene involving a radiator, a blindfold and my first true love at twenty and an abortive effort toward switching that shocked my first true love when I slapped her face unrestrain edly as she lay bound at my feet. I recounted my childhood and teen years relating to a family that desperately desired to its core not to be one, which horrified her—a reaction which was not uncommon, yet which never failed to surprise me.

We discussed careers. Then we broke down potential scenes. The food, the service, the atmosphere, despite its excellence, might just as well have never been at all. I was dining out on her and she on me. It was as if the air itself was dark with the thickness of our connection—or was it yearning? I couldn't say lust, or desire, it was something past that, something metaphysical that occurs only when the physicalities involved have been firmly and unutterably crushed. Beyond the confusion of our opposed personal histories and storytelling technique, we appeared to have an understanding.

She got up from the table and motioned me to follow. I hesitated looking at the delicately unappealing dregs of my food before I did. She led me to the bathrooms. I began pushing the door to the men's room, but she stopped me. "Not there," she said, "but *here.*" She opened the door to the ladies' room and glanced at the opening for me to enter.

I went in first and she closed the door behind me. Unlike the men's' room, the ladies' room *locked.* She removed my jacket and had me grasp one of the short metal beams of the flesh-tone toilet stall. When I did, something slipped from her jacket and glinted harshly in the light. She reached up on her toes and clasped something from in front of the beam to my hands.

Handcuffs bit into my wrists.

"Not too tight, I hope—they're my Smith & Wessons. Had them since high school."

I shuddered, let out a reflexive moan and she had my pants down around my ankles. She removed her top and bra, as the doorknob jiggled and two tentative knocks came and went. She gave the band of my underwear a crisp snap and soon had them down by my socks with a single gesture. I resisted trembling, though I was cold, apprehensive and now exposed.

"Nice," she said, squeezing my cock for firmness like a piece of fruit at the supermarket. "I was hoping you had a good one."

Her leering smile and the glaze that came over her eyes were nothing short of resplendent.

Her body was not. Though she should have had the physical aspect of a youngish suburban *maedchen* under her jeans and jacket, she projected that of a *hausfrau*. Her breasts seemed ruined and depleted somehow, her compact body weighted with dappled fat at her thighs and buttocks. And although she had the healthful-seeming pudginess of a small child at the arms and shoulders, her skin seemed wrong, somewhat loose and ill-fitting. I noticed again her hair was thinning.

I didn't care; her grip on my cock was precise and knowing. She spanked me brutally, worked my cock expertly to exercise control of my reactions, not allowing me to come, but using my own copious lubricant against me. My wrists lost all sensation as she beat me hard against the cool, now delectable metal of the toilet stall even as my ears turned sharply toward the doors. Just behind the echoing slaps of skin against skin, I could hear the forceless knocking and the weak though growing persistence of voices.

She bit me, and I let the blunted commotion outside the door continue as it may without me. It would anyway.

"You want to be my little toy? My little piece of property? Say it!"

"Yes!"

She inserted her index finger up my anus and worked the glans of my cock to a lathered frenzy. My brain was startled and it seemed as if my head whirled around.

She reared back and slapped my face yet again, though this time I was braced enough not to be too addled when she whispered, "Beg me!"

"Please," I said.

"Louder!" The slaps themselves were certainly louder—and the pain had increased, though my endorphins had managed to keep pace. She was using a small black leather paddle she had kept in her purse, obviously well-prepared for this moment.

"Please," I repeated an octave higher then froze as I heard a key in the door, my erection marvelously unaffected.

Karenina rushed toward the door to keep it shut while I, like the bell-ringer Quasimodo, swung about to the left from the tether of the handcuff chain into the stall to get a tentative footing on the toilet seat. I had managed to shoulder the door shut, my feet trapped in the pants about my ankles, my arms firmly restrained and twisted at the wrists.

It was the maitre d' at the door. Karenina bullied him out though sheer force of trumped up feminine outrage and relocked the door.

It appeared—from the diffuse chirruping muffled on the other side of the door—that the gaggle of hens was somehow involved. I could hear them outside as Karenina hurriedly released me and helped me with my clothes. We had inadvertently dammed the flow of middle-aged matronly excrescence, among several other lesser venial sins.

We laughed, red-faced, blushing not with embarrassment but with exuberance at the knowledge of having just barely gotten away with something deliciously inappropriate to any accepted sort of social conduct at the Heritage—indeed, to any accepted sort of social conduct anywhere. With intrepid spirit, Karenina unlocked the door to face the gauntlet of capon harpies lined up in a desperate queue just outside in the little antehall. I hesitated to pick up the black scarf she had dropped into the moistness of the tile floor. I emerged to a chorus of exaggerated gasps, obstructed by the convergence of prim dour faces, chubby elbows and plump trunk-like legs of the parade of dowagers by the door. I mumbled a reflexive "excuse me" as I pushed my way through their haughty resistance to catch up with Karenina.

As I rounded the corner, one particularly plumose harpy screeched at me: "You should *never* be excused!"

Karenina heard this as I came up behind her, and just as we passed the sneering, cigarette-sallow maitre d' with our most solemn and controlled expressions, we broke down and bawled with laughter.

Back in the grandiose, absurd Mercedes, Karenina insisted on driving me to the offices of the *Register* where I was going to meet with Bahamian whether or not he wanted me to. Karenina liked the idea that I was entering a professional meeting fresh from a D/s scene, the aura of the afterglow affecting my every subsequent move. There was some extraordinary tension and pull in our baffled looks and smiles toward one another at the end of the ride outside the register as I got out and turned to face the car and that snaggled grin bearing down on me from the open window of the driver's side.

It somehow hurt to see her go.

I shook it off and used my still-valid security card to get in past security and reception to head straight for the elevator bank that led up to editorial. As I waited for the elevator and waved away the usual lethal murk of cigarette fumes, I noticed that their progenitor this time sported a hugely bulky posterior reigned in by a belt cinched in one notch too tight and a pair of ill-fitting, laughable, badly pleated trousers. "One of the big plug-uglies from sports," I thought, who always managed to look like over-the-hill jocks freshly rejected from a tryout they were sure would mean either a comeback or a pro shot. "Oh no," I thought, "It really couldn't be—"

He turned and puffed a gout of smoke directly into my face as the elevator doors sighed open. He batted his pretty, sensitive eyes at me, his mouth curled with a more informed version of the Elvis Presley sneer as he greeted me with a grudging "Patetick," loosing more smoke. He looked down on me, a sort of triumph over bad posture.

"Happy Boy," I said with what I hoped would pass for a grin instead of a grimace.

Crane flipped what remained of his lit cigarette into my corner of the elevator with deadly prep-school accuracy. I though about hitting the emergency stop button and then perhaps that little pug nose, but erred as usual on the side of caution.

"Last guy who called me that wasn't very *happy* having his jaw wired."

He pushed the button and I saw then the true error of my ways. There was no alarm—just another slow elevator bank.

I shook my head and feigned a chuckle. He actually believed he could get away with something like this free and clear. This fact, regardless of whether he could, disturbed me. "We having an impromptu meeting, Happy Boy?"

"Fuck you, *Pathetic*—your story's dead."

I became brave with anger. I moved my hand fast and he flinched. 'Put it here, *bitch,*' I wanted to tell him, pointing to my cheek, making a little kissing noise with my lips for punctuation. Instead, I shrugged and went for the bluff: "Maybe. Maybe not."

"What do you mean maybe? No *maybes* about it. You're story's killed, you have no reason to be here. So, when I get off, you can take the elevator straight back down and blow."

"Guess again, Crane." I was pumped with S&M adrenaline and nothing was going to stop me, least of all Happy Boy. "You remember our feckless, superstar managing editor—your boss? The one who unaccountably likes me?"

"He *doesn't* like you."

"Well, as much as he likes anyone. It seems he thinks your story approval was a hot idea—he congratulated me on managing the trick of working with you again. I credited *you* with the idea, naturally. I faxed him an outline and— you know how hands-on he likes to be — he contributed what he felt would be a good lead. I'll rework it of course."

"Bullshit."

"No need to believe me, Crane. Check with *Dickie*. Maybe he'll buy you a drink out of his bottom desk drawer."

"It's dead, I said—*you're* dead."

"Who am I to argue? Take it up with Dickie. You're much better at these sorts of political pissing contests than I am. Who knows—

maybe you'll appeal to his budget consciousness and he'll assign the piece to *you*. After all, it was your undeniably brilliant concept to approve an S&M lifestyle piece to run in—what does Dickie like to call it? "This all-purpose family rag?"

That seemed to hit.

Happy Boy started the elevator with a violent smack of the back of his spatulate hand on the emergency stop button, his face as red as if it were sunburnt. "Bluff," heaved Happy Boy quietly. "Stupid bluff."

"No doubt," I said sympathetically. "It could just be at that." The doors opened to the blurred, subdued cacophony of Editorial. Sue Horoschow was waiting impatiently to move past Happy Boy brandishing a laptop. "Really, there's only one question for you, Crane: How much do you have to lose running it down, querying our jolly, avuncular, always-forgiving editor-in-chief, and then second-guessing his judgment if it comes to that? I wouldn't worry— except maybe about getting caught in the avalanche path of his career slide downward when you poke that bear with your usual *schtick*. But you move quick for a big guy with a big gut, don't you?"

I jerked my arm up to my forehead again and he perceptibly flinched again. Then he blinked.

I had him and he knew I knew it.

"This is the *last* time I want to see you here," said Happy Boy, seemingly stranded on the threshold of the elevator, keeping the doors from closing with a stiff attempt at a nonchalant pose against them, blotting out Sue Horoschow as he might a ray of light.

I winked at him.

"Stay happy," I said, and moved from him past Sue quickly through the hostile electricity of the corridor toward Bahamian's cubicle, all the while thinking up the appropriate lies to swap for the continued life of my story and therefore what remained of the life of my career as a journalist.

Bahamian smiled warmly, flipped off his monitor to give me his full attention, which meant he was not glad to see me. I took a breath and went into my song and dance.

It was a long one.

FOR DAYS AFTER THE INCIDENT AT THE HERITAGE THERE HAD BEEN nothing but broadcast silence—no phone calls on the fly away from the permanent glower of the "huz," no stolen moments of dialogical typing deep in "chat," no clumsy pages from the main menu of Dreams-Come-True. I wrote a long e-mail describing my addled state and the admixture of eroticism, terror and exaltation that I found in being cuffed to the stall. I had finished up some remarks about the capon harpies that clucked their sterterous outrage at us in the antehall.

One day, as I began sketching out the actual outline for my piece, I popped onto the board for a little diversion and there at the entry prompt was a piece of e-mail from Karenina, written in her stylistically ingenuous voice of enthusiasm and resolve:

"Prop!"
I couldn't believe how beautiful your letter to me was about our little stolen moment at the Heritage. I want you to know that I laughed till I wept at your term for those biddies, "capon harpies." I suddenly contracted some kind of flu, or bronchial thing the day after and just couldn't do anything. The huz had to take care of the children while I lay in bed clutching the printout of that precious letter, wondering to myself if I was delirious. Did we really meet and actually have that scene right in the ladies? Did the maitre d' actually barge in on us and we still both managed to get away with it? Was that a look of boundless joy that you saw on my face as I took control of your cock while you dangled? And I was relieved and of course delighted to find that you had such a nice one.

As I told you, I may like to take the submissive role, but all my dreams are dominant—could this in fact be the dream of dominance I have within my submissive fantasies? I don't know. What I do know is all I did for

the last few days while lying in bed fending off the huz
was clutch the printout of your letter to me, repeating
"Propertius, Propertius, my sweet Propertius—was it
real?" And if it wasn't, can we make it real. I am nervous. I feel we have somehow gotten into a thing.

Then that line came, the one she would repeat so often, the one
that sticks and won't come free:

But whatever happens—you know I always make all
my dreams come true.

Yours breathlessly,
Karenina

She had every reason to be nervous. I had for every silent day
suffered that wrenching sensation which meant it was nothing but
likely that we were somehow falling into a *thing*.

This of course, and all the overt external resistance to such a
thing, made it irresistible but to continue, compulsively impossible
to stop.

We needed to have a serious private scene, Karenina and me.
And now that we knew that we could in fact have it, where to have
it was the question.

Karenina relieved me of finding that particular integral during
one of our lengthy, furtive exchanges in the clumsy and backward
"chat mode" proffered by the stagily inelegant software environment
of the Dreams-Come-True BBS. We essentially typed malapropish
love notes and heated exchanges to one another with the silent ferocity of two newly deaf acquaintances cozying up to one another on
the phone for dear life. She left it that I would simply be waiting
for her one light spring Saturday when Ms. Right—never one to
entrust key printing and drop-ship tasks to contractors when she
could just as easily do them herself—was away in Western Chichester ensuring the timely production and continued dissemination of
her magazine of good health and sane living that she had perpetually
lost sleep over and which, by then, had utterly destroyed our sex
life.

As the magazine suggested: "Breathe though the pain. Keep breathing."

So I kept breathing.

And I did so uneasily until that Saturday, that absent Saturday after I had packed Ms. Right off in the morning with all her accessories—the rain simulator so that she could sleep, the extra electric fan, the fruit and water for the ride, her special pillow that reminded her of home and us—when, regardless of our buzzer, the series of fatal though peculiarly jaunty knocks came at the door. I heard them easily, despite the distance of several rooms and one floor, took a long final breath and readied myself to let her in and perhaps my life out.

I tensed there for a moment, hesitating on the threshold of the stairwell, gazing forward into space. The knocks came again, insistent, but not importunate. I saw nothing. I opened the French doors and lumbered down the steps in some sort of twilight state, braced to welcome the pain.

NINE

"Hi," she had said. "Invite me in."

I recalled some indistinct myth about the Devil having no power over you until you invited him in, ignored it and did.

What I remember next was the cool of the floor, the smoothness of it as I skittered across it, chewing up and marking the polyurethaned wood forever with the dangling nickel-plated steel D- and O-rings of my cuffs. How clean Ms. Right kept that floor, how good to the touch it was at that precise moment when Karenina and I began our first private scene in earnest.

I still hold fresh in my mind's eye the cool sheen of that floor and my own fumbling nakedness upon it. I was like a dog—not that hackneyed puppy image that every would-be submissive male used with the same presumptuous abandon that every novice female dominant did with the term "goddess." Puppies and goddesses—that summed up the handy self-imagery held by our little Miltown scene. Strangely enough, Karenina and I considered ourselves to be neither.

But she didn't entirely escape this consensus imagery any more than I did, for she needed the dog-on-a-leash simulacrum to be in control just as I needed to be a pet of some kind in order to be the object of that control—in order to be abject under that control: the control of a goddess.

She danced me about the living room on my hands and knees, paraded me about as she commented about Ms. Right's sparseness of decor, how immaculate and unlived-in she kept our place and potential that it possessed so shamefully unrealized. This room here would make a perfect dungeon. A metal cage could go there, a suspension rack with winch would do well from that ceiling beam.

The whole attic floor could be a suite of minidungeons. *We could hire them out!*

I can see her even now at the door, as I opened it into the lurid heat of the midsummer's midafternoon, grinning her broken grin, dressed like a ten-year-old tomgirl in jeans with a threadbare hole at the knee, worn white sneakers with pink stars and purple comets fading out of sight, preposterous sunglasses well out of date and a white cotton pullover with tiny barnyard animals and a Peter Pan collar—such was the prefiguring dress of intimate S&M. She was sitting on the porch railing as if she owned what was on the way to being our house—Ms. Right's and mine—kicking her legs like an overindulged child eagerly awaiting some new surprise.

It wasn't at all a long leap from a moment of small-talk civility to me on the floor stripped bare, jingling about as I slipped and slid in matching wrist and ankle cuffs.

It was hardly any leap at all from dog on the floor to submissive in the bed—Ms. Right's bed. (Ah, but then as now, was anything ever really mine?) Karenina led me there, whipping and flogging me with fresh ferocity on the buttocks and upper back as I made my way with supple clumsiness to the bedroom.

Or was herded there by her awkward punishing strokes, delivered with absolute certainty whether they hit or missed.

With a burst of surprising strength in the bare little bedroom, in the shadow of the armoire and in the light of one undraped window with a broken shade, she dragged me up by the collar onto the bed. The cheap Harvard frame upon which sat the standard boxspring and mattress affair quivered even as I knelt still on the absurdly expensive embroidered reverse duvet. Karenina pouted, and I was given leave to rise, pull off the duvet, flat sheet and blanket and set them folded neatly on the rug as a unit so that she could repeat the same move again with less restriction. Once I was back on the bed kneeling again, she stepped out of her clothing. Then, with a bunch of C-clips in her mouth she proceeded to fight me down to the mattress. Sadly, I gave her only token resistance, as I wanted the scene to continue. But I made her fight to claim me, and fight she did. I watched her muscles strain against mine, sweat mixing with a tear or two and splashing down to my chest as she gradually—and with near-failure each time—clipped each restraint to the tenuously steady frame of the bed.

With the last clip of my left wrist secured, she set about the terms of ownership.

"My little piece of property," she whispered.

Without much deliberation she produced a small cylindrical bottle of Astroglide and began working my cock, which, although previously rigid, had now become urgently steel, the glans slick with preorgasmic lubrication flowing and mixing in with the Astroglide. Her enthusiastic hands and tongue located the pinpoint break of where my orgasm kicked. She worked that point with timing that kept me hard and kept pressing so all I could do was buck and come, buck and come, intuitively responsive to her control.

Like I was getting electroshock.

Like I had found a place to be which suited me—what was it?

Like I had been loved in a way that reached me.

From my spread-eagled position she had me splash her injured breasts and sallow skin with my come until they were fairly well-coated. Despite this and her sallow skin, her broken smile and wily expression, I thought then as I sometimes think now, that she was the most beautiful woman I had ever seen—a stirring woman, a striking woman, a final woman. I flooded her skin again with my come, and when I moaned, she braced my head with a moistened hand and smacked my face. Again and again. So many times I was dizzy.

Her beatific grin, it made her look like a child in an exaltation of satiation after having been presented with a dreamed-for, much-coveted toy. There was light of a kind that shone from her complexion, and stars danced in and out of that light as she slapped my face again and again.

So how could I refuse when she fed me my own come, had me lick every square inch with the flat of my tongue till dry? How could I refuse to do something I reviled, that disgusted me even when trying to do the liberal-minded thing of *imagining* myself in the position of being someone wholly different from myself, such as a homosexual sucking some other guy's cock? I couldn't suppress the gag reflex.

Oh well.

At least it wasn't piss-drinking or scat.

And it was only me.

I wasn't half bad, I discovered, having finished my last response to her fingers' command, blowing my saliva dry upon her skin with pursed lips. She embraced me in the haunting way that women have when somehow you have moved them beyond sentimentality into that fragile realm of trust. It was just like Ms. Right all over again, with that embrace that flowed over me and seemed to draw the marrow straight from my bones.

Fuck Pecksniffian and his remark about coffee. If I had any stab of self-awareness at all then that hit me, it was simply this:

My come was the least bitter thing about me.

IT WAS OVER JUST LIKE THAT. WE WENT OVER THE ENTIRE APART-ment carefully, making sure to clean up the most infinitesimal speck of our little scene, as Ms. Right was hypersensitive to anything out of place within her own small empire of order. I lamented the subtle scratches made in the urethane of the floor and Karenina laughed.

"Nobody would ever notice those—not even someone who keeps a place as gorgeous as this so sterile and spare."

"She likes neatness and order."

"I like my children too, but I'm *thrilled* when their father takes them for the afternoon."

"She's going to notice," I said, pacing from room to room. "She'll know it from how we made the bed, the scratches in the floor, the drops of baby oil on the carpet."

"Just like a little submissive—so worried." She stood up on her toes to kiss my cheek.

"She can tell. She loves this place. The rhythm even of how we move within it belongs to her, not me."

"No," she whispered and kissed me again. "It belongs to *us*."

We made a final sweep and headed out for the car. Gentleman that I am, despite its being a pleasant summer's day in a safe neighborhood, I just had to walk her. I felt the risk of being seen by our affectionately adoptive landlady, Mrs. Tsumashedshy, was worth taking. After all, this was Trinity, where young men and women could be friends and consort without a breath of scandal or disapproval. Of course, Mrs. Tsumashedshy came from that part of the Trinity working-class heritage where everything was scandalous, which made life tolerable. But what was there to hide, really?

There was no romance involved, no secret plan for elopement of any kind. I was just playing with my new friend Karenina. We shared interest in a hobby, a sport, as TechnoSlaver might have said. We had never even so much as *flirted* with idea of fucking (too staid for us, too—*mainstream*). We were simply erotic explorers, companions marking out our territory in the uncharted vastness of D/s. If anything, this would strengthen and save my relationship with Ms. Right, making it possible for me to stay with her, to do her deal, now that—at last—I was getting what I needed, albeit from the outside.

After she got into her indigo-blue monstrosity and started its monotonously puttering engine, she rolled down the window as if to give a wave and instead said to me, less loud than goodbye but loud enough perhaps even for Mrs. Tsumashedshy to hear:

"Was it just play, Perry? Or are we having an affair?"

She didn't wait for my answer, just drove off smiling that smile that seemed so much older than the existence of alligators, whose primordial smile, it comes to mind, it resembled nonetheless.

Are we having an affair.

The L-word.

Shit.

BEFORE I HAD TIME TO RECOVER FROM THIS AND OTHER THINGS, I could hear Ms. Right pull up alongside of the curb in her father's car, the rattling of the aging engine being unmistakable. The unlikely pitch of it, in fact, carried easily on the summer breeze through the open windows into our unairconditioned apartment. It was my alarm within the quiet reflection of my worried brooding.

She galloped up the stairwell and through the French doors all sunshine and smiles, waving in that fetching limp-wristed way she had, looking like a little girl playing grown-up in her floppy straw hat, loose floral-patterned dress and oversized glasses that really could only be described as "spectacles" in and of themselves.

She loved me. She was glad to see me.

As I loved her, was glad to see her.

Or should have been. The fact of the matter was that I felt nothing, a void of emotion. Perhaps it was shock of a kind, perhaps it was the denial of an onrush of emotion. I no longer felt any love nor delight in her warm presence. And my discovery of this at the instant of her first warm and yielding kiss invoked no feeling of guilt, no sensation of shame, no poignant recrimination. I was dead in her warm, grasping, and desperately living arms. Where were my emotions? Where had they gone?

Gone to D/s, every one.

Long time passing.

And I did spend an eternity in her arms, neither loving nor denying them. Then her second great love, our place, had to be greeted and seen after her long trip. She went from room to room as I began dragging all her necessaries from the car into their various places of storage. I took up her two electric fans, her comforter, overnight bag, special pillows and a favorite stuffed animal (an ersatz child in this story) who shall remain nameless.

I have to confess that it hurts me more than the needles I had my last professional decorate my chest with as I writhed helplessly tied to her bed of bondage to say that name. It hurts me more to say it than the fist up my backside hurts.

I admit it here and now: the name of a stuffed animal embodies the pain I can't face.

All such couples, it seems, have such small silly-sounding miracles that exist between them so easily held up to ridicule, yet so lasting.

Ms. Right screamed.

I rushed to her, thought she had either fallen or burned herself. When I reached her, I realized this couldn't be the case because, although she was lobster red, there wasn't a single tear. She was in the living room, pointing down with tremulous arm—unbelievably enough—at our polyurethaned hardwood floor.

"It's scratched! You! *Some*body scratched it!"

Then, before I could levy some commonplace common-sense response, she made a little sprint toward some more remote area of the floor skirting the oriental in the dining room. "And here!" she shrieked. "Here and here and *here!*"

"Are you sure they weren't there before?"

That went completely unheard as she strode over toward me, then delivered a sound little punch to my upper arm.

"You bastard!" she screamed! "What have you done and who have you been doing it with! Tell me now!" She stamped her foot so hard, I was wondering how long it would take before Mrs. Tsumashedshy, who lived below us, would let herself in and make her way up the stairs.

I rubbed my arm thoughtfully.

"What have you done?"

"Not the floor," I answered, convinced of a weird kind of truth. "That wasn't my doing."

And it wasn't—it was *Karenina's*. I had given her my will at the time, it was not my own.

Oh, yet another refuge in the spurious law.

I embraced her, convinced her too of my own weird truth, trying to comfort more myself than her as she burrowed her face into the crook of my shoulder—"the notch," she called it. I wanted to experience her love, feel my own leave me perhaps as I would give it to her, but nothing came through. I might as well have been a wax dummy, but for my mind arching a laconic eyebrow and muttering to itself, "Well, this is interesting."

A new thing for me to be recognizably in love and so well loved within it and so totally lacking in feeling, so perfunctory in my performance of it.

She ultimately believed my assurances and I was spared her tears.

Chatting idly, I followed her back into the bedroom and she began to change the sheets, as was her custom upon returning from the hotels of Chichester, where she would stay to deal with the print production of a given month's *Alpha Waves*. She loved making the bed, and had swung from being distraught over scratches on the floor and terror at my possible infidelity to brimming with positive cheer as she tucked her hospital corners.

Something winked at me in the corner of my eye.

It was coming up from the rug on the floor.

Suddenly, I began to feel something knifelike and extreme.

My heart leapt within me as I saw what it was.

There, gleaming on the floor by her feet, was a shining, nickel-plated *C-clip!*

I suppressed the need to dive for it and instead wrung my hands, as had seemed to have increasingly become my habit. They slid and slipped against each other, as Ms. Right went on chattering and making the bed, covered with sweat as they were. She managed to step around the C-clip, her feet dancing about it tantalizingly in her mules, as if to deliberately torment me. If she stepped on it, that would be it.

Would everything come out then? Would I feel relief as our life of seven years together came crashing down?

All I could feel then was slight fear as my mind raced for miles, only to smash amid spectacular din and flames into dead ends, stolid wall, doomy barriers I could not breach. But as she did her unknowing C-clip dance and the sweat beaded on my forehead at least I could recognize that I was alive. She was making me feel something. She could still do it.

The only problem was that it was still a function of D/s, which I realized, transfixed by the glint of the C-clip, owned me. And I could do as much about that as I could if Ms. Right's feet made the fatal discovery.

With one crisp tug, she tucked the duvet in place and smoothed it down.

"Fresh sheets," she said. "They'll be cool and nice to sleep under tonight, with the breeze coming in from the windows."

She approached me and wiped my forehead with the back of her hand, which was icy band smooth. "You're hot. Have you been drinking enough water? I know you, Perry Patetick. I'll bet you haven't been. You are *such* a child."

Incredibly, she left the room, stepping over the fatal item. Was she toying with me? Did she *know?*

If so, there was nothing to be done and I would know soon enough. If not, then, for the moment, our way of life was preserved.

I dove for the clip and pocketed it quickly. A flew flecks of sweat flew from my face and splashed against my bare arms as I did.

I straightened up just in time for Ms. Right to return with a full, cold glass of water. I drank it down in a single swallow while she watched and smiled approvingly.

"MAKE IT *SKIN* DEEP," HE CAUTIONED, LUXURIATING IN HIS LITTLE cloud of smoke. "In deep is no good. It's always the depths that get you—I'd stay out of them."

Dwight DeSeigneur laughed his phlegmatic, liquid-center laugh, sprawled back in a Danish-modern leather recliner at a desk more cluttered with ivy-league citations and memorabilia than with any real work and lit a "lite" cigarette, squeezing his thumb and index finger desperately around the air holes about the filter in order to get maximum smoke. His blue eyes twinkled now that the bifocals were off.

"Spoken like a man on his third marriage with two separate sets of daughters," I said, sipping coffee.

"And one son."

"And one son," I concurred.

"You're next," he said with a burst of energy, dangling that treasured cigarette from his lips in a style long gone out of fashion. "It's the late bloomers that leave all of us precocious reprobates in the dust. After your unintended, I have a hunch you're due for a few more semipermanent heartbreaks. When you get enough money for a ring, make sure you spend half of that sum on a good attorney first."

"They're only semipermanent? That's so hopeful."

"It is," he agreed. "Nothing lasts, not even Madonna." He hated her with a lust that bordered on admiration. So, improbably, our conversations always included at least one reference to that trash-pop icon of schmaltzy music and kinky sex. "There are just two things that are eternal: death and god."

"If you believe."

"If you want to hedge your bets, like that frog philosopher—"

"Pascal?"

"Exactly. You know, you always did have a bit of the geek in you. Chess squad in high school?"

"Worse. I ran the local communist cell."

"And put it on your Trinity application as an extracurricular activity."

"If I could have lettered in it, I would have."

Dwight's face crinkled as he gave out with his liquid-center cackling again and another "lite." "Spoken like a true nerd. If we'd have gone to the same high school, I'd have kicked your ass."

"Never happen," I said. "Choate would never have had me."

Dwight arched an eyebrow and sighed out smoke and honesty: "No, they wouldn't have, would they?"

"You were talking about god and death."

"Well, screw God then, for the moment. Death is eternal. You can grant that. So anything held within this temporary life of ours is all the more so. Heartbreak, romance, orgasmic satisfaction, money, professional success—the best and worst of it all are, at their most extreme, just semipermanent. Everything is enlisted in the inevitably lost struggle against death. Even this *mishigoss* you've been talking about."

"*Mishigoss?*"

"Yes," Dwight puffed, wielding his cigarette for emphasis. "This *chuzzarai*. The D/s crap, this woman, the *rebbetzen* you've been *shtupping*."

"*Shtupping?*" I asked, playing dumb. One of my greatest pleasures then was to hear the patrician, Miltown-rounded accent of Dwight DeSeigneur continually mispronounce Yiddishisms, even as he would readily interject them here and there and employ them correctly within the scope of our banter. The more I pretended not to understand, the more he would use them to express a subtextual kinship with me, my having lived once in New York City, and his always assuming that I was Jewish, which I wasn't—just one of the darker Dutch having grown up (if the term can be used loosely) in a Jewish suburb. Dwight was proud of being amphibious to a certain degree, a Breed's Hill Brahman who knew Manhattan well enough to quote Fashion Avenue Yiddish *patois*, but never, *never* with gutturals and always with the broad "a."

"Yes! *Shtupping* the little rebbetzen whose boots you've been licking, for Christ's sake! That S&M stuff you've been handing me of late." The spate of coughing began.

"You love it," I countered.

"More than you love hearing me rattle off Yiddishisms, *schmuck*. I must confess, I've always had a certain desire to spank a few lanky little girls I've seen here and there. There's this very lithe little mulatto girl working PR for that dolt State Senator Forrestal—keeps him out of hot water and threatens to get me in some. I think she'd be willing. I detect a bit of a winsome wink in our luncheon conversations."

"Oh yes: Forrestal of the diluted gene pool. Well from what I understand, his family definitely knows how to pick them."

"Almost as well as you, *bubbelah*, believe me. So tell me what you and your rebbetzen have been up to at the club you frequent—Pere Ubu?"

"Ubu Roi," I corrected. "Mispronounced of course."

"The only way," he shot back, eyes darting mercurially, once again sucking down his "lite" to the filter. He swallowed hard, coughing down with the smoke.

"Hey," I said straightening, noticing that Dwight was having a deleterious impact on my posture, as he was always sprawled or slouched or leaning and when I was with him I for some reason tended to do the same. "I thought you limited yourself to three of those smokes a day—if that?"

Dwight's teeth leaked smoke as he chuckled. "I do, I do, but when I know you're coming, I save them all up so that I can enjoy them during our discussions. I believe I have one more coming."

"If what you say is true, I believe you do."

"Never mind that, I want the skinny—I want to know how you can live life on your knees, in one relationship and out the other. "Give," he said, lighting up.

So I did. I told him the whole thing, start to finish amid his anteroom office cum library that sat by the entrance to his triplex Breed's Hill townhouse—the single area allowed him by his prim third wife, who ran the household like a start-up company whose chief product was their one child, a son named Charles. For all his bluster and dominant talk, his wife Alice overtly, and much to his relief, ran the show. It didn't jar me in the least to discuss the recent history of my D/s peregrinations in a place whose decorator must have used J. P. Marquand's *Late George Apley*, for both inspiration and guidance.

Dwight chortled with approval throughout, and at the end, said, as he played impatiently with his mostly full pack of cigarettes: "Don't leave her, your unintended."

"Why," I asked. "Afraid I won't produce offspring fast enough to be in that club of desperate deductions you keep pulling me toward?"

"God no. You'll get there soon enough. No, the Red Menace loves you. Go have your fun on the side like the gentleman you aspire to be and come home to her at the finish."

"But I do that as it stands."

"Good. Do that and it will stand. There isn't any life in that collection of defectives you call D/s."

"D/s is the practice. The collection of defectives is called 'the scene.' "

"Whatever. There isn't any life there. Not one of substance that will carry you beyond the most temporary—which I grant you could last years."

"I'm not so sure of that."

Dwight put down his cigarettes and put us both at a standstill while he rode out a spontaneous coughing jag. When he finished and wiped his lips with handkerchief from his desk drawer, he said quietly: "Take me to Ubu Roi."

I of course said that I would.

"And we both will never tell the women, will we? First and last mistake. You know that's true."

I sighed and agreed.

We adjourned on a handshake, Dwight standing behind his desk in a slouch, towering over me nonetheless, looking craggy and handsome, wincing slightly in the throes of what I could only guess was yet another nicotine fit. I left knowing as one of the few sure facts that I could safely rely on that what we had so firmly agreed upon just a moment ago would never happen. I felt sure at the time that Dwight was aware of it too.

Of course, I know that now.

"Todeskampf," Dwight coughed. "The D/s thing you do is just a death struggle—an effort to overcome the knowledge of mortality. There's no life there. Get out of it what you can then get out of it *while* you can. The things that seem to overcome death often kill you the quickest."

I heard him. But it didn't register. Dwight had a tendency to moralize a bit on the conservative side. It never seemed to be what he believed in the sneering scatology of our usual conversations. I passed it off as being yet another of Dwight's burbling post-mortems.

It's like that paraphrasing of the old song:

"When will I ever learn?"

I HEAR DWIGHT'S VOICE IN MY MIND EVERY NOW AND THEN SO stripped of posturing in that moment of flirtatious vulnerability, "Take me to Ubu Roi. Take me to Ubu Roi."

Would that I had. Not for him, but for me, as a selfish act that might have changed everything. But oh no—I was too pleased with the mere fact that he already, at this remove, seemed to be hooked.

I would get to it somewhere along the line, I thought, but first things first. And I had places to go and people to see. Priorities, like the Wednesday-night alt.sex.bondage munch at Sidereal Mall, always an early crowd during the week, the penultimate shutdown of the mall being only around nine.

And Karenina would be there.

So I had to be.

After an eternal ride on public transit and a long, brooding change of lines, I made it to the black-ballooned food court in the icy fluorescence of the dumpy-shopper–crowded Sidereal Mall. They were mostly there, in addition to a contingent of Baruch University students who'd begun yet another cliquish subsection of postings on the alt.sex.bondage newsgroup. Tutor, glad-handing, backslapping and bragging in his brittle fashion as always, Mount, focusing his energy on any Baruch student receptive to his great height and greater age, Auntie Maim, holding court with a group of suits, and Deprav-o, sitting by his orange tray of cheeseburgers as placid as some gargantuan junk-food Buddha.

And Karenina, hanging out with the skanky custom-leather-worker/security guard Manny and the even skankier thrash-metal rocker wannabe/mental health day orderly Wally, in her best street-corner society attitude and argot, always at ease in the company of men, especially when of a vulgar, lower order. She had confessed to me during our numerous urgently poetic confabs on-line that I was too refined and elegant for her—too delicate. I simply wasn't crude or crass enough, not enough of the "diamond in the rough." I know that that was likely how she had settled on marrying Bennie, the huz, a man so patently beneath her, only to find no diamonds there, just iron pyrite, or fool's gold. Those were my sympathetic thoughts at the time.

I approached her to the mutterings and chagrin of Manny and Wally, gave them my own token greeting, then tugged her aside. I took her hand and clasped the offending C-clip into it.

"You left this behind," I said.

She grabbed the C-clip nervously, closed her fingers about it. She looked at me with heavy apprehension in her now agate-streaked hazel eyes and sighed. "Our undoing?"

I told her the story of the near miss.

With an aggression that always took me by surprise (and does still in memory), she clasped my left hand with her own—the one that held the C-clip—raised them both together then added her other hand. She kissed my fingers where the clip was now. "No," she said delightedly, dramatically. "Not our undoing. Our *beginning*."

There was a lump in my throat of both outrage and desire, fear and determination.

Why was I doing this? Why was I jeopardizing agreed-upon sense for the senseless?

Once again the aggression that should have shocked me but instead provided an inexplicable ease asserted itself: Karenina took me fiercely by the shoulders and bit my neck hard enough to make me scream.

The icy fluorescence spun away.

Then I knew.

TEN

Somehow, in a backward canting ambition born of hope for a forward motion, I had fallen into a New York excursion. Things I had read about in the sexual psychobabble trash that never quite made it into the popular consciousness (but had become a secret focus of my own) were about to be realized. TES—The Eulenspiegel Society, the oldest most respected, most politically dedicated to internecine struggles and play-partying S&M group—was having a bash at that rickety old dive in Manhattan's meat-packing district with the deliciously D/s-fraught name of the Vault. Because she was so often priming the pump of my admiration with boasts (and I wanted to be her match or at least complement her in all things) I let it drop to Karenina that I was taking a trip to the Vault.

What a coincidence!

She was bringing the kids to stay with her mom—a vain, selfish, manipulative, somewhat negligent gourmand who had divorced her beloved though philandering father. She had aptly nicknamed her "The Snuff"—short for "Snuffleupagus" derived from some Muppet show or other. Owing to this delight of a mother and her keen interest in whatever D/s could be extracted from perhaps its national capital, Karenina was going to be in the city at the same point I was. It was uncertain she could get away for enough time to see me there, however. Her mother would keep rigidly to her own pursuits, kids or no. Oh, she was a doting granny all right—but only in small and careful doses.

I remember typing in the amber light of my dumb-terminal screen which punctuated my pauses with uncertain flickerings: "I have this thought, a fantasy—that when we're there for check-in time on Friday at about noon in the lobby of the Sojourners' Suites, you come bounding out of the elevator all full of your impossible energy and throw your arms around me right there in front of god and everyone."

She typed back: "I don't know—there are logistics problems there. I don't know when I can get away. We'll at least see one another that weekend, this is for sure."

I felt then I lost her in the void, as I so often did: "I would love it."

My cursor flashed and nothing happened. What was going on? Had the huz found her out? Did she disconnect to hide us from the obsessive mindstalking of that lowbrow twit she had married to protect her from love—to protect her from me? No, I would have been booted from chat mode back into the teleconference after that chilling error printed to the screen, "NO CARRIER."

The ringing phone broke my concentration followed by an even more keening shriek.

"Who keeps hanging up on me!?" I heard loud and clear from the room off the stairwell behind the French doors. Ms. Right repeated herself and I heard the phone slam resonantly against the wall, a fine tinny fading ring acting as a grace note and counterpoint to silence.

The letters typed in slow as Ms. Right burst into the room, her pink sweat-shirted chest heaving like a robin's:

"You know I make all my dreams come true."

"What about my dreams?" I hurriedly typed.

"Your dreams ARE my dreams," she shot back.

Then I was blasted by the stark "NO CARRIER."

Ms Right screeched about a suspected infidelity and the abuses of her private line. I let her squawk like an unfed chick. I had other problems. Fielding the next potential hang-up, I discovered the following:

TechnoSlaver had had trouble with wifely alibis and wanted to leave for the city later.

Widow's Pique couldn't meet us halfway—as a practicing vampire, it was a bit difficult to get up at a time she should have properly been going to bed.

Auntie Maim wanted curb service and made it plain that whatever time was established for pick-up, she was going to be late. She believed—being new to any socialized concept of female dominance and having a preference for traditional deferences given the fairer (never weaker!) sex—she was convinced that such allowances were not only her due, but incumbent upon her as a *Mistress*. It was to be as much a part of her newly obtained title and position as a pair of thigh-high boots. So we simply *had* to come and get her.

Ms. Right stamped her foot: "What are you doing going to New York without me and with all these new people from I don't know where? Who are they? Who's the woman who keeps hanging up on me. If you want me to leave just say so. I can't be made crazy like this. It's like you're living some sort of secret life and I can't live with secrets."

"Unless they're yours," I said.

"Unless they're mine," she agreed.

"What do you want me to do—you said you wouldn't come."

"*Couldn't* come," she corrected. "Couldn't come. You know I want to. You know I would."

"I don't know that anymore."

"Yes you do, Perry Patetick. You know damn well I want to come with you."

"Then come with me. We'll go together."

There. I said it. A moment had come at last that threatened to end everything yet continue it, a moment I welcomed into the heart of my life with all the anxiety and commotion of a casual toss of a cigarette butt into the gutter. I said it, and I meant it. The moment was there before us. The face of the woman I loved stared into mine without guile, without manner, with nothing but the purest resignation to her own best truth. I could feel a sweet hitch in time, a fleeting chance into which my life would lock and stop the course of everything from flying apart into some unknown melee of bizarre sex and familiar betrayal. I didn't dare exhale. I couldn't risk it.

"I can't," she said. "So stop."

Failure.

The other phone in my office rang.

"I'll get it," she said hurrying from the dining room I used as auxiliary office, whose table held the dumb terminal that was the meeting point and interstice for all my virtual assignations. I heard

her put on her best social greeting voice, honeyed, eastern and cold—
so opposed to her natural southern lilt when she was relaxed and as
close to being herself as I could determine. It was obviously someone
she didn't know, so it was either someone on the other line I knew
who she didn't or someone totally outside. "Perry. I forgot to tell
you that your other girlfriend is on the other line—you know? Lilly?
The one you're *leaving* me for?" I presumed her hand wasn't cupped
over the receiver when she said what she said, which wasn't for my
benefit alone.

I assumed it was TechnoSlaver with another engineering problem. I left Ms. Right to interrogate him with a round of searingly
disarming small talk while I made for her dark, remote office on the
other side of the French doors to our cozy realm and just off the
landing of the stairs in our clammy plaster stairwell.

Widow's Pique had apparently been left hanging and was, to say
the least, *piqued*.

I argued, I inveigled, I cajoled—she fumed.

"Why can't you do for me what you do for Auntie?" she accused.

"Because you don't need as much as Auntie does. You can handle a little distance. You'll get curb service on the way back."

"You're testing me, Prop!" she yipped.

"Yes—and you're a consistent high scorer."

"I know that."

"I know you do."

"Then maybe you can remember to *treat* me that way." She
sighed and deliberated for a moment. I could hear Ms. Right's efforts
to pump TechnoSlaver for information through the door and across
the stairwell landing. "See you at ten in front of the Quick Chick."

"The *in*convenience store?"

"A good checkpoint from which all good things flow."

"Like coffee?"

"At least."

I didn't have a sense then as to how much I was beginning to
sweat as I rushed back to my office to stanch the flow of Ms. Right's
interrogatory. Too late. She was sitting there amid my papers, my
jumble of CDs and cassettes, tangling herself in my miscellany, waif-

like by the phone. White-complected, pale-lipped, she looked at me with wide, glassy eyes of pure green. Her look told me that she needed reassurance, that she wanted some kind of renewal of faith, something to add to the insistence that we go on as we had gone on—but with the additional boost of marital blessings.

And a cooing baby, of course.

I sidestepped it.

"That was Bill, wasn't it?"

"Yes. He told me to tell you he'd be on-line."

I made straight for the terminal and paused reflexively for a moment before sitting down at the keyboard. Something whizzed past my ear. There was a splatter followed by a tinny crash. I turned and watched a graying spot spreading over the white chintz wallpaper like a shadow.

"You're leaving me, you bastard!" she screamed when I left the room.

"Only for the weekend," I said, suppressing a shudder.

"Liar," she said and I knew she was right. But I also meant it and wanted it to be true. Her emotions still reached me, moved me. Even in our comfortably resigned distance, I did the thing I knew she wanted me to do. I went back to my office and I held her close even as she fought to get away—but not too hard. No she didn't fight hard enough to make that happen but instead slumped into the hug like an overtired child. It wasn't so long a pause with her in my arms clinging to me both sweaty and hopeful, subsumed by our awful crumbling love, before I was able to get her back to her office yet still not miss TechnoSlaver's electronic presence on the board in time to argue him out of further elaborate and time-consuming plans.

"NO CARRIER"

That meant my phone in my office was about to ring again.

I dove for it.

It was Auntie.

"Darling," she announced with bright severity, "I've decided that Mountie will be coming with us and that's all there is to it."

My head was reeling. The loud, huge buffoon would not only cramp up TechnoSlaver's van but his bluster and pumped-up pontifications would destroy the camaraderie of the ride, such as it was. I knew her tactic would be to put him on the phone, and there he was.

"Propertius, *friend*," he boomed—Mount *always* boomed. "Your mistress has ordered that I accompany you on your trip—I must say I've been looking forward to seeing the Vault and branching out into TES for the longest while." It was always pronounced TES, like of the d'Urbervilles, never "The Eulenspiegel Society" or the formerly Offenbachian *Til* Eulenspiegel society.

"I'm sad to hear that, Mount, because there simply isn't *room* for you. You could always follow us in your car."

I knew he couldn't—he drove a leased vehicle and was vehemently and paranoically obsessed with both mileage and damage.

"You'll think of something."

"I don't think so. Auntie's order simply violates the laws of physics. You ought to talk to Bootlicker—that's more his specialty."

"I thought he was in computers?"

"He is—but he's just such a technodilletante, you know he's got his hand in there somewhere."

"You mean his tongue."

"I mean you can't come."

"I most certainly can—and I think Auntie will drive home the point."

"The point is she's not driving anywhere and you won't be riding along. Sorry you don't fit, Mount. But I'm sure you've heard that before."

There was a scuffle of white noise and a yulping guffaw that mimicked the tone of a whine before Auntie presented herself on the line once more. "You've upset him, you know."

I heard Mount hollering indecipherable epithets in the background. "I know. But he doesn't really fit—and if we squeeze him in, how will you get your foot massage and smoke your cigarettes without having to breathe in his? Besides, you know he'll be all over you throughout the ride. And—in addition to less space, less air, less conversation *and* less comfort, how can you explore new prospects if he's always hanging around moping, boasting and blowharding away. You know how unsatisfied you are with fucking goofy. And how are you going to do better when he makes you look so much worse?"

"You're right, darling, of course. But you'll still have to be punished for putting him off. Mountie *must* be appeased, if I'm ever going to get what I want out of him."

"But you never will—get what you want out of him."

"I know, darling, but let's pretend it isn't true and beat you up anyway."

The phone went dead for effect at that moment, as I thought it might, and Ms. Right stood watching me in the hall, her eyes glazed with tears. She'd been listening.

"It's all a lie. You're not just going with Bill—*she's* coming too, isn't she? That *bitch*—the one that's stealing you." She sobbed the question and followed it with a dignified sniffle. "I don't know *what* you're doing anymore."

"I'm not doing anything," I sighed, battling the red streak of anger that shot through my mind at her insistence, her suspicion, her very compulsiveness. She had to cling, to pry, own me and possess me as close as she could—yet another instance, I thought then, of nonconsensual disorganized D/s. Wasn't that what characterized what held us together? Wasn't that the undercurrent? Her love was nothing to me then, of course, her enormous hurt and confusion, only a practical annoyance to be put off. I wanted to give her back some of the years of anger now referenced in my beleaguered brain, but she was keeping her control this time and I'd be damned if I was going to lose mine. I'd make this thing work if I had to spontaneously combust to do it. "I'm really not," I added softly, laden with Christian tolerance.

"Then it isn't what you're doing," she returned to me in a small voice. "Just *who*."

IT WAS RAINING THE NEXT MORNING, WITH A LITTLE HAIL AND SLEET mixed in as a little reminder of the cold underlying truth. I liked the idea of profound natural indifference to the course of my life. It bolstered both my conviction and faith. And Ms. Right was both loving and considerate in seeing me off as I waited at the bottom of the stairwell behind the storm door, sipping coffee, watching the windswept precipitation turn to mist and fall.

Sweet, tender, loving and absolutely bereft of connectedness, was how we spent these lingering morning moments together. There was no intensity, there was no vibrancy, just a stale rote pattern of autonomic emotionalism. And love. Plenty of love. Plenty of poisonous wrongful, destructive *love*.

Why was it poisonous and wrongful? Just wait and see.

I don't know why, but when we kissed goodbye, I bit her lip. She recoiled, looking somewhat pained for a moment, a haunted expression overtaking her eyes. Then she laughed. I laughed with her, tousled her mop of red hair and TechnoSlaver pulled into our driveway—gesturing wildly for me to hurry out in the usual catch-up flurry of his chronic lateness.

"Yowcho," she said. *Yowcho.*

We suffered peals of laughter.

Ms. Right blew kisses and gave me the exaggerated childlike flopping of her hand and a silly, open-hearted grin. This too was a reminder, an emphasis placed on our perceived bond: we could be children together. And in being children so long, our adult desire had gotten lost, shut out of the comfort of our clinging infantilism. I waved back and Bill gunned the van.

It was stop and go along Divinity Ave. to the Quick Chick, where Mossman waited carrying his ancient valise, wearing a tan overcoat threadbare at the hem and mispatched at the elbows. He would have been towheaded but for the soapy gray steel-wool color his thinning hair had taken on. He nodded noticing the van, his face suspended in his rictus of a smile—sardonic, wry, resigned. Widow's Pique was covered in a home-sewn cloak with the obligatory vermilion lining, her blackened hair frizzed out in the frozen rain, her lips swollen with red lip gloss, her eyes a lurid Egyptian mask of liner and mascara.

I sprang for the coffee and spent the ride to Auntie Maim's smoothing over all our logistical squabbles and avoiding traffic. When we got there, Mount was helping her with her bags. There w simply too many of them to fit and too much Mount to make a getaway. I went out to help Auntie with her baggage and Mountie presented himself in his typical fashion as a blustering, fustian one-man *commedia dell'arte*. And, as usual, he was in the way.

"Good to see you, Prop. Why don't you go help Mistress with her bags while I take care of mine?"

There we stood in the cold rain on Hassock Street, a steep incline that led down to the Bay, Auntie in repose on one too many suitcases smoking a cheap "lite" cigarette in a black plastic rhinestone holder. I looked at her, and she shrugged, which gave me leave to handle things as I thought she wanted them. It was obvious she never told goofy he wasn't going.

"You're not coming," I said.

His mouth gaped, slack, and his toneless bleat of a voice remonstrated like a small child up past its bedtime. "But Auntie said I should come. You're her submissive, so cooperate."

"When I said there was no room, I meant it. And we can't fit in all her bags—and now I have to gingerly make her aware of that, then help her pick, choose and consolidate. I'm staring at a project here, and I don't think it should include you."

"You have no say."

"Oh yes. That's right. Mine is just to obey. The only thing is, Auntie doesn't want you along. She just left it to me to handle you diplomatically. And before you start making a scene with her, you might want to check the van. There's a united front sitting in it all-too–patiently waiting for me to get Auntie and her gear stowed so we can make time. You go argue with them; I'll go argue with Auntie."

"Maybe I will."

"Then grab one of Auntie's bags when you do—preferably the one with all the fetish. I don't think Auntie will want to stint on that."

"We'll see about that."

He marched over to Auntie and all was lost.

After a few lip-licked whispers, a bit of tonguing and some formidable grabbings in places that may have been less so, Mount acquiesced, repacked all her nonessential toiletries and day wear for ⸱er there on the steep street in the rain, while it took both Auntie ⸱ me to lug her bag of clattering toys and fetish garments to the Bill honked impatiently as we did the lugging. Bright sun glimmered sporadically through broken clouds even as the rain, no longer so icy, fell all the harder.

We left Mount losing his footing on the hill with Auntie's extra bag, waving goodbye, loose-jawed and perplexed, in the rain. His snow-white pompadour of hair was collapsing matted against his scalp, leather highway-patrol jacket sagging and what I thought was a shirt tail sticking out.

We all had a laugh when she explained that it was his oversized boxers that got pulled up a bit too far during their final entwining grope as Auntie's regal person was coaxed into the van. The ride was eventful only in the delighted air of conversation—an inevitable though lively dissection of what we collectively and individually conceived "the scene" to be, a confession as to favorite practices, and even I went on about skin: how to worship it, the whys, wherefores, techniques and the products best suited to aid in the practice. I even dozed, watching Mossman so artfully suck on Auntie's blissfully pink toes.

I woke to find Widow's Pique laving my cock with her tongue. I mumbled something about lack of safety. Bill commented that I was belted in and not to worry.

I asked her softly why.

"I'm angry at you—it makes me hot." She nibbled just under the head, making sure I was helplessly, urgently erect. "This way you're mine to control. And sucking your come makes you part of me . . . almost as good as blood. There's even some blood in it."

Auntie continued smoking, giggling intermittently as Mossman continued with her toes.

Widow's Pique controlled my orgasm with rote expertise.

"Not much more to say, *is* there, Prop?" She stroked my shaft, licked and teased. I sweated. "Nothing to say?"

"No," I grunted.

As I came again, I heard Bill's low, approving bacchanalian chuckle.

THEY WERE RENOVATING DOWN AT THE THE SOJOURNER'S SUITE which was set amid the knotted throng around 42nd Street. W raged the car and negotiated our way three stairless flights in clogged, tentative, seemingly temporary elevators. We shambled out to a half-built lobby affair whose disjunct elevator banks continued upwards of forty stories from the other side of the plaster-dust and board-arrayed expanse. Bill went through some complex negotiations at the desk to get his corporate rate locked in for the room and garage. Mossman, Auntie, Widow's Pique and I sat in overstuffed naugahyde chairs, chatting and waiting, our sacks, bags and valises huddled by our feet. Widow's Pique grabbed my crotch and squeezed hard. "That's it for the weekend, you know," she whispered as I reeled in my seat. "I just wanted you to have a good start. You're too sub-missive for me—I need to be topped, and by someone who knows how."

"I don't top," I croaked.

"You don't switch?"

"No. I don't feel it. I just don't think I was born to dominate, my life reflects that."

She gave a low chuckle and settled back into her jacket, looking quite dowdy, the harsh light dappling her skin causing all its inherent defects raised to a sharp relief. "What makes you think that the most pitiful, the most subjugated and put-upon in their straight lives aren't the ones with the biggest reason—and biggest desire—to be domi-nant when they're kinky? *Especially* if they can get sex out of it!"

It was, like most clichés, well-based in experiential truth and insultingly trivial.

The converse was clear: Those who were in fact most in control, or felt themselves to be, needed to lose it in submission. I didn't have to say so. It was laced between the teeth of Widow's Pique's incipient grin.

Karenina.

But what was I?

I had no control over anything. I made my choices, I directed my will, I anticipated, acted and reacted, yet I controlled nothing. I was on a course determined by a longing, a need, at whose direction and pleasure I moved. It was like a deity of some abstract eternal ~~lue~~ like hope, faith or truth, but the value in this case was D/s. ~~ays~~ D/s.

D/s.

And Karenina was its *avatar*, the messianic savior of the desire that was the undercurrent of my life, which I could not control.

"You're all the same," Widow's Pique chuckled waving her hand, her blood-red nails chipped and frayed. "You all top from the bottom. You direct everything—the dominant is just there to serve you."

"We're all the same," I said, looking into her eyes. She nodded.

"No we're not," said Mossman. "I'm nothing like you. I'm better than the both of you."

"Really?" asked Widow's Pique. "How?"

"I don't really do any of that, I only seem to. When it comes down to it, I really just have sex and do feet. Sometimes at the same time."

The elevator doors opened and Mossman knelt, looking into her pallid face, crinkling the corners of his eyes.

"Do *yours?*"

I was looking over his gray, balding head at the elevators. Something was moving at the edge of my eye. It was headed straight at me.

A befuddled and breathless Karenina bounded out of the elevators and ran towards me, her little leather backpack bouncing in the air. She leapt at me, clutched at me with her hands, threw her arms around me, pulling her face back to gaze at me from time to time so I could see that snaggle-toothed smile.

"In front of god and everyone," I whispered.

"I make all my dreams come true," she whispered back and kissed me hard.

Bill came back apologizing for having to go back to the car and look for a key card with a special corporate ID number. He didn't notice Karenina and I locked in a wondrous death-grip of an embrace, while Mossman distractedly rubbed Lilly's—Widow's Pique's—stocking feet as Auntie Maim sat and smoked, tapping hers impatiently.

I didn't know or care. A sweeter, more forbidden kiss I had never had—we might have been in the middle of a busy, half constructed New York hotel lobby, but we were so rapt in the ment we might as well have been back in the ladies room at the Heritage restaurant. By the time Bill got back from the desk with extra key cards for us all, Karenina and I were still kissing. I heard Mossman mutter, "It's beginning to border on the disgusting." If Lilly didn't grab us and kick me smartly in the shin, we might never have made it up to the room.

I remember hobbling to the next set of elevator banks, carrying Karenina's extra bag. I remember her laughing, her bright eyes looking at me with wonder as if I were a vision of some future event, foretold, yet unbelieved.

Her eyes held the weight of an intolerable love, and what I wanted most was that weight to rest upon me. The intolerable love Ms. Right held for me was just that. This was different, weightier, truer to the essence of what I had determined to be my own heart. Her eyes held the ephemeral aching moment of meaning. I had to grab it.

The intolerable be damned and me with it!

BILL HAD SQUARED US AWAY AN ACTUAL SUITE, REPLETE WITH TWO rooms and two convertible couches, which meant sleeping accommodations for all. With the discovery of the extra room, Karenina pushed me into it backward upon the bed. She had things other than clothes and toiletries in her bag. We fell quickly into a scene, where I was roped, belted and spread in a delightful impromptu arrangement on the queen-sized hotel bed. Bill opened the door unexpectedly. Karenina had my legs up at a ninety-degree angle and spread wide apart, anchored from my ankles to knobs on the night stand on either side of the bed. She paddled me with one hand, pressing a pillow to my mouth with the other so that I would not audibly scream. Bill looked like an uncle at the door watching children at play, hardly a "TechnoSlaver."

"I've never seen him happier," Bill observed innocently—or at least his tone was innocent.

"Oh," she said, "he's about to become much happier still."

When Bill shut the door, the amusement and bonhomie both

brimming from his face, Karenina broke out a long, vibrating dildo. She used the pillow case as an improvised gag, tied compassionately to allow the comfort of breathing with a minimum of noise. "You want this now, don't you?"

The thing was molded to seem made up of balls, each growing progressively larger toward the base. I nodded "yes" avidly, and she proceeded to give it to me, ball by ball, sliding each in with a good, slow stroke.

"I could get to like being dominant," she said, that snaggle-toothed grin splitting the image of her face into a mocking laughter my pain barely allowed me to recognize. She wrapped herself about me and bit and caressed me, again and again.

We lay chaste like that for hours until it was time to for her to go.

KARENINA LINGERED—COULDN'T PULL HERSELF AWAY ACTUALLY, BUT not entirely because of me—it was the activity of preparation that she had yet to participate in as we all suited up in our best fetish to make our New York debut at The Vault, somewhere in Manhattan's dingy meat-packing district. I wore the cock harness and chaps, exposing my behind, Mossman wore frayed shorts, sandals, and some homemade harness affair that tempted both criticism and confusion, Widow's Pique wore a fishnet bodysuit, tasteful leather bikini reserving modesty beneath, and TechnoSlaver wore his rainbow-colored nylon windbreaker, having yet to discover a fetish outfit that worked as well for him—a possible aim of the weekend. Beyond Cruel and Unusual, there simply was no boutique or clothier except the gayboy haberdasher headshops selling image and not much else in the cold environs of Miltown.

Auntie Maim, gloved, corseted, bustiered and booted up to the thighs, her close cropped Audrey Hepburn—coifed hair freshly lacquered, looked as brittle and immobile as an exotic plant blown from black glass. She struck an impatient attitude with her cigarett holder, too uncomfortable to either stand or sit down.

We covered up with long tee-shirts, jackets, khakis, wh

would fit over the fashion statement of reckless sin and caught a cab whose first stop would be Penn Station so that Karenina could make a timely train back to Long Island. She squirmed in my lap along the way, and our faces mashed together in deep communion.

"Isn't young love disgusting?" offered Bootlicker.

Not love, my mind screamed as my mouth was busied with the force of Karenina's kiss—*never love!*

"Hose 'em down," chuckled Bill.

"Lock them in the trunk," said Widow's Pique mordantly.

I won't regale you with the cliché of parting on the platform by the train. We looked at one another and the concept hit us both so that we nearly said it at the same time, "Separation anxiety." Then she skipped off to get a good seat on the train, shooting me a curious look back as she did. I didn't know if that look held lust, or a hopeful yearning promise. I thought it might be both at the time. Now I don't know anymore. She had something definite in her eyes, I can still see it as if it had somehow superseded memory and become some organic compound integral to my vision. What was it?

Belief.

She had found a truth. She *believed.*

It tore at me as she left.

The demon Love, rending at me again, denied, only to find yet another method to get at me: D/s.

Having rejected love, I must have been wide open for it, completely vulnerable for love to take me in any new way it came. Demons love disguises.

I wasn't the only one who knew. Karenina was open to everything. Perhaps she had let the demon in.

I'd like to think so now.

Here's the trick: I wanted what I had rejected. I wanted the cheap Hollywood sticky moon candy of the plastic, beautifully acted redemptive kiss. I wanted transcendence in the idyllic idiocy of a perfect love that should have made the proper D/s jade I saw myself becoming gag back on his tongue. Yet, it was a tickling, seductive of a whisper in my ear I heard tell me that the love I had with Right, so wounded in its intolerable blandness, so compromised

in a habit of comfortable misery would be love of a superior kind
with Karenina.

Demons deceive, and few demons are greater than love.

Few demons are worse than ourselves.

And I was counting demons then as being among my closest
friends.

So they were.

I got lost amid the hectic run of our little group through the
streets of Manhattan to some sushi place in the Village, where S&M
regalia was covered only so far, chained accessories peeping out here
and there and Widow's Pique's fright wig of teased Gothic hair and
red nails at a length that threatened to curl all made us seem well at
home at our cramped little table amid the MacDougal Street crowd.
The sense of liberation was intoxicating—it was all we could talk
about. Especially TechnoSlaver and me. Perpetual student that she
was, Widow's Pique was as free as her parents' grudging endowments
allowed. Mossman was never free, as he was either too poor or too
parsimonious to spend the money to facilitate such freedom, but he
was always *available*.

Ms. Right was far behind—even Karenina, in the glowing moment of our heady potential, of my life's apparent resolution on the
very brink of the Vault itself, had left my mind entirely.

WE WERE A BIG, BLACK CLOT OF ANTICIPATION AS WE CABBED OVER TO
the Vault. Cabbing in New York City was the way to go—no pushing against sinister crowds and malicious *hoi polloi* in the mildewed
labyrinth of the violent, ancient subway. We needed to carom
through the streets in the overconfident hands of some overambitious
and recently immigrated Pakistani. We needed reckless speed and no
delays.

Finally we stopped by the almost invisible Little West Twelfth
Street at a seeming meat-packing warehouse adorned with too much
rotting plywood across from even seamier, semioccupied buildings
I could see the Hudson River as I fumbled out, not knowing w'
was paying, not caring.

A pleasant-looking man with a short, skinny build, bushy mustache and wide-brimmed hat was directing people away from the main entry line of the club. And there was a line, mostly a gaggle of youngish single becapped men in warm-up jackets or rubbing their arms in tee-shirts that provided inadequate warmth on a more autumnal than summer's evening so close to the river. We went for the line and the man—who had a thick accent that mimicked perfectly that of a comedic TV priest I had grown up watching.

"Are you a here for the TES Party?" he asked with dour joviality.

Mossman asserted himself as group leader. He began reminiscing with the priestly man about his D/s exploits and contacts when he was in graduate school in the city. The man stepped away from Mossman as if he had ceased to exist, as if we had shrunk as a group and were simply too small to bother with, and hollered into his hands as if into a handy megaphone: "If anybody here is a TES member or member of some related group, please show your card to the lady behind the ticket counter." He repeated it.

I was the only one among us with a card—it was a courtesy card for reduced admission to Athena's Fetish Friday—but it served to get me something off the admission, which was only about four times what would be usual anywhere else. The man in the hat gently pointed out to us—with a voice hoarsened somewhat by periodic announcements meant to keep the line directed and moving—that the crowd of jockish men and their scattered few hive-haired women were going to the actual club, the Vault, in the basement, looking for kinky-sex pick-ups or possibly a low-priced prostitute, cross-dressed or otherwise. The actual D/s party where the scene-players were headed was on the first floor and that's where we wanted to pay our exorbitant ticket price for admission, present our cards that affiliated ourselves somehow with some even far-flung kinky-sex–recognized organization for a discount, or remind the cashier that women—TES members or not—*always* paid less.

While I waited by the exasperated, thickly made-up cashier who ʳhed a garlicky sigh at me as I stood next to her window, the rest ·ır group made its way to the front of a newly formed first-floor ʼlding up the smoking Auntie Maim to keep her from falling.

The aluminum-faced door with an ancient mechanical bolt that swung across it was pushed open by an obviously amateur bouncer relying on his immensity and not much else to keep the throng in check.

Somehow his slouch, loping arms and vapid grin made me think that any one of us could have kicked his ass. I was more concerned about the little viper types flitting about whose grim expressions signaled a dark comprehension of the value and meaning of everything: they knew what we wanted, how to control us through it and would kill us all for a nickel if nothing stood in the way. We were grimly sized up and primly ignored before we even made it through the door.

It was a barn.

It could have been some forsaken structure in the middle of Neenah Menasha, Wisconsin, for all appearances.

But within the rickety, ragtag confines of grayed, distressed wood was nothing but scene after scene of denuded play. Floggers and paddles dappled the darkened, sporadically lit air as the group of us huddled in and tried to make a space within the evanescent circle that had drawn us in.

In the center of it all was a wrought-iron cage in the center of the room with hardly any space to see though its bars to the center due to the bodies of portly women and paunchy men with chests more X-rays than flesh bound to it. A woman spread-eagled in the center—an unusually pretty one, tall and lithe—was receiving oral sex from a hefty blue-jeaned bulldyke wearing crepe-hair sideburns and goatee dressed as a stevedore. How did I know she was a bulldyke? Her black tee-shirt identified her as one from the back. I should have said "screaming bulldyke," as did the shirt. We busily insinuated ourselves into the crush of new arrivals checking jackets and bags by a closet with a halved, hinged door. At the counter that divided the closed lower section from the one opened above, a frizzy matron who must have been in her seventies fought with dusters, windbreakers and a barrage of black canvas tote bags, complaining about the lack of tags and tickets as she crammed our belongings into hidden nooks we could not visually track.

A svelte woman, looking one or two steps down from a model,

but perhaps one above some Seven Sisters ingenue, walked by in a fishnet bodystocking, her body almost totally exposed but for the enhancing shadows of the netting. Bill gawked, Mossman savored, I coolly glanced. We didn't exist to her. Widow's Pique ran a caressing hand near her netted buttocks, but stopped just short of touching.

The netted woman blew her a perfunctory kiss.

At the bar we ordered expensive waters and sodas, alcohol being proscribed anywhere genital nudity was allowed. And was it allowed!

Everywhere I could marvel, genital nudity was clamped, clipped, fisted, grabbed, tormented—never groped, never gently caressed but flogged with minifloggers made of deer for the purpose. A weasely, skeletal man named Jim casually bullwhipped with a nine-foot bullwhip some blond and aging gamine who cried for her daddy through tears of mascara. A lithe, statuesque executrix femme with a dragon tattooed on her rippling back lay on a tabletop by the bar as people drank and ignored her as if it were some lover's tiff. There was no rapt fascination—except possibly on my part as I watched her fisted slowly and thoroughly by another slack-shirted, leather-vested workmanlike male dominant with a graying ponytail and egocentric leer. He was in the standard uniform of the Gepetto-men: little gnomelike craftsmen of pain, unapologetically homely.

Her passion was so invested with effort as to seem a job of method acting, but when she fulminated into a dainty orgasm, the room was hung for a moment with an erotic expectation and salaciousness that steamed up as if from the pores of our collective skin, not like sweat but like a fine mist. The back of my neck was beaded with moisture as the Gepetto's rubber-gloved forearm undulated within the tall businesswoman's seductive lower quarters. I made my way slowly closer, and Widow's Pique was behind—her hand gently clasping my crotch as if placed across my heart to feel its beating. I could hear it in my ears. Mossman presented me with a seltzer. My hand trembled a bit taking it.

"That's just Ed and Lisa," he said.

"Ed and Lisa," I repeated. The beating in my ears was gone. Widow's Pique had disappeared, as did TechnoSlaver.

Auntie Maim found a comfortable spot on a bench on the other side of the cage in the shadow of a femme-to-femme spanking with three shirtless, gray-haired men massaging and licking her feet, as she smoked and fidgeted, ignoring them. She looked somewhat ant-like sitting there indifferent to preening, her eyes drooping in sym-metry with her cigarette, the workers busied below her. There was a stage—weatherbeaten, wooden and battered—and to the side of the stage was a buffet. Fetish-dressed folk, fat women and slouching Gepettoes splintered off in little cliques chatting. I skirted Ed and Lisa's scene and made my way toward the food, not out of hunger, but out of a need for an identifiable sense of direction.

The fishnetted vision blocked my path.

"Nice outfit," she said, indicating my cock harness, chaps, col-lar—the usual array. She didn't yank on the ring as seemed so cus-tomary back in Miltown. "Who are you?"

"Propertius," I said.

"Really?" she did a doubletake that might as well have been the mockery of one. "What an odd name. I'm Susan."

She extended her hand then withdrew it with the fleeting action of avoiding a hot stove as I began the motion to kiss it. I nodded, she gave me the frozen headlamp stare of some escaped, exotic gazelle and loped off. I had no urge to follow, and I watched the netted motion of her ass with something akin to scientific interest.

There was a bit of activity on the stage—though nothing com-pared to the scenes below. There was literally scene upon scene, mis-shapen, grotesque, delectable, desirable, nondescript bodies either overdressed or stripped of everything but the merest suggestion of modesty; so much play, I would later say to the clique of naïfs who made up the Miltown collection of fetish splinter groups, that you could hardly take a step on the floor of the Vault without falling into a scene. I sat by the stage and watched a petite, dowdy secretary gamboling across the stage in what I thought was a ruffled, pale, somewhat diaphanous pair of—of all things—silk boxer shorts. I moved closer and sat on the edge of the stage as our wide-brim–hatted greeter traded jocose paddle spankings with a zaftig latex-clad women as if they had invented a new sort of close-order ping-pong. The secretary was exultant, intoxicated by some rampant sexuality—

believe she must have seen herself whirling like Salomé to the throbbing call of the music, though in reality her motions were confined to a hesitant gyration and tentative sway.

It wasn't boxer shorts she was wearing.

It was a trick of the light.

It was her pale jiggling cellulite-thickened flanks I had mistaken for pale, lightly colored lingerie—mottled flesh for rippling silk. She briefly noted my stare and continued exposing herself to me in her stiff dance, her thighs dappled greenish-blue with healing bruises, yellowed with a plum-colored mark like a recurrent smudge here and there. I understood what she was doing, I understood why her eyes were shut in drugless beatitude.

The depravity of flesh had set her free from the flesh—just dreaming of her beating at the hands of a superior who had claimed her, who had subjugated her will and body to his own or (in my own hope) *her* own—had transported her. She had been allowed to release her autonomy, the seemingly vast responsibility for her own life, her own persona, into dominant hands, to present her sexuality as a means of leading her away from her own desire, to be released from desire.

The dowdy little secretary was clueing me in, pantomiming for me the great cliché in sexual terms.

Freedom in slavery.

It was every submissive's excuse.

The touch of Zen Buddhism mixed with endorphins and forced orgasms amid the flaccid corruption of mature flesh made me dizzy with an anguished nausea. I had to leave. I walked into bullwhipping Jim, who jumped, then gave me a suspicious look coupled with a mumble. I pushed past him. Trembling by the bar, I fell in with Mossman who was surveying the splintered floor for suitable feminine feet as he sipped spring water. Susan stopped by to chat, though Bootlicker was unable to converse, ogling her breasts and nearly bared fishnetted loins as I held up both our ends of the conversation, outlining for her what intricacies there were in the Miltown scene. Elton, who wore his hat and comedian's mustache, came over to chat as well. We were curiosities, rustics.

They were TES members. We were fresh meat—for TES memberships, I suspected. From Susan's hard glare, I further suspected we were good for little else. We met some other members, forming a group whose good fellowship was marked by a concerted efficiency. I recognized some of the errant moans, as in the light of the stage I could see TechnoSlaver's silhouette working diligently upon the wall. I could only hear Widow's Pique's screaming, so I had to imagine just how her body responded to TechnoSlaver's finely pointed ministrations—the colored, hotly burning molten wax, the latex flogger, the plastic cane, the fur and rubber glove.

The place filtered to emptiness around three, and of course outside there was a crush at the corner for cabs—a few arguments that could have advanced to greater asperity proved an obstruction, but Bill led our little group several blocks away to a lot where we could intercept one before it reached the meat-packing loading dock where everyone waited in their suspect state of overdress. It was too hot for trenchcoats and slickers, but there they were: huddled and obvious for not so obvious reasons.

Some things are considered to be too much even in New York.

Back at the room, we shucked fetish into respective heaps—but for me who meticulously hung it all away—then divided accommodations by indifferent suggestion. By the time I got to put in a word about it, TechnoSlaver and I had already been given the main bedroom where Karenina and I (to make a new verb transitive) had *scened*—the women wanted the larger room with the two convertible sofas. Mossman was content to be on the floor by their feet, laying beneath where he could both see and imagine their legs and whatever familiar secrets lay beneath. But first came the champagne. Bill had iced several bottles. Widow's Pique sipped a bit, but stayed close to Auntie, keeping herself nervously shy of the always gentle, meticulous and now quietly perplexed Bill. Mossman abstained, citing his twelve-step oath against alcohol. He occupied both charming women with footrubs.

"That was a bit of all right," said Auntie, ever the blasé anglophile. "But at the end of the day just another club scene."

"I thought it was fun," offered Widow's Pique glumly.

"It was much more than that," Mossman volunteered from the floor.

"I thought it was great," TechnoSlaver said, gulping champagne and wiping his chin errantly on his sleeve. Widow's Pique's already wide eyes widened and her face flushed. She kicked her legs against the chair like a restless child.

Things fall apart.

I said that didn't I? Whether Yeats or Dr. Seuss, the references are now all the same, as childishness masked as maturity steers us continually to the end of the light. Us? Oh yes, I forgot. Never you— *just me*. These things are mine; I own them alone.

Things fall apart, I said, and they fall apart exactly at the point where they seem most to be coming together.

ELEVEN

The following day—a Saturday—was the kind of day you believe will never come again, the kind of day that, while you're living it, you know will never end as well as it began, never reach, much less fulfill, its delectable promise from morning to morning. It was a day to make you ache, golden and cool, woven with hope, shot through with unobstructed possibility. The perfect day to betray you.

It was, as were so many, a day of pain—but of such sultry quality and delicious character that the heart could only cry for more. More.

That was her rubric, her assigned epitaph: "More, more, more."

"On my deathbed, I'll be asking for more," she would say. "That will be my last word: 'More!'"

Karenina showed up at the room at nine am to rouse us. The girls—even Boot at the foot of the bed—threw shoes with poor aim at the doorway at the first sign of her ebullient, excited cheer after Bill let her in. She flew into the room before my eyes could focus and was on me before I could even properly raise my head. She smothered me with kisses and closed her hand protectively round my cock, cuddling into me under the covers like a little juggernaut, all harshness, knees and personal force.

Through the magic of coffee in styrofoam cups brought in a white paper bag, she had managed to keep Bill and I conscious enough to start the day with blistering hangovers and shaky appendages. There were murmurs of "Silence" and "Shut the hell up!"— I think that might have been Auntie Maim—from the floor of the next room as Karenina chatted and cheered us on, occasionally clapping her hands and—while chewing on a bagel—she found my jeans, boots and wallet while I teetered about in the bathroom. Bill hardly said a word, but apparently was resigned to drag himself along wit' us to wherever our expedition might lead. And we each of us tacitly knew that where it led was worth fighting hangovers, early hours and even precognitive wolves for.

Fetish.

We were about to do the time-honored out-of-towner fetish crawl.

After breakfast we cabbed it down to Christopher Street, heading for a place called The Leatherman, which I'd heard was a gay sex shop that stocked a good deal of necessary outfitting for the scene. As usual, I was wrong. It wasn't a gay leathersex shop, but *the* gay leathersex shop. The display window was the usual unexceptional harnessed mannequin, really not much more enticing than our own Cruel and Unusual back in Miltown. The entryway, like many of the older Manhattan storefront entrances, was crabbed and narrow, positioned hard by a cash register and counter, clogged with a few large men trying to get in and out, check their bags, pick them up, get information or cash out. A bald spindly faunish little man dressed in faded black studded leather worked the register while a younger pretty boy with milky complexion, moussed hair and cupid's bow lips checked the bags with little slips of laminated cardboard, each having its own wise-ass sexual slur typeset on it, such as "Cum Sucking Pig!," "Fist Buddy!" or "Everybody's Favorite Mary!"

Just looking up by the entryway, there was a pegboard crowded with every sort of conceivable armband and g-string, from chainmail to vinyl. The counter was a showcase for handcuffs—stainless steel, nickel-plated, flat black, English Darbys or even German Clejusos. There were padlocks, keys, studs and all-important sexual-freedom political statement or top and bottom identifier tags, bespeaking, "Master," "Slave," "Lord," "Serf." Leather motorcycle jackets and chaps dominated an entire wall of the oblong space. There was a low carbon-steel cage at the end of it all that made Karenina kneel by its cool smooth bars and admire it with eyes as wide as those of a child's fascinated by the overkill of some toyshop chainstore widow display at a strip mall near Christmas.

A narrow wrought-iron spiral staircase as stingy and severe as those similarly outfitted for nuclear submarines led down to the sec-nd level. After negotiating the steep and twisted steps without fall-

ing, Bill having to go extra slow to account for his size, we found
ourselves in a well lit basement that shared the oblong shape and
dimensions of the upper floor, but not its stock. We were surrounded
by toys, landing amid a melee of well-packaged flesh-toned disembodied rubber penises in all shapes and sizes.

"It's the dildo superstore!" exulted Karenina.

We all laughed helplessly.

Whips, bullwhips, shortened bullwhips (three and four-foot signal whips), paddles, canes, crops, quirts—a tasteful, plentiful array
of all these sadomasochistic implements, utensils—toys!—lined the
walls and filled the racks of the left side of the well-lit, impeccably
clean, though cramped and crowded, space. It seemed that the hulking, shaven-headed or buzz-cut men in outdoor wear were everywhere. Karenina was radiant with enthusiasm—her skin shone with
it, her jerky mannerisms and tentative fondling of device after device
betrayed it. She was utterly at ease and unselfconscious of being—
at that time of the morning on a Saturday, amid a pride of bearish
gay men—the only woman in the place. Bill went for the head harnesses and bright orange ball gags and Karenina smacked her forearm
with various crops. Before I could ask too many questions, a bald-
pated sales clerk with ropy muscled arms, striated, bulging deltoids
and pecs straining at the fabric of his muscle tee as he moved,
grabbed me and started fitting me for a variety of harness called a
"Texas tank." I liked watching the veins in his biceps pulsate as if
in some outsized erect penis. They both looked ready to blow as he
worked, running his hands gently over my body as I stood next to—
but not in—the row of changing rooms at the far end of the room.

In a moment I was stripped naked, exposed and harnessed up
in the middle of the crowded basement floor at Leatherman, being
shown off by the aging muscle top who had fitted the straps and
buckles round me. He started spanking the bare flesh of my buttocks
with sensitive expertise and I did not object.

Naked, spanked and harnessed at 10:30 am in the middle of the
floor of a retail outfit in New York City in the heart of the Village.
It was like a dream I should have had but didn't, which further
hammered home to me its exigent reality with every flat-handed blow
that landed on my ass.

"You look so awesome!" Karenina said.

Bill nodded with approbation, still processing an acceptable set of verbal responses to this unexpected situation, and chuckled with near-spontaneous throaty pleasure.

Muscleguy's smacks increased with force and intensity until I nearly lost my footing. Then he stopped, massaging his hand across my sensitive buttocks. "This one's good," he said directly to Karenina, having determined who was in charge. "How much do you want for him?" He was sizing me up as if I were a horse for sale.

A group of admiring gay men came to inspect the harness and me in it, letting fingers slip from the straps to my skin by playfully deliberate accident.

"Not for sale," she said, moving through the group to grab herself a strap and causing them to disperse.

Muscle guy took back the reins and patted my flesh while helping to gently extricate me from the harness. "Borrow him maybe?" He winked.

"Maybe," mused Karenina, appearing to ogle me surreptitiously out of the corner of her eye, her head slightly turned, while lingering over the thought as an obvious gesture. As always, she was sizing up options.

I was still undressed when she grabbed me with exaggerated harshness at peril to my balance and I allowed my weight to fall into her and she embraced me, dovetailing at that moment, contour to contour as I huddled into her for warmth, naked and vulnerable in a public room of large men, whose eyes were all over me, just like a dream I once did in fact have (but I was nine at the time). They waited for us. Nobody broke us up, nobody intervened. It had been informally decided, apparently, the S/M hets could have their moment. And have it we did.

We hit the Blue Contusion next, not really a shop but a sort of outlet in transition run out of Elton's condo—a place he had claimed and remade by hand, formerly a talent agency for dancers, magicians and the sort of borscht-belt comics who worked bar mitzvahs. Elton was leaving the almost obligatory New York City position of contactor in favor of retailer. The cozy eclectic new-age-appertained at room of the condo held the future elements of his storefront—

down to the indigo-blue bunting and curtains we could easily tell were newly hung. We sipped tea—he had no coffee on hand—while perusing his mail-order stock of latex and leather fetish clothes, floggers, quirts, canes and paddles. I had something special and furtively planned, something I had called in during one of those bad moments at the nadir of a clash with Ms. Right—a fantasy item ordered out of pique and revenge and lust and longing. But I ordered it and had put down the irretrievable credit card number and so, I assumed today, without having even called, that there would be a fitting. At the time, Ms. Right kicked in the door at the end of the transaction and beat at my chest with her fists, accusing me of having been murmuring ardent pleas to a lover, rather than a tailor of leather, buckles and grommets. As I savored this thought, Karenina modeled outfits and browsed toys.

Elton consulted with a somehow-harmonious combination of insincere retail floorwalker patter and obsessive enthusiasm. Bill discussed the merits of some items, the flaws of others as I sat limp in the chair, my O-ringed boots playing against one another, nodding attentively, lost in a fog.

Karenina was there, naked, shuffling through racks and hangers of dresses, tops and skirts, a look of determination to find the right item. She meant business.

She stood before me—and Bill and Elton—both of whom showed no lack of composure. Her flawed body shone in the sunlight, and she was an unprepossessing woman. Her face seemed slightly jowly at the cheeks, her breasts had bits of withering and wrinkling, and one had a chunk of a scar from a lumpectomy, removing a tumor yet saving her breast at some risk. She had said that her sexuality had meant her life to her and in this too she meant business. Deposits of fat had gathered in the usual place around the thighs and hips.

She stood before me, waiting for me to come up with something. But I gawked, and tried to hide my gawking. I was struck by an awful if not terrifying fact: Ms. Right, that red-headed urbanized southern belle, was so much more classically beautiful than the little naked rebbetzen who stood before me—yet I was overwhelmed by such a physical love, it felt like some sort of urgent tragedy building in my chest, like I was on the verge of cardiac infarction. I strained

to appear relaxed in my chair, evaluating outfits she held as if I were
a client at an *haute couturier* in Paris.

I loved her.

I loved the idea of her, the freedom of her, the possibility of
how we had mapped out our lives, dreamed and planned, that stood
in such dark contrast as to how I drudged through each day now
with the delectable but so personally shellshocked Ms. Right. What
could I do?

There was only one obvious answer.

Submit.

"The black latex dress, the *Loco.* Try that one." My voice was
rough and dry.

"I couldn't get into it—it wouldn't fit." She pouted.

"No, that will fit, I think," Elton said, sizing Karenina up with
his hands, more tailor than lecher. "Should look good."

"It'll be tight."

"It's meant to be tight, I think," said Elton. "You just need some
help getting into it."

"Try it on and see," I added as Karenina gave the black rubber
garment a look of doubt and concern. "Elton ought to know."

While she changed a line of people entered the room—I was
chagrined to see a largely Miltown crowd: LadyPain (kyphotic and
rondentine as ever), Floyd, Deprav-o, Muffy and—husky, ruddy and
round as a pastry *bombe,* "O." There were several others I had recognized as neophytes like me or grizzled old hands, gray, flabby
faced, nondescript or downright haggard. There were the cursory
acknowledgments of head nods and grunts, but they for the most
part trundled forward to the racks of fetish and toys, rubbernecking
and expressing their inexperience with a volume of overspoken regional aplomb.

Karenina looked as slick as a black fish wriggling on a line, as
seductively vicious over her inchoate dowdiness as a fashion-
magazine editor out for a night on the town as she modeled the latex
dress, flexing her muscles and enjoying the confined feeling of rubber
over skin. Elton and I sprayed her down with silicone and she lux-
uriated under the cold stream of the spray as the black rubber cock-

tail dress began to gleam. We both stood back and paused for a few seconds of silent admiring approval. Then Elton went into his spiel of care and treatment while smoothly coaxing the credit card from her and briskly running it through his hand-held Veri-Fone machine. I looked about and noticed the surprise contingent of Miltown shoppers had utterly ignored the mythic vision of Karenina and her latex sheen as they hemmed and hawed over racks of merchandise and their own irrelevant scheduling—but what of it? They might as well have never left Miltown. They could have been picking bargains at some suburban discount warehouse, for all it seemed.

In the physics of our world, they weren't really there at all.

The moment was ours.

And we were so emphatically *there* within it.

We hit the Noose afterward, a fetish boutique nearby with as cramped and well secured a storefront as a retail jewelry operation. It was stocked with beautiful fetish objects, 7th Avenue mannequins replete with nipples and bulging groins to make leather and chainmail gear stand out in some relief of unreality. I noticed a rack of hanging braided bullwhips, three and four feet long, new, shiny, stiff and black. I removed one and held it, rigid as a cane. Karenina was busy with nipple torture devices well out of our price range, comparing notes with TechnoSlaver. The item I held was a three-foot, small, thin and lethal.

"Twelve-plait, kangaroo-hide" said the rangy, gaunt-faced clerk. "A good starter singletail."

"Singletail? You mean a bullwhip?"

"*Signal* whip. Dog-racing whip, actually. Here—let me show you." He skittered through the chunky crowd of butch dykes and hulking gray submissive gay men, jaws and eyes both drooping agape at collars and restraints in display cases. He dipped behind with a nervous and jittery motion, then ran the gauntlet of clientele back to me with a worn, somewhat grayed, coiled version of the stiff whip I cradled so tentatively in my hands.

There was an explosion and I jumped.

The little whip flickered by me and exploded again.

The gaunt, obligatorily leather-vested counterman grinned a

near toothless grin at me, his salt and pepper goatee glinting with spittle. "Seven hundred and fifty miles an hour breaks the sound barrier every time."

All eyes were on us and the little whip that he swung out and back nonchalantly like some outsized serpentine tongue. "It's a showboat move, but it gets a response no matter where you play—or with whom."

He extended his arm, the thing now coiled in his hand. He made a gesture and demonstrated. With a fast snap of my body, I cracked it, then promptly jumped back. Karenina's eyes widened watching me. TechnoSlaver—as he did so often—looked bemused.

"That's good," said the counterman with serious eyes, "but don't do it that way, or you'll whip yourself to death."

"To death?

"Sure. You could off someone with one of these things if you wanted—but the point is to learn to play with it so your submissive can enjoy it."

"My submissive?"

"Who else?"

I saw Karenina watching fixedly, her eyes sparkling now with sentiment. Her face lightened as an unmistakable smile of admiration played across it. Before I knew it, he had my credit card and I had the whip.

I also had a tiny tub of what looked like suet.

"You take that treatment and work it into the whip once every six months, working the plaits against one another with a twist, like an Indian sunburn. Then, it's just like getting to Carnegie Hall."

"What, you mean like hailing a taxi?" I threw my arm up in an excited motion, imagining my hand held the whip.

"No," Karenina shouted—then she and Bill said it together: "Practice, practice, practice."

He grinned stupidly, handing me the wrapped, bagged whip and I turned the trick of feeling both exceptionally dull yet extremely snobbish all at once.

Outside, Karenina and I embraced. She whispered to me, her tongue flirting with my earlobe: "I thought you were just submissive."

"I am," I nuzzled back.

"Someday maybe you'll switch for *me*."

"I don't switch," I said loud enough for Bill to overhear. He smirked.

"I'm going to switch for *you*," she said, a minor note of defensiveness creeping into what was meant to be a tease. "I already have."

This, unbelievably enough, did not play to guilt. Instead, I felt touched by the meaning of her conviction as I perceived it: love overriding need. I clutched her to me. I wanted to be able to make her happy, to remain and even to exceed how important I might have been to her then, or knew myself then to be becoming.

"I don't feel like a dominant," I murmured with absolute honesty. "I don't connect with it. I don't feel that I've ever taken or had that much control in any other aspect of my life, let alone had it evoke an erotic response."

"I know," she said, with affectionate condescension, "you even *dream* submissive."

"I'd like to switch," I said. "Maybe sometime I can try." I searched for some conviction when I said it that was nowhere to be found.

She shook her head as our bodies parted and Bill bided his time by the window. "So submissive," she sighed and stroked my hair. "Maybe we will. Maybe we will sometime when you can feel it." She winked. The wink was to tell me it was okay.

And then I was sure it was so much better than okay.

"Maybe when I feel it," I agreed, happy to get out of it. "May-*be*."

Next stop on the crawl was the East Village.

The day had turned even more sunny and magical by then, as we stopped to eat steam-table salad-bar food from the nearest grimy deli, sitting amid the garbage-strewn, leaflet-blown detritus of yet another demonstration of disgruntled homeless beggars and their radical agitprop advocates. Apparently, there had been a riot. My mind referred back to the newstands we had passed and I realized the top story in the major papers had to do with the now quiet garbage-strewn park in which we sat. Like good little educated right thinkers, Karenina and I expressed sympathy for them as a group while deploring them individually. Bill, having more pioneer traditions in his Midwestern social economy, expressed regret at their condition, and hatred of their weakness and what it made of them.

His hunter's ethic suggested they be shot down out of a sense of brute mercy and social utilitarianism.

George Orwell once observed that the impulse upon seeing an obviously hungry man pass by in the street was to kick him—perhaps out of resentment for having to imagine his privation and pain, for feeling it incumbent upon ourselves to care about such hunger when it had no immediate practical bearing on our own lives whatsoever, except perhaps to fear it. He never did explain this hatred, or the even more modern over-reaction to coat it over with apparent es-poused decency and kindness. The sentiment just rang—and still rings—bitterly true. Beneath the mannerisms of all the warm talk and the cold shoulder, *you just want to kick him.*

What would it be like now, I wonder, if you saw me pass you in the street? How would it be if I stood in your path and for that angry, suspicious second that distills our fears and prejudices down to the condensed pinpoint timing of a yawn, what would you feel? How much violent disgust, how much hate or fear?

Perhaps it would be your one final well-placed kick that would do me in.

Even with this book in your purse or clutched awkwardly in your hand passing me by, you'd know I was in for that kick. You'd want me to have it, and I'd be wide open for it. My eyes would ask for it, look straight through you, give you absolute license to *kick* me.

But, then, it really is too late, isn't it?

No point kicking a dead man.

And here, right here, at this point in the recollection of my end, it would be far too soon to want to kick a man who was so very alive, so engrossed in life—plunging himself as hard into the heart of his own obsession as his physical risk would let him, directly in the midst of learning by living it out all over again (or so he thought, perhaps even for the very first time) what it was to love, what it was to revel in the fertile power of lust, so full of the savor of erotic longing, so tempted by every taste of its ultimate satisfaction and renewal. It was

all so possible and true, as everything must be in the bright, kaleidoscopic vision of love alloyed with carnal fervor, thoughtful hope
and spiritual yearning, the madness that psychopharmacologists and
pop gurus still hope to approximate.

No. Orwell might just as well have said: "You don't kick a man
on a winning streak walking down the street with his own true love
in his arms, moving towards a perceivable goal. You don't even
want to."

You want his secret.

And of course, you *have* his secret.

Eye to eye, at the exact minute of your arrival at the stop of
self-revelation that brings you to consider this, you could just as
easily become the detestably considered target for the toe of someone
else's shoe. Or boot.

You could be the despicably ruined and hungry one glimpsed
irrelevantly on my day in New York when I could feel my love in
my arms, my winning streak holding.

Love. The sheer enmity of it, the leering craftiness of that ancient demon, was working itself upon me amid all my calculated
denying of it!

St. Michael's Emporium. That's where we headed next—the site
of my furtive vengeful financial transgression against my soon to be
former life under the regime of Ms. Right. We had split off from
Bill, as he had rightly deduced that we were getting far too lovey-
dovey for any detached person's stomach to tolerate and he needed
to interview some local mistresses for potential experiences (which
could have been a book in and of itself).

The Emporium was a cramped one bedroom apartment on Second edging on Alphabet City. We were buzzed in and before we
could find the apartment, a tall, Nordic figure in a black blouse and
jeans, with long reddish-blonde hair and close-cropped beard strode
to meet us, ushered us into his place which turned out to be the
showroom for his wares. St. Michael—as he called himself—crafted
fetish. Gothic renaissance fetish, or garb and gear for "the new dark
ages," as he referred to it in his catalog.

He was a towering yet friendly faced man, with a loose gait and
gangly motions that belied an edge of tension when he moved, the

model for the huge suits of armor featured in his catalog and worn routinely to the Renaissance/medieval recreation fairs and fantasy role-playing events so popular among the colleges and their fringe elements. But of course he was in the scene, and of course, because there weren't that many of us, he would make adjustments just for me. Karenina was both immediately awestruck and enamored by the items on display—the Apocalypse Chaps, the Dark Angel Armor, Herculean Shoulders, Diamond Bracers, the Armored Basque corset, all harsh tooling leather, steel buckles, rivets and not always in black, sometimes bright green or deep vermillion. Karenina's eyes were wistful with delight and what was becoming known to me as her usual pitch of enthusiasm. I was learning that this enthusiasm was how she would approach the first blush of exposure to any new D/s phenomenon, whether it was warranted or not.

Enthusiasm was her cachet, her calling card, her chief trait.

Such a bundle of personality, my Karenina.

Surprisingly, though he had been written up in the big magazines and was recognized as the hippest of the New York scene *haute couturiers* of fetish, St. Michael remembered both my name and my order. He went into the back workroom to get the piece. Somehow Karenina managed to take advantage of my poor balance and have me leaning on the wrong side of a display partition over a workbench by a dusty computer terminal. She had my pants unbuttoned, one hand around my throat, the other around my balls. "You're mine," she said as I heard Michael hammering in the back, smiling and enjoying the game she knew I wanted, playing the scene to make it feel right, working it to better fit my own ideal, her hands travelling over me and under my clothes.

I could see Michael standing at the doorway, a bemused expression on his face, deciding what to do with us, our getting intimate if not blatantly sexual in an off-limits quadrant of his little showroom where all the how-to books, works on historical armaments and reference volumes on mechanical engineering were shelved. He did the only and—in this Goth stronghold of the feral East Village—unexpectedly civilized thing he could do:

He cleared his throat and pretended not to notice.

As we got ourselves back together and made our way out from

behind the partition into the legitimate area of the shop, he wryly suggested that I strip where I stood. After all, since I had no compunctions about doing anything *else* behind the partition, I might just as well do so in front of it.

I remember Karenina laughing.

When he was done she sank to the floor by my feet, huddled against my leg, looked up at Michael and said: "It's beautiful. It's just so positively beautiful."

"This is my fantasy meets New York commerce," I said, my body rippling with gooseflesh.

Michael chuckled and tightened.

"And thus you see the result," said Karenina.

We both looked in the oblong mirror at the fitting of the leather, dragon-scale plated harness and my cock and balls hung in the nickel-plated ring, strapped in by unforgiving tooling leather between my legs and up my butt so that the thong went virtually unseen.

All three of us—for vastly different reasons—beamed at the reflected image.

THEY SHOWED UP AT THE SUITE, LOOKING DISREPUTABLE AND SURLY, which is how I immediately knew they were of our scene. There they were, Tutor and "O", looking haggard and suspicious, shuffling uncomfortably, distorted in the lens of the peephole, somehow not out of line with their natural aspect. I let them in while Karenina showered and Bill outfitted himself with—to my surprise and consternation— two St. Michael bracers, which Widow's Pique buckled for him in an attitude of mock submissive servitude. Tutor and "O" brightened with blinding speed and glared at all of us with grimaces of goodwill like we were some long-lost rich relatives come to town to revise our respective wills. Tutor pumped my hand and made lascivious jokes about women to me in my ear, as if I were one of the boys—as if he had *ever* been one of the boys at any time in his life, which from his stiffness and unnaturalness I felt to be far from likely, regardless of who the boys were. His military claims rang like brass in my ears, the scars on the backs of his hands developed a different origin. I knew that I was tired of him, which somehow gave him boundless energy to go on as I foolishly held my tongue, drinking in what was nevertheless a wonderful if not wondrous moment: the fetishists dressing together in near contentment. Even Auntie Maim's whinings and grunts of discomfort could not belie her own level of excited ease. She was as high-strung, chirpy and ebullient as a debutante getting ready for her first cotillion.

"O" doted over Karenina as she clambered into my spare pair of wide grommeted leggings which I loaned her to go with her spandex-netted leather bustier top, black of course. She braved a spiked collar and wristbands, even to the point of wearing makeup, which, having reached maturity in the thick of the earth-shoe epidemic, she was normally dead-set against. "O" seemed genuinely tremulous—nothing like those trumped-up, gelatinous undulations she threw herself into atop Tutor's quavering knee whenever she was due a public spanking. It was the sight of Karenina—once a preserve for punitive probing to be done by her and Tutor alone—recreating herself as a dominant.

"You're *switch* now, aren't you?"

Karenina reached over and stroked my leather-chapped thigh with a motion that was less deft than it was direct. She slapped it once sharply, gazing at me with the undistilled sentiment of romance, her glistening eyes showing how utterly moved she was by her own observed understanding of the moment. "I am now," she said, the responsibility of that gaze as crushing as was the love behind it.

This fascinated her enough to be unable to afford even just one passing glance at Tutor's ongoing effort to recruit the disinterested Auntie Maim as a submissive. Her mannerisms betrayed an eager disgust. TechnoSlaver made efforts to lure the single-minded Tutor away from his prize on the earnest pretext of comparing notes on dominant stylization. Mossman perfected his already practiced grovel, gorging himself on the toes and soles of the boots of Auntie Maim. Karenina finished herself by the mirror, talking her favorite talk, which was always the talk of logistics: how do we get there, what does it cost, where is it in relation to this or that, the mechanics and underpinnings of the night. I stepped back to watch them, engrossed as they were, united by their lascivious interest, and took in the room. Though we were nearly fully dressed and ready, we were a strange diorama of contrasts in the sterile, anonymously modern box of rooms at the Sojourners' Suites, all leather and nickel-plated steel, black and daringly exposed, our flesh adumbrated and reformed by dress until we exuded nothing but the promise of vicious forbidden sex acts while the room stated comfort, familiarity, sameness and would regardless of who was in it or what took place there.

We knew, as she suddenly joined me at my remote point in the room, watching as Mossman finished lacing Auntie's thigh-highs, that we had arrived at a perfect moment of scene camaraderie, a reality of our sexual bent culminating after years of pining in New York City among supporters of the same blissful sin of painsex, of dominance and submission, of lust.

IT SEEMED WE MADE IT TO THE CLUB IN A HEARTBEAT, GROUND ZERO, which for five or so hours tonight, would be the D/s club Paddles and my heart was pounding with the full force of the sexual unknown. We made our way through the usual darkened dogleg tunnel to the expected complications at the coatcheck counter. This time a haggard bearded aging hippie biker type I could have sworn had a solid career as a movie and TV commercial "type" bit player from whatever the modern equivalent of central casting was, clothespin tagged our bags and "coverage" and gestured us in with gruff exaggeration and a wink. He cackled with performer's zest at some offhand acting comment I made, as if I too were a veteran of the cattle calls.

Inside was a darkened maze of broken and in some cases half constructed walls. The ceiling reached easily twenty feet, the walls, only eight or as even as low as six. Tutor and "O," though obviously as uncertain of the layout as any of us, did their best to seem almost bored by the immense, seamy and tortured beauty of the place. As I raised my eyes, a high stage met my gaze and on it a youth with a waxed and pointed goatee did a woman with knives. When I say "did," I don't mean he killed her, stabbed her, maimed her— but certainly he did torture her. The blades played heavily across her skin, slicing, probing, pricking, caressing. She sucked and licked one knife as the other slid with slow, sinuous deliberation directly up her pink, bare vulva. She lay across a leather-padded sawhorse that in itself was nothing deluxe or elaborate. The woman was fair-complected, fresh-faced and blonde with peach-colored, metal-flake lipstick that glittered in the hot light, and was stripped naked but for a slender adorning chain about her hips and one overtly though delicately locked about her neck. Her *dominant*—it might have been far-fetched in this context to assume he was her boyfriend, though that was most usual—was slender, perhaps as much as she, stripped to the waist and wearing the requisite slack fit black jeans and O-ringed motorcycle boots of the younger, more rock-club cross-over S&Mers. They were, as personages, nothing special, just skanky X-ers.

Oh, but their scene, so tight in with the knife, so lubricious with that dollop of clear fluid gleaming like a single jewel in the light suspended as if from a strand of Karo syrup dangling down from between her thighs as he worked the knife so slowly and carefully not to cut and she sighed, heaved and moaned way above the music, fervid yet delicately pitched. That scene, their scene, *that* was something.

We watched transfixed and wordless, all of us, not even noticing Tutor and "O" as they turned away to set up for what must have been in their minds something potentially so much better. It *must* be better, it must! And that would be seen as a necessary end of their professionalism.

I was grateful as they left us watching, that what they saw inspired no further comment from Tutor. Even he recognized that, in seeing what we had seen, there was nothing he could say. There was no spin to be added, no commentary to be made to his advantage but to simply walk away.

The dominant suddenly finished her in a modest, non-theatrical move with a clean removal of the knife. When he did and stood over her with approving eyes, drinking in the sight of his handiwork, it was as if I had been permitted to breathe again. I hadn't really noticed up till then that I had stopped but, confirmed apparently by both my light-headedness and dizziness, I had.

Oh, but that wasn't the end of my dizziness just yet.

There was a call to applaud that hung thick in the room when they were done. No one applauded, of course. They might have done that in Miltown, but not here. Not in what I knew then in my palpitating heart was the epicenter of the scene. Soon they clambered down from the stage, the young dominant guiding his submissive by her hips down from the stage to the floor, halfway lifting her. They moved unselfconsciously through us, making their way to the bar. I could see she was covered with a light sweat that glistened like quartz on her skin. They would have spoken to us, seemed ordinary, open-faced and affable, but we somehow couldn't bring ourselves to speak to them.

I could hear her giggle warmly as they passed, his hand curving gently about the gooseflesh of her behind, its cleft so firm it was almost prim.

Karenina cleared her throat. "Shall we?" she said.

"What?" I said regaining my bearings.

She grabbed my arm with a good deal of strength and guided me. We went on a tour of the rooms, alcoves, racks and points of anchor. There was the usual amount of foot worship, and we spied the always-eager Mossman sucking the vinyl toe of some obvious pro who beat the denuded buttocks of a man who might have been a lawyer, an executive or even a high-school principal, his boxer shorts, pants and belt around his ankles, his center-pleated jacket and blue Brooks-Brothers pinpoint Oxford flapped up onto his flabby hairy back. He held her business cards in his mouth in a plastic sheath. There were one or two over-the-knee loving couple spankings going on, mostly yuppies in suits and dresses, fetish being best expressed for them by more black than they might ordinarily wear. In every one of these that I could see, the man gave and the woman received. There were several skulking "grays" moping about unaccompanied. At least two were in torso harnesses, more wore either jerseys or tee-shirts. There was one very distinguished though exceedingly mourn-ful "gray" in a suit and tie, his silver hair elegantly marcelled. They all had one thing in common: no pants, no underwear. They ambled about, heads bowed and guts protruding, on a shopping expedition, if not for a mistress then for a scene of the type that would be right enough for them each to take their respective cocks in hand and masturbate right then and there to the quiet loathing, appreciation or indifference of the club at large.

Signs hung on chains from high ceiling beams, white and catching the ambient stage light, clearly legible: "No Unprotected Sex. No Oral Sex. No Mobile Masturbation."

From what I could see, at least the third rule was taken seriously, though the grays to a man all had both a grasp on the situation and on their respective cocks, should the moment and the ardor together arise.

A close look revealed that all the play fixtures or "furniture"— the X-style St. Andrew's cross a la Milt Pecksniffian, the winch rack, the "Grecian bench," or just chains bolted into the masonry of a half-finished wall attached to ankle and wrist cuffs—were all unstable and in poor condition. We, Karenina and I, ambled about just like the grays shopping for a place to play. She led me on a leash and I realized we were getting looks. Karenina stopped to chat with Tutor, who was busily securing "O" to a patent-leather–covered bondage bench. He grabbed the center ring of my new harness and the heavy tooling leather creaked and bit angrily into my skin.

I debated the merits of kicking him, but decided against it.

"Hey," he leered with his head turned toward Karenina, "in that get-up he's about the best-looking thing here."

"He is," she agreed. "I like showing off my little toy."

"Glad to see I still turn you on," I said to Tutor, whose cheeks instantly colored.

"No," he said, his voice going up an octave, sounding both crotchety and old, "I have nothing against that sort of thing, but I'm a red-blooded perverted heterosexual."

Karenina looked at him adoringly, which caused a confused on-rush of emotions and made my stomach tense. "We're both raging heterosexuals."

I bit my lip and shrugged.

She borrowed extra cuffs from Tutor's play bag, which seemed to be as full of kitchen utensils as it was S&M toys, and yanked my leash taut indicating where we should go next. At the end of the room was a simple rectangular suspension rack. She demanded I sit

by it and by our own playbag on a straight-back chair while she went
to get a glass of water from the bar. When she returned, she bid me
to strip off my chaps, which I did. Soon my boots were removed
and I was cuffed in, all four points. She forced my head down, told
me not to speak unless spoken to, the safe word remaining our last
inviolate means of verbal communication.

She slid my leather zipper g-string down my thighs, letting it
rest at my knees. My cock shriveled with the cold air and exposure
to the coolly uninterested women smoking, chatting and observing
me, sitting on a bench in the murky light just opposite from where
I hung. Karenina fondled it for a moment before disappearing altogether from my senses. I hung there and waited, my adrenalin pumping and my breathing both deep and rapid. I felt cool air blow like
a breeze over my exposed and vulnerable loins.

Then came the rain of blows.

She started with the heaviest and thuddiest of the suede floggers,
not a comfortable mooschide tressed item, but a much coarser, more
incisive, steer whip. I gasped at the shock of the first wave of pain
as she lightened her strokes, letting me catch up. She was working
the bring-up now, experimenting. The deer came next, which was
like a massage given by several gently slapping hands. Then she went
back to the steer, which riddled my ass with a number of precise
and full-out strokes and caresses which just about put me into arrest.
Then I saw blinding lights as the collective ends of all the bull flogger's tresses landed hard into my groin, giving me the single most
effective punch I had ever received there. My eyes teared with anguish and I cried out, shaking my arms in my bonds, insensible. I
contemplated using the safeword, but became unsure as to whether
this blinding blow was deliberate when the onrush of endorphins
rolled with a thunderclap through my brain, paralyzed my tongue
and rescued my body. My head bucked and sweat flew from my
now-matted hair.

I was ready for more.

There was the flash again and my knees buckled. How the endorphins rolled. I was devastated. My legs no longer supported me.
Instead, I hung limp from my wrists. It was a bad wrap, the tresses
winding about my waist to smash me in the groin. I knew it was

bad. I was about to say so, when my back was cascaded with hits, smacks, whacks and slaps from the heavy moose tresses of the "Bullwinkle" flogger, causing me to bow more fully and more satisfyingly beneath the weight of the impact and pain.

My eyes were open, but they didn't seem to focus well as I felt the bite of two nerve wheels play over my back, the inside of my thighs and across my buttocks. When the room started to resolve in my view, it blackened with the crack of the heavy steer flogger across my back, which oddly enough by then felt comforting. I relaxed into it and hung slack from the cuffs of the rack until a sudden warmth overtook me. I could no longer hear the voices in the room, the rushing of the air or the swirling diapasons of the techno-industrial's wailing slapback. Then the crack of the whip had vanished.

I had a dim awareness of the scattered lights, the ambient rushing sound of the club, the lingering subsiding and lifting of the fog of pain. There was a galaxy of little embers of gray in the air, swirling to the center of my vision then hanging like a mist, diminishing as I hung, slowly revealing a sense of the club as I struggled to lift my head.

Another blow—harsh, wide, possibly two-handed—crushed my posture spreading across my back so my head was slackened again.

My vision, which suffered no outside obstruction, such as a blindfold, or strong, yet feminine hands pressing upon my eyes to keep them shut yet make them see, was a good while in coming back.

When my vision was restored and I could see, my head still hung, hands not yet either caressing my back with blows nor grabbing at me to assert ownership, what I could finally see was boots.

A sea of boots, brown, black, cowboy and not, snakeskin, leather, polyvinylchloride, D-rings, O-rings and buckles, silver skull bedecked and bootstrapped winked dully at my sharpening eye. I could only see the sea of boots, obviously attached to legs, presumably attached to onlookers. I struggled for motion, but was stopped dead again by hard certain hands, grabbing me, positioning me, cautioning me not to move.

I hung limp. Her knee pressed against my back and lifted me forward as her arms crossed about my waist. Then there was that airy cool vulnerability. She'd snapped off my g-string and my flaccid cock was prone and visible to the dark environment of the club. It felt drafty, chill, and I had a sense of growing humiliation. She took both cock and scrotum with both hands and began to manipulate, then massage.

I was cold and wet again—she had squirted me with something.

Baby oil. I could feel its heat, and then she took command, forcefully, with machine-like regularity.

She gave me orders, softly, licking my ear. She told me when and how.

With a grunt, I shot an arc into the crowd.

I kept doing so until she turned herself to pain again, yet kept doing so afterwards, keeping still as she had one hand on my cock, the other on a knife that played over my back like a dancing stinger, a wave of slicing edges, the remorseless scratching of a lover.

The spines of the Wartenburg wheel ran under my cock, yet I still came. But I saw and heard no approval for my continued performance. Just boots. Boots so inert they might have been just kicked off and set to dry higgledy-piggledy in some dark cloakroom. A disarrayed, disembodied assemblage of boots that did not move at all.

I pumped so much cum, I was almost as ashamed as I was sexually exalted, blissed-out by the surrender to a torrent of orgasms no longer my own.

Then she had me lick myself greedily from her hand, and I began to sense movement and noises among what had formerly been just a crowd of boots, but I wasn't sure.

When I finished cleaning her hand, I heard unmistakable murmurs of appreciation. As I trembled, spent, she climbed up on a chair to massage my numb hands and set them free. My wits collected again, I looked up about the rough chambered room, then back down, but of course the boots now were nowhere to be found.

The rest of the night at the club, another hour or so, was spent socializing. I chatted with the pretty young knife-people, who claimed to enjoy Karenina's scene with me as much as their own. Other introductions were made, and Karenina, Tutor and "O" went about promoting their sense of the Miltown scene, pushing their wares, glad-handing furiously. I went seeking Mistresses, and one fine brown leggy woman, whose muscularity and femininity were seamlessly portrayed in a shimmering black dress and bright white high strap-in mules, introduced me to a spring-loaded Catherine wheel set into the masonry of the wall. It was without much of either time or fanfare that she had me spinning at speeds much higher than those of the rollercoasters and Tilt-a-Whirls of my youth, such that I could barely see the changeover of Paddles into Boys Town as the throng of young men in their hip-hop gear, backward baseball caps, overalls without shirts, prison jeans slung low and shirts open to the navel showing chests shaved down to the same. You might find it hard to believe, but even amid the pump and throb of the sex-boy music set for wild dancing at the highest volume, they all stopped and gawked, watching me spin and spin as the brown mistress kept hitting the lever until Karenina got me down and I lurched into her arms.

And that's how I remember the height of my sensations that night, the depths of my desire.

That's how I went submitting to the flood of moments.

Spinning, spinning, spinning.

When I came down to her, dizzy, prone, exultant, it seemed I had never really come down at all.

Before we could fully collect ourselves, I was borne out of the club by a seeming sea of hip-hop–capped and overalled gay boys, as if I had scored the winning touchdown for the Army-Navy game. They rushed us into the seamy streets of industrial darkness lit now by passion, hope and a tantalizing sense of incompleteness. Karenina made some plaintive remark about the time, showing us her oddly out of place, somewhat-dated diver's watch.

She was making a point about the train. She was on the clock.

From the frozen faces of TechnoSlaver, Widow's Pique, Auntie Maim, Bootlicker—the offended, leering of Tutor and "O"—could see how obvious it was to everyone that we both were.

Karenina and me.

Our clock was ticking.

TWELVE

Laughter.

Life is full of it—laughter. The indifferent, hulking guffaw of a *nouveau riche* businessman, the cackle of the office crone, the open-palmed chuckle of the desiccated administrator, the laughter keeps at us. In the foreground of every chortle you enjoy, life has already reared back with unheard laughter to snap its jaws shut as you pursue with reckless seriousness your own crushing punchline. I should have known that as we were laughing dopily in Bill's van speeding Karenina back to her mother's place on the Island. I should have known then just what the laughter meant, throwback to adolescent innocence that it was, seasoned with the ironies that only adults who have known abject and terrible defeat could light-heartedly delight in.

It must have been near dawn in the ancient-seeming steel gray of the parking lot by the train station in Massapequa, when we embraced. We stopped there to let her off to avoid the havoc of a mistrustful mother's discovery. It was chaste, electric with unexpressed emotion, punctuated by the lightest of kisses, her lips barely alighting on mine, our faces hanging in the air like aimless helium balloons. Bill hung patiently in the driver's seat as Karenina lavished him with praise. There was a reference to our next mobile New York play date, and we all laughed.

A slight and buoyant moment of detached gaiety, of *esprit de corps,* of laughter.

Bill and I laughed all the way back and the miles melted, as we refined our S&M technique through conversational delectation and critique. There was a contretemps with the concierge when we tried to regarage our car, Bill gave forth with some of his Wisconisnite LaFollete-esque outrage and we later found the front tires of his van summarily stabbed through to the tube with long, rusty concrete nails when we were pulling out to head back to Miltown-and-environs the next day. We changed them, cursing, laughing.

We had left Bootlicker, Auntie Maim and Widow's Pique lying in a reckless heap and tangle of snores, half-moaning and muttering pleas for extra time under the covers. Auntie declared she would take the bus rather than arise at such an ungodly hour as noon, seconded by Boot and Widow's Pique, who daintily continued simulating death. Auntie was helpless with sleep and laughter like a sigh. Bill at least secured a 5 pm checkout for them through the not so strangely obliging concierge. We shook our heads, laughing.

As we drove uptown on our way out to stop for brunch, Bill slipped me a note. It had been left under his name as he had booked the room. The message had been written in the widely looped cursive handwriting of an obviously female clerk, and addressed Bill by name, but was clearly directed straight at me.

To William MacCollar:
I want to thank you for one of the greatest nights of my life. It was really wonderful, special. I have to have you like that again soon, where you belong. Hoping always for better and, of course, more, more, MORE!

Love,
Karen

Where I belong.

I finished reading it for the ninth time as Bill parked the van by some arch little brunch place in the West 80s with a cute blue awning. He snatched the note out of my hands with a cruel motion and tore it to bits.

"Hey—"

"You still love your significant other, don't you?" he asked with schoolboy seriousness.

"Of course but—"

"Well," he said studiedly, "things like that will destroy you."

"That little note?"

"I've had my own close calls," he said. "She's the primary. You don't want to mess with that, trust me."

Of course, I just had to watch the bits of note blow down the street. We had one of those long conversational rides back across the expanse of Northeast highway, with all its fits and starts and construction bottlenecks. We undertook the usual conversational detours, potential mate-swapping, elaborate outdoor scenes, suspension bondage technique, social etiquette and propriety among dominant woman and submissive men, and vice versa, and we discussed *alignment*. Alignment was what enabled Bill to pursue his S&M activities with a bunch of anonymous fellow enthusiasts, bringing his wife along in time to join in or perhaps supplant them all. Alignment was the positioning of his life that made sense. It was his *summum bonum*, his *sine qua non*, his level and plumb.

Ms. Right and I were misaligned, he said. We needed to repair that alignment, perhaps redefine it altogether, or all would be lost. At least the "all" that seemed so basic and important to my life at the time. In my narcissistically astrophysical view, however, I saw my alignment shifting to where Karenina and her universe moved in, and Ms. Right and all her stardust and debris dispersed away into some black gravity. Closing my eyes and feeling the miles tuck under me riding the solid suspension of Bill's minivan like some kind of mobile massage-equipped Barcalounger, I replayed the night at Paddles, shuddering pleasantly with each recollected blow of pain.

I smiled at the thought. I had the solution, of course.

"You're glad I tore up that note now," he said.

"Glad all over," I said.

"WHAT HAPPENED TO YOUR BACK!" SHOUTED MS. RIGHT, JARRING ME awake from a bondage fantasy in which I was more prop being worked on than anything else, starring Karenina with Tutor in a supporting role as Igor, the demented hunchback. "It's purple!"

"Accident," I yawned. "Tire iron."

"Who hit you with a tire iron?" she said with hurt accusation in her voice clipping her tone. "Who hit you?"

"Nobody," I said. "Like so many other things, I merely backed into it."

"Yes," she said bitterly. "Like you backed into this. Are you doing something *weird* with Bill? Did he hit you with the tire iron? I know he's some kind of freak, the way he stands there and stares at me."

"Bill just likes to process his thoughts before he expresses them. He's an engineer—says he's digital, not analog, if you don't give complete answers to questions. Or the right answers."

True to form, she hit me with her pillow.

I didn't level mine at her—I could feel a total absence of play in the blow when it connected. A pillow fight now might end in further violence or tears.

"He knows you then doesn't he. He knows you won't tell the truth no matter what. He's not digital—you're just a fabricator. Are you doing kinky stuff with him? Is Bill hitting you to get his faggot rocks off?"

My best defense was laughter. She wanted to love me, wanted for everything to be all right. For her, my laughter was a signal that the fear had gone, that there was hope for tomorrow's being some sort of normal, stable day. She laughed, close to crying.

Her heart was wrong. Everything was wrong. She was trying to right it all.

My laughter was the axis for her effort.

"Can you imagine me and Bill in an S&M affair? I mean—would he even be my type?"

"Who'd be the man?" She turned red, wracked with shudders of mirth.

We embraced and turned out the light once more.

MY FIRST ORDER OF BUSINESS THE NEXT DAY WAS TO CALL KARENINA at her unlisted private line. It rang enough times for there to have been a machine, but instead, at the cut-off, I heard voices and a minor scuffle for the receiver at the other end. "Hello," she queried, slightly out of breath.

"It's me."

"Oh—John! It's been awhile. How's Marie and the kids?"

"I'm not John."

"Yes, Bennie's right here—would you like to speak with him?"

"Shoot me first."

"Sure. I can do that. But why would I want to? There's a few other things we can do. Hang on?"

Muffled voices—one of them was the nasal regional honk possessed only by those of the lowest order of the rigid Miltown social caste system. The other was the high muted yet keening falsetto of Karenina. The phone fumbled again and she was back.

"He says you're a bastard for not helping with his business plan."

"His what for what?"

"Well, he thinks I'm talking to one of our friends. He's sulking in the basement now because he's an illiterate."

"Really." Not knowing altogether that much about her, I had to ask. "What does he do for a living?"

"He rides my coat-tails is what he does. I made a real estate business, he made work for me pissing off clients, associates and lawyers, getting in the way with his ego and drove me crazy. I made profits, he made complications. Why? Because he's simple-minded. He barely budged enough to allow us to pull out of the business before the bigtime bust."

"He sounds retarded."

"He is. But he has just enough crude brain power to dog me, browbeat me and get in the way of any forward movement toward anything in our lives."

"What about the kids?"

"He's a good dad—at least I always thought so. Who knows now, he's so bitter and angry."

"About what? Sounds like a good life—collect the rents on the properties, cook up more business schemes—"

"Like I said, he's in the basement trying to write a business plan for a Safety Club projected franchise of strip-mall stores dedicated to protection against home invasion, robbery, so forth. Countermeasures."

"Paranoia products?"

"Absolutely."

"Sounds like a money maker. What's the problem?"

"Well, apart from the usual one of not wanting to spend

own money on it, there's the fact that he can't get past the first paragraph."

"He needs your help, obviously."

"Fuck him. He's always needed my help."

"His was a case of marrying up?"

"Yes. He's been using my life to try to get over his."

"Hasn't been working?"

"Well, it has up till now. I made him a yuppie for a year or two—got him a job brokering special deals at some tidewater branch of an investment bank, but he screwed that up with his usual native disability. They fired him and he sued."

"He's the type they pay off, isn't he?"

"That's how it went. He cried so long and loud and made so many scenes they either had to pay him off or have him arrested. The former seemed neatest."

"And you lobbied for it."

"My kids need their daddy."

"He sounds like a job and a half."

"He's what I *undo* for a living."

"And what do you do now."

"I'm coasting until the next big score comes along. Looking for a deal—but he's sucking through the money, refusing to get a real job because he can't, and because he can't stand the idea of his working while I raise the kids."

"I thought he was Mr. Vanilla."

"He is. But he has to have everything even-Steven, he says. If I have it, he has to have it. Even if he has to take it from me to get it."

"So he's a feminist—"

"In that he wants me to go to work to support him? Yes."

"Piece of work, your Bennie."

"Piece of something, all right. Hold on."

I could hear her shrieking muffled by the hand she clasped tightly over the receiver. "Oh, he's on me again. He's always on me, like a bad-smelling, distempered dog."

"Should I go?"

"Maybe. In a minute. Have you thought about our next foray?"

"Nothing but."

There was banging—not knocking—on the door that led to the stairwell and the room across from mine where Ms. Right's office was. It was behind bookshelves and stacks of miscellany. It didn't matter.

The shrieking on this end was loud and clear: "Who are you *talking* to in there? I hate hearing you talk on the phone, you sound like such an *asshole!*"

"My turn," I sighed into the phone. Then, cupping the receiver none too thoroughly, I called back in return without anger, "Just another editor, honey. Trying to scare up work."

"Sounds like you're having too friendly a conversation in there for that."

"But we want to make friends and influence people."

"I don't care, Perry! Just do something, will you, and stop farting around?"

"Stop *eavesdropping!*"

"I can't help it—it's what you make me do!"

I went back to the phone. "Still there?"

"Yes, unbelievably enough. Though the huz is on one of his cost-accounting rampages. I went shopping this morning and he's about to make me return some food items that were not bought at bargain prices."

"What about those bulk warehouse clubs?"

"Oh, he loves those—that would be a winner except for one thing: he hasn't figured a way to get them to waive the membership fee. He's been working on it though. Makes a call to office head-quarters once a day."

I heard the shouting of numbers in the background; sarcastic, whiny, in an extremely personal interpretation of the worst of the Miltown lower-class accents.

"What are we doing?"

"A scene, of course, my beloved Prop. I'll get back to you with time and place. I have to go. The huz."

I heard her lips kiss the outer rim of both the phone's receiver and my imagination before the line went dead.

There was an immediate ring. I thought it was her finding a

other brief time window through which to call me back, getting another chance to tell me more, but it was only Habanero Bahamian telling me to check the newsstands.

BY THE TIME I WENT OUT IT WAS LUNCHTIME ANYWAY, AND BEYOND what little work I could get from Dwight DeSeigneur and his dilapidated string of inner-city vanity-style throwaways, there was nothing for me. So I took Bahamian's advice and went to the convenience store on the corner. I picked up a sandwich, some coffee and the newest *Register.*

"I can't believe they get away with publishing this shit," said the counterman ringing me up.

"No accounting for taste," I said.

"Yeah, well they could do with putting out a bit of news, those guys, ya know?"

"I know. Nobody likes news."

"They might as well all be writing fuck books," he said as I gathered up my change and left.

"You have a point," I said, letting the shutting of the door and the ringing of his antiquated bell make mine for me. "They might as well," I mumbled, as I stopped in the hot gray gloom of threatened summer rain to look at it.

There it was in all its bilious glory: It hadn't been edited; they ran it whole!

"Smitten With A Whip: Miltown's Kinky Sex Scene Uncovered."

True, they blew the concept by having a yuppie scrub the floor for a callow looking waif-girl gotten up in black vinyl boots and mistress gear, none of which quite fit her, eating a donut as her slave slaved. She wore an overtly false blonde wig shaped in Bettie Page 50s bangs. She looked bored and he looked confused. I was offended.

And then I laughed: The parody that had missed the mark had mirrored the truth.

All the mainstream flaws in perceiving sex, in finding some place within in it that wasn't furtive or duplicitous, its furthestmost alternative reaches had been captured in that unknowing, cliché-humored cover tableau. Bored, exploited, clueless. An excellent counterpoint to my article, which was all but frothing with enthusiasm, romance and poetic appreciation. I let everybody gush and quoted them voluminously. I let them beat their breasts with sensible pronouncements of self-importance as if celebrities, as if Hollywood stars with a social conscience. They expressed their ideas, their opinions, delivered their message.

I felt hollow and disappointed. I had only pulled off the usual journalist's trick of succeeding in creating art where having captured an ungainly truth with an enumeration of facts, a listing of unspun events without a local hook, would have done much better. It would have told something unexpected and unknown, would have educated, but would also have violated the most sacred modern canon of the press, which is to flatter the ignorance of the public, shocking only in acceptable patterns that the public knew too well, never calling any basic assumptions into question, which most real news always does, before we report it.

Not news reporting, just news processing.

Of course, I wrote it in the features style, which mimicked the slick magazines and which meant I had made a pleasant bedtime story out of everything to be dreamily glissaded over within a few moments of the intellectually somnolent daylight working hours. The counterman almost had it right, but we weren't so much writing fuck books as romance novels.

I made my way home just as the rain hit.

When I bounded upstairs with wet copies of my latest public moment, all I could hear was Ms. Right concocting more new-age lineage extensions with her usual good-natured somberness. She was in a sweat—nattering, spinning her wheels desperately to please whatever shark steeped in spiritual lingo and mind/body products for eternal well-being was trying to extort lower rates from her on the other end of the line. I picked up my own phone and called Karenina as thick droplets battered my windows in the gray light.

KARENINA KNEW THE HARDWARE STORE AROUND THE CORNER FROM THE dogleg of my street. In fact, she had an account there so her various

contractors could pick up essentials for the maintenance of her properties. She was there in twenty minutes as our miniature Miltown
monsoon began to predictably subside. There she was, my Karenina,
hanging out of the window of her godawful navy-blue Mercedes
Benz station wagon, wearing sunglasses, the snaggletooth grin making her features appear both lurid and absurd in the struggling sunlight as I crossed Divinity Ave. toward her window. She was
cartoonish, more squat than petite, but believed herself a femme
fatale.

The illusion carried. I believed her too.

"Excuse me, I'm lost," I said.

"Why don't you hop in my car, little boy, and I'll help you find
your way."

"I was told never to ride with strangers."

"None stranger than me."

"I was told not to."

"I have candy."

"Rots your teeth."

"Well," she leered, "I have other things—toys."

"Like what?"

"Come and find out."

"I don't know."

"Do I have to get out of this car, wrestle you to the ground and
drag you in here?"

"Is this a kidnapping?"

"Of course."

"Well, why didn't you say so?" I got in and she mercurially
cuffed my hands with a pair of peerless stainless steel.

"You're just such a problem," she said and attacked the traffic
patterns, driving her station wagon like a Porsche. "Always late.
We'll have to save the wrestling you to the ground and dragging you
in here part for later."

"Where are we going?"

"To the graveyard."

It wasn't just any graveyard, it was the Trinity Mount Olive,
which was as much of an actual historic park rife with machicolations, battlements and turrets as any that had been preserved and

dedicated to life. There were paths and structured, pamphlet-marked walks among the rolling hills and charming knolls among which mausoleae, catafalques and garish monuments to stoic political leaders and grandees were points of either awe or indifference. We walked to a tower that could have served as a model for the representative Tarot card.

We clambered up shallow steps five flights to the topmost turret. I was still cuffed. Before I could admire the scenic view of the graves among the green hills, winding paths and gnarled, tortuous trees, she spun me about, kicked the trap door shut with her heel and locked the center chain of the cuffs to a rusty iron hasp set in the granite as an anchor, perhaps for a winch. She had my pants down and began clamping my cock with some item I couldn't see that made me writhe and scream.

"I can have you wherever I want you? Isn't this the perfect place? All cool stone, high winds, graceful sky? How does the breeze feel against your painful cock? Soothing?" She licked and sucked the flesh against the clamp. "Does this make it better?"

"No," I moaned.

Then she applied oil to the slick area she had licked. She worked her fingers under my cockhead where she knew I could not resist. "Does this?"

I was emphatic, but lost to the wind and the pain. "Nooooo. . . ."

She presented her palm in front of my face with a wide, glistening trail of fluid seared across it.

"See this?" she asked.

I nodded.

"This is you. This is your erotic longing, your need, coating my hand. This is your essence distilled. Do you want it?"

"Yes," I cried as she wet just under my nose with it.

I extended my tongue to lick her hand, but of course she withdrew it before I could connect even the tip of it to the glistening skin. She bent, thrust my legs apart and began to go to work on me with her fingers. I struggled against her motion, my pants about my ankles, the cuffs and the disturbing chill of the wind. Then there was a gasp that was not my own.

Nor was it Karenina's.

Some ungainly matron with a tow-headed toddler in tow had unknowingly followed us up to the parapet, no doubt to avail themselves of the wonders of the bleakly rolling panorama of graves made so inviting by the gray cast of the sky. Bits of rain were flung down upon us as Karenina shielded me from further viewing even as the matron, bug-eyed, prepared to level some outraged moralistic Miltown bluestocking commentary our way. She kicked at the trap door before their feet had reached out level, forcing them down. She continued kicking as they retreated, the toddler whining and the matron huffing without being allowed by either opportunity or oxygen to wrap her outrage about any choice words or phrases.

I could hear her flustered voice gather around unintelligible syllables for a good distance down behind the trap door.

Karenina placed her bags on top of the door, produced a flogger and went after my shanks, indifferent to my screams, indifferent to the occasional wandering figure way below who might catch the some of the meaning of the scream, before looking up, seeing nothing and moving on. After I was panting with pain, and the effort to pace my endorphins to meet it, she uncuffed me and loosed the clamps about my cock. I winced at the surge of fresh pain caused by their removal and she briskly pulled up my pants and buckled them, returning to me the use of my legs.

We held hands like chaste lovers walking the path back to the car. We shared in the rain those long, liquid silent gazes that speak of a fiery yearning for completion far beyond procreation and the brute comforts of a contented home. We had tapped into some governing passion whose food and drink was pain and sex, and whose subtle and refined needs were to sap our pasts and futures dry to the bone, blend them, make them one.

We were so stupidly in love, it was positively *normal*. The ablatives were all by twist, by quirk, by hook and by lie. The objectives were all honeyed with the hopeful sentimentality and uncaring worldly obstructions of a perfumed romance novel. Anyone who saw us would have nodded with approbation on the strength of the connection, the palpability of the romance. It would have been more than acceptable that we were spousal cheaters steeped in unspoken practices of S&M. True love finding its way was at the heart of all social sexual fetishism and the kinky sex, and well, between true lovers, these things were smilingly allowed with a nod and a wink.

As long as we were bound by the stricture of true love, it was a fine thing. As long as we had bowed and engaged in every perversion and treachery we could find in the name of true love, we were virtuous, as romantic flaws can efface even capital crimes under the right circumstances.

It was as sacred and undeniable as the fact of children, an unquestionable good.

We parted back at the hardware store where, after a cinematic kiss wherein our thoughts were unspoken but well expressed, I left to face the gray rain and anger of Ms. Right.

Why was it so difficult to stop kissing, petting, gazing?

"Separation anxiety," she said. "My kids have it."

I COULDN'T HEAR THE DEMON LOVE LAUGHING AT ME AS I RIFLED MY pockets for change. I didn't hear its wings beat away from Ms. Right and alight on the specter of Karenina, whose snaggletoothed visage was ever fixed in my mind.

I dropped the change in, sweating and trembling, protecting my area like a convict.

I was becoming a slave to the pay phone.

Rather than discuss my cover story in The *Register* with Ms. Right, I had to go out for some air. This meant I had to run out, find a pay phone, my not being spendthrift enough to have a cellular phone (and Ms. Right was convinced they caused cancer), and talk with her to help capture that brilliant, amorphous future that loomed so tantalizingly just above the crest of our playing. I just *had* to talk with her—hearing her discuss sex, love, kink and promise was better than a drug, I simply could not get enough of Karenina.

I knew better than how I felt. I knew what was what.

Fuck it. I had to do what I was driven to do. Hesitation, planning, caution were for fools who had never been exalted to this level.

How many times in my life had I felt this way? How could I be suckered into repeating the same misleading excitements of youth, simply because when they occurred, they felt so different each time, so new?

I could do it because of love. I had been loved, been brainwashed for love, had my refined dissatisfactions and lusts *focused* on love, even as I had struggled so pointedly for its opposite, for a purity of kink, for corruption that had no civilizing or redemptive quality mimicking the virtues of the straight, vanilla world of suit and cap-wearers, of sexual lemmings running off their respective cliffs, chasing down lifelong one-of-a-kind love and well-being as served up in the datastream or in hand-out magazines with slick covers like *Alpha Waves*.

This time I had it right.

The demon Love had told me.

Karenina had told me, my partner in crime—the crime that was redefining my life.

D/s.

I called at the lone pay phone by the student entrance to the decrepit and diminishing Catholic school at the end of the cul-de-sac where our house sat squat amid other historic working-class structures of the early post war period. As usual, after I dialed, there were enough rings to kick me into the answering machine. I got Bennie just before and hung up.

The windows of the school, the convent, even those of the chapel were dark with diocesan downsizing.

I stood in the shadows of the rectory, pacing pathetically by the lone payphone, eyed now and then by an intermittent dogwalker. I dialed again—Bennie. His voice was cheery, filled with brio. "Hell-*oooo*," he called into the receiver like a jolly tourist standing over a ravine. I walked around the block in the darkness, bathing myself in the buzzing glow of the liquor store's ancient neon and beer-brand aureoles.

I would not be denied! Again and again I went for the hail-fellow-well-met voice of an obvious fraud. Each new "hello," smoldering with a darker edge of anger. Time was passing. How could I account for this lapse with Ms. Right, make the interminable length of my night-time stroll sensible. I didn't care. I'd tapdance, sidestep, make light of it all, find some diversion to skew the focus of her razor-straight suspicions.

I winced at the anticipated fury in the saccharine greeting, but instead, was exultant to hear the weary, exasperated voice of Karenina.

"I can't talk now—I have to get out of here. I'm trying to make it to my submissive women's support group."

"The huz is trouble?"

"You have to ask?"

"He doesn't stop. Hear him in the background—droning on and on about my *subversive* women's group? He just doesn't get. Wants me to be the stay-at-home wife and mother, serving his whims."

"Would that satisfy him?"

"It never has. He hollers, complains, fusses. He doesn't know what he wants, but he thinks he wants to be rich and secure."

"Don't we all?"

"But he wasn't happy when we were. It was as if we were still broke and struggling. It was as if *I* were still struggling. All he ever did was sweat and mope and get in the way."

"He sounds retarded."

"He is! I think he's brain damaged, learning disabled. Oops— have to go. He's coming. Love you. Bye."

I didn't even get the dial tone before I hung up.

"SHUT UP, EVERYBODY! WE'VE MADE THE COVER OF *THE REGISTER!*" screeched Athena. With a Bianchi handcuff key worn about my neck as a new trademark, I was dutifully helping the stage mistresses in the dressing room with their boas, prop whips, crops, snapping and yanking them into unpolished latex as they squirmed. It was hard to bend and kneel in my usual harness and chaps, but I began to enjoy the tooling leather riding up the crack of my ass as I labored on the pouty girls' raiment. I could barely hear Athena screaming, *"Shut up!"* I was on my knees busily spraying silicon on Chlamydia's latex skirt when I heard faintly amid clamor the horror-movie pipe organ that was Athena's herald and then yet more indistinct squalling. I did my best to make it out, but Chlamydia extended a boot for me to lick, a reminder for me to pay attention.

"Hey—*shut up!!!* I said we made the *Register!* We—*us!* Our crowd! Somebody *finally* gave us our due—right here in the good ol'" Milltown *Register*. Look around you! Look at the guy in rubber and chains next to you! I'm telling you all these people dressed up here in the fetish of their choice are the bravest people in the world. And tonight is their night! So you go introduce yourself to one of them and buy them a drink. Show them your appreciation for help making Fetish Friday the best and sexiest night in town! You'll find copies of, the *Register* in a box by the entrance to the main room— pleeee-aaaase—"She played the mike like Elvis here, dipping as if she had a stand to go with it instead of wireless air. "*Pleee-aaase* tell your friends. Now—right now—everybody go see Akasha! Buy a drink for a fetish friend!"

There was a good deal of mixed milling, approbation and scorn, catcalls from the cap-wearing boys as well as subverbal cheers from the tourists having drunk too much to bolster their courage only to find that it gave them desires different from the ones they came in with. The crowd seemed to close in about the stage and there weren't many takers for the newspapers in the box. *Registers* wound up on the floor and underfoot. How would I know? In the middle of my worshipful duties to all the delectable mistress wannabes, I was dragged upstairs by Daisy May Arcana, who tonight was in butch booted, belted male attire, meaning he had come to the club straight from work.

The punching sound was Athena's black press-on nail tapping the mike.

"Propertius! Where's Propertius, that little son of a bitch! Come on up here, honey! There he is! There's the genius that wrote the article about us that told the truth! Bring him on up here!"

My stage humiliation fell flat, as I knew it would. What was there to say about the article? It was one of those slick little features that sounds plausible and true, flatters everybody, attacks some general imprecise evil—more as a concept than anything else—and adds to all the initial misperceptions and confusions, layering them with

a patina of dreamy simplicity. I held up *The Register,* grinned, did a
little exaggerated kneeling so I might receive a hokey spank and leave
the stage. Athena loved it because she wasn't misquoted, wasn't de-
monized. I made the scene look harmless and cute, like upright
housewives playing at wicca.

I downplayed the sex, which made everybody happy. In fact—
as a sex scene—I made it look immaculately sexless, while adorned
with pretty boys and girls (all the ambitious club pros desperate for
paying model work) each one looking as if they had just emerged
from the raunchiest of orgies with barely enough time to pull on
their skimpy vinyl or latex at the last minute. I wrote a wholesome
social trends psych piece, lying all the way, striking a compromise
between the hard lines of propaganda by playing up the most credible
elements of both and eliminating the unacceptable, loathsome facts.

After my little turn of worshipping at the size 11 boots of Miltown's Ultimate Mistress, and receiving a few customary butt
whacks, I was allowed to leave the stage.

When I did, I found Karenina once again surrounded by the
skank boys, Manny and Wally, basking in the attention, her wounded
(and long since healed) left breast, flopping somewhat out of her
bustier. I put the idea and vaguest concept of infidelity out of my
mind. Infidelity—cheating—simply couldn't exist in an open play
relationship! I laughed off any sense of low creeping jealousy and
dismissed it, even as the demon Love beat its wings silently behind me.

I came up behind her and she embraced me, as I did her.

It was the lovers' entwining.

Manny blithely went on discussing his plans for a better bondage
business, his hand on Karenina's ass, but even Wally had busied
himself elsewhere.

It was the usual cacophony of students in Gothic mufti, semipro
mistress/callgirl/strippers in PVC minis and thigh-high boots and
frustrated aging remnants of the self-aware seventies swinging scene
meandering about, all looking to make their own special brand of
connection. And I had made mine with Karenina—or so I thought.

With Athena's blessing and approval, Karenina gave a little demonstration, stringing me up on the unsteady black lacquered pine

rack by the stage and practicing her whipping as I stripped down to a tasteful "g." The crowd of decrepit older men focused upon us, Karenina fielding insipid questions about finding a mistress like her and pushing them back with the gestures of her authoritative hand. Floating beneath the waves of her keening blows, watching the little mascaraed go-go goths gyrate full of empty, incomprehensible promise, I smelled thick cigar smoke, but only for a moment.

Bootlicker danced, bouncing his belly to and fro. Auntie Maim basked in the attention of uninitiated men, smoking cigarettes in her long cigarette holder, as drunk as her audience's interest and ability to keep buying her drinks would allow her to be. Chlamydia did some sort of Asian dance presentation on the proscenium, with a bevy of writhing slave boys and go-go Goths aplenty, doing their best to strut the stage with the conviction of the undead, all giggles and jerky gyrations of baby fat. Widow's Pique hung with Marion, clawing at his enormous pecs while he in turn grabbed his boyfriend Ned's crotch and held it hard in his leather-gloved hand, sipping cranberry juice seltzer and lime, no doubt this time containing some quantity of urine. Mount handcuffed college co-eds and made them squeal, in his state police outfit.

As happy as I'd ever been, I thought at the time.

We were starving, hungrier almost more for food than for more of one another's company, pouring out into the street with the late-night throng as the swaggering, lanky boy-men with walkie-talkies charged with security bullied and herded the drunken revelers off public streets as if they had a legal right to—which they didn't. We all went along with it anyway. We didn't want to blow anything at Ubu Roi. The pick-ups, transactions, altercations were always all too fascinating for me to watch, so I was usually pushed away by some gothic clod sporting muttonchops and an attitude.

Gazing like loons entranced with the sensitive, diaphanous poetry of Alfred de Musset, we ate steak and eggs in an unlicensed all-night joint boarded up on the outside to look closed. I knocked back bourbon after coffee, but Karenina could only drink water. "I have a thing about fluids," she said. "They have to be pure."

"No alcohol at all? No coffee?"

"No, not even Coke. And besides, there's always poison that settles at the bottom."

I'd heard this before. For some reason, I enjoyed hearing stock personality traits like these recounted again by her. It was, as always, a trick of love.

"Poison," I repeated. "And how is it with *come?*"

She smirked her little practiced smirk, the one that was supposed to show she held a secret. "Well. You seem to like yours. It must be pure enough."

I clasped her hand, my fingers greasy with steak. "I can assure you it is of the lowest purity possible."

"Well then—I'll just have to be the judge of that, won't I?"

COMING HOME WAS THE USUAL ISOLATING EXPERIENCE—MS RIGHT HAD ceased to exist for me in the present moment. There she was, nestled in on her little loveseat with no room for me, her mouth slack with dreams and stale air. I shucked off the fetish, ready to collapse on the bed now too big for just one to set my dream-blurred sights on next week when Karenina could squirm away from the house, the huz and the kids and begin designing with me the idyllic future that lay unspoken between us.

But I didn't give in to bed just yet, still jazzed from my night at Ubu Roi.

In a frenzy of pure whim, I got out my new acquisition, the little black signal whip I had bought at the Noose and cracked it over my head twice rapidly. I jumped at the crisp explosion. In the silence just after, the air ringing with the aftermath of the gunshot burst, there was no stirring. I practiced aiming for the drapes with little noise—worked the stiff whip almost limber, teasing drapery material with the cracker until my right arm was nearly numb and my brain ached for dreams of the future. I was barely able to conceal the thing somewhere Ms. Right-proof before I was swallowed by the ever-expanding horizon of my empty bed.

I awoke to the phone.

"Hey, *compadre,* busy today?"

"Always—the normal social context of weekends means nothing to me. I'm a freelancer."

"You should come in. It's quiet and we can talk."

While I groggily collected my thoughts, Ms. Right, who was already up and cleaning our brightly sunbleached apartment brought me coffee and encouragement. She could always smell an editor on the line when her senses weren't clouded by love and jealousy. Of course, my brain was so clouded by a romantic longing that itself was so poisonous that I had lost reasonable cognitive function long ago. I was in a mist of illusion palpable enough to make the reality of my life just a thin shell around it, protecting my delusions and intangibles as if they were a nourishing meat.

Crack it all open, though, and all you would get would be air.

Ms. Right mussed my hair and I went on.

"Why come in?" I was at my most articulate, greedily downing coffee.

"That piece was great, man. I haven't seen you in while—this might be a good time to lay out a follow-up strategy for that transgressive series we've been toying with. You know: piercing, body art, raves."

"What?" mouthed Ms Right.

I cupped the receiver. "They want me to come in at the *Register*."

Her eyes were bright, her smile broad and her red hair gleamed like polished copper in the light from the shadeless windows of my office. "I'll drive you," she said, and gave a clipped nod.

I sighed, correctly feeling outnumbered. "I'll be there. Brew coffee."

"Hey, buddy," he said leaning back—I could hear his chair creaking even over the phone, "for you, the *hazelnut*."

I was still asleep when we got there, or felt that way, my lungs still occluded by the variegated smoke delivered by sweat and exhalation across the stale wafting air of Ubu Roi. Ms. Right brought a book and was determined to wait in the car and read—*The Bridges of Madison County*, I think it was, or some other thin and frilly volume of embarrassingly romantic tripe—despite there being numerous perfectly suitable waiting areas inside. The place spooked her, she had said.

As you know, I never really gave Ms. Right the appreciation she deserved.

Nodding past the weekend make-up people, the editors in their impeccable weekend leisurewear, looking like the kings and dowager empresses of the shopping malls and the indoor tennis and squash courts that their privileged sophistication had made them. Dilettantes and political connivers at best at work, they were all near-professional experts at a leisure so rarified they could fill hours of your time merely describing it. I navigated the maze of cubicles and their wall extenders until I reached Bahamian's office, an actual building struc-ture with a door. He was in his characteristic pose of wary yet relaxed reclining, sipping from his oversized Three Stooges coffee mug. He was schmoozing—it could have been the phone, it could have been someone in the room.

"Hey Hab—am I interrupting?"

"Come on in, stranger," Bahamian said.

I was about to say, "None stranger than me," but something caught my throat.

Standing in front of him was Happy Boy, big and bloated and living up to his name.

"Patetick," Happy Boy stated like some sad fact as he glowered at me.

"Ambushed again, *Chemo-therapy?*"

"Don't look at me pal," Bahamian sighed. "I just work here," implying strongly that he had no intention of taking the slightest risk of discontinuing to do so.

Happy Boy's eyes were red-rimmed and sagging. "Your piece was a disaster for us, Patetick. I'd like you to print an apology."

"To whom?"

"Our readers of course—this whole fetish thing was a mistake. We've had two advertisers cancel already."

"Out of how many?"

In typical style, Happy Boy threw the issue in my face—literally. "Enough!" he shouted.

"So—I guess there's going to be no transgressive series on piercing, no new sexual proclivities of the Generation X grunge coffee-bar set to make my career on? Hab, I feel set up and betrayed."

"Don't get that way, buddy. Everything's kosher. Just keep pitching your stories here directly to Crane here and we'll use them." I thought I saw him wince after saying that.

"We might use them," said Happy Boy. "But we'll have to have someone else write them up who knows what he's doing first."

"So this piece didn't get a lot of attention? Didn't wind up on one of the local affiliates somewhere?"

"Oh, it did," said Bahamian "—and Crane was quoted as saying we'd never do such a thing again. Chet Whatsisface gave it his stony-faced hard-news nod of approval. How *dare* we approach kinky sex as a local issue!"

"News is news and sex sells," I offered.

Happy Boy glumly looked at his watch. "I'm not here to argue with you about what is and isn't journalism. Just write up the apology, sign it and leave it on my desk. Then I think we're done, Patetick."

"But I'm *not* done and *it's* not done. Editors are the ones who make the apologies for the writers—especially freelancers. Running what's run is your judgment call, not mine. And you can't really run an *erratum*, can you? I mean, where there is no error?"

"If I say you're done, you're done. Leave me the apology, sign it and then you can leave. I don't need to argue this—just read you the riot act. And if you feel the urge to deal with anyone at the *Register ever* again, you can call me first. Then I'll tell you what to do."

"Haven't you already, though?"

Bahamian looked embarrassed, seeming to shrink into his chair. Happy Boy swung his bulky form toward me and stood close by, sweating, looking down on me, his eyes aimed with threat.

"You really shouldn't be around here anymore," he breathed. "We don't have anything for you. Isn't that right, Hab?" he added loudly.

Bahamian shrugged to cover a flinch, obviously wishing he were home watching videos of spaghetti westerns. He looked nervous, flimsy.

"Really?" I asked, submitting at last to the demands of the moment. "No place for me in an organization where inferiors routinely fail upwards? No slot for another pushy, cronied-up ambitious failure?"

"Just write the fucking thing up, sign it and get the hell out," Happy Boy growled.

I was cornered. And whether I had in fact cornered myself or had simply played out a hand whose cards offered little or no other conclusion was beside the point. I had arrived in the corner and it was time to do as Happy Boy demanded: Get out. There was no other option.

I smiled good-naturedly, winked at Bahamian and shook my head. "Crane, Crane, Crane. You do realize that I have to tell you to go fuck your apology as well as yourself in the bargain. I mean, you're *perfectly* aware that that's really what you're compelling me to do––that this meeting was all one big goad. There's no need for me to apologize for anything and you know it."

Bahamian swiveled his chair away, tucked his knees under his desk and began clicking his keys, looking studiously at his monitor. Happy Boy backed me out of the room with his superior bulk, edging close to me to press a physical confrontation. I could feel his belt buckle.

"You're out of here, Patetick." He clapped his hands loudly and Bahamian jumped.

"Well, that's why you called me in, isn't it? Oh, that's right. You had to have somebody else do that."

"Good*bye*, Patetick!" He picked up the phone and uttered those immortal words that every freelancer lives to hear: "Hello—Security?"

I had adrenaline bravura left: "Next time, Happy Boy, it won't be an ambush!" I apparently caused one or two peeking heads to emerge from behind hutches and cubicle walls when I said this.

His last words: "If there *is* a next time, it won't have to be *Patetick*."

Last-word freak, I thought, biting my tongue, letting him have his final threat. I'd fix the fucker soon enough.

That stopped me in my tracks just before security came. How positively *dominant.*

More laughter in my head as I moved on.

The pimply, blue-clad, chubby boys of security were striding perhaps several lengths behind me as I made my way out to the car, where Ms. Right was waiting. She threw her book down to the seat and twinkled large green eyes brightly at me as I got in. Her embrace was as light as that of a bird enfolding its wings about me. "How'd it go?" Her voice was breathlessly expectant. She was hoping to hear news of a job, a raise, a title—*anything.*

"Great," I said. "Everything's on track."

Her features fell slack and her eyes glazed over as she pulled the car out of the lot and back onto the highway. Then she said quietly, as much to herself as to me, "Somehow I knew it would be."

I laughed, but it fell flat.

THIRTEEN

The Miltown summer weather had become a clear, sunny and oppressively cheery as the normally cloistered Miltown inhabitants were filled with a dim gray stiffness. In the glowing heat, it seemed everyone was suffering a luxuriance of weather normally marked by storms and indecisive overcast.

So I wasn't surprised that our romance—and it was purely that, a romance, perhaps in the strictest of senses, a far-fetched fantasy of ethereal luster—should be sealed with a death.

The heat was already suffusing our apartment with a palpable haze and Ms. Right was busying herself about the place in oversized white Bermuda shorts and Hawaiian shirt to summerize our environment. She was on a household cleaning frenzy, raising up gouts of dust and the staccato racket of finicky personal industry, which caused me to shut my door in an effort to focus on the usual morning task—finding a way to find work. I was pushing back the morning fog, knocking back cup two of coffee and facing my desk of prospects.

I was recovering from two days of lethargic depression, where all I could do was loll in bed, take expired headache medication and call Karenina obsessively, only to hang up on Bennie's cheerily phony greeting. I admit I did get something out of cutting off that artificially affable voice. I rubbed my eyes to clear my aching head and was contemplating getting cup three of coffee.

The phone rang—and it was Karenina, sniffling.

"Are you all right?"

"No." More sniffling.

"What happened. Did the huz get rough?"

"Him? I'd clean his clock. He's no match for me."

"Then what—"

"Hedda's in the hospital—she's going to die."

I mussed my hair and ran my hand across my face in an effort to court clarity.

"Who's Hedda?" I had to ask.

"Don't you remember? She's part of my submissive women's group? You met her at one of the munches? She's Ally's wife."

"Ally." I repeated and wracked my brain, trying to concentrate amid Ms. Right's banging on the wall. "Alistaire. The Englishman. The down-at-the-heels, sad-sack Englishman. He ran his submissive wife as a pro-dom sex worker to make the rent."

"Harsh, unforgiving and totally you to say so."

"That's a shame. I sort of like him. He's depressed, disillusioned and wry with black humor, sparing no one and nothing. Not even himself." This was true and a little of him went a long way because of it. His unacknowledged despair was a steady vacuum that made it hard to physically breathe. He was like the little cartoon character Droopy—a dog whose very physique was dragged down to the earth by the gravity of his comic depression. He had been physically shaped by it.

"He's a bad man, he treated her badly, cruelly. He humiliated her, calling her an old woman, comparing her to the young things at the club and trying to take them home, threatening to make her walk home."

"Don't tell me," I said. "She loved it."

"I suppose she did. But it made her miserable. She was an artist, an intellectual, a novelist—"

"And he was an engineer and a bad sci-fi writer. Both so poor she had to be tricked out to support them both."

"She loved doing it for him."

"And it killed her."

"Not yet, my love. But probably soon. Meet me at the hardware store?"

"Fifteen minutes," I said.

I didn't fashion a lie for Ms. Right. She was glad to see me go, as I was in the way of her cleaning. She looked dowdy and severe in her tidying, rushing back and forth between rooms, refusing to miss any calls from advertisers as well as any areas of dust in the gain. Ms. Right only had to observe that I needed light and air and that the dust was bad for me—so my getting out was as approved of and ignored as my presence. In my skimpy thin bluegrass, tee-shirt and threadbare jeans, I was hit by the warm blast of the day like a warming slap of hope that mocked and teased.

Karenina was waiting for me in the gleaming haze mere blocks away, leering at me through her sunglasses with her snaggletoothed grin. Members of Karenina's submissive women's group were visiting Hedda in shifts, so we were bound to be in a group at this time of day. Hedda was in the ICU at St. Anselm's Mercy, curtained off in a little ward, writhing, seeming to be only asleep and struggling to wake from a bad dream with a quart or so of bloody fluid that had been drained off from her brain suspended by her bed. Two fat frizzy-haired S&M witches hovered over her bed in cheap-appearing black lace, one of them cooling Hedda's unfeeling brow with a wet washcloth.

"I think she's rallying," said witch one.

"You must be right," said witch two.

Karenina rushed over and placed a teary kiss on Hedda's cheek. Hedda's expression was filled with unrest, her brow furrowed, her closed eyes unnaturally placid. "I think she may—she looks like she wants to open her eyes."

All I had to do was look at the bag of fluid drained off her brain to know she was already dead.

Sun streamed in from a carelessly curtained window and made the blood-streaked bag of fluid glint like a jewel.

I looked into her face. I recognized it. She was the ditzy, frilly-dressed matron in the wide-brimmed hat I thought ridiculous—a somewhat pretentious anglophilic funny-aunt type wearing a daisy-festooned pinafore I had briefly chatted with about Thomas Hardy. One of those perhaps lesbian adulator/emulators of Gertrude Stein, hoping for prestige and appreciation without the privilege necessary to secure it. She spoke with an English accent that bore heavy overtones of Lancaster, Pennsylvania, wearing granny glasses, her once flaming-red hair dyed black and worn in a spinsterish bun.

Writhing in bed, fighting for a consciousness which perhaps already fled, her body adjusting to a total absence of mind and approximating its own death throes. It should have been sad, but a was, seemed just another set piece in my own drama, ascent, decline, whatever. I wished I had known her, but I hadn't.

I wished she would live, but I knew that wouldn't happen either.

"Where's the fucking bastard?" asked witch two.

"Licking his wounds, going through the mounting bills and inventorying her possessions for sale," witch one replied.

"Pro-dom mistresses lack for health benefits," I murmured but went unheard.

"I saw him this morning," Karenina confessed, her dog like eyes nearly spilling over onto the face of her nearly dead friend.

After all the hugs goodbye—or I should say the women hugged while I just stood there watching Hedda hopelessly squirm—Karenina and I rode off in her car with time on our hands, always dangerous. "Ally taking this well?" I asked.

"Sure. He was feeling well enough to try to force himself on me this morning."

My back stiffened. "Did he—?"

"Nah." She waved her hand. "He's not strong enough. He tried to push me down to his knees. Pathetic. I did let him spank me though—but I wouldn't let him until he put his little weenie away. He's fairly brutal, but thankfully as weak as a kitten."

"You're all right then?"

"Of course I am. It put me in sub space pretty quickly." Sub space was the mindset of proper sexual submission that allowed the most extreme acts to be committed upon a person to wilder screams and paroxysms of pleasure than could be arrived at though normal channels of tenderness. It was a pun of the science-fiction nerds, geeks and conventioneers who overflowed into the ranks of the polymorphous-perverse remnant-hippie contingent of S&M. Ally had been one of them, writing long, incomprehensible novels about multidimensional bondage and artificial intelligence as an implement of torture all neatly inflicted almost exclusively upon young female lieutenants in panties. A lot happened in Ally's alternate worlds of subspace. The term had taken hold as a standard, at least in the Miltown region.

"So he's not too broken up."

"Oh, he's destroyed. I can't believe he's able to keep from breaking down and blubbering, or whining mournfully. He loved her, depended on her. Now his life has been cracked open with everything running out of it like an egg and he can't stop the flow. But Ally is *all* stiff upper lip. All acid self-depreciation and wit at his own expense."

"Deprecation," I said without thinking.

"It's the huz," she said. "All his gutter-rat attempts to sound more educated than he is have rubbed off on me."

"Would you have fucked him if you didn't know me?"

"Of course not."

"And where are we going now on this day so wild with sunshine, fresh air and abandon?"

"Do you love me?"

"We've said that word—yes I believe I think I almost *want* to believe." I didn't know how to put it anymore. My understanding of love had been so raked over, roughed up, deranged.

"And I believe I love you, Perry."

We soul-kissed vibrantly even as she drove the Mercedes wagon about the narrow cowpaths and conflicting one-way streets of the Westminster section of Miltown in circles, navigating by instinct and running at least one or two other vehicles onto the shoulder of the road that I could see out of the corner of my eye. Our lips parted and a modicum of safety returned.

"If you really love me, Perry, then I have something to show you."

She parked the car in front of sprawling, ancient Edwardian house just blocks away from St. Anselm's Mercy. "We didn't get very far, did we."

"Depends on what you mean," she said.

"Whose old house?"

We went up the path. "Guess," she said.

I didn't have to. Ponderous and slovenly as always, "O" opened the door. She clapped her hands together and enthused: "Oh, you brought Propertius! Is he going to watch?"

"I hope so," Karenina said, then fell into the flaccid, withered arms of Warner Cousins, "Tutor," embroiled in a lascivious kiss, an exaggerated tongue-to-tongue.

Turning his face from Karenina, Tutor brightened his normally sour expression and beamed at me, holding her off balance, spitting: "Prop—always good to see you."

"And you, Warner. You seem to be popping up more and more places I go. You're getting to be as ubiquitous as Mistress Athena."

"Don't even mention me in the same breath with that fraudulent fuck-up! As Karenina will tell you, I'm the *real thing!* I brought you into it all, didn't I?"

"If not for you, I don't know where I'd be," Karenina said, giving me a wink.

We went upstairs to the second floor. There was a third floor that had been rented off to a bickering pagan married couple—the Farmers—continually fighting over which sex-magick ritual to attend apart from one another. This was made clear, as we could hear them fighting as we passed the door to the shallow stairs that led to the sort of cramped, shabby overstuffed rooms I could only guess at. Karenina observed this and that "O" was the house's actual owner. Warner—not surprisingly—was there at some sort of subservient sexual sufferance. How she suffered him, I'll never know.

Opposite the quarreling pagans' door was a room—a very plain room—with exposed wood ceiling beams, windows without blinds, uncarpeted hardwood floors; a smallish room with a high ceiling. The sort of room a student might rent as interim lodgings before either assembling or joining a collective household. The room bespoke Miltown as the house bespoke New England: all antiquity and crabbed smallness, crafted and exact.

It echoed.

As if in some grotesque ballet, a gross example of surrealism minus Diaghilev, Cousins and "O" stripped Karenina bare as she wriggled and stepped out of her jersey with no sure sign of obeisance. They began behaving somewhat coldly, with grim expressions dragging down their already-tired faces. Karenina, on the other hand, was good-humored and excited, chattering away as they hoisted her up by one compact thigh each and put her in a cloth-banded seat suspended by common links of chain from eyebolts in the ceiling to the side. They cuffed her in, blindfolded, her smile as wide and snaggletoothed as I had ever seen it. "Isn't this just over the top, Prop?"

I had no time to consider a real reply to "over the top," watching a droplet of drool sail down to Karenina's white shoulder from a long glistening strand originating from the upper portion of Tutor's discolored, whitish beard. "It certainly seems to be," I managed to say, watching her struggle, Cousins and "O" both sweating to keep her bound and in tow. "Shut up—she's in her head space now!" said Tutor.

From what I could see, Karenina was chatting away glibly, making blind efforts to kick "O" in the face and clawing at Tutor's mossy beard.

All I could do was stand and watch dumbly the half-naked Tutor slapping, pinching and prodding the woman I loved as the slatternly "O" bit and caressed her, rolls of fat and barely recognizable breasts flopping freely. Tutor was like some mythic gnome laboring at an oven, rubbing his hands together with glee and fidgeting as he applied a back-massager to Karenina's sex. My girl squirmed and squealed, shrieking refusals, but no safe word that I could detect. The air hung with the misty scent of her sweat. My empty stomach churned and twisted in on itself.

It was a hellish thing to watch—those ugly, sneering sex fiends working on my baby. Getting their spittle on her skin, making her intimate with the rotted odor of their degenerating pheromones, forcing the fetid taste of their self-besotted kisses on her tormented lips. I was dizzy with the vision.

My hopes and dreams were at the mercy of these unkempt geriatrics whose aimless lust and personality defects made an effort to swallow anything worthwhile in their path. I focused my will on suppressing the urge to vomit. Then Tutor turned his rich and porcine belly toward me and with a leer asked the following directly to me, headspace or no, loud and clear above Karenina's ungagged protestations: "Propertius—will you go over to that chest by the wall and get me a dildo?"

"Sure," my voice cracked.

"And make it a *moist* one!"

My disgust turned to laughter inside me. His horn-rimmed glasses, his ridiculous spittle-flecked leer, his elfin attitude hunched over my squealing future mate as if she were a little oven—it was all too absurd. "Get me a dildo!" I walked over to the chest to do so, slightly bent, as my insides were now cramped with suppressed laughter.

Sure enough, there was a Ziploc bag filled with rubber, prelubricated dildoes of varying sizes. I tossed Tutor the bag, which he nearly missed catching. He fumbled, then gave me an audible snarl.

I should have handed it to him.

I walked back over and waited for the pain to subside, holding the nausea at bay.

At long last, Karenina came, making a shrill, childish sound and holding it like the note from an aria. That signaled the end of the scene. When I moved forward to help her down, Tutor simultaneously stamped his foot and held up his hand "no."

Tutor and "O" made a sandwich of themselves with Karenina the meat between. Inexplicably to me, she seemed to love it. With the graceless nonchalance of firefighters suiting up in a locker room, they dressed, kicked legs into pants, chatting discordantly. They commented on their scene with the thuggish elan of Sunday suburban sportsmen analyzing a sanitized pickup game of basketball, with a great deal of self-congratulation and complacency that skirted lingering doubt.

The goodbyes—at least on my end—were cool and perfunctory, although it appeared even to Karenina that we had just been hurried out.

Back in the car, on what should have been an aimless drive but which instead pointedly deposited me back in front of the mom-and-pop hardware store, Karenina asked the fatal question: "What do you think?"

"You mean of the scene?"

"I mean of *my* scene."

"Well, to tell you the truth, I was a little taken aback."

She chuckled with a bit of smugness. "I wouldn't have expected anything less."

"I won't lie this time, since what we're doing has already made a magnificent liar out of me."

"Weren't you one already?" she asked with what I then took to be forced innocence, but which could just as easily have been a force of innocence.

"All survivors are, I suppose."

"I don't lie," said Karenina, believing every word of that statement.

"What do you call what you do with the huz?"

"Playing for time."

"What do you tell him?"

"Stories he wants to believe because he hasn't the courage to face anything. Not the D/s we've tried to do after he dangled it in front of me to get me to marry him."

"But not lies."

"Never lies."

"No lie: it disgusted me, that scene."

The clouds were coming, predictably enough—if there was anything at all predictable about Miltown weather—as was the trickle of her tears.

"You want to hurt me."

"No. You wanted to know. I had a hard time with it. I knew I would. It was just unbearable to watch them doing to you what they did—and I find them both so physically if not personally revolting. But I'd do it again for you. I'd do it for us just to have no illusions about it, if that's the direction you want to be heading sexually. I hated seeing it, but I *needed* to see it."

Her eyes were still teary, but her cheeks were now flush and her lips had softened with passion.

"You love me?" she asked, half mocking innocence, half pursuing it.

"Like no one else," I said—yet another disconcerting truth told.

We shared a hot, wet embrace as the summer shower bombarded the Mercedes. We kissed and sniffed in the high and breathless emotions of teenagers. Then I burst out into the storm from the passenger side, running away from her and looking back toward her.

"Separation anxiety!" I shouted.

"I know," she shouted back as I disappeared around the corner behind the oil trucks. "My kids have it!"

When I opened the door to the stairwell of the apartment, wet and breathing hard with excitement, Ms. Right was standing there waiting for me.

THINGS WERE BEGINNING TO GO BADLY. SO, AS IT HAD ALWAYS seemed when things were at their absolute worst, there had to be a party. I let Ms. Right know coolly that I was going off to another Fetish Friday at the Roi, to which she responded with sad indifference. If Ms. Right was worried about what I was doing, she didn't show it. She had accepted my Friday nights out as her chance to reel me in with extra lengths of rope, yet taking enough time for herself to do those sensitive feminine things I wouldn't share with her, enjoying the quietude of well-marketed feminine bunk. Ms. Right was as secure in our impending marriage as she was in anything, which was to say comfortably nervous, ever watchful and suspicious.

It was an eerie feeling to live together in the wake of love, the deadness plain between us, yet hopeless and vestigial yearnings cementing us together weakly as the ghosts of our feelings for one another drew all heat and light away from our presence.

I packed my backpack with my usual strategic change of gear for the club, which I was aware she knew about. If I had done any less, her suspicions would have raised a delaying argument. And we couldn't have that. *Not tonight.*

Her loveseat was right by the door, on which she was already *in situ*, huddled in for the night, the trailers for other romantic and soul-searching videos blaring away with sonorous old men and husky-voiced women reading off their tantalizing hype. There was no way to avoid final contact before I went out the door—but at that moment, I wanted to avoid her lingering soft kiss and bird-like embrace with all my heart.

I knew Karenina was waiting for me outside in the blue Mercedes.

It was an average parting, but not an average Friday.

Tonight there would be no Roi, but instead a play party at Tutor's house—a big one, to which Karenina had not only been invited but had even overseen some of the set-up of the play stations. And if Karenina had been included, then I would have to be grudgingly invited as well. Why grudgingly? Tutor's imagined scene power base worked on hatred and exclusion. If I was a heterosexual male and neither a toady nor a fool (well, not an *obvious* fool, anyway), then I was to be excluded from the Tutor events that "O" paid for, put together and generally would oversee. There would simply be no advantage to having me there and every appearance of my being a threat, as Tutor was in fact a fearful little man. Of course, this was outweighed by my connection to Karenina.

Fearful as Tutor was, he had no fear greater than that of losing his meat, having little means of attracting more to him other than his aged pretense of being a teacher. Therefore, I had to go.

This would be our first party together—yet another rung on the D/s ladder to the hallowed permanent lifestyle of 24/7 D/s.

There she was, in the dark under the light by the hardware store, her face devoid of make-up, with that snaggledtoothed smile at its widest as she leaned out her window and greeted me. We kissed a kiss that was as alive as the one I shared with Ms. Right just moments ago was dead. She drove off in the wrong lane at first, breaking all speed laws to get to that party ahead of everyone else and it seemed like moments before we were already passing by St. Anselms's Mercy where Hedda lay struggling with her coma.

"She's going to die," Karenina sighed.

"How do you know? She was fighting pretty hard to come back when we saw her."

"I just feel it. I have a dead feeling about her. I think of her and all I feel is cold emptiness. I'm clairvoyant you know."

"You told me. You're probably right. People just don't come back from having their brains flooded out with blood. That bag of fluid beside her was drained out of her skull. How did it happen, anyway?"

Karenina pulled the car into the last spot in Tutor's driveway, blocking several cars in for the night. "They're not going anywhere anyway." She turned to me and said without humor. "She had a headache and it killed her. Her headache's name was Ally."

"So he killed her?"

"As surely as if her had beaten her to death—which he probably did, being as vicious as he was with her. He beat her emotionally. He humiliated her, tricked her out to other men, lived off her, rejected her—"

"So he was a successful male dominant?"

A smile flashed across her face. "At times I think it's a very good thing that you're just submissive, Propertius."

We did the lovers' rocking embrace again and I lugged her bags out of the car and up the path to the Tutor's vestibule. She had brought every toy and sexual device she had ever owned, that we had, in our Friday outings, secretly acquired together. It was all there and the weight of it nearly broke my back.

A piece of typing paper taped to one of the French doors read crudely: "Thataway." A scrawled arrow pointed the way. I ignored it and entered the doors normally, stepping into a great, *grand guignol* of ugliness so casual and vast it made me gasp.

I dropped the bags in the front room where a fire was roaring, which wasn't so ludicrous taking into account the various states of undress that the figures who lounged on the furniture or lay sprawled on the floor were in. Tutor scowled, but his expression lit up when Karenina followed behind, carrying our last and smallest bag. This little fire-lit setting and its corpulent loungers could have been a scene from the cutting-room floor of Fellini's *Satyricon.* I greeted the sprawled, sweat-speckled players who interrupted their animated conversations to give the comparatively young scene lovers their due. After all—we were living the dream. We were a love couple in a play relationship. We had settled all the issues of who was to do what and to whom, all of which the scene was an eternal hunt for, masqueraded thinly from time to time with bits of politicized consciousness raising, constitutional stumping and power struggles so microcosmic they might as well have been for a world that didn't exist.

The house was well-laid out, at least for such a party. The dining room had been devoted to a buffet of pot-luck food more impressive than the usual equivalent for a local democratic fundraiser or satellite political-action committee, and for the dissemination of rules. These rules were photocopies of a jaggedly laser-printed page whose numbered entries basically amounted to checking with the hosts for any extreme play, honoring the house safeword (the unimaginative "safeword") and obeying the hosts whose word was law that both abrogated and superseded the rules at any time. The downstairs livingroom was outfitted with a spinning wooden St. Andrews (or "X") cross, which was set at an angle so it barely skirted the ceiling. A long, slender, black naugahyde-upholstered table studded with steel eyebolts served as a bondage table parallel to the high, curved stairway that led to the second floor where three rooms served as dungeons—dungeon number one being where I watched Karenina get her fill of Tutor's dildoes just days ago. A futon had been thrown on the floor for recumbent play comfort, and chains were hung by the gambrel window, with plastic stirrups for a suspension rack.

Dungeon number two boasted a wrought-iron bed frame with extra mattresses and add-on tie points, with a wooden gymnastics rack bolted into the wall for various sorts of four-point bondage. A lacquered Japanese screen hid a small futon flanked with pillows and blankets for encounters of a more discreetly intimate nature, safe except from those most prying of eyes. These items were, respectively, the slut bed, the stretching rack and the nest. The slut bed was, according to the rules, a place where if you placed your slut (or yourself) on the bed you were there for the taking by almost whomsoever pleased. Anyone you wished to exclude from working on you could be named on a list, as well as any practices you might find too unseemly to engage in. The stretching rack, well, was to be stretched upon, and the nest was the worst of all. The nest was the one thing, the one place or play station or device of exquisite torment or what have you, that sealed my fate within the scene for keeps.

What about dungeon three? That was the upstairs bathroom— the watersports area, for toilet slaves, showers addicts and coprophages of various types.

Mossman was gorging himself delicately at the social space table, one hand with a cheesy cracker to his mouth, the other hand selecting a morsel from the hot canapé tray as he worked on his usual line of cajolery with Auntie Maim, hoping to get a scene with her. Auntie, meanwhile, surveyed the cramped social room for marriageable prospects, older men who would take care of her, try to dominate her and have a tug-of-war ratio of success with it. She was in a black strapless taffeta in her Audrey Hepburn bob. Tutor and "O" were there regaling incoming guests changing into gear and stowing bags away in a little unkempt room off the social area that served as Tutor's office. After Karenina and I moved our bags from the firelit room of lounging bodies, she snapped a leash on my collar and pulled me close by the ring.

"I have to keep an eye on you to make sure you don't stray," she announced more to the room than to me. For this she in fact received some quieted attention and noises of amusement. She led me on a quick a tour of the available party space wherein we reviewed the options dungeon by dungeon to reveal that there were none for us.

TechnoSlaver was bringing a surprisingly toned and lovely ingenue to her point of erotic surrender on the slut bed. I dwelled on her muscles rippling as she came, succulent with smooth skin made electric by sweat. Her mouth was pouty and Bill had driven the exterior world aside in favor of the beauties of his own field of concentration, however vividly that may have mingled with his fancies.

Rotted-toothed, lisping appliance salesman Pasquale was being done by LadyPain and Floyd in the swing where I had watched Karenina worked on similarly by our hosts. He was writhing in the swing, dappled by black wax as Floyd in a tutu and the ever-rodentine LadyPain tormented him, a dildo routinely squeezed between his inflamed butt cheeks. He was squealing like a girl on a rollercoaster.

Some goddess or other was spanking a man with both palms at once hung in the suspension rack by the window. The air had become acrid with smoke as Karenina lounged to trade comments with Catspaw, a young mother of four going through a second divorce, with a fifth child on the way, and her new dominant, Riley, who had drunk too much and was leaning his considerable weight on his equally hefty submissive. The smoke was coming from an abandoned upstairs kitchenette—"the smoking salon"—which was, not surprisingly, packed more fully than any other room. The tall, older man who was suspended yowled with the landing of each of the goddess' blows, though admittedly she was throwing all her body weight into each strike.

Meandering out to find a place to settle in, we heard shrieking and bellowing a bit more spirited than that belonging to painsex. Apparently another polyamorous D/s couple was hitting the skids and doing their preliminary break-up psychodramatic song and dance. We weren't going to be like that and we couldn't be like that.

We hadn't even gotten together.

We were also of course as one to one another, intuitively attached and desirously intertwined. When our gazes locked, our bodies followed. When our lips kissed, it was as much an effort to consume each other as it was just some symbolic show of affection. As most lovers think, we thought at the time that no kisses ever existed that were as vivid or electric as our own. As most lovers think, we replaced most of our thoughts with dreams.

We injected the waking dream of life, the dull reliance on habitual, consensual illusion, with the superior electricity and vivacious, lustful embrace of our dreams for each other in a widening vista of D/s sexual exploration. Nobody could touch us and everybody could touch us. It was mastery and surrender all at once, both yielding and command.

So we demonstrated it, Karenina doing me for all to see in any and every rack we could find in that dismal house of corpulent, sagging, poorly arrayed flesh. And then the thing happened that always happened. It was why we did it, it was why such gross venues as Tutor and "O" 's were more than tolerated, but were sought out, savored, prized. The world of the ordinary was surmounted by passion and will, the capacious sins and corruption of the flesh, the paltry squabbling, petty playing at personalities, dropped away like a butterfly's discarded chrysalis and the purity of play took flight.

There may have been politicking downstairs. Athena and his horde of clubbers may have been absent. There may have been a Tutor and "O" push to be something more than merely dedicated players in the scene, but all of that was as trivial and beside the point as its progenitors were puffed up with the windy importance of their need to be important somewhere, *anywhere,* making the S&M scene their fragile court of last resort. The paranoid self-interest masked as community interest may have been as rife and bland as your average Greenpeace meeting, but all of that paled and died beneath the mildest of scenes played just a few feet above upstairs.

Somehow—as if by faith, as if by an even more puissant form of ritual magic effected in those makeshift, jerry-rigged dungeon rooms than the continually bickering pagans upstairs had ever hoped to conjure—somehow, overdrive had been reached. The voluptuous intensity of the swinging whips, the flashing blades, wind-whistling canes, had swallowed whole yet simultaneously surmounted every element that could have been considered disgusting, leaving the beautiful pain, the exquisite torment, the absolute focus and control of all erotic force to the exclusion of all else, especially and particularly of death.

The *grand guignol* had been replaced by an *auto da fé.*

My own screaming was a comfort to me. The crowded slut-bed dungeon of players was a confirmation and restraint to be overcome by the power of absorbed sensation, of delicious need to be broken down, unmade and undone, peeled away to my most basic need within an approving group whose understanding acceptance and complete solipsistic indifference was as essential as the scene itself.

A scene within a scene of course, which made the bonds so strong and necessary, which gave us always the poisons of politics and the false grandeur of the self. The poisons spread downstairs in the lecherous honk of Tutor as he strove with usual failure to be charismatic and voluble.

Could I ever hope to explain it, the sporadically fulfilled need that made all life surrounding a coarse dead husk as gray and wretched as the average body of the experienced player? Could Ms. Right snoozing at home on the gold embroidered love seat with her video ever know?

How could I tell her?

How could I leave one life for another and never return to that dead, dull gray dream that passed for consciousness, that substituted for a life?

It all ended in the nest.

Covered with sweat, stripped of our fetish and curled up within the pillows as smooth and concave as an egg, we nestled, without even the merest thought of coition, drunk with intimacy of another kind. "I can't give this up," she whispered stroking my hair as my face burrowed into her shoulder. "I'm not going to give this up."

"Neither am I," I rasped, not knowing anything anymore, past caring beyond what my body could cling to, beyond the freedoms experienced who knows how long ago when I was hanging from my arms crying for mercy and god.

We nuzzled there sleepily until Tutor kicked us out.

FOURTEEN

I should have been working. I should have been working on getting some sort of work before the entirety of my savings were drained. It was another morning, so normal by appearances, so ordinary. I had my coffee. I had my agenda. I had Ms. Right frantic on the phone in the room across the stairwell landing chasing after money from the delinquent subjects of her magazine *Alpha Waves'* aquiferous advertorials.

My phone rang and I felt spoiled with delight that it was Karenina.

"Hedda's dead."

"I'm sorry. When?"

"Days ago—when we were partying."

"She would have wanted us to party."

"I know that. You don't have to tell me that. There'll be a funeral. Sometime tonight at Griselda's farm way out in Wessex. You know Griselda?"

"The whore of Babylon? Of course." Griselda was a tall, russet-haired doyenne of forced femininity who called her sexual choice "a political preference." "She's the lipstick lesbian publisher of *Penis Envy*. A pay pro-domme for older men, soaks vanilla marrieds to pay for the harem out at the farm and the paper and printing costs of her hobby. Maybe blackmail. A lot of people seem to do her expensive favors."

"So you know her?"

"No. You?"

"All I know is that her soft-focus girl-on-girl stuff leaves me cold. And that she hates Ally."

"Well, we won't make that. How could either of us explain it to our significant smothers?"

"Yes—it would sort of push things. Bennie's suspicious."

"As is my girl. But they're always that way."

"Yes. They are. But we aren't ready to tell them yet, are we?"

"No. And we don't have our own plans yet at all—who lives where and with whom."

"Perry, I've thought it out carefully. I've gone over it in my head again and again until I could scream. I don't want to lose my family, my children. And I have no intention of losing you. I will lose Bennie, though. That fucker is always in the way, clinging, whining, bullying. He's an idiot. I am moving forward. I am not going to wait until I'm near dead to get what I want."

"Like Hedda?"

"I learned a lot from her."

"So we're really doing it."

"Yes, we are."

"I'm going to say goodbye to Hedda right now."

"This minute?"

"Well, I have to drop off the kids at Nadia and Bob's, Swansea's answer to the Huffingtons, and then I'm heading off to Trinity Mount Olive. Wanna come?" If a voice could have winked like an eye, that's what hers would have done.

"What else is there that I'd rather do in my life?"

"I knew you'd see it my way."

I don't even think Ms. Right noticed that I left—or if she did, her phone conversation was too urgent to pull away from and deal with my footsteps and the slamming of the screen door right then. She was there, her Mercedes idling. She didn't wait for me to close the door before jerking the car into gear and tearing up the placid traffic of Divinity Ave. as we headed for Trinity Mount Olive. I followed her to the crematorium, a surprisingly pretty, chapel-like building, a sort of charming gingerbread house of death. A cardboard box the size of a coffin lay resting on a catafalque of crates outside the window-sized griffin-worked iron doors where the corpse was to be slid in to burn away.

An unnamable creepy feeling came over me when Karenina told me that the cardboard box was the coffin.

"Say goodbye to Hedda."

"Hedda," I half whispered. "Let's say goodbye like we said hello."

Karenina got teary, approached the box and stroked it, whispering her gratitude and memories that I both couldn't and didn't want to make out. Her tears splashed on the white finish of the cardboard bringing up dust and dirt.

"Why cardboard?" I asked in an effort to change the subject, lighten her mood.

"It's all Ally could afford. Hedda's death ruined him in more ways than one."

"Hospital debt, loss of income, loss of consortium."

"Loss of play," she added. "No one in this scene, will ever have anything to do with him ever again, he was so horrible to her."

"I didn't think Ally was all that bad."

"She worshipped him, served him, doted on him, and how did he repay her? With cruelty and indifference."

"But isn't that what she wanted as a submissive?"

"Yes," she said with glistening eyes. "It is."

"And he obviously loved her. At least it's obvious now."

"Everybody knows he's suffering. Everybody thinks it's just."

"Just. Though he gave her more dominant cruelty and pure D/s than most ever dream of getting."

"You know," she said as if it were her own idea, "I believe the chances are at least good that she may have died happy."

"But that Ally's still a bastard."

"Yes. He is. He loved her too late."

"So what happens now?"

"Ally said it would take about six hours to burn her up completely. Then, tonight, they scatter her all over the waving fields of Wessex."

"She was a scattered person in life, I suppose that's how it should be in death."

Instead of laughing, as I stood rigid, tense and somewhat numb, my Karenina dropped to her knees by the cardboard coffin with a sudden sob and cried so loudly it echoed:

"Oh, Hedda! From your ashes I am to be reborn!"

———

I WAS BEGINNING TO LIVE A LIFE THAT REVOLVED AROUND THE
phone, ever attuned to whether the morning ring might be Karenina, whether she might ring through on Ms. Right's line if mine
was tied up with modern, stalking available and functioning pay
phones everywhere I walked, as I was too poor for a cellular. People could see me on practically every street and corner store in
Trinity, at every atrium and mall, pumping change into pay
phones for a moment of uncluttered communication and to avoid
key charges from popping up on the phone bill, causing the inevitable explanation. I would have put off the inevitable forever, if I
had had the choice.

Meanwhile, Ally had become my best friend—of course I had
yet to meet him.

When I told Ms. Right about the death of Hedda and of Ally's
legendary stiff-upper-lipped refusal to fall apart even as his own life
was unraveling about him, she encouraged my meeting with him to
console him about his loss. By her lights, a distraught Englishman
would make the perfect pal to set me straight, as long as she was
kept from knowing that he had a penchant for whipping women till
they bled. Thanks to Ally, I had my out for meeting Karenina, my
carte blanche to leave at a moment's notice when Ally was either
despondent or freaking out, accounting for both late night and mid-
day forays into the Miltown morass of traffic and smoggy industrial
haze. As long as Karenina's schedule would permit—as long as she
could ditch the huz and find childcare, we could mourn Hedda and
support Ally's preferred lifestyle with the reverence and care dictated
by the circumstances.

We could do legitimate things—couple things.

We could be romantic and dream those sweetly constructed couple dreams made so vivid by the shortness of available time and by
the entanglements that so directly thwarted them. If Ms. Right and
the huz only knew how much they added to the passion of this
horrible, breathtaking love. This love like a nova that was the un-
making and remaking of everything even as it collapsed in on itself
and exploded.

We could walk together holding hands in public.

There was a single moment I recall like some frozen shard pricking my skin that Karenina was too expert in this, too note perfect. Whatever was left of the journalist in me hollered suspicion. I decided that experience certainly counted as much as practice, and that Karenina was nothing if not experienced. I let the rest of what I once was go.

The strategy of love became all.

Karenina became Ally on the phone so Ms. Right barely listened anymore, keeping her shouted interjections through paper-thin walls, her knocking on the door and her rantings as to how I sounded to near nonexistence. She respected death and pain with the same depth as she would laugh at them both in a joke.

We met near Trinity Commons in a Chinese restaurant. I sat at the table and watched her canter in, dressed in a modest black cocktail dress that covered her up to her neck, and sheer black stockings. I quickly learned her joy had more to do with the restaurant than it did with me. She explained that exactly as much as she loved Chinese food was surpassed by the huz's loathing for it. All recognizably ethnic food was an offense against his beloved traditions of prepackaged white bread sandwiches, freeze-dried, frozen convenience foods and cans—all desperately down-market eating that had broken her palate years ago. These were the foods that had made him the splendid man he had turned out to be, the foods he was most familiar with. He would teach Karenina to eat properly, if it took him to retirement, which he hoped would come soon. Though he doubted it would, being essentially pessimistic. Her diet, her culinary and gustatory senses, all had been ruined by subservience to this tyrant of the imposed low standard of cuisine. I listened to all this willingly, even enthusiastically. I wanted to hear, wanted to solve her problems.

I was stupefied with love in Karenina's presence.

She gushed over and gratefully savored every bit of mediocre Cantonese food delivered out of sequence by our surly waitress who had an overbite so extreme her breathing moved napkins about on the table as she wrote our orders. Then Karenina got into it, the plan. "We have to move," she said.

"Literally or figuratively?"

"Both." She grinned that grin which made me know that I was in trouble. Fascinated, I slurped won ton soup as she continued. "You know how I'm in real estate."

"I thought the huz put an end to that."

"No, I did. If he'd of had his way, we'd have gone bust with the market when it did—but it just so happened I was able to drag him out. Besides, you know that real estate never ends. You're never really out of it."

"So, you're getting back into it. That's good. At least one of us will have a career."

She loudly put up a cry for more soup, which at this restaurant hardly seemed out of place. Amid the blustery service, she continued. "Don't worry, we'll do something together. You're my property. I always take care of my property. Who knows?" She winked. "Your writing might even come in handy."

My food was cold, but I ate despite that and the lump in my throat. How could she be so calm and confident? I was a wreck. She took my hand.

"You look after the magic," she said. "I'll take care of the mundane."

"Okay, let's be magical. The next step is we go right from one life into another. We leave in order to enter."

"And tell them both."

"We would have to."

"I live in a quarter-million–dollar home with my children. I am not settling for less than I have. They'll have to live with us, of course. And we'll have to do so in a house—one that's an improvement on the one I live in now."

"Too rich for my blood," I countered.

"No question. But not for mine. And this time our blood runs together. That being the case, I ran the numbers."

"What numbers?"

"The ones that pertain to this little two-family I have my eye on. It's not far from Trinity, yet just at the edge of Sussex County, which means I could keep my kids in the same privileged Swansea school district that they are now. Things will be tight for a while during the divorce—Bennie will fight tooth and nail and try to spend us both down to the last penny."

"He's that stupid?"

"If he can't have it, nobody will. And he knows that without me, he'd be the manager of a retail store somewhere off the highway. He's been trying to send me to work to support him while he stays home with the kids and daydreams about Safety Club."

"Still on the same paragraph, I see?"

"Just where he left off—angry and bitter that I won't write his business plan for him. But let me tell you about *our* business plan." She laid it out right there on the table, jotting numbers down on napkins, her mini pocket calculator trembling beneath her fingertips as if it were my soul.

Karenina's numbers came out solid there on a napkin stained with jasmine tea. She could make the down payment without selling her own disputed house which the divorce would inevitably tie up. With the rent from the apartment below and the mortgage she could structure with her connections at one of the loan clearinghouses out of Texas, we were in business. I'd be paying the same rent I was paying now—but it would all be going into equity.

"Equity," she said. "Isn't that an exciting word?"

"It never has been before."

"Oh, but it is. Think of the freedom and possibility that comes with property ownership. Think of what it will be to be a member of the landed class."

I always harbored the Bakuninesque notion that too much property wound up owning you rather than vice versa, but her eyes were so deep and wide with conviction and purpose, her voice so laden with tender enticement, how could I protest on behalf of some half-hearted worn out scholastic politics not upgraded since my junior year at the hellhole that only recently had stopped garnishing my wages? I was still trying to resolve in my mind how Karenina could be an ardent anarchist, member of the temple sisterhood and Block Beautification chairperson.

"Once you own property, you wind up owning more and your credit increases. You can flip one house into another and then two and then several more, since real estate values always increase, even when they seem not to—they just do it more slowly then. Soon, you have all your property producing for you and all you do is manage it. I'll show you how. And there are always other benefits."

"Such as?" I asked, suppressing tremors deep in the thick of my heightened sense of unreality.

"Dungeon space, of course. As if you didn't know. We could have parties that would make us world-famous in the scene."

My throat was dry. "We could."

She sighed. "So nervous, so submissive. Don't worry. It will all turn out alright."

"Will it?"

We paid the check and walked out onto Morris Place in the back-blast furnace of heat of the still summer evening. It was harsh and dry. I unconsciously rolled up my sleeves and sweat gathered in the fine dark hairs over Karenina's upper lip. I unconsciously allowed my as-yet-unformed suspicions to flit away and ignored some dim echo of good sense fading away in the back of my mind. She pressed against my side and bit my shoulder, holding my flesh with her teeth. The pain quickened my step and hers alongside. She let go slowly, so the pain would increase with the release of pressure on my tissue.

With the taste of endorphins came clarity, comprehension and belief—or something so much like it as to avoid detection altogether.

"It will turn out just right. I promise. Remember: I told you I'm clairvoyant."

"That's right," I said. "And you always make all your dreams come true."

We walked arm in arm in the shadow of the Trinity University chapel as a street guitarist called Archtop belted out grittily "The First Cut Is the Deepest."

She put her lips to my ear and said: "Yours too."

"DO YOU EVER INTEND TO GO BACK TO WORKING FOR A LIVING AGAIN?" asked Ms. Right with lack of both patience and emotion.

I looked up from my truly obsolete machine, my computer,

which seemed to serve more as a sex toy than much of anything else, and smoothly addressed her sarcasm.

"Of course I do. What do you think I spend most of my time doing?"

"I don't know—and I don't know if I want to know. But if you do intend to get back to work and start holding up your end of things again, you better go talk to your old friend Bahamian. He's on the line."

"Where was he when *I* was on the line?" I asked thoughtlessly, knowing the answer already.

"Just go do it. Talk to him. You can always say no, which is what you usually do anyway." She seemed resigned and depressed, but this wasn't out of the ordinary, being that she was at the crest of the *Alpha Waves* ad cycle and in the frenzy of being behind in her onerous quota. I shambled into her office where the receiver lay like a gutted fish amid invoices.

"Et tu, Bahamian?"

"Hey—you ain't no Caesar, pal."

"Why are you calling? You heard Happy Boy. I'm out of it now."

"You could always come down and work in paste-up. You could get off that PC and learn to use a Mac."

"My thing is so old, I don't even know if it's a PC—I think it's a Texas instruments calculator."

"Really? Just like some of the old boys upstairs."

"I imagine that's right, as I seem to recall that we have some Texas rejects in bolo ties that came in on the *Post* conglomerate thing. *Yee*-hah. What do you want?"

"Not to be the cowardly shit my life is turning me into."

"Don't give me that. And don't throw your wife, kids and the guilt thing at me again, either, okay?"

"I'm a senior writer at a local daily: I have no guilt, I have no shame. I cover Arts and Leisure."

"Fine. So what's your angle?"

"I need to do a favor for a friend which luckily may turn into a favor for you. Besides, I hate to be hated. Suppose I need something from you sometime. Well, I'd want you to feel you still owe me."

"This is going to be good."

"You tell me."

"It's excellent-paying grunt work for the agencies of greed. You can literally phone it in. It goes like this . . ." The job was for Chattels and Pelf, a financial reports clearinghouse, on businesses, industries and geopolitics. They were an up-and-corner, a local start-up swallowed recently by Global Fund Watch, which meant they were looking for more personnel to chew up and spit out and more creative and pointless ways to flex their newly developed, capital-rich muscles. They wanted some work-a-drone to sit at home, access a random sampling off all the major wire services of investment-related international news, put it in order, pare it down to the bare essence of investmentese (for which I was to be given a manual of style), code it up for possible printing and then save the work into a waiting queue of similar files for processing into god knows what. Of course I jumped at it and Bahamian relaxed his guard as much as he could.

"I love doing a crony a good turn. Warms the cockles."

"Of what? Your heart?"

"Of course! You wouldn't believe it! We all have hearts around here. That's what makes us the cut-throats we are. We've been hurt. We have frustrated dreams. We live in fear and are too goddamn sensitive."

"You're all just a bunch of Happy Boy wannabes, aren't you?"

"Why you didn't fit in. You just couldn't say *yes* enough times."

"Giving me a job lead doesn't make you any less a coward, you know."

"But you respect me."

"As much as I ever have."

I heard a handclap. "And that's what we're in this business for!"

"I'm not in it anymore, Hab."

"You will be again. You need the abuse. You need to have a clearcut dream that can be taken away from you on a daily basis."

"Everybody needs that, Hab, though I prefer to save it all for my personal life."

"It's better at the *Register*. At least you know where you stand."

"No, Hab. I know where *you* stand."

"That's gratitude."

"Yes: *Register* style."

"Okay, buddy," he said flatly. "Go and call the guy already before I start feeling more pissy than guilty."

I hung up and did exactly that, which gave me a headache, last-word freak that I am.

Within the hour I was down at the Miltown docks unshaven in my shorts, scouting out the rehabbed location of the new financial-reporting powerhouse. After weaving my way through the sooty brick warehouse fronts that masked immaculate glass and chromium electronically secure lobbies, I wound up in a cubicle among thousands of square feet of cubicles in a room like a slow-motion parody of a newsroom as casually dressed workers shambled about with printouts and reams of documents, and filled the air with less-rapid keyclicks of concentration than I was accustomed to. In this cubicle, I sat opposite a ruddy-faced, gaunt overt homosexual dressed just as I was. I was under a wall of photos of boyfriends in tropical settings, and cats. We had a pleasant chat about the weather, shook hands and that was that.

I could have phoned that in too, apparently.

The most important thing was not to save any of the stale wire-dump information into my own computer. Chattels and Pelf would deliver a dumb terminal to my doorstep to ensure this— keyboard, screen and external modem. Just as long as I made no copies of any of the extracted product I was creating. It was proprietary. I was not to use the outdated news abstracts in any way, shape or form after creating them. My hours were my own. I was given what was viewed by my interviewer as a difficult quota. I concurred as to the difficulty when of course it was an easy lob, especially for someone used to hoofing and grinding out four stories a week while close editing at least twice that a day. As long as the quota was met, I was in business. Just drop by, file timesheets, collect the all-essential check.

Corporate job title: Reports Editor

Translation: Electronic File Clerk.

I didn't care. I took it with joy and relief at being able to leave yet another newsroom environment but this time with a continued rather than truncated income. I fairly danced from the building, and though I noticed the bits of clerkish commentary on my oddness escaping from the massive tables of the proofreading division, it only confirmed the reason for my light-hearted mood.

I could take their money and have nothing to do with them.

I blessed Bahamian's cowardice, guilt and cynicism and turned my mind to celebration.

I was a bit too far from the suburban wilds of Swansea for an assignation with Karenina. I resolved to pay an unannounced visit to Dwight DeSeigneur, who would be happy that I now had less need to hit him up for use of his considerable connections. It was still early enough. He'd be home making schmooze calls from that broad desk by the antique paste-up table where I used to slave away getting editions of his local community news rags out when I was dead broke without a lot of options. He'd be conning his way in to some exclusive event that he may have had title to, but no wherewithal to get to go to on his own. He'd be sneaking a cigarette.

Fighting the slant of Breed's Hill, I jogged to his townhouse door with the heavy brass door knocker, pressed the button for the electronic chimes and stood there, sweating and panting from the climb.

Dwight was not glad to see me. He seemed harried, flustered.

"The protocol is to call first, then show up. As usual, you have it backwards."

"You're saying there's no room for the spontaneous here? Invite me in, Dwight. You can watch me have a drink."

Dwight grumbled and complied. Something wasn't quite right about him. There was no acerbic small talk. "I'm an old fart," he said waving me in. "These irregularities don't sit well with me." He was out of the room before I could sit down in my usual chair. He came back with some obscure single malt in the correct wide-mouthed tumbler, water back in a high, thin glass. "My favorite," he said.

"Joining me?"

"Hell no!" He leaned back in his plush leather office chair, his hands around his knees and entered into a long coughing jag, which always seemed longer than it was. "You're drinking for me," Dwight gurgled through sputum and managed within a hack to add on, "Enjoy."

I sipped and noticed Dwight looked a little off. His craggy face was covered with little cuts, as if from a bad shaving job and his hair seemed about to detach from his head at the scalp line.

It hit me that he was wearing a very pricey toupée, grayed precisely, matching exactly his shade of reddish auburn, salted so well it looked just like his own hair—doffed as a cap. He noticed, reached for the baseball cap of the failing local favorite team and turned to face me, composed. "I don't have a lot of time. So drink up and let's get to it. I'm not really on my game today."

"Just a social call, Dwight. I landed a job today, through every fault of my own."

"Cause for celebration, then. Drink."

I did, and was filled with that glimpse of warm overconfidence and authority which would, in substance, forever elude me. I went for more of his whiskey and ignored the water altogether.

"Good," cackled Dwight. "Now, for a dose of reality: Don't do it, kiddo. And don't say, 'Do what?' Just don't."

"You mean throw over the Red Menace in favor of the D/s girl?"

"Just don't. You have a good thing with her. Just do the thing already and move on with your life. You can't stay young forever."

"I see how it's worked for you."

"I'm different—different class, more privilege. I'm allowed."

"Come on, Dwight. I'm allowed to fuck up in grand style just as well as anyone who inherited a comfortable life and squandered it away."

"The rebbetzen is not a ticket to the life you think you want to lead. You don't really know what you want—like your whole generation you're obsessed with novelty, insecure about missing out on things you don't deserve and which are just not that important anyway. Listen to me and dump the broad. Hitch up with the menace. She's right for you, keep you out of trouble." He rumbled in his throat so I could barely hear it: "She loves you."

"Too late for that—I'm moving on, then moving in."

"With her? It's a mistake, you know."

"I think it's that true love thing that everyone talks about."

"True love." Dwight made a face and cleared his throat. "They all talk about it because they don't have it. They find out what a cheap, life-destroying drug it is, find they can't get out of it and so encourage you to get into it to justify their mistake, get validated by the crowd the way they always have. Oh well. Time for my one and only cigarette of the day."

"Saved it for me, did you?"

"I would have if I'd have known you were coming." He lit up some reduced-tar number and it seemed to restore him. "You'll want another drink, of course."

"Of course—but I won't be having one."

"This S&M scene isn't turning you into a stoic, is it?"

I laughed. "No—just a more studied hedonist. But the joke of it all is, I'm in love and we haven't even had sex yet."

"Haven't had sex? You mean normal sex?"

"Yes. You know: the risky, lovey-dovey kind?"

"I've heard of it. So you found some sort of chaste, perfect love who screws you from behind with a dildo after she whips your bony ass?"

"It's an uncanny thing—we have some sort of personal syn-chronicity, some sort of soul connection."

"You're sounding cliché."

"Love is a cliché, but that's what it is."

"The great journalist is a romantic—redeemed by true love. You have truly swallowed some of the foulest refuse of my generation." He was about to cough, but the cigarette repressed it.

"It *is* romantic, almost Victorian—and why should that worry you? You also like the idea of what I've been doing."

"I do. I wish I'd have done it in the first place, gotten into this thing you're into, but it's too late."

"Not really."

"Yes, really," he mocked in a midget's voice. "For a whole host of reasons. But you need to know this." He leaned forward. "You never, *never* fall in love with the other woman, scene or not, and switch your life for her and her demimonde. Never, ever. No matter what! It has never worked then and it wouldn't work now. Don't give me any of this Walter Lippmann shit—I knew people who knew Lippmann and they said his second marriage was even more miserable than the first. And besides, he was a Jewish Machiavelli and you're not."

"I don't think I'm either Jewish or Lippman. I just think I'm in love. We're getting a house together, you know, Karenina and I."

"A house? And how's a semiemployed scholarship boy like you going to afford that?"

"She's in real estate. She has enough property now to get some sort of mortgage. She ran the numbers for me. They seem to be much the same as they are now on my end."

"You think the husband is going to stand for this? Just let you walk in and take what's his—or what he thinks is his?"

"She made all the money, did most of the work. She gave it to him, she can take it away. Besides, he's far from the brightest bulb on the tree."

He shook his head. "You're violating the law."

"Only one? I thought I had at least a few going."

"You know I mean the law of sensible conduct, the law of what's done and what's not."

"You know that's over."

"Is it? Well it shouldn't be." Dwight was getting red-faced. He patted himself unconsciously for his pack of cigarettes, caught himself and stopped. "I want reports," he said.

"Reports?"

"Yes. I want to know just what mishigoss you and the rebbetzen are up to. What kind of *shtupping* you do, who gets spanked, whipped, whatever. I need to make some decisions. I'll want facts."

I licked the rim of the tumbler and felt the warmth, the ancient renewing taste of fine scotch.

Dwight cleared his throat and lifted his rangy form from the chair. He stood over me and sighed, grabbing the empty glass. I felt his hand on my shoulder for the merest of moments before he turned to leave the room.

"I think we both need that other drink," he said.

BRILLIANT SUNLIGHT SHOWED HER EVERY FLAW. HER SMILE WAS BEA-
tific. "Isn't it beautiful?"

It was a big, dull red clapboard house with a clerestory added
on and a two car garage in back I know for a fact Karenina picked
for its dungeon possibilities. She was dressed like a twelve-year-old
girl in cut-offs, cartoon character sneakers and jersey, and sporting
Ray Ban sunglasses. Her six-year-old son, Mike, played in the high
brownish grass of the uncut lawn with one of the Dragon Men action
figures, tossing it up and down as he mumbled to himself, oblivious
to the surrounding adults.

"It's nice," I said.

"You're the first people to see it," the well-browned and cigarette thin real estate dowager announced brightly. "So, are you and
Bennie looking for another rental property? Because I also have a
three-family—"

"I really don't want Bennie hearing about this if it's all the same
to you. We're separated."

The dowager lowered her voice. "Really. I hadn't heard. It
doesn't seem to have gotten around yet."

"This is just between us."

I got goosebumps when she sidled up next to me and placed her
arm thoughtlessly about my waist, mostly from nerves. "And I want
to do another walk-through of the place with you so that I can get
Perry's opinion on everything."

"Really?" One well-plucked eyebrow arched, distorting her crag-
gily tanned face.

"Oh, yes. He'll be living here too."

Mike followed the falling Dragon Man out into the street, lisping
and mumbling at unbelievable speed, capering such that Karenina
had to rush out past the car to drag him back. She fussed over him
and instructed him to stay nearby, which, like most children, he
insisted he had been doing all along. The dowager switched gears
and lulled Karenina into a conspiratorial exchange regarding her own
separation and impending divorce, which appeared to genuinely

shock and take this woman aback. I was un-nerved because Bennie and Ms. Right both knew nothing about this. The dowager was sure to get word back to the hulking, shambling huz.

The dowager kept an eye on the light of Karenina's life while she took me through the rehabbed old colonial. It took me back to the time she did a walk-through of my own place, identifying what could, should and would have been done with each room under her stewardship. She had the entirety of the place planned and accounted for. There was an attic room perfect for an edge-play dungeon. She pushed me over the railing as I looked down at the problematic angle of the stairwell for hauling up equipment, and as I lost my balance she steadied me. "I could do you right here, right now," she said, unzipping my pants.

"You couldn't. Your son is outside."

"I could. He's way downstairs, out on the grass with the dowager, as you call her." She pushed me further back, and I allowed her, feeling an enormous relief in the seizure. She chuckled. "The dowager," she repeated. With a bit of a workmanlike sigh, she forced me to come and directed I do it so I shot drops to the floor. "This is our place," she whispered hot in my ear just before chewing it roughly, causing me to squirm and nearly fall over the railing down the shallow stairwell. "I want to anoint it properly, mark it as ours."

"I'm glad you're not into scat," I said, zipping up.

"So am I," she laughed.

The dowager lowered her voice to a cautionary whisper when we approached her at the end of Karenina's tour. "I hope Bennie's okay with this."

"Why?" asked Karenina.

"Well, you can hardly get the mortgage if he wants to encumber the property in probate, unless the title's solely in your name."

"It won't be a problem. I'm going to get things rolling before he has anything to say about it."

The dowager chuckled and shook her head, making a note on her clipboard. I hardly noticed the cigarette dangling from her mouth. It seemed such a part of her. Mike played intently on the grass with his Dragon Man, unperturbed. He made mouth sound explosions, gun blasts and what could only have been death-ray bursts—which it was nice to note that high-tech had not affected all that much over the years. His lisping obliterated the sense of his whoops and battle cries, so it was impossible to identify the source cartoons. He was hiding assiduously and thoroughly in his play.

"You'll want to submit an offer and get a P and S together. It'll take a few days, then you can start the mortgage application process."

"Sounds about right," Karenina said, dragging her son up from the ground as he struggled, more with the Dragon Man than with her.

"You're sure you both want it?" The dowager was still incredulous.

"Are you sure, Perry? Are you really? With poverty and kids and all?"

"Poverty?"

"Things will be rough for awhile when the huz and I start dissolving things. Lawyers, taxes. They'll be cramped: you, me, two kids and the tenants downstairs who'll help us make the nut."

She fit hard into my body as the dowager nodded with sage detachment, sizing up the validity of this potential sale. "Let's do it," I said, feeling light-years away from the condemned man who also uttered those words. "Let's do it."

Back by the car Karenina introduced me to her son, who shied away by his mother's leg. In protest of having to acknowledge me, he tossed his Dragon Man into the air yet again. I caught it and gave it back to him. "Ice cream now, I think," I said to him, bent over.

This cheered him up and I began—in the tiniest way—to exist in his world as we went around the corner to a premium ice-cream shop chock full of whiz-bang local press reviews of glory framed on the walls. Mike began bumping into me almost as much as he did his mother, communing with Dragon Man and his invisible fellows amid the double-fatted ice cream and languid adult chatter at one of the vacant antique wrought-iron soda-shop tables by the window. He had no way of knowing to what proportions my tiny existence was about to grow in his delicately violent world and how different it would be from all the other monsters that lived there.

He had no way of knowing that as far as monsters went, I left much to be desired. *Then.*

FIFTEEN

On the evening of our ice-cream foray, I was in such happy confusion about the future, I cavalierly asked Ms. Right as she nibbled on supermarket roasted chicken in her heron stance by the sink, if she thought that it was possible for someone to get everything they wanted. "Do you think I'm blessed?" I asked her, swaggering with secret satisfaction, the dream of a life together with Karenina hanging before me as real as the reports I had to process at the dumb terminal to make my quota.

"No," she said chewing. "I think you're riding for a fall, like everybody else."

"You really think so?"

"Of course," she said, perfectly balanced on one leg, "because you're making a fundamental mistake that prevents you from ever being truly happy."

"And what is that, pray tell?"

"Marrying me, of course!"

We both laughed at the same time, but hers lasted longer and ended with the touch of a sob.

"What do you think is going to make your life a happy one? Those friggin' Friday nights of yours?"

"I don't know."

"Well I do! I'm smart, I'm determined, and I *love* you, Perry Patetick—I love you for the person you are, not the one you want to be. It comes down to realities, Perry! No one loves you like I do and no one will ever stand by you the way I will! I won't let go without a fight!"

I stood dumbly, watching her red-faced and holding in tears, refusing to complete the delicate segue from light laughter to profound sadness.

"I'm the only one who's going to make you happy, god damn it! You know that! Admit you know it!"

So much for being "blessed." Another "yes" I just couldn't get my mouth around.

I just stood there, dumb, deserted for the moment by everything but Ms. Right.

That was just before the week to end all weeks.

It was a delicious confluence of circumstances, a scheduling gap of absurd opportunity we simply just had to take. Ms Right was driving upstate to Chichester to oversee the printing of the latest *Alpha Waves* at a new, cut-rate printer. And it was Mother's Day weekend, the day in question falling on a Saturday. What did Karenina want from husband and children for Mother's Day? Why a very long weekend, thank you very much—with me.

She had arranged for the huz and Mike and little Christa to stay with neighbors on the Cape. The neighbors—two Mussulman Turks who owned a chain of delis in the Ripon slums of Miltown—would be delighted to put them up and take them out on their twenty-foot sloop *Gratis* (a great temptation for the huz, who took items and services he didn't want as a rule so long as they were free), the catch being that she would stay home and reflect, gain great, renewing epiphanies of inner peace and introspection, undisturbed. The huz bullied and fumed, insisted she come along to help with the kids, but the damage had been done. He couldn't resist the free weekend under solicitous neighborly care and a chance to appear the hero to his children; taking them around in a boat he had no responsibility for and had no clue about captaining.

Karenina could meditate on the error of her ways, learning to appreciate and miss him during his absence. It was an apparent gift to her which would actually be putting something more in his pocket—a Bennie kind of deal. He bit at it and Karenina, filled with gratitude and solemnity, laughed. Or could barely keep from laughing inwardly, making up for that as she related everything to me while I pumped change into the battered payphone of a nearby strip mall.

After seeing off our respective spouses—after my packing and repacking Ms. Right and double-checking, then triple-checking, ho-

tel arrangements, phone numbers and provisions—Karenina and I
played house at her house for four days straight, or kinky, if you
have to put it that way, because when we played house we played it
D/s style.

We hung from the rafters. Or again, to be more apt, I should
say I did.

All we did for what seemed days on end—a glorious four of
them, sequestered and savored through guile and manipulation, Karenina and me—was to play and engage in attempted sex, something
we hovered over and teased each other about doing, but which we
never did. The delight was so much more in wanting than in having,
the torment so sublime.

I started out chained up in her attic and worked my way down.
Our initial defiling scene in Ms. Right's rooms was nothing compared
to the defilements of Bennie's suburban dreamworld, as every room,
from Christa's still pink and precious nursery to the rough-hewn
crafts tables and sawhorses of the garage was the setting for a scene,
each more intense and gratifying than the last, I had no aperture that
didn't feel insertion with pain, no sexual tendency that didn't find
its nearest gratification in the eagerly accommodating roughfuck behavior of a leather-collared, severe-bustiered mistress in stilettos
swinging toys of delicious abandon, cranking my desire for pleasure
with pain, spinning orgasm after orgasm into a spellbound purgatory
of lust met end to end with pain.

Capering about one morning, naked with coffee and amusement,
dappled (at least me) with red, purple and plumose, smoke-thick
watercolor sunsets of vermilion bruises shot through with a black
plum color, we playfully logged on to the Dreams-Come-True BBS.
Or, rather, she did. I simply preferred to hang naked and watch her
milk the chat lounge for her usual round of adulatory attention.

We telnetted in.

Member Menu (PAIDTOP)
Make   your   selection   (T,H,O,S,E,Q,F,V,R,A,P,C,G,K,J,I,!
B,L,W,? for help, or X to exit):
P

You are in the Main Public Room!
Type "LIST" to see a list of available Rooms.

Manny, "O", Tutor, Big Fat Dick, Daddy-OH and Muffy are here with you.
Just enter "?" if you need any assistance . . .
***
From Manny: Hey Sexy!
From Tutor: Karenina, my playmate—how is your butt?
<WEG>
<WEG>? What's that?
—message sent—
From Tutor <To You>: Wicked Evil Grin of course—I have to update the glossary here sometime. Keep people up to speed.
***
Well, my butt is being pretty good, since it's mostly been playing with Propertius.
—message sent—
From Big Fat Dick <lamenting>: I need a butt to play with . . .
From Manny <To Big Fat Dick>: Play with your own.
From Tutor: That's nice—Propertius needs to be broken in. Glad he's under such a strong hand.
From Tutor (whispered): "O" and I think it's time we got our hands on you again dear.
From Manny: She beat me armwrestling!
From Big Fat Dick <lamenting>: I wish somebody would beat me . . . armwrestling or not . . .
From Manny: Go beat yourself.
/tutor I'm sort of busy with Prop these days.
From Tutor (whispered): What does he matter? I'm talking about playing!!! Remember—I'M your master.
From Manny: How are things going with Prop—you guys seem to be quite the item.
***
Well—he's right here with me, lying naked at my feet.
—message sent—

***

Tutor has left the room.
We've had four days so far of nothing but D/s with—with more in sight!
—message sent—
From Muffy: I'm jealous—Prop's cute. I'd like to take a whack at that bottom.

***

It's been a fuck feast!
—message sent—
From Dicksey Chick: Anyone here want to meet a tall, sensual TV for some real time action?
From Manny: Blow me.
From Dicksey Chick: Me first.
From "O": A fuck feast. You must feel very lucky.

***

We do. I think this is the one. We're going to be together a long time
—message sent—

***

Well, I have some further bonding to do. Or in this case, binding. Bye everyone!
—message sent—
From "O" (whispered): He looks good lying there at your feet?
/"O" Tantalizing!
From "O" (whispered): I figured. . . . You're lucky you know. It's what we all want. The dream.
/"O" The Dream?
From "O" (whispered): Yes! D/s with someone you love! Love, kink, exclusivity, diversity. What we all want! The dream! 24/7—D/s as a life! With someone you LOVE!
/"O" I always live my dreams.
From Big Fat Dick <lamenting>: I want to do some binding!
From Manny: God.
x
Member Menu (PAIDTOP)

Make your selection (T,H,O,S,E,Q,F,V,R,A,P,C,G,K,J,I,!,B,L,W,? for help, or X to exit):

x

Exit

You are about to log off the Dreams-Come-True BBS. Press (y) to terminate your connection, (n) to return to the TOP menu, or (l) to re-log.

y

"You exaggerated," I said as she closed out of the telnet program and logged off the net.

"You think so?"

"Well, we haven't really actually fucked yet."

"Fucked. You mean vanilla sex."

"I mean entry and everything."

"That's next then," she said smirking with approval as we adjourned to the bedroom and instead got so lost in the toys all laid out on the bed that the vanilla convention was simply forgotten.

THE APPOINTED HOUR CAME TO LEAVE AND I SIMPLY DID NOT WANT TO go. We huddled and snuggled on the upstairs attic futon, the only freshly made bed in the house that was clear of the detritus of our play. I nervously checked my watch between smooches and smacks. We were like two teenagers stealing adult kisses well before their time. It was appropriate to think that, as high school was Karenina's favorite time of life just as it had been my most despised.

"You have to go soon," she observed, identifying the problem before I could say it.

"We have to clean up first."

"Don't worry about that—I can get it done in an hour or so without you. I'm a mom, remember?"

"Yes. I hear special powers come with that position."

"Speed-cleaning is one of them. The other is timing. Our only known weakness is school vacations."

No laughter, just kissing.

"Ms. Right could be home now or tomorrow morning. She

wasn't home an hour ago and it's almost two now. Odds are she got stuck at the printer's and crashed out at the hotel before she could call me. Or—"

"She's on her way."

"That could be."

We both scampered up from the bed and quickly dressed. We shared a cup of freshly nuked coffee in the Mercedes on the way to clear our heads, laughing hysterically about the huz, for some reason, calling on a cell-phone from the *Gratis* while I was bent over a sawhorse with a dildo up my ass, a ball-gag in my mouth and all aglow with stripes from a rattan caning that covered my lower thighs to my upper butt. Bennie kept asking if she had learned her lesson.

Karenina had said yes. She was learning more all the time.

Parked discreetly on the corner of my street, the Catholic school looming above us like an abandoned factory, we could see the windows of the apartment were dark and no car in sight in the driveway of the house. "It could go either way," I said.

"Why not just come back with me and risk it? She has to know sooner or later."

"I know. But I'd like to be in control of that—pick the time and place. You wouldn't want Bennie to just find out, would you?"

She chuckled. "He could never do that."

"Sure he could—even he's not that stupid."

"He's just a coward. He couldn't face it. He'd make up any lie to not believe the truth. He's been doing most of my covering up for me. I just lie to make it a little easier on him."

"He's your charity case, isn't he?"

"In a manner of speaking."

"Well Ms. Right isn't mine. I need her to know in some less destructive way than her just finding the evidence or working it out in her head. She's a little detective, you know."

"So you've said."

"She would have called and left a message. She's compulsive like that, needs to dot the I's and cross the T's. I've got to go."

"Whatever you have to do, Perry, is okay."

We kissed. I opened the passenger door to leave.

She grabbed hard at my shirt.

"I want more!" she whispered as if shouting.

I mouthed it so the neighbors wouldn't hear, so Mrs. Tsumash-edshy, who lived on the first floor, wouldn't hear. "Me too. I want more."

She gave me that snaggletoothed smiling leer as she leaned out the passenger door to close it and drove off, her tires squealing.

It wasn't more than ten minutes after I hit bed that I could hear Ms. Right lugging her baggage through the stairwell. I clamped my eyes shut and pretended to have been asleep for hours.

THE WORST DAY CAME DOWN ON ME HARD AND FAST AND CAME OUT OF nowhere. Withoug precipitation, without any grand escalations. It just emerged, like the morning itself, bustling in brightly before all the sleep could be wiped from my eyes. It was less than a week since I had seen Karenina but when I awoke, I was thinking of her and coffee. I stumbled for the coffee in my striped pajamas and found Ms. Right sitting on her loveseat arranging travel folders on our coffee table. It was a brilliant morning, warm and sharp.

I shambled into the living room and started to thoughtlessly put my coffee down.

She slid a plastic coaster beneath the mug before I set it down.

"Getting ready for the trip—my parents' remarriage."

"That's coming up soon, isn't it?"

"Soon? You really don't care about anything or me do you—just that fat suburban S&M bullshit you do on my Friday nights! You don't give a shit!"

"They used to be our Friday nights."

"Lots of things used to be, but we're different now. We aren't in love that way anymore."

It was an oncoming freight train. Rather than sidestep it, I decided to ride.

"How are we in love?"

"Like brother and sister—and the joke of it all is that you're sexually obsessed."

"This isn't the time to talk about it. I haven't even brushed my teeth or dressed." I got up and made my way to the bathroom, feeling tense and desperate inside, miming control where there was none.

"So," she asked coldly, "when are we going to break up?"

I turned, feeling as cold as her question, still tired yet relieved. This was an habitual query she would continually make to force us back together, a painful bit of mind-gaming as annoying as it was repetitious that had long ago lost its poignancy, I decided then and there, feeling a bit ticked in addition to all the layers of my conflicted emotional confusion over which my love for Karenina lay like a thick sheet of ice.

"I think now is as good a time as any."

Her mouth gaped and her green eyes widened. That was the wrong answer. That was not what I was supposed to say. I was supposed to say, "Don't be ridiculous, we'll work it out," or, "Don't talk like that, you know I love you," or the ever-popular "I could never let that happen—you don't have to drop the bomb between us to work out a problem."

But the bomb in fact had to be dropped, and the decimation of its explosion could not be retracted. We were helpless onlookers at the destruction and carnage that kept moving forward, whose force sucked us in, whirled us about, dragged us along to its final conclusion.

"It's not true. You don't really mean it."

"But I do," I said, standing there sagging in my pajamas. "We've been heading here a long time. Now we've arrived."

Why I thought she'd be relieved at our facing a hard truth that had become essential to us and approach it with calm, productive resignation, I'll never know. I was grasping firmly to a control lever that was even more firmly attached to thin air.

She trembled; her hands folded in her lap, feigning composure. "You're serious," she said.

"Of course I am."

"No," she gulped. "You're really serious."

"It's serious between us."

"I didn't mean it. I really didn't. I want us back where we were." Her face was red. She bolted up from the loveseat and ran at me;

nearly knocking me over she grabbed me to stop herself. "No—you don't understand," she shrieked. "I really didn't mean it! I love us! I don't want us to stop!"

"We have to." I peeled her off me, realizing that I could make it through this moment because I felt nothing at all except an urge for comfort of some kind. Any kind. My emotions went on sabbatical, left no forwarding address. Even my love for Karenina was, at the time, analogous to a craving for a certain kind of sandwich—a variation on a physical need one could do without.

My need had become then almost purely intellectual. My future was at hand. I had to grab it, or be forced to take something that would have been so much less. I was oblivious for a moment to Ms. Right's squealing and pummeling at my chest. Her hysteria of crying and pleading brought me back to her and the moment.

"You know we're over. I'm the one admitting it because something else has entered into it for me."

"You mean some*one*, don't you?"

I made for the bathroom. "Why not?"

She paced slow circles about the room, like a descending glider. "It isn't that funny-looking little girl in the sneakers Mrs. Tsumashedshy warned me about, is it? Not that little creature! I won't have it! Mrs. Tsumashedshy said she looked like a young female Winston Churchill."

"No," I lied out of habit. "It isn't her." I closed the bathroom door and took a breath. "And Mrs. Tsumashedshy is an old biddy who doesn't know what she's talking about," I shouted. Something told me to lock the door, which was good because it was only a moment later that I heard Ms. Right's bird-like body thudding against it.

"You aren't leaving me for another woman. You aren't!"

"I am." I ran the water.

More thudding.

"She isn't going to have you! You're mine! I can change! I'm going to be better! I am! I can do it! We'll do the S&M thing! I'll do whatever it takes! You're-not-leaving-meeeeeeeee!" She squalled all of this like a toddler in her terrible twos throwing a tantrum to press against all her parents' limits, thudding herself against the door until I could hear her collapse and slide down against it. She began alternately screaming and crying piteously, "I can change things! I really can!"

I was unmoved.

I felt so calculatingly desperate, I determined that I could afford neither sadness nor empathy and so rejected them both.

There was nothing to say. I waited, shaved, brushed my teeth and then felt an unseen weight lift, an oppression disperse. I detected that the pressure against the door had been removed, then heard hurried, excited footsteps move sharply across the hardwood floors then muffled against the carpeted steps of the stairwell. The outside door slammed and I opened the bathroom door just in time to hear the phone ring.

Karenina.

Or was it Ms. Right from down the street? All I could hear were viciously hiccuping sobs barely able to articulate my name.

No, it was Karenina—and I couldn't make out what she was saying, tangled as it was in a knot of heaving sobs. I got the sense that she needed to meet me right away and the words burst through somehow that this was to be at Skinner Park. She kept repeating, "My family, my children, my family, my children."

I told her to drink some water, take a breath and together we would fix what was wrong.

I was treated to a blast of more of the same. I slammed the phone down and ran to the park, already out of breath, already covered with sweat. She met me there, her face distorted with hysteria and tears, carrying a blanket and clutching it to her body. In the boiling brightness of the day, she met me under the spreading leaves of an oak, staggering and crying like Christa, her eight-month old.

She hadn't told Bennie. The thought of leaving her family suddenly occurred to her to be far too real. The life she had led in Swansea was disappearing before her eyes and she simply could not let go of it, of being a suburban married, of the Block Beautification Project, the temple sisterhood, the strong illusion of belonging to a neighborhood with good neighbors whose fences were so much better than good that she never really got to know them, but for the Mussulman Turks. She couldn't leave the crest of her expensive realty hill in Swansea, dissolve the life that wasn't working and, with its assets, conjure the life that might.

She liked us better as dream than as reality. And who was to say she wasn't right?

Me, of course.

I fought crazily with every Socratic argument I could weave, passionately inveigling her until my voice was hoarse. I recounted our every mad exploit and explicit passion, our irregular and disordered vows and pledges—all the romance that passed between us like a shared blood supply. I wore her down, renewed every experience I could think of that brought us to this point. Then I concluded by asking how happily could her children grow in an environment where it was overt that both parents despised each other? And did she think she could ever hide it so they would never know?

She had to say no.

We embraced and she collapsed into me, clutching her blanket still. The kids had to be shuttled to their play dates and she had some discussions to have with Bennie about their marital state. I posed no argument and walked her back to the Mercedes, unaware of the tantalizingly warm breeze and the pleasant, soothing arboreal fragrance of the summer air. My mind was racing to find some way to make things work. My mind was racing to salvage what was plainly breaking apart.

I had the sense that no matter what I did, there would be no turning back, even though factually and practically it may have been possible. The life that someone who loved me as much as Ms. Right did had in mind for me was something I could no longer bear to think about. No, Karenina and I were moving forward, come what may.

Either I won it all, or I would lose everything. And like every soldier who has marched willingly to battle, accepting the odds, knowing the risks, I felt sure that I would not become a casualty of the events that were about to take place. Yet I already somehow felt a casualty of the future.

Karenina had agreed for us to meet on Saturday morning with the dowager of real estate and make an offer on the house. The future was approaching—I could feel it in every wound I stanched and moved through so as not to feel.

All I had to make it through was two more days!

Two more days!

Striding up Divinity Ave. lost in thought, I walked square into a thick, older man, nearly knocking him over, experiencing the unpleasant heaviness of his body against my own slight frame. Wretched cigar smoke assaulted my nostrils. I looked up—a familiar face.

"You don't have to say excuse me."

"I know you."

"Not very well."

"From the club."

"I'm surprised you recognize me in the cold light of day."

"Nothing cold about it." I wiped the sweat from my forehead.

"Oh, this is Miltown. It's always cold enough. Have you given it up, yet?"

"Given what up?"

"You know." He winked. He was dumpy, large, overdressed in a brown, ill-fitting suit and sickly blue polyester tie. "I sort of pointed the way for you once, remember?"

"Yes. But to answer your question, I'm not giving it up. Not now, not ever. I'm going through with it. I'm going to hold everything together. It's going to happen."

"You seem pretty nervous, hyper. Things not going too well?"

"They've been better—but I can handle it. I'm just in a transition phase."

"They all say that. Well, my advice is to turn back. Fix what you're leaving behind, hold to what you've got."

"What I've got is the future."

He laughed a short laugh like a bark. "Nobody has that. You're mixed up."

I felt a stabbing headache. "Are you for real?" I shouted. "Are you something out of my head? Who the fuck are you?"

"I never said, did I?"

"No. You didn't," I fumed. "So say it now!"

"It's better I don't."

I rubbed my eyes, the sweat trickling down my neck. "Then leave me the hell alone!"

"I may, and I may not."

I tried to walk past him, but he stood in my way.

"Move, fuckhead!"

"Don't get tough with me, Poindexter, you're not equipped."

I was not to be messed with, near trembling, unbalanced with recklessness after the earlier events of the morning. But he was bigger than I was, fat yet solid. I didn't need to add assault to my list of woes at this point.

No, I was too vulnerable, too prone to error. I had to play it smart.

"What do you want?"

"Nothing yet," he said and chuckled, spitting loathsome cigar flecks my way.

"Then get out of my way!" I made a surprise rush and success-fully elbowed my way past him, power-walking home.

I could hear his laughter, long and loud, as I refused to look back and made my way away as fast as I could without breaking into an all-out run. He was having a belly laugh for god knows what reason. I chalked him up to being one of those truly strange and confused creatures that inhabited the less active fringes of the scene and thought no more of it. When I got back, there was no sign of Ms. Right.

In the unexpected moment of peace, I determined to settle my-self into a bit of work so as not to jeopardize my new income stream. I logged on through the dumb terminal only to find out that my high hourly wage depended upon a so-called "bonus quota," which I had not yet made. Therefore, my hourly wage was to be lessened until the quota had been made and sustained for two work shifts.

I was now making less than the average teenaged hamburger handler was at the fast food chain of your choice.

I lay down in the bedroom, which was the coolest room in the house, owing to Ms. Right's insistence that the blinds be drawn to keep the bedspread from becoming sunparched. I lay down on the bed and found myself both unwilling and unable to cry.

Sharp sun bit at the corners of the shades, made impish rhombuses on the opposite wall.

I heard Ms. Right calling my name with forced and artificial happiness from the stairwell as the storm door slammed shut. I clenched my eyes closed so hard that it hurt and refused to answer, aiming for darkness but seeing only red.

I imagined that this was how a condemned man might feel and discovered I was too paralyzed to laugh at myself or at the thought that dispassionately criticized everything, repeating itself over and over in my brain until Ms. Right entered the room and lay down beside me:

"Was any of this really that serious?"

SIXTEEN

I was numb and vibrating in the increasing summer heat and the threatening overcast. I was in a Karenina blackout even as Ms. Right was reaching enlightenment. She asserted it in a frenetic daze. She loved me undyingly and would never, ever quit. Things were going to improve between us, just wait and see. She could do it. She was both committed and determined.

What was I?

Lovestruck? Sucked into D/s as if it were its own separate world, a realm ruled over by dreams, desires and delusions whose regency was avarice and the weak, squabbling behavior of insecure biddies? Somehow, I found this better than any other kind of life.

What was I?

So lovesick over the prospect of a new life I could not properly live the life I was living? So in love with hope, had I mistaken the all-too-human Karenina for that and made her the object of it all?

No.

I shouted "No" out loud walking the street, standing alone in the apartment, browsing books in the second-hand shops that littered the fringes of the university.

No!

It was real and true! Far more so than the sham and shallow love that Ms. Right was giving. Deeper, more trenchant and filled more fully with affirmations of vitality than the sick, codependent hanging-on through weakness Ms. Right was using against me, against us, against the tendency of life to live. It was life denying! I had to get out, before I choked in some eighth-rate compartment where I did not belong.

Like most, I had the bold, daring and entirely unfounded id' that I was so much more than I in fact was.

Two days more. That's all.

I only had to make it to the appointed meeting with Karenina and the dowager of real estate on Saturday morning. The rest would fall into place after that.

Of course, I couldn't work. I couldn't even BBS on Dreams-Come-True without electric shocks of enthusiasm and despair running through me on alternating current. I avoided as much of Ms. Right as I could by combing the streets in direct sun, revisiting old haunts alone, even venturing into old sections of Trinity University that had gone unchanged over the years and wondered where my life had gone.

I was being premature.

It had gone nowhere—yet!

My heart leapt—as it had been doing for days—when I heard the phone ring as I ran up the stairwell. Ms. Right threw her arms around me as I entered the door. I struggled free and made the connection at the sixth ring.

"Hello, darling—this is awkward, as I never call anyone, you know." It was Auntie.

"Yes. I know."

"We've dropped out of one another's lives, it seems."

"This isn't unusual in the scene."

"I'm not calling to ask you back—you were a dreadfully unfaithful little toad."

"What are you calling for?"

"To cry on your shoulder."

"Can we do it over lunch?"

"If you'll buy."

"Mistress—how could I not?"

She laughed. "Oh, so you can now, but you couldn't then—but that's the way of it, isn't it?"

"The way of what, Mistress?"

Her voice trembled: "They never really love you until they've left you."

We met by Vannevar Bush Tech at a Japanese noodle shop ﹍ned Dojo Dojinsm, whose walls were plastered with lacquered comic-book pages. Over soba noodles and soup, I told her about the travails of my new life with Karenina.

"She's a funny-looking one, isn't she?" said Auntie slurping. "But it's obvious she loves you. Of course when love comes into it, it ruins everything."

"How so?"

"It'll destroy your life—human biology does not work in concert with the civilizing desires artificially imposed by society."

"Weighty stuff, Auntie."

"I got it out of a magazine. But it's worked for me. Or hasn't."

"What do you mean?"

"Mountie and I are finished. Over. Done. We broke up."

"Really," I slurped with unconcern. "When?"

"Oh, weeks ago while you were off doing your thing ignoring me as usual."

"I'm sorry."

"He's such a good-for-nothing bastard—he wants everybody but me and I told him that last night."

"Last night?"

"Yes. Oh, of course we're still seeing each other."

"But you're broken up?"

"Absolutely. He's such a pig!"

"So you see him anyway."

"Why not?" she sniffled. "I love the big buffoon and. . . ." She trailed off here and shoved her face in the generous paper napkin supplied by Dojo Dojinsm.

"And," I repeated.

"And I want to keep him close enough to me so I can do him some real damage."

Soon I was into the platitudinous phase that all good comforters face while she cried with lusty abandon, irrespective of the patrons of the Dojo. I kept talking sense, giving advisory reassurance, telling her it wasn't as hopeless as all love tends to be—being so in love myself (and so full of hope!)—and giving her implausible scenarios for the rosy futures that none of us ever really seem to achieve. I fed her all the right lines it was appropriate for her to hear, the simp solutions to problem so hard won they could never be applied because so much emotional effort went into making those problems insoluble.

After a jag of open weeping, she collected herself, replenished her store of tears with slurps of soup and proceeded to dish scene gossip, which I was counting on her to do.

"Athena's on the outs at the club." She had commandeered my soup by now and was daintily digging in. "Mouthed off once too often to that little weasel whatsisname."

"Quinnie," I volunteered.

"Her little partner split for some community college somewhere—took her TV husband with her."

I dimly recalled a night at Ubu Roi where stripped down to a PVC g-string I handed up the rings to the happy couple as the ring bearer while Athena officiated and frat boys in caps cackled. I thought it was all for show—turned out the little teapot had actually married the tall drink of water.

"I thought they were doing the baby thing grunge-style."

"Sure they were—till Lady Daisy May got wind of the fact that Chris O'Beryl's family would give her a tidy sum if they made baby whoosis legitimate."

"One can't blow the horn forever in hopes of a windfall," I said, hungry and anxious, attentive to both my food and her gossip, one going in her mouth, the other streaming out.

"So Virtuosity wants to be queen. So—"

"So Merv wants to buy her the throne."

"Hubby Merv needs to keep his consort busy and happy, and hopefully away from horny boys like you. Which happens to be her preferred type, as you well know, not little pudgy sods with thistly red hair everywhere but where it's supposed to be."

"Virtuosity get her own event yet? Hosting public play parties hoping to cover with the take from the gate?"

"She's a suburban wife and mother in a bedroom community. A Junior League wannabe. Merv's corporate with a Fortune 500 or some other number ranking his company. He can't really afford the ~ual high level of public indifference that we're wont to get. He ~ht get noticed."

"Then how does she plan to run things?"

"Merv shoved some cash into Dreams-Come-True."

"And Athena squandered it all?"

"He's got a good heart, but his head like his finances are both up his nose—and his wazoo."

"This all happened recently?"

"Not really." She did in the last of my soup with a long spoon scouring of the bowl. "That's been happening all along. Just background."

"What now then?"

"Merv and his bitch are taking over the board. They had Grody, their techie cohort, break into Athena's and swipe everything."

"He's pressing charges, Athena?"

"Nah," she waved her hand dismissively and accepted a refill of tea from a demure and boyish waiter. "He's in denial. Talking boyhood scenarios of revenge including flaming bags of shit placed on their doorstep. And apparently Merv has the papers to prove his point. Athena was never too careful about what he signed and who he trusted."

"So they control the board."

"The BBS."

"Maybe the other board too. For now."

"But the BBS does put them out there. What about child safety and corporate appearance for the high-tech exec and his suburban block beautification wife and mother?"

"Oh, they could never risk being that in-your-face about it. They partnered up with someone who could act as the public front. Someone who'd get off on that more than money."

"Someone without a life?" I ventured humorously.

Auntie snickered, seeming relaxed enough to have forgiven me my desertion and subsequently successful (at least in theory) D/s love affair. She took me seriously. "Well, someone whose life is an attempt at a full-time public display of D/s, anyway. A display for those who care."

"Someone without any visible means of support?"

She chuckled dryly, dabbing a soiled napkin at her perfect blood-red-lips, "Or someone whose means of support is screamingly obvious. Someone who has someone who's willing to chuck large sums of money out on maintaining this one's shaky sense of self."

"You're not serious," I asserted, focussing in on Auntie's dry giggle.

"Nothing could be more serious than "Tutor Presents Your Dreams-Cum-True." You haven't logged on lately, have you, darling?"

"No, I haven't."

"You really do need to keep up."

"Yes," I said absently. "I really do."

CHLAMYDIA EMBRACED ME AS I ENTERED THE FETISH-CRAMMED PORtals of cruel and unusual. She was again half-naked in chains.

"Want some Coke?" she asked. The store was empty but for us and the suffering mannequins.

"I don't do that sort of thing. My only drug's at the club and beyond."

"I meant a pop, silly." All at once I detected her Midwestern origins in that single phrase. To hear the bit of Midwest twang in the word "pop" pleased me.

"Sure. That'd be nice."

"I'm having vodka in mine, you know, some in yours?"

"I'll pass."

She shrugged. "Life's just too damn boring to do without a buzz of one kind or another."

"That's what Baudelaire said."

"He used to do security for Quinnie at the Roi, didn't he?"

"I think so," I said, ogling her pale skin, the light hitting her high cheekbones just right, adding to her face a shapely luster that otherwise might not have been there. Her breasts looked conical, pert and firm, braless under her shirtwaist of mail. I couldn't decide if I wanted to bite or lick them more. Since I realized that that would be entirely up to their owner, I opted for neither.

I sweated in the closeness of the barely ventilated shop, watching the crack of her ass appear and disappear among the shadows of the chains as she bent to get the cans of Coke from the minifridge behind the counter, then the cheap pint of vodka from which she added to hers. Despite the fridge, mine was warm. I drank it down greedily despite my usual indifference to soft drinks. It had a coppery after-taste. I made a face.

"Diet," she said. "Tastes better with the vodka."

I waved my hand, killed the can, tossed it.

"Not much new stock," I commented, still erect from her fleshy though strictly social embrace. My worn blue shirt had dark sweat blossoms growing out from under the arms that threatened to meet in the middle and kiss.

"We have some new toys, floggers from Adam in New York, some of Tito's paddles."

I recognized the names—toymakers whose business and pleasure was S&M.

"Really?" She saw my eyes light up and suppressed a smirk.

"Sure. We haven't even taken them out yet. No point. Most of the customers just want to stand and model, shock mom with a spiked collar and a Bettie-Page tee-shirt. Those we have out nice and prominent."

"May I see them?"

"Maybe," she said with the coyness of a high-school cheerleader withholding a view of her breasts from a somewhat less than adroit jock boyfriend.

"If I'm good?" I asked, pressing the button to start the game.

"Where's your little, funny-looking top—the one who replaced me?"

"Karenina? She's, uh, she's . . . working things out at home."

"Got a boyfriend not into the scene, huh?"

"No—a hubby and two kiddies lost somewhere amid the sub-urban sprawl trying to find her way out."

She pouted charmingly, swinging her long stem legs with insou-ciant grace from the stool behind the register. "In for a rough time, I bet."

"Things are under control."

"But are you?"

"Not really."

"But you should be."

"Yes."

"Well, who's going to control you?"

"I have no clue."

Two more days. Two more days.

"You looked like you were asking that question the first time you walked in here."

"I was."

"And it was me then."

"It should have been, but there was no control."

"Yes there was—don't contradict me. I was first, wasn't I?"

I was breathing heavy, sweating more, waiting for the blunt electronic chimes of the door to signal the approach of some unwanted customer Chlamydia was laid out and attired specifically to entice and attract. There were none. "You were, yes."

"First and best."

"The first always is," I lied, not knowing at that moment precisely why. No, I knew. I wanted a scene with her right then and there. I wanted to bite, to suck, to be beaten by firm patient, caring hands. In love with Karenina as I was, I wanted Chlamydia. I had no shame about it and even less care. My strictest goal right then was to manage my breathing in order to prevent light-headedness.

I was in love with the play.

As in love with Karenina as I was, and she with me, we both knew the play was the thing.

I believed with near wholesome idiocy: Our hearts were exclusive, never our D/s.

And I *needed* the D/s so very badly—but *never* as badly as I needed Karenina, I told myself of course, my self-criticism all but slipping away.

She dismounted the high stool with a sigh, strode out from behind the counter and grabbed my shirt collar, towering over me in her heels which she would have without them anyway, at least several inches. "All right you. Let's see whether the dusty old bench still works."

"Right here, right now?" My sweating skin sprouted pinpricks. Yes, yes, my mind pleaded as my throat was stuck.

"Sure. The worst that could happen is that we get someone to come in and buy something—or call the cops, who'll come in and buy something."

I ignored what I thought to be her naïveté.

"Okay," I croaked, and she dragged me up several steps to where the main racks of stretch jeans, PVC minis and leather pants were. In the center of the above floor in the widest row between the racks was a leather covered sawhorse with eyebolts screwed in as anchor points. She pushed me forward, having detected my slight disequilibrium. I went over the top of the sawhorse lengthwise and grabbed its legs tight for support with my hands. Kneeling, Chlamydia clipped cuffs to each eyebolt. She grabbed my hands and feet with tender directness and strength, which put me in the proper mood. She kept turning her back on me, noticing me out of the furthest corner of her eye noticing her lower quarters. She brought her soft, taut inner thigh close enough to my face so that I could just about taste her sex.

She lifted the mail skirt with agonizing slowness.

My sweat was as thick as a fog. Breathing had become something to consider.

Her black satin g-string was damp. Little curly hairs shot out from the sides like tiny ruined springs. "You want this, don't you?"

I was stricken and couldn't speak. The best I could come up with was a clicking sound, a sound one of the African Bushmen or an Aborigine might make.

Two more days. Only two. Two more days.

Things were getting dark—she stood in the way of my vision. No, not stood. She was straddling my head. Her thighs were heavy and powerful about my face. I was urgently erect and restrained, struggling for freedom of movement and the minimum of release necessary to enjoy what was before me, but there was no way I was going to get it. I was to be a pleasureless supplicant. And as I thought that and experienced my own slow wetness, I realized the exquisite tantalizing pleasure of being that way.

"Worship me! Lick and suck now and do so until I tell you to stop."

I was unsure for a moment until I felt the inside of her thigh smack me briskly on the cheek.

"Do it—through the g only!" she shouted.

Her weight on my head felt terrific, the pain in my awkwardly positioned neck, less than bearable, but I did as she bade me with far-reaching alacrity. I nibbled, adding a dimension of my own imagination to the affair, locating her clitoris beneath the satin, positioning it between my teeth, pebble-like in hardness as it had become, and sucked gratefully. She emitted controlled yelps and yips of approval.

She stood stock still, her legs braced against the sides of my head. My life had become completely heady with the overwhelming odor, taste and inner penetration of her perfume. Her g-string had become both soaked and superfluous, yet remained in the way of either of us achieving our own best pleasure, but most importantly prevented me from achieving mine. I worshipped nevertheless with all the more fervor.

Her last yelp was cut short and the pressure about my head became so bad I was forced to relinquish her clit and cry out myself. She stood balanced forward on the balls of her feet, her thighs sweat-sticky, perfumed sweet and pressed hard against me. I felt her tremble, then go slack. The weight was lifted, the pressure relaxed, the now-warm metal skirt slid from my face as Chlamydia moved away and composed herself.

There had been no customers, but I had detected the recorded message for Cruel and Unusual playing once or twice as I was either entering or leaving my moment of submission; I can't remember which, only after what had seemed interminable electronic bleating. She moved behind me, murmuring, "Very good. Verr-rry good," as if she were sizing me up for purchase. I felt a draft just as my head was clearing and I couldn't place where it was affecting me.

Then I could.

She had yanked down my pants.

Before I could protest, she had already begun to spank me wildly, with little regard for the conventions of "the bring-up" or any other of consensuality, for that matter. She must have been right, as I gave in more than willingly—hungrily, abjectly, instantaneously. She let loose with a wooden paddle, peppering my buttocks with slamming blows, dancing about me in her rain or cascade of violent strokes, or I imagined she did, as I couldn't see her. I was just able to vaguely detect her lilting laugh as my body clenched head to toe and made futile, involuntary efforts to buck against the sawhorse.

Then it stopped.

Door chimes.

I could hear her turn and stand in front of me to hide me from the line of sight of whoever it was who ventured in. I was both grateful for the interruption and profoundly disappointed. I could tell it wasn't anybody she felt might have been offended by my lying restrained over a sawhorse with my pants down in the middle of common retail space in the middle of the Miltown afternoon. I could just about get the content of what they were saying over the pulsing in my head, but I was still caught up in the brute sensuality of it, tasting her still around my mouth mixed with the salt of my own tears, which had been streaming down my face profusely as she beat me, despite my joy in the moment.

As they streamed hot into the corners of my mouth, I thought they were sweat, not tasting coppery enough to have been blood.

A hand touched my face gently—a man's hand.

The voice was familiar.

Who was it? I could tell by the lusty, subdued chuckle.

Mossman.

"This is good timing and bad timing, as I see it, fellow surfer."

I forced my dizziness to subside in vain, catching a hint of Chlamydia on the phone to whichever boyfriend might have been paying the rent for that month.

"Why is that?"

Again, the chuckles. "Well, dude, bad for you because I blew your scene with the muffin dominatrix. Good for me though, as my old roommate is back in detox and I need a new one in order to keep my place—and I hear you're about ready to leave home."

Chlamydia nattered on laconically, her voice filled with lilting pleasure void of either conviction of enthusiasm.

I nodded as Bootlicker dutifully and skillfully helped unbuckle the cuffs. Getting over the ache as I straightened up too quickly, I pulled up my jeans equally as fast in a ludicrous gesture of modesty

Two more days. Two more days.

"I'll think about it," I said.
"I knew you would." He patted my ass.

THE GREAT DAY CAME AT LAST. I AWOKE TO BRIGHT SUN, WARM—IF NOT
hot—on my face, my eyelids' red flesh burning the cornea of my
eyes until they filled with the blue skylight flash of day. I lay in bed
half under the sheets drinking in heat and daylight. It was a beautiful
summer morning and the air through the screen of the open window
was moist and tangy with the freshness of the hour and sultry with
the promise of oncoming heat. Birds twittered, distant voices laughed
and shouted, and—thankfully not too close—lawnmowers hummed
away not unpleasantly.

My stomach tightened.

The time.

Had I missed the appointment with the dowager of real estate?

The digits of the clock sharpened to clarity and I realized that
I had two hours and change until the entirety of life changed. I was
exultant, filled with episodic snippet visions of a future life with
Karenina: play in fantastic fetish venues with Karenina, a whirlwind
of business successes and wealth accumulation with Karenina (it
would be a nice by-product of exciting deeds and not the point of
them, of course), and travel, living well with Karenina and the children. The children! As if they were mine. I hadn't even gotten to
know them yet. But I would get to know them. I would. And maybe
I could right some of the wrongs of their actual jackass father.

I dreamed of our space. Our space—a place where we could just
be. A place for play of the mind and body. Someplace apart from
the world belonging only to us. A place that was truly mine, not an
abdication made up of weariness and indifference such as I conceived
the place I had made with Ms. Right to be. A place that would be
mine.

I thought of all my scenes as a cinematic mélange, arranged in
kaleidoscopic counterpoint to one another. I thought of submission
to Karenina and her ownership and masturbated softly. The harsh,
wounded red behind my eyes softened to black.

"Perry?" It was Ms. Right. Her tone of voice was tremulous,

lost. Hollow-eyed and slight in her night shirt, she had the aspect of a little girl who had awoken from a nightmare shambling meekly into her parents' room for safety.

But there was no safety. And the dark swallowed everything up before the goal was reached.

"Perry?" She queried again.

"I'm awake," I said, sounding asleep.

"Are you going to have coffee with me?"

"If you want me to," I sighed.

"It's ready if you want it."

"I do." I roused from the sheets and stretched naked in the sunlight. I caught sight of Ms. Right. She was shaken, vulnerable. Her voice couldn't suppress the trembling beneath it, despite all the apparent effort to do so. Her face held the hallmarks of recent tears and her stance was unsteady.

"Your cup's in the living room," she said, turned and left, adding, "with mine."

I put on my robe and joined her.

We sat looking at one another, entering into an aimless whimsical chat about people in our neighborhood. It was as if everything was as it should have been, as if I had never entered—even in my most hopelessly far-fetched day dreams—into any other kind of life. As we were talking, sharing a laugh at our Welsh neighbor who was forever struggling against his doomed garden, she placed her hand on my thigh and said with delicate firmness: "You're not leaving."

I gulped coffee.

The moment stays with me now as I tell you this. It's fixed and frozen, hanging in all its promise and wrongfulness before my eyes like a defect in my vision brought about by a migraine. I can see it, like a ghostly cobweb I cannot wipe away. The moment hangs about me inextricable from my life—an ethereal fresco or frieze: an icon of my failure.

If there was ever a time that god had forsaken me, that was the moment. That moment and none other.

There she was, the woman steeped in love for me, refusing let me go, willing to forgive me my every hurt, injury and gression against her, willing to make some sort of life with n

I threw her away. I threw her away calmly, without recrimination, without even a second thought. Why would I do such a thing? Why would I chuck away the virtue of a good—albeit flawed—woman who loved me deeply, bitterly, who cared to the depths of her soul whether I lived or died? The answer is simple.

I felt nothing for her.

I held no emotion whatsoever for Ms. Right as she abased herself and pleaded with me not to leave, pleaded with me with everything she had, tossing dignity and decorum out onto the mulch. She let loose entirely focused on me.

I should have felt something.

It was necessary, incumbent upon me after seven years to feel something. I should have felt something. If I could have felt something, anything, some nano-emotion even close to love or pity, I would have stayed. I couldn't have resisted her pain, her utter lovingness and heartbreak in my violation of it. My stubbornness and my resolve would have crumbled as I retreated back into the safety of our lovingly comfortable misery, once so acceptable to me but which I could now no longer stand to think about. I would have surrendered my strength to that great demon, love. I would have because not only was I already in the grimly determined process of surrendering myself to it, but I was surrendering her as well.

I felt no anger toward her, no resentment, no animus. I harbored no grudge—there was nothing of the pent-up anxiety and repressed sense of injustice at last unleashed that characterizes so many broken relationships. I had none of that.

My problem was that the demon Love had placed its hold on me elsewhere.

There was no love left for Ms. Right.

The demon Love had deserted her even as it had chosen me.

And there should have been love for Ms. Right. No one was more deserving.

But in the new dictionary of our time, to morally deserve is to practically do without.

It was at precisely that moment when I needed to love her most I could not love her at all.

ouldn't.

It wasn't within me. If something, if anything, if god would have let me love her I would have. But I couldn't. It was shut off, gone, null and void.

So I made my future:

"But I am leaving," I said.

"Where will you go?"

"Well, I know you love this place, so I'll have to find another."

"You can't afford it."

"I know. I'm going to have to start small." I picked up my coffee and drained the chipped mug dry. Her hand stayed where it was. "In fact, later this morning I'm going to meet with someone who might rent me a nice room not far from here. Right near Swansea."

Ms. Right slammed her mug down on her grandmother's gilt leather-topped table and didn't bother to wipe away the droplets that had spattered out from its mouth. "That's where she lives, isn't it?"

"What difference does that make?"

She shot up from her loveseat as if receiving an electric shock, then marched from the room, hiding her face from me. "She'll never love you the way I do, Perry Patetick!" she shouted. "Never!"

Before our bedroom door slammed I heard her shriek: "She's never going to have you, Perry! Never."

In all of that, I still couldn't bring myself to feel either love or hate. I could muster neither. I calmly had another cup of coffee, dressed and left.

The only feelings I could detect as my face and arms were pleasantly bathed by the incipient heat of the day were mild exasperation, excitement and a longing that matched a sensation of extreme physical fatigue.

When I got to our little house at the edge of Swansea at the appointed time the dowager of real estate was there to give me a practiced, expert warm greeting. She said she was sure that Karenina would be along any minute now. Karenina hated to be late, she assured me, and prided herself on punctuality. The dowager congratulated me again, not only on my excellent choice in future housing, but in future spouses as well. She was firmly in Karenina' corner as far as Bennie went. Bennie was a loathsome creep, an F Trinity gutter rat more suited to conniving ways of receiving

bility checks than functioning as husband, father and provider amid
the complex social strictures and strata of suburban Swansea. She
was sure I would be better choice. After all, it was clear that I had
light-years more education and finesse—and hadn't I been to Trinity? She was certain I was the one for her.

And I drank that in.

Here was a long-standing friend and colleague, a woman of obvious rectitude, coming down squarely on the side of our love, forbidden or not, D/s or not.

I was being endorsed by the dowager of real estate.

Karenina would be here in just a few minutes. Would I care to take another tour of the house?

I walked the place again and—seeing through what I imagined to be Karenina's eyes—found it perfect. My imagination peopled each room with a happy, thriving relationship of true lovers surrounded by the unending exploits of her two irresistibly mischievous children. It was a wild life of corruption mixed with an innocence of hope I viewed in each room, ignoring sconces, cornices, sashes, outlets, molding, heat vents and everything else I should have been responsibly looking for.

It was going to happen! It was actually going to happen! Any minute now she'd come bursting through the aluminum storm door in the summer light, that ragged smile beset with joy, dragging one of her playful little pygmies in tow, and the buying process would begin. It was real. It wasn't just the waking dream I imposed on each room as I walked through. It was real and true.

Real and true—just as a love should be.

Any minute now.

The dowager interrupted my reverie, banishing images of the dark, intimate little scenes Karenina and I would have up in our cozy attic dungeon, shattering the memory as I stood in the precise spot where Karenina had me come. Cigarette smoke followed her like a bitter promise. "I don't know what's keeping her. I put in a call—discreetly of course—but her husband Bennie said he hasn't seen her since early this morning."

"What does that mean?"

The dowager shrugged. She adjusted her oversized, oblonglensed glasses, looked at her watch. "We'll wait a few more minutes, but then I really will have to run. I have a few more houses to show before the day's out." She skipped quickly down the shallow, spiraling stairs. "This really isn't like her," I heard her call back up to me as an expression of concern that sounded a tone of salesmanlike sympathy.

A few more minutes. She'd make it. She had to!

It—was—happening!

It was so close.

And then, of course, nothing happened.

Nothing.

An eternity of nothing, falling upon me like a ballast of sand, knocking me down so hard I could barely stand, all within the space of fifteen minutes.

I sat in front of the house on the overgrown grass for what must have been a long time. I watched the dowager leave in a puff of smoke, exchanging pleasant reassurances with me to minimize my embarrassment just in case a sale could be made at a later date. I was slipped a card and entreated to call her—especially after I heard from Karenina.

She was also concerned.

I must have been there for an hour, working it all through my mind, weighing fear and rage against worry and sadness, breaking it all down in an attempt to calm my agitation.

How could she not show on this most crucial date after a communications blackout of three tortured days?

I concluded that nothing had happened because something had happened.

But I had no way of knowing what.

The walk back to where I (for the moment) lived with Ms. Right from the locus of my (now) uncertain future was a long one and brought me back covered with dry and sticky sweat in the middle of the afternoon. The air was heavy, humid, but something more than the weight of the day was on me, making it hard to move, to breath. I felt pushed down, offering a token resistance against somet' that was slowly crushing me to the ground.

I needed to lie down in a dark room and think.

I no longer had to escape the brightness, however, as the day had lapsed into a muggy, dank miasma of gray. My knees were buckling with every step I took ascending to our apartment. I looked out of our shadeless living-room windows as I resisted the urge to fall down on Ms. Right's loveseat and weep. Why wouldn't it just rain and get it over with, already? Let it happen.

Leaden and trembling, I made it to the bedroom where my wish to lie down in darkness was granted.

I awoke from nullity to the caressing hands of Ms. Right, whispering her love for me, telling me everything would be all right as long as I stayed with her. I shook and focused myself on suppressing that shaking.

The threat of rain still had yet to be realized. All I could hear other than Ms. Right's breathing was the disharmonious crying of birds.

She would take care of me she said. Everything would be fine.

"My room fell through," I mumbled and sighed, more piteously than I would have liked.

"You see?" she said brightly. "You should stay. It's fate."

I was about to speak, but she clapped her hand over my mouth.

"We're not going to talk about it. Today, we're going to relax. It's Saturday. You need to calm down. We're going to have a good day together. You'll see. Then you'll think about staying."

"But—"

"I don't want to hear anything about that funny-looking little bitch, Perry Patetick. Nobody knows you as well as I do. I know what you want and why this is happening. I'm going to save you from yourself and save us." Her eyes were wet.

I tried to speak, but she grabbed my face.

"Don't say it. Don't tell me you're leaving! Not today you aren't."

Her hands descended slowly to the bed.

"I was going to tell you I agree," I said.

"You do?" she asked, surprised.

"Yes," I said. "There's nothing to be done right now. Nothing

"

t exactly. We can do anything you want."

"I don't know what I want."

"I'll help you," she said. "First off, we'll get something to eat."

"You don't like to go out."

"I do now. Then—how about a movie?"

Dinner and a movie. The lost debacle of two years ago now clearly won. And on a Saturday! How could I refuse, though I still felt nothing but a hollow sense of disaster?

I nodded, finding it hard to speak.

She led me from the bedroom by the hand, took me out, grabbing an umbrella on the way while prodding me on to the car. We drove off in the gloom and ate macrobiotic food prepared by a cordon-bleu chef at Lemuria, Trinity's new hot spot. For once, Ms. Right didn't stint on the ordering, having appetizer, main course and even dessert, no doubt helped by the fact that it was all macrobiotic. I barely spoke, much less ate. Ms. Right did all the talking, saying things to make me laugh, being as cute and winning as she could be, which, I admit, was a formidable thing to behold.

I found myself laughing at times, and if not actually feeling warmly toward her, acting as if I did.

It gnawed at the back of my brain that no matter what happened, I simply had to find a pay phone and make the call to Karenina to find out what went wrong. It simply couldn't have been a change of heart and mind, a fickle decision backward. It couldn't, though the pessimist in me felt that it might.

I had to know and I couldn't wait.

Dinner lasted the millennium. Then she suggested, as gloom thudded down to a thick, damp darkness, that we go see a movie. "The air conditioning will feel good to us," she rightly assumed. I murmured my assent. I could see my reticence worried her. Her forced cheery facial expression seemed to have a pall cast over it in between her hastily spoken sentences. I wanted to be chatty, voluble, keep up my end and not make things more difficult for her, but it felt profoundly true to me then that speaking required the supreme effort. Just uttering a few words sent a dull ache that spasmed through me deep as an abyss and as weighty as a cannonball thrown down into it.

To speak just about made me quake with pain.

The line for the movie was a long one. It was the most highly touted and saturation advertised flick of the summer, a movie about public transportation explosions that would occur if one fell below a certain number of miles per hour. It starred former child actors playing adults with a former teen idol now playing a middle-aged madman. It was supposed to be an hour and fifty minutes of safe sensation and approved daydreaming, looking pretty all the time.

I could hardly stand the idea.

I needed a pay phone and the space in which to use it.

We passed one on our way to the theater in the strip-mall parking lot next door.

I had a falsely beatific moment of being bolstered by my cleverness. I excused myself to Ms. Right, expressing the need for fresh air as we stood in the crowded line for tickets. She couldn't help but understand.

I tried to pace myself as I left, wanting to run out explosively into the gravid, sticky night, blasting my footfalls toward the damned pay phone. When I was out of sight of the ticket line, I ran till I was out of breath.

I got to the payphone under a buzzing twenty-foot high streetlamp and fumbled through my wallet for a number. I strained for thought. Calling Karenina at home would be no use. Every call I made during the blackout of the last three days had been answered by the boorishly affable "Hello-oo-o" of the huz. I was unable to get past it and simply hung up each time. As an offhanded precaution during one of our Chinese meals, Karenina had given me the number of Kimmee and Jimmy, a married couple she had described to me as being "cool people," meaning people she trusted, nearly to the point of divulging her D/s passions and practices to them. They were intimates of both her and the huz. I should call them if anything happened.

I considered nothing happening to be just as good a reason.

The number was on the back of one of Karenina's business ards, folded in half and hidden behind a card compartment in my ⅃et as a hedge against Ms. Right's snooping. I took a breath and a soft, luxuriantly feminine voice answered. I introduced myself with a false first name as a friend of Karenina's.

The voice became sharp, defensive.

"I'm a friend," I repeated. "I had a very important appointment with her this morning. She never showed up. I've been trying to call, but her husband has been— shall we say— less than helpful. She had given me your number so maybe I could call in this eventuality. From what I understand, her husband has been quite an obstacle to her getting certain necessary things done."

I heard a sigh and the voice softened again.

"Yes, I suppose that's right," Kimmee said.

"Well I was calling to make sure she was okay," I said, I lied. "I didn't meant to bother you."

"It's no matter," Kimmee said. "You were doing some kind of business with Karen?"

"I don't think I can say."

"I see," Kimmee said sadly. "Then I guess you haven't heard yet."

"Heard what?" I asked with fraudulent coolness.

Then she made me hear.

Then all the weight of the night, of the unfulfilled rain, of the atmosphere of the deadening world fell down on me.

Then I couldn't stand anymore and the earth spun on its axis faster than I could tolerate.

Then I sank down and dropped the receiver, Kimmee's voice buzzing away like a little mosquito until it clicked to the flat wail of a dial tone.

Then I fell to the tar of the parking lot pavement without feeling it.

My head felt crushed, as if it had received a blunt and direct blow—I was as dizzy and nauseated as I would have been upon receiving a concussion. It was too hard to stand.

Then it rained.

Thank god for the rain.

The rain was hot on my hands.

Tears.

The sky, at that point in time, had no interest in crying.

A car drove up beside me—I barely noticed.

Ms. Right found me, shouted at me, shrieked at me wildly, her face turning that famous shade of "Red Menace" red.

The dangling pay phone receiver swung slightly to and fro by my head as I shook and cried, heaving sobs that were likely loud enough to drown even Ms. Right out.

Recognizing this, she stopped her demonstration, pondered my state for a moment, then helped me up into the car, which she had driven round to find me, having abandoned the fast-hit summer movie. With all her strength and several repeated tries, she used leverage to pull me up to a standing position. I leaned against her bird-like frame at every step with my full weight as we both staggered into the car.

"It's all right, baby. Ms. Right said, smoothing my hair and starting the car. "It's going to be all right."

Ms. Right's words were like a foreign language to me. I simply couldn't comprehend them.

Breathing was a struggle.

When I leaned back in the seat the world started to fall very far away.

Kimmee's voice spoke I language I knew.

She had said: "You'll get it all on the news pretty soon, anyway. So I guess I can tell you that she was found very badly beaten up in one of her and her husband's vacant properties earlier today. They hospitalized her, but it was just too much for such a little person to bear."

Too much to bear.

"She passed away a couple of hours ago."

Passed away.

And I went right along there with her.

Then the rain came—or was that just Ms. Right repeatedly punching my arm?

SEVENTEEN

The dismal, gray spiraling down into the gyre that had become my life began and didn't stop.

I was tossed about by it, lying alone in the sweat-dank sheets of my new bed, trying to block it out, trying to distance myself from the persistent imagery. It was a stabbing thing, the recollection at god-knows-what time in the morning. I didn't need to see it, didn't need the ashen dry taste in my mouth, or the burning sting of salty tears.

Violent lurching to a different position in the bed only made it worse.

The moving out was so wrenching, remembering it now makes me feel a physical cramping, as if I were lifting the heavy boxes again all alone.

Or almost.

Ms. Right was there to help me, blue, disconsolate and now apparently cold. I couldn't warm her up, as I had shut down, as the popular phrase goes, and it was true. I was like a machine, after the news, that no longer operated properly and so had to be run only on the most basic level. I became oblivious to the scene. I tried once in the middle of another sleepless night to log on to "Tutor Presents Dreams-Come-True," but I couldn't make it past the clumsily worded formal death notice of long-time member Karenina. A special interest group, or SIG, had been set up to deal with thoughts and feelings about the incident, the first message posted there presumably containing a summary of all available information about the incident, but I couldn't bear to see it.

Just as I was logging off, I was paged by Virtuosity.

The page read: "How are you taking it?"

How was I taking it?

Taking it.

I had no knowledge of how to take it. I had in fact stopped taking it altogether.

Sleeping in a bed of love and mourning with Ms. Right huddled close into me, preparing to leave, feeling nothing for anyone, not even for myself, stuck in a grief so total and overwhelming I was unable to fully experience it. It wasn't long, no, not long at all, before I had left that bed for the convenient discomfort of Bootlicker's apartment.

Ms. Right drove the car with me back and forth as Boot and I hefted boxes up seemingly interminable steps. Her face was wounded, and she seemed to be continually biting her lower lip. Her manner was nervous, her voice, hoarse.

When she hugged me good-bye, she felt limp and insubstantial, like a sick animal unable even to cling for comfort.

Every trip was a tragedy, and she insisted on being the one to make each one of them with me. It was like some sort of grisly duty to her. She could only look upon the squalor of Bootlicker's apartment, shake her head and sigh. Boot persistently lay on the futon couch in what would have been a living room if it hadn't first been converted to a trash bin, half-naked sprawled like some dying form of marine life, surfing through soap operas and game shows. He waved his arm weakly as Ms. Right surveyed the wreckage.

Then the moment came when there were no trips at all to be made anymore.

Ms. Right seemed to be taking it well, and where god had left me before he seemed to be right back with me at last.

I felt nothing.

Nothing.

Only a man who felt as I did could act as I did.

I made that last sweep of what had been our place together with unhurried thoroughness. When I was sure I was all cleaned out, when it was sure that all the years of junk and carefully arrayed sentimentality were gone, I reported the fact to her as she fussed with papers on her leather-topped coffee table, now bereft of my ⁀n mug and clutter. Ms. Right's face suddenly became ashen, ⁀n. Her pale lips faded paler.

"That's it," I said cheerfully.

"What am I going to do?" She asked it as if I weren't meant to hear it.

"Do?"

She ran toward me, then stopped short several feet away and extended her palms out to me. It wasn't a scream or a sob, but a sound much more final and terrible. It was the voice of Love the destroyer, the demon Love speaking right through Ms. Right's possessed and shaken frame, her broken nerves and wounded heart:

"What am I going to do with the love I have for you?!! What am I going to do?"

God was with me though—god or madness.

I was protected. None of it got through to me, none of the moment seemed to register then. I captured it, stored it away, kept it dormant like an incubating virus, like a time bomb, like a rich poison to be slowly absorbed over the years.

"What am I going to do?" She cried beautiful tears.

I did what any man would do who felt nothing.

I turned on my heels and left, saying nothing.

I knew she was looking at me, red-faced, tearful, wrought with sadness. I knew. Therefore, there was no reason to look back, was there?

Go ahead and argue.

Go ahead.

It's too late.

I took the ghost of the moment with me for another time.

I took it with me out the door.

The only thing that really was forever, that dead end.

The drinking crept up on me, like one of the strippers huddling next to me in bed when all that lay between us was our skin and treachery. It seemed, in the most oppressive and brutal summer heat as we edged with thick slow motion toward its finish, that I was gradually and inexorably freezing to death from within. My core burned with unremitting frost and cold. I would pause, think and shiver. I couldn't concentrate on anything, not my revolving bed of sex, not even the happy vapid frenzy of the ever-phlegmatic Boot licker's telesurfing frenzy that dominated our rubbish-heap den

turned blue with inertia and frigidity trying to work as I sat in my
bedroom, vacant but for the desk, dumb terminal and festering bed,
whose sheets I seldom cared to change and which I had long since
given up making up.

Bootlicker and I connived our way into every minimal fetish
night held anywhere in Miltown and environs. Soon, I became the
favorite toy of the bored and inexperienced strippers who wanted to
get their feet wet in S&M, reasoning that it might be good for business. As always, it was too attractive a concept to ignore: abusing
men and getting paid for it. And even though it was well known that
it never, ever worked out that way, I was happily willing and able
to exploit their exploitation of me, keeping up a consistent drunken
buzz to keep me protected against the cold.

The pro dominant women are the most subservient prostitutes
of all, forever trapped in the supposed submissive male image of
themselves, remade by the fantasies of those who would pay to submit to them, giving in to the desires and needs of the sub john, no
matter how loathsome or denigrating. But they would have to learn
that the hard way. So Boot and I sought to teach them, *mentor* them
at their feet the way some would by spanking the bottoms and torturing the nipples of the anxious female submissive neophytes.

Bootlicker, considered a grotesque in his obesity and homemade
harness, was left in the lurch by the strippers, but longing for them
so as he did, it was necessary to blame me. So the rancor may be
traced to my watching him standing dumbfounded by the goth
guards smoking outside the roped off entrance of Ubu Roi as I pulled
away, giving a weak wave from the backseat of a beaten-up station
wagon sprawled across the fragrant, fishnetted legs of the Gen-X
mistresses-in-the-making.

I was to be their practice dummy.

In return, I could drown in the fresh inexperience of their flesh.

Having been elected to serve, I became ashtray, pincushion, torture dildo, feminized boy and—dressed in full latex catsuit that
maxed out my last credit card—piss target for the neophyte strippers. I was like an animal captured by curious children who wanted
ᴐ learn by forcing it to perform. And perform I did. I ate and drank
ir clumsy, ham-fisted dominance and sadism with greed and grat-

itude at their swollen silicone breasts and shaved pubes. I sucked cunt as I was commanded to, bit, licked, laved and slaved. I took it all including plugs up the ass.

I was rewarded by stripper housecalls, which drove Boot crazy, making him crank his TV both to drown me out and announce his displeasure.

They thought I was cute and safe, the strippers, so the lonelier ones, each and every one of them in thrall to the demon Love, came and fucked me one by one.

I was the carnal equivalent of a teddy bear.

But what did it matter? What concerned me was getting it up while drunk, which was a definite performance crippler.

I received a regular six-hour paddling from a 6-foot-6 dominant TV mistress who figured that if she kept that up she'd get lucky and bugger me with the enormous cock she kept persistently whispering to me about every other stroke, licking my ear. This was at the rock club MU, where the management used us as a lit centerpiece on the dance floor while some given local band got their unpaid jollies up on the stage while I got mine suspended in the center with my pants down.

D/s a-go-go.

Bootlicker made it clear to me that we were quits. Not because of my sexual perversity—he envied me that—but because I had utterly violated his twelve-step approach to D/s I had made it a drunken bacchanalia in which I wasn't even doing endorphins anymore, according to him. We were quits. No more surfing on the couch anymore, no more collective proffering of ourselves as submissive objects to the goth rock-groupie girls without a clue—but so desperate for what they mistook as being freakish.

I could stay, because I paid the rent and bills on time.

He managed to elude touching on how I was paying his share.

I laughed, joining in with life at last.

For some unknown reason—perhaps drunkenness—I twisted my ankle as I made my way down to the wharves where Chattels and Pelf loomed large and discreet along the docks. Drunk and limping, disheveled and with the good-natured mien of the truly bla I pleaded my case grandiloquently for a month's unpaid leav jecting well-processed bourbon fumes into the face of my gay and ruddy boss, admiring his thick red curly hair that camouflaged pale legs up to the hems of his Bermudas. He gave me two instead and personally escorted me to the door, hoping I wouldn't injure myself further—at least, that is, until I left the building.

It rained as I headed for the subway. I slid into a puddle upon my purple, well-paddled ass and laughed and laughed.

Life will out! Won't it?

No.

Voices called to me, mumbling.

I heard Karenina screaming. Was she saying my name?

What did you want, Karenina, from just another submissive?

Why the demon Love? Why press for that when we had D/s?

Voices.

Shut up!

No.

Phone.

I rolled, twisted up in the sheets again, let my arm fall toward the source of the noise and missed. I whacked my wrist on the edge of the bed frame. Managing to bind myself up further in the bedding, I grasped the receiver, fumbled against dropping it and launched it to the mattress. When it was secure against my face I sank back to the pillow.

"Hello."

"It's too late to be in bed, you know."

"Too late for too much."

"You don't sound good."

"I'm not good. I may never be good again."

"I don't want to hear it. Not why I called."

Ms. Right. "Why did you call?"

"To tell you what an idiot you are, Perry Patetick!"

"It's too late for that too, don't you think?"

She sighed. "Yes. I think. They came looking for you, you know."

The little gnomes working regular shifts at the iron forge in my all clocked in at once, bringing about the standard amount of head-splitting agony. As the pain in my frontal lobes heated up, I began to feel cold again and needed a drink. "I'm cold," I said softly without thinking.

"Cold," she repeated bitterly. "It's in the eighties."

"Sorry," I said, fighting for an upright position as the gnomes did their number. They all looked like mini-Tudors in their leather aprons stoking my own little Beamer furnace of pain.

"Fuck," she said. "Don't be sorry. I guess no one's as cold as you."

I wanted to say, "Maybe my father," but let it go, asking instead, "Who was it who wants it?"

"Nobody," she said, matching me, ice for ice. "Just the cops."

The pain was lessening. Now it was only the usual monumental language that was making me dizzy. It was still too much effort to go into the whole of Jack on my desk.

"And I bet you told them everything."

"That's a bet you'd lose, Perry Patetic, because I didn't."

"What did you say? How did you account for my whereabouts? You didn't lie?"

"You bet I did—straight through my teeth. Another life you would have lost, Perry old chum. But then you knew that when you lost me, you lost everything."

"Thanks for hammering that home."

"Anytime, bucko."

"So they don't know where I am."

"I don't know about that, Perry, but you better get moving. They think you offed the funny-looking babe."

"Offed?"

She giggled bitterly, perhaps to camouflage enraged quavering. "You know."

"I know."

"I mean it, Perry. Get dressed and get out."

"Why bother—they're probably already here, aren't they?" All I heard during the curious pause was Boot's TV once again permeating the walls. It seems he was watching my old Bettie Page video I had duped off a dub of a BBC broadcast.

"Just go. Then you can answer their questions on your terms."

"You mean where they can go at it on *their* terms? No thanks.
I'll hang here."

"No, Perry. You'll just hang."

"Cute. But I didn't do it. You know that."

"I know that. You never do anything."

"So it would seem." My stomach was knotting for some unaccountable reason. Daylight made fugitive shadows on the wall.

"Why couldn't you just be normal and marry me? Why couldn't
you have stopped all that role-playing nonsense. I was the only one
for you. You knew it."

"That was the trouble. I knew it and everything I knew was
wrong."

"So it's right now, then?" Her voice would have dripped with
acid if she hadn't been sniffling.

"I don't know yet."

"Be careful, Perry," Her voice was fearful, worried.

My door exploded open, kicked in by the thick blood-brown
cordovan shoe of a hulking graying man with a bad mustache.

"I will, honey," I said cheerily, "but I have to go—company's
here. Love to all the children."

"Children? *Jesus, Perry*—" her voice said tinny as a fly as I
fumbled to slam down the receiver, which did in fact make a slamming sound when it connected with the cradle.

I reached for the bottle of Jack, but the thick, tubby-grub fingers
of the aging hulk standing over me got there first. "Look what we
got here, one of those kinky sex people. He looks sort of cheap. Are
you a cheapie there, cowboy?"

"Midnight cowboy," said another voice. A stouter, unmustached
hulk entered. His suit was charcoal gray where his partner's was
babyshit brown.

"I'd offer you a drink, but I don't even know you guys."

"Since when did you have to know someone before you fucked
them?"

"Or beat them to death," added the new guy.

"Okay. Either you're the police or two of the stupidest burglars in world history. Of course you could be both. These days I hear the cops *are* the robbers."

"The whores are right—he *is* cute," said the primary.

"Just precious," said his partner. He made a mocking kissing noise with his lips.

"Isn't he though? And in the buff. Did we disturb your slumber?"

"As a matter of fact, you did. Why don't you guys wait outside, I'll get dressed, then you can ask me what you need to ask me, whatever that is."

The junior partner grabbed the primary's sleeve and said, "Let's wait for him outside—he ain't going nowhere."

The primary shook it off. "Fuck that. I ain't letting the little worm out of my sight. He can dress right here in front of me."

I sat up fully in bed, the sheet barely covering me, rubbed my eyes then shrugged.

"I'm not here to ask you anything, I'm here to tell you."

"Ease up, Ellroy, for Christ's sake," and the secondary grabbed again for the thick shoulder of the cheap suit.

The gnomes were hard at work, as my head clanged with consistent pain. "What are you guys supposed to be—bad cop, *worse* cop?"

"Exactly," said Ellroy as he sucker punched me straight in the face. Red images reeled before me. I got a close view of Karenina's broken and bloodied corpse, and winced, just as Ellroy followed things up with a smash to the left side of my face. I bolted up, and he pulled his Colt. "Let's do it right here, baby," he said. He made a little kissing noise with his lips. "C'mon, plant one on me so I can plant you."

I paced naked and dabbed blood from my shirt.

My hair was tangled in blood and felt like a clot in my fingers.

His partner tossed me a towel from the bathroom and I dabbed away. My nose was swollen but, apparently, unbroken. There would be a swelling on my jaw but it too was intact.

Bored for a moment, and distracted by the heft of the police special in his hand, Ellroy holstered it.

"Maybe he wants his lawyer?"

"Maybe he wants the phone." The secondary, named Healy, tore the phone out of the wall and threw it at me, barely missing my head. I in turn casually tossed the towel at him and bloodied his suit. He made a move toward me as I was sitting on the bed, groggily pulling on my pants, but I spat blood at his shoes and he stopped, more waiting for a cue from Ellroy than anything else, perhaps needing permission to land the next projected blow to my face as Ellroy had staked it out as his personal territory.

Bootlicker had not yet rallied to the rescue. I suspected he wasn't going to.

"Gee," I said. "You guys here for fun and games or just to ask me to your tea dance?"

"Let me tea dance on his face," said Healy, the secondary.

"Allow me," said Ellroy, stepping closer to where I sat on the bed and crunching down on my toe with the tip of his shoe. I resisted wincing.

It occurred to me he was off balance, so I recoiled in pain and as he smiled I leaned forward and yanked suddenly on his arm hard enough and purposefully enough to bring him down. He fought against it, but his weight won the struggle and down he went.

Ellroy swung but I stood before he could connect.

The barrel of Healy's gun was hard against my left temple.

"When you guys are finished with your sex and violence thing, maybe we can talk about it after."

I was braced for another blow as Ellroy righted himself from my bed, but none came.

"No sex, faggot."

"Too bad for you," I said. Blood was still trickling down my nose. I searched for the towel.

"Read the twerp his rights."

"You'll be read yours when I prefer charges."

"The lardball in the next room will swear it never happened. We had a chat." Ellroy actually looked angry, Healy, bored and offended, his gun barrel following me in my search for the towel.

I found it, dabbed, and received a short but effective punch to the stomach, courtesy of Ellroy. I doubled over but did not fall.

"We know you did it. All your little scene buddies ratted you out—no surprise there."

"It's true," piped Healy. "They gave you up without a struggle. Someone named Warner Cousins, also known as Tutor, explained it was a scene gone bad."

"A scene is when you beat her instead of fucking her like a man, isn't it?"

I controlled my heaving and managed to blurt: "You have drool on your mustache, detective."

He put his sleeve to it and I added, coughing; "Don't wipe it off—it's a good look for you."

Ellroy looked like he was coming forward again, but I began heaving a bit and he thought better of it, recalling my blood on Healy's shoes.

Healy gave me what I wanted finally: "You were the jealous boyfriend of a married woman. She wanted to go back to her husband. You couldn't stand it. You played one final scene with her to say goodbye. Give her the real, full-out treatment."

"But it was her death scene, wasn't it?" Ellroy droned.

Nearly recovered by then, I was overcome by laughter.

Laughing along with the wonder of life! The joke of it all come home: true love as murder!

I welcomed it!

I was overcome and back to the bed I went, reeling with laughter.

"He's cracked," Ellroy mumbled.

"I don't know," said the secondary, pointing his gun at me as a I cackled, somewhat forlornly. "Could be something else. Maybe drugs."

"You have it all wrong. Should I wait for my lawyer to tell you why you have no case? That's right. You didn't let me call. So why don't you take me outside to a pay phone so I can call, or arrest me and bring me in and I'll make the call from there. That's still how it's done, isn't it?" Of course, I had no lawyer to call.

Ellroy shrugged.

"We can take your statement now, if you like."

"A confession would speed things up," the secondary oozed.

I rolled on the bed laughing and they didn't know what to make of me. I sat on the edge, pulled on a clean shirt and the fun began. "Did you ask anyone else known to be in this 'scene' as you call it who knew me?"

"We did," said Ellroy.

"And what did they say?"

"We don't have to tell you anything."

"They said I was submissive. They said Karenina topped me— beat me as you put it. Did they ever say I beat her?"

"They said you could have."

"Sure. And you can skydive, but you don't. I'm identified as a submissive. It's a type. A submissive doesn't go against type. They don't beat their dominants."

"They could." Ellroy was unimpressed. "We know about switchables."

"Okay. What's my motive?"

"Revenge, jealousy, the usual."

"Why not the husband?"

"She was going back to him, for the sake of the kids."

"Who stands to gain more if she dies, me or hubby? Who winds up with more? I think all I stood to gain was, well . . . what did I stand to gain?"

"He's clear, the husband."

"Clear?"

I put on my shoes.

"Clear. We investigated him. Alibied to the hilt. He has witnesses as to his whereabouts. He was on the phone with some realty lady around the time of her death. He was with a bunch of people at the time, for Christ's sake." Ellroy looked smug. "He's been ruled out."

"Cool," I said, looked up and grinned. "My alibi is his alibi."

"It is?"

"How?" asked Healy, almost interested.

"I was with the realty lady when she made the call. Ask her. My alibi is just as good as the guy who gets the house, the money, the kids and the retribution on a cheating wife. The realty lady called the husband looking for Karen and I was there with her when she did it. Tell me: do you think he had as easy a time getting witnesses to lie for him as you did getting lardball to agree to lie for you? What am I *saying?* Why would hubby *ever* want to do that."

"He's been cleared, I said." Ellroy was dour, his eyes searching my room for anything incriminating and coming up only with me. "He had more than one witness see him."

"Then clear me too, while you're at it."

"We'll have to check."

"Yes, you will. Going to read me my rights now?"

"You have no rights."

"Then I'm not arrested, am I?"

"No."

"Then get the hell out."

"No."

"Okay. But I believe this has been what they call 'a roust,' isn't it? It's what I heard it called when I was a reporter. I used to be one, you know   technically I still am. I freelance for the *Register.* You know how the *Register* just *loves* cops. I wonder if a roust like this in a murder case might be considered newsworthy. Think it is?" I finished dressing, opened the door and made my way into the bathroom to do my hair and stanch the bleeding. They moved aside, making no effort to stop me.

Healy grunted.

"Hey, Bootlicker," I shouted to the shape on the couch watching TV. "The soaps any good?"

He murmured something incomprehensible.

I heard Ellroy begin poking through my possessions as Healy watched me shave.

"Go ahead," I said genially. "Toss the room. You won't find anything incriminating. I don't do drugs, I don't receive stolen property, just alcohol and sex with pretty women, strippers. You know, the kind you guys fantasize about?"

I was ready for the next attack. Surprisingly, the detectives were docile. They seemed uncertain. Healy cleared his throat and spoke: "You can account for your whereabouts?"

Trying not to cut myself by suppressing the tremors in my hand: "Sure. I was having sex. You remember sex don't you—something you used to do when you could still get it up?"

"That's it!" Healy shouted and stepped next to me. Could he see I was nervous enough to crumble?

"It is," I said. "So, like, if you guys are finished assaulting me, you can go. If you aren't, please go ahead. But you'd better just kill me in the process because I intend to squawk good and loud—get my attorney on the case, alert my colleagues—you know."

Healy bore down on me, nudged into me, straining for a height advantage he plainly lacked, breathing hard.

"Ease up, partner," said Ellroy coming up behind Healy.

"Why?"

"Because I said so." Ellroy pulled Healy back from the bathroom and at long last flashed his shield. He dangled a little Ziploc bag of white powder in front of me for hypnotic emphasis. "You know what that is."

"Looks like a plant to me."

Ellroy nodded and smirked. "Could be. Could also be one of your strippers left it here without your knowing, by accident. Sort of by mishap. Most of them do it, don't they?"

"They do. But I don't know any who'd forget a fix."

"Hey," he clapped one thick mitt on my shoulder without a shred of violence implied. It was almost a gesture of warmth. Not surprising with cops, as they usually blew both hot and cold. "Do you know any who have anything in their lives that squared away—even when it comes to heroin?"

"No," I admitted.

"You have the right to remain silent. . . ."

I WAS DOCILE THROUGH IT ALL, WALKING IN A DREAMLIKE STUPOR, as they booked me, photographed me and locked me in a holding cell alone where I lay down and let it all spin down till I could catch up with it. All this was helped by the mild concussion caused by the battering about the face and head I took as Ellroy and Healy body-checked me down the four flights of stairs to the street. There were

no remarks—that I could pick out anyway in my befogged state—
about my appearance from any of the officers who processed me
through to the cell, despite my obvious battering, torn shirt, bloodied
lips and teeth.

I was just another criminal.

They treated me as if I were drunk, which I might as well have
been, my speech slurred, my vision blurred, my gait tentative and
wracked with imbalance.

Before I could fall away into the gyre, accepting the whirling
laughter of my life, a thick and heavy hand dragged my up from my
padless steel cot.

I had been bailed out.

She was standing there, glassy-eyed, ready to escort me back to
Boot's crabbed domicile of debauched slobbishness—I could hardly
choke back enough in my throat to call it home. Her lower lip trembled, but her body was set with determination. My girl no more,
Ms. Right, dutifully saying goodbye by greeting me at the precinct
desk. The paperwork had already been done, and it seemed weird to
me to be released just as quickly as I had been detained, but then,
as I had been concussed, everything seemed weird to me.

And it occurred to me I had no sense of time anymore.

I felt profound affection for Ms. Right then, disgust for myself
and oddly at peace with the world, as game and ready to laugh as
was life, and just as ready to fend off the demon Love should it come
at me in any of its devious or tempting guises.

Her face blanched and the trembling lips pulled back. "You
bastards better be ready for a monster lawsuit and some criminal
actions—look at this! You've beaten him half to death!"

I smiled bloodily, being too much out of it to jump back into
my bruised skin and make some sort of noise.

The desk sergeant, a beefy, hulking probable lesbian, crinkled
up her pug nose until her freckles disappeared and retorted, sternly,
"You do what you have to, ma'am. This is the condition he was
delivered to us in. If you have any complaints, you can fill out this
paperwork at that desk over there." She thrust out papers and indicated a bare wooden chair and table for one in the corner, obviously
decades-old salvage from a school. I grabbed the paperwork feebly.

"We're going to file a complaint."

"I'll see if the lieutenant on duty for Community Relations is free."

"I want to go home," I said more softly than I wanted to due to my ravaged throat and tender split and injured lips.

"You can file your complaint any time you like," said the police lesbian, halfway ignoring us.

"We will," said Ms. Right and pushed me toward the door. "Home," she repeated as if no one could hear her say it—quite possibly because she knew I no longer had one.

"Yes. Home."

I was dizzy and my footing reflected it. She was forced to take my arm rather than watch me stumble.

"I wish I could say I was enjoying this," she said, her face flushed with anger, suppressed sadness, or both. Her tone of voice was as neutral and casual as it used to be when we were first dating years ago.

"And you aren't?" I said by rote.

I felt painful vibrations as the car started and pulled away. "I die inside seeing you this way, Perry. It doesn't make me hurt less to know the misery your affair has caused. It just hurts me all the more. I have so much hurt now."

"It was supposed to cause us to be free."

She gave a practiced scoffing laugh like a cough. "The only real freedom is death. No hurry to get there."

"You sound like me."

"Why not? I've carried you inside me like a child for seven years hoping you'd be born."

"But I'm calcified instead. We must chalk that up to another joke on god's TelePrompTer to the great comedian life."

"What *are* you talking about?"

"I don't know. I probably have a concussion. I'm not my usual sensible self."

I got no laughter from that. "I'm going to drive you to the hospital," she said.

"Forget it—I'm uninsured."

"It could be serious. You need to get looked at."

"I've been here before. Like everything else, it'll pass."

"Well, I'm driving there!" She gunned the engine to emphasize her seriousness.

I cracked the passenger's side door. "I'll just get out then." She glanced at me, her teeth gritted. "I'm not going in to have my head examined. It's too goddamn late for that." No laugh there either.

"Fine. I'll just take you to—that place."

"Yes. Take me there." I slammed the door shut.

Traffic was frustratingly slow. I attributed it to the usual Miltown rubbernecking at the usual police stop that was no doubt up ahead.

"You could always take me home," I said.

"Home?" Her eyes glazed. "You just told me—"

"Home," I said. "You know: *Home*-home."

"You mean *my* place?"

"I guess it's that now."

She shook her head, eyes riveted on the road and the slow bumper-to-bumper line of cars. "Oh, Perry, you don't really mean that."

"I do." Something wet my face. A tear! Could she see it? My eyes ached and swelled. They were so heavy they dragged my head straight down. "I really do. I do. I want our life back." Oh, I was stopped up with so much needing to be cried, with great mucosal blubbering agony, but all that I could manage was one anemic tear.

"No, you don't. You know you don't!"

Damn. She was outcrying me as I sat stonily and watched.

She spoke between sobs and gasps. "You were right, Perry, so very right. But I was afraid to do something about how right you were. I couldn't face the pain of it. You faced it for us—you were the brave one. You need things I can't give you—I lied about even trying. They disgust me. I'm sorry they do. You don't know how I wanted to, but I just couldn't. It's just like you and being a father. You aren't ready. You knew it, you told me so. I wouldn't listen. I'm sorry!"

"I don't know about that. I could try and find out."

"Oh, I know you'd do it, and not just because things are bad now—but it would be suicide for you. And things are terrible enough for you now. You don't know how much it hurts me to know it. It hurts me." At the next dead stop, she pulled out a tissue and sniffled into it, overwhelmed it and grabbed for more.

"You don't want to live the way I need to live in so many ways."

"But we did it together for so many years."

"Yes—and you know why. We depended on each other for our worst insecurities and fears. We were each other's protection, but that was it. You know it! We *both* know it! We played at satisfying each other's needs that way without really doing it. You stopped loving me—you couldn't be like me. I changed one way; you changed another. I know you don't love me anymore. I know it! And it's okay. I will never love anyone the way I loved you, except my child, Perry, the one I'm going to have no matter what! Oh, it was such a special love, Perry. And it's here with nowhere to go." She paused and added: "You were my child, Perry."

"But I do love you." This pain was beating me. This was the one I couldn't master, couldn't consume rather than be consumed by. "I do."

She kissed me and her lips burned as hot as a lit match to my cheek.

"No, you don't. You love her—and she's dead. And I love you—and we're dead. And that's the truth."

"I could come back," I said in a dream. "I could make the effort."

"No," she kissed me again. More burning, more anguish in the tentative motion. "No coming back from the dead for us." She took a breath, exhaled. "Perry, I've met someone."

"You don't—"

Her delicate hand went over my mouth. "I don't. You're right. But he's a good man and will make a good father. He's not what I want, but what I need. And he's ready for it."

"How can you live with that? It hasn't even been that long! Just days!" How long it had been, I really didn't know. Had it really been days—or weeks? I was bluffing and she knew it. "You're crazy."

She wiped her tears away and said bitterly: "No. Determined. Besides, you did it with me for seven years. I can do it with him at least that long. With a child, maybe more. And you know the other thing, don't you?"

I sank my eyes down into my palms. My head was a dark ovum of pain.

"Don't you!"

"You're pregnant."

"No." She started to laugh but it died within her. "No, but, I've been testing for it both night and day. And when I am at last, I know I'll be happy. Truly happy!" It always amazed me how delicately she could cry, how demure and without hysteria the real tears could be, the ones invested with depth, the ones that were more than a momentary indulgence. "Happy," she said softly. She looked up at me. "You know what else, Perry? You what else? He *wants* me to be pregnant."

"Should have been ours, shouldn't it?" I said, growing frigid with pain.

"Yes." Her face betrayed a weariness of mind. What did mine show? I was so busy warding off the busy little Tutors of pain, I couldn't possibly know.

"I don't want to know about him."

"No. You don't. Not the way I know about her. You don't want love letters and photos they way I got them. You certainly don't." She stated this matter-of-factly, without bitterness, like an accounting. It was sure to strike at me more effectively that way. And it did.

She pulled the car up by the curb with an obscene crackling of gravel. "We're here."

I kissed her on the cheek—which was cool and slack—gave a painful nod. "Good-bye. . . ." My throat choked when it came to saying her name. I couldn't do it. I fought to keep the world straight in my brain, focus what was left of my eyesight as I no longer had vision to speak of.

"Bye." I managed to squeeze out awkwardly, clearing my throat.

"Good-bye, Perry."

We locked that last look hard then broke it.

She drove off quickly, still gazing at me, her expression hollow, haunted, wan.

I stood wavering in the hot breeze and watched the car corner. Then, the demon Love and I strolled slowly hand in hand back to my apartment.

EIGHTEEN

No point fending off even demons when you're freezing to death at the end of summer and starved for company, so the demon and I made peace. We watched television together on Bootlicker's couch amid candy wrappers, empty pop cans and one or two sticky, fly-ridden ice-cream cartons, Mossman being blessedly gone for once. The demon Love joined me in a drink—which was wholly ill-advised, my having a spanking-new concussion and what appeared to be a full-blown drinking problem, but I was cold despite the heat of the day and my continual sweat in the still air and the Jack Black warmed me up, made the demon Love better if not tolerable company.

We had a good laugh. It was good to confront life then love, both of them laughing fully at me at first, then with me as I joined in, helpless in the drifting current that I had leapt into with such abandon.

We watched the TV tabloid trash news show *Inside Affairs*, laughing at the swinish behavior of the Hollywood elite, state politicians and redoubtable suburbanites from such enlightened communities as Marion, Ohio. We all laughed and I sucked down Jack Black, watching stalkers, sex criminals, forgers and embezzlers reveling in money, ostentatious luxury and the word of god.

I was slipping into drunken hopefulness, an ability to cope and, if not somewhat delusionally, to thrive, until something totally unexpected popped up on the TV screen.

My face.

It was really my face—a big, bad twenty–four inch picture.

I laughed so hard I vomited. The room spun.

This was not uncommon in concussions, let alone those mixed with liberal doses of alcohol.

It was the photo from my driver's license, which, blown up, made me look like a paranoid sociopath, which all such images do. It's either that or some malefic moron caught in a headlight moment of harried unconcern. It was obvious what had happened: They had pirated my image from the DMV! Why?

Apparently, I was the top story on *Inside Affairs*.

I raised the volume after I staggered back from the toilet, still clutching my bottle of Jack Black by the neck. The show's anchor, a dowdy matron in a frosted fright wig and power suit, was announcing events excitedly after the flashed black and white photo of a woman who had been beaten and horribly disfigured who was now most likely dead.

Karenina.

". . . Patetick had only a 'no comment' for our *Inside Affairs* team, currently investigating this brutal and heinous crime. Patetick, an unemployed freelance newsman, was being held on a separate drug possession charge while at the same time being investigated as the prime suspect in the murder of his married girlfriend, but has since been released on bail. Despite his release, according to law-enforcement officials and investigators, Patetick has *not* been dismissed as a suspect."

I thought they'd cut to Ellroy, but instead some thick, aging brown-shirt bouncer with a boxtop haircut, craggy squint and lantern jaw I had never seen before filled all America in on my perfidy. His face reeked martial authority.

"Mr. Patetick is still being considered a suspect, but he's legally out on bail now pending a hearing on a separate drug charge. What happened to this woman was a brutal, heinous act tinged with the worst elements of sexual perversion. Whoever did this must be taken off the streets to prevent this from happening to some other wife and mother."

"But wasn't she asking for it by participating in a kinky sex scene?"

"Nobody, I don't care what their sexual preference, asks to be raped, beaten and tied onto a cross, then brutally and deliberately murdered. Nobody."

"Have you any other suspects?"

"No. Her husband—who we thought was a right guy right from the get-go, a man at the mercy of things he didn't completely understand—put everything he had into helping us. He's been ruled out as a suspect by a number of witnesses. Now, this character Patetick, though—he's something else altogether. And I'll tell you this," said the ranking suit pointing his finger, presumably at the absent me, "although we have no further suspects, we're going to be watching *very* closely the one suspect that we do have to prevent anything like this from happening again, until we can put the perpetrator where he belongs."

Freeze frame.

Cut to slideshow photos of Karenina and children playing. Cut to lovey-dovey stuff with hubby, which to me looked stiff and somewhat tentative, but I was drunk and concussed, so what did I know? It seemed false. Even then, Karenina's eyes were haunted with longing.

Cut to Karenina's high-school yearbook photo.

Voice over: "Pretty, vivacious Karen Poshlust, whose late father started the celebrated estate planning firm of Poshlust and Chichikov over thirty years ago in New York City, was a typical wife and mother—until she met up with this man."

God—more of the driver's license photo! They zoomed in on it by rigid increments for shock value. I looked like hell—even though the image lacked my two newly blackened eyes.

I tried to slump down to the futon, but my body just wouldn't go.

I supposed that at this juncture, the image was not wholly inaccurate.

"Freelance Journalist Perry Patetick, a graduate of Trinity University and a journalism-school dropout, was into kinky games—sex games. He was known for scouring the Internet and local electronic bulletin boards for potential partners in these dangerous games, which is where he first enticed Poshlust away from her husband and family and possibly to her death."

Cut to the grieving hubby. He looked just right, too well

groomed, which on TV comes off well, holding back (none too successfully) discreet tears.

"I tried to keep her away from that damned computer—tried to physically pull her away, you know what I'm saying? I tried to keep her from that machine, but it was too late—like dealing with an addict. I let her have her space, gave her options. I was a good, liberal husband, and now Karen is dead."

Cut back to the matron.

"Oh yes—and what about the computer that caused it all? Bennie Poshlust-Middler says—*he smashed it.*"

I shut off her smug grin before I followed Bennie's lead and smashed the TV.

I was learning all about the details of the murder of love from TV. This seemed to me somehow just, as I might just as well have learned about the creation of love from the same source.

She was found about midafternoon of the fateful day of the bid on our house, tied to—of all things—a St. Andrew's cross! The photo they flashed of the scene showed it. The cross was in a vacant loft somewhere on the Miltown docks off Thrasher Street. Karenina had been raped—her attacker used a condom—while she was tied, or to be more precise than the reporting, strapped onto a piece of custom-made bondage furniture.

She had a gag stuffed back in her throat.

Cause of death was due to the severity of her wounds—someone on *Inside Affairs* guessed tachycardia due to internal bleeding. It could have been shock, it could have been blood loss. Whatever.

She had been beaten more than she could take— every inch. The flashed photos, whether of her or not, implied it.

I was the chief suspect. I was the *only* suspect. Hell, anyone could see from the misappropriated license photo: I did it.

The aggrieved hubby was an obvious good guy overwhelmed by forces he couldn't *hope* to understand. Why were there no cameras, phone calls, fellow journalists all ganged up to get a comment?

There was no story in me—I was obviously guilty. They were waiting for the ax to fall, for the investigation to gather up enough to make a murder charge stick and the arrest hold up in

court at hearing level. That would be the story: my arrest and ar-
raignment.

I was useless until then, except as someone who could try to
exploit any and all press attention to declare my innocence *before*
being formally charged. Until then, I was firmly in the background
with my drivers'-license photo all over syndicated TV. In a hot new
murder case I was a nonstory, not yet a suspect, not yet dismissed
as one. I was an irony in the background jockeying with fate to be
in the foreground.

Damn!

I ran to my room, drunkenly caroming off the wall, spun around,
hit the bathroom and doused my face in the fine waters of Trinity.
Dripping wet I made for the phone. I called all the numbers to get
me to the staff of *Inside Affairs*. I needed one of their damned celebrity reporters. It took over ten dialings, some due to my drunken
clumsiness, to get through to a voice routinely habituated to saying
"no." But I wanted that matron anchor and I was going to get her.

"I'm the one who did the bitch," I said, and added on some
heavy breathing.

"Excuse me?" The voice was offended, but interested.

"The SM Murder . . . I'm the one."

Suddenly, I began noticing a beep on the line.

Tone change.

"I need to speak with Kitty O'Shea, please. I have some material
to offer her in that story."

"You can tell me."

"I can hang up."

"Who are you?"

"You know."

Phone fumble, voices, interminable Muzak, but only for a few
seconds.

"This is Kitty O'Shea, can I help you?"

Without missing a beat! They were ready. Yes, the beeps meant
I was being recorded. I wondered if they got my opening line?"

"Can I help *you?*" I offered

"What do you mean by 'you did her?' "

"Did I say that?"

"I have it on tape."

"Well, Ms. O'Shea, you may or may not have that, but I had to do *something* to get your attention."

"You already did. You beat a woman to death—SM style."

I had to laugh, join the silent chorus of laughter.

"No. I didn't. But you're making it look that way."

"You're a reporter, Mr. Patetick. I don't have to tell you we present facts without conclusions."

"No, you don't have to tell me you present facts and imply conclusions while evading commitment to them, but so what? My point is if you need more facts, look into hubby."

"Hubby? The husband—"

"The huz, she used to say, my Karenina." No tears, just a blur.

"That's a little obvious. He's been cleared by the police."

"They could be wrong."

"They could be—"

"But it isn't news without dead-bang proof is it? Because people expect the cops to be wrong, but want a suspect they can hate."

"Not exactly—"

"And that's me, isn't it. Look at what you pilfered illegally from DMV—of *course* it makes me look like a lunatic! Did you identify where that picture was from, no-oo-oo!"

"Have you been drinking, Mr. Patetick?"

"Have you been whoring, Ms. O'Shea?"

"Anything else, Mr. Patetick?"

"Only this: look into who had the most to gain from Karenina's death. Perhaps alibis can be fixed."

"Karenina. You've said that before. Was that what you'd call her *scene* name?"

"A nickname. Look—you said I gave you no comment on the show. Of course, you never contacted me, so in a far-flung sense perhaps that's true. But here's your direct comment now: I loved her, I never hurt her, I didn't kill her, and the person who did is getting away with it."

"I see. You're being set up. That's our story then. We'll go with that. Thank you for your time, Mr. Patetick."

"No! I set *myself* up. *Somebody* used that. But the police won't charge me and you won't keep insinuating I did it, wanna know *why?*"

"I think we have all we need here, Mr. Patetick, but thank you."

"Wait! Here's the kicker: his alibi is my alibi. Break mine and you break his, meaning *either* of us could have done it. Maybe we did it together! There's your angle, the facts are there! Go after them."

"I said we have enough." The voice was pensive, flat, almost speaking by rote. There was a pause. Either the hook was baited or more time was needed to confirm the best of what I said was on tape. Either way, I had changed things, perhaps even so much that they might go my way. I heard activity and a clicking in the background. "Thanks very much, Mr. Patetick. We'll be in touch."

I hugged the phone to my face and caught this in the background as I hung up: *"Beautiful, Kitty!"*

I made another call, as my adrenaline was now pumping loud and clear through the warm, alcoholic fuzz.

"Bahamian—hit me!" said a voice after two rings.

"Patetick—been hit!" I rejoined.

"The man of the hour!"

"None other," I slurred.

"How does it feel to be famous?"

I hiccuped not very loudly. "I have to drink to kill the pain."

"Know who's looking to talk with you?"

"Happy Boy?"

"Nah, he's off somewhere gloating, passing out morgue copies of our SM issue. The managing editor wants a word though—"

"Gunn here," a voice cut in, preempting the unctuous ease of Bahamian's voice. "We've missed you, Patetick. Everyone's talking about you."

"Dickie!" I said, drunk and uncaring. "You actually *miss* a free-lancer?"

"We do Perry. Or should I call you *killer?*" The way he said it made us both laugh.

"Well then, why not give me the old column back?"

" ' 'Round the Towne?' That old saw? Nonsense, Perry, we have bigger things to discuss."

"I want a column," I said.

"Well, let's talk about it."

"There's nothing to talk about, Dickie." Dickie of course was the running joke about the *Register*—the reporter's encoded way of saying *dickless*. "Give me a column or we're done."

"Then you have it," Gunn said soothingly. "Come in tomorrow and we'll work out the details."

"Like whether or not I get paid? We'll do them now," I said.

"Perry, Perry—you have what you want. No one works it out final on the phone. You know that. You can phone in a story, but you can't phone in a contract. I'll have legal get us something and we'll meet tomorrow."

"Make it afternoon."

Gunn laughed. "Oh yes. If anyone understands rough mornings around here, it's me." He gave me an opportunity to laugh. I gave him silence. "I think a column would be a very good place to start talking about your innocence, Perry."

"Nobody's innocent—least of all me."

"Just so," said Gunn. "But you won't talk to anyone else until you talk to us, Perry. After all, you're family. And you don't want to queer your deal."

"I didn't talk to *Inside Affairs*, did I?"

"Of course not," said Gunn.

"Well then—who else would I talk to?"

"I told you he was reasonable," Bahamian clicked in.

"We miss your brand of tough-minded editorialization at the *Register*, Perry. See you in my office at one tomorrow."

"Me too, buddy. Bring your sense of irony with you."

"Happy Boy doing a sit-down with us, Hab?"

I had no idea whether Gunn was on the line or not. I suspected he had moved on, exhausted by the perfunctory nature of the pleasant exchange; he knew we hated one another. Then again he knew that he was universally hated at the *Register* anyway.

"Heaven forfend!" Bahamian laid on thick enough so neither of us could tell how thick. "He's strictly out of the loop."

"Wonderful, Hab. Bring your airsick bag with you. I think I'll be taking mine."

GARY S. KADET

Uncertain laughter. "Okey-dokey, Pilgrim."

Beautiful, Kitty, my mind echoed.

I hung up, delicately cradled the phone with a supreme effort, then fell to my bed, sick and dizzy.

The room spun and I allowed the darkening spiral to take me.

"Fuck you!" I tried to shout, but must have moaned, then promptly gave up everything I had to the void.

NO DRINKING FOR ME WHEN I GOT UP THE NEXT MORNING—I WAS APproaching this visit to enemy territory, straight and sober.

I wore a suit and then—the tie! My old school tie, the one that was such a joke between Karenina and me. I wore it for luck and protection. I wore it for irony.

It took an overheated uncomfortable two hours for me to reach the post-industrial suburban enclave of the *Register*. And when I made it up to the city room, which still observed the antique convention of having the editor-in-chief's office at its head, every head turned and a pall was cast over idle conversation as I passed by. There was no pretense about it. I may have added up to little in the outside world, but here among the ranks of local tide-pool journalism, I was fast becoming a story. I had inspired awe, jealousy and contempt all because I had jumped the fence, becoming what was written about instead of staying the nonentity who was doing the writing. And—as a story—I had yet to fully break.

I knew they assumed that I was about to break as I opened the door to the editor's office and shut it briskly behind me.

Of course, the fact that I looked like some sort of mutant raccoon due to the beating about the face and head I'd received from Miltown's finest didn't help matters—or maybe it did, making me seem like no one to mess with.

Before I could declare my purpose to the ruby-lipped sorority maid secretary, eyeing her pink chemise and strand of pearls, Gunn charged out of his office, overpoweringly tall, stooped and wretched-faced from alcohol, pumping my hand.

"Patetick! Come right in. We've all been talking about you." He draped his arm over my shoulder.

"All of you? That can't be good."

"Of course it is. It's always a good thing when talent and hard work are recognized."

"That can't be me," I said.

Dickie laughed a disarming laugh that made me long for a weapon.

Bahamian was there, waving me in and an unknown in a suit, a young up-and-comer, the sort editors routinely use as eager slave labor, sat uneasily next to him in a chair.

"Hey Hab—who's the shmoo?"

"One of Dickie's minions. He's recording secretary."

The shmoo gave me a crisp unsmiling nod. "Mark Foment— just here to take a few notes."

"Why do we need notes, Dickie?"

"Minutes to the meeting, of course. Make sure everything re mains official." He leaned back in his green leather swivel chair to avoid piles of unreviewed material and a precariously positioned monitor. His desk was an avalanche waiting to happen and even his office resembled that of a low-rent lawyer's, expecting to impress, but not trying too hard to do so.

"Like my contract?"

He made a church steeple of his fingers and blew out a sigh. The shmoo adjusted himself in his chair and Bahamian yawned. "Especially that."

"Like we're on the record?"

"Yes, Perry, everything here is on the record."

"Buddy, we're just outlining terms." Bahamian looked jumpy, his expression straining towards open and cool.

"Can I hear them please?"

"Legal is drawing them up. A standard contract with add-ons."

"Let's hear the add-ons."

"We can get into that in a minute, Perry."

"Why not now?"

"Well, I think the paper has promotional issues to address first, Perry." Bahamian's face seemed to shout: "He shoots, he *scores!*"

The urgent, burning need for a drink rose up within me. I crushed it.

Dickie was like an enthusiastic guidance counselor. He leaned into me earnestly, spoke with gravid tones: "Exactly, Perry. First we need to print what happened—the whole story. We'll give it very big play."

"Your story," said Bahamian, looking wearily focused, "told in your own words."

The cold feeling was growing again. I needed the heat of a blast of alcohol. I locked in on reason.

"You told me legal would get us something and then we'd meet, Dickie."

"They're working on it. And while we're waiting, we can concentrate on your story."

"It's just promotion," Bahamian dismissed.

"The shmoo here—he's got the assignment, hasn't he?" I thumbed toward a solemn Foment.

"Assignment?" Dickie gave a minishrug.

"You know—covering the SM murder and my alleged part in it."

"We just want you to tell your story. To promote the column." Gunn was insistent.

"It'll be the ideal kick-off." Bahamian was selling.

I slumped in my chair, shook my head, took a breath. "Okay. I get it. Hey, shmoo. Start writing."

After glaring at me, the shmoo obliged.

"That's the boy," said Gunn.

"Do you mind if I stand?"

"Whatever floats your boat," Bahamian chirped.

"Float is about right," I began while clearing my throat. "Well, here it is: This is the whole story."

I unzipped my fly and urinated zestily onto the carpet.

Gunn jumped up and back, Bahamian flinched but sat where he was. The shmoo scribbled away with mad calm. "He's out of his fucking mind!" Gunn shrieked, with a tone of voice that amused me because I'd never heard such sounds coming from him before.

I zipped up, flung open the door and elbowed my way through

my concerned journalistic brethren, as it was strictly the men who piled up by the door after the incidental crash of Dickie's monitor to the urine-soaked rug. "No—all too sane. It's exactly what you guys were already trying to do to me. I simply beat you to the punch."

I wanted to tell the shmoo to quote me, but I had to run.

There seemed to be just one opportunity to make my exit throng the throng of confused men who were now at the end of their hesitation and were beginning to zero in on me as the target for whatever action they were going to take. I hunkered down and slowly walked a zigzag path through the cubicles doing the defeated walk of the journeyman journalist. Blending in as just another harried droid made it easy for me to get to the ground floor and out of building past the beleaguered woman at the front desk routing calls, just before security caught on.

I was dull and staggering in the blunt sun amid glinting cars in the parking lot.

Someone grabbed my arm. I pulled away and spun about. My mind flashed: Security!

"I'm sorry—I thought you were someone I knew."

The shortish graying dumpy man who stopped me looked almost as unsteady as I was.

Edge.

Edge Tatty.

"Patetick! It *is* you! You look positively, well, *pathetic.*"

"I've heard that before, thank you," I said. The heat and glare were making me ill. I knew I must have been hungry but my body was pounding my head for a drink. I was sweating.

"You look, in fact, like you've just been in visiting editors. They must be interested in you because of the *Inside Affairs* thing. And it *is* interesting, I have to say. I hope you did it, by the way. Innocence is so boring, protesting itself this way and that all the time and so forth."

"Look, Edge. I'd *love* to stand here on the molten tar of this parking lot soaking up all the passive solar heat from the glare of these cars with you and trade *bon mots*, but I'm fairly parched and dehydrated from just having dumped a full bladder of piss on Dickie Gunn's carpet." My hands were shaking.

"You're just being literary. . . ." He trailed off then added: "Aren't you?"

"Dead serious. I peed on the managing editor's rug."

Edge's face split into a beaming smile and his voice into the burst of a guffaw.

"You're not serious!"

"I just said I was."

"No! Really!" He exploded into guffaw again, composed himself, looked at his watch, then guffawed once more, this time with flecks of spittle. "I have a phone interview in ten minutes," he said catching his breath, "but this is just too good. I want to hear it all. Come. I'll even buy. No such heroism should go unpunished."

"It's just what my battered ears were hoping to hear."

"To the Roisterer then—the charmless bar with the charming name." He added: "Oh, I only wish I had known you were *this* much of a bad boy beforehand."

The Roisterer was, thank god, a short walk from the parking lot in between the *Register* and the highway. It was a faded shamrock-bedizened dive that served the local cannery for years until that operation closed, only to find itself saved by the relocated newspaper whose politics and presence its owners loathed. What made things worse was that the newspaper had taken over the cannery's physical plant. As a gesture of revenge, the owners put less money than ever before into the bar, serving the cheapest brands of liquor and beer, and letting it fall apart by slow degrees.

This of course made it the bar of choice for hard-core reporters and even the editors who wanted to show solidarity with those doing the grunt work of the news, making a point of doing their after-hours drinking there. It was the owners' last laugh: using the news world's illusions about itself against it.

I followed behind close by Tatty, suppressing the impulse to stagger.

Someone walked toward us with a furious gait. The face came into focus.

"Pecksniffian!" I grumbled, not at the fact that he hadn't

moved—I knew by then he never moved—but at having to face another colleague whose loyalties were unclear.

He stopped in front of us. "Is that *Perry Patetick?* What happened to you?" He put his hands on his hips, leaned back and sneered: "Didn't you used to be cute?"

"Oh, believe or not, Milt, he's gotten even cuter."

"I've been under some stress," I said, taking extra care to enunciate clearly.

"I heard," said Pecksniffian. "You a celebrity yet?"

"Hell—I'm not even indicted."

"You did it, of course."

"Sorry, no. Even they know I didn't. It's just newsman's revenge, their leaving me on the suspect list. That and the fact that I'm the only one on it."

"No indictment forthcoming?"

"No—I have an alibi they won't break."

"Won't or can't?"

"Maybe both."

"I hate to say this Per, but you seem to have the shakes."

I shrugged.

"Okay. Maybe I don't hate to say it."

"Oh," Edge interjected smarmily, "but you haven't heard *why* dear Per has the shakes, have you?"

"No."

"It's too hot—I'm heading for the bar," I said, overwhelmed with a need to leave both the heat and the *Register.* Edge started walking to keep up, leaving Milt Pecksniffian standing exasperated in the sun facing the cannery buildings of the paper.

"I have work to do, you know."

"You won't believe how good it is—makes quite a bumpkin of our lush-living lord and master Elston Gunn."

I picked up speed with the determination to leave.

We left Pecksniffian quite literally in the dust—or were leaving him, when amid the cloud our footfalls raised, he shouted: "Oh, all right. Fine. It better be damn good!"

"You don't know how good, Milt," said Tatty, happy at the prospect of vicarious enjoyment over fresh scandal. He was so happy he didn't mind holding me up when I nearly collapsed after tripping on the broken stone and concrete as we left the broad parking lot of the *Register*.

DESPITE THE LACK OF CONVERSATION, MILT SUFFERED FITS OF laughter at the story Edge and I related to him concerning my new column and Gunn's old rug. Edge kept the cheap drinks coming while searching the morgue of his mind for an anecdote that would top mine. Sunlight moved across the stained wood and cheap vinyl and Formica of the Roisterer as we drank, barely keeping sloppiness and nausea at bay.

Register staff came trickling in as the sun ebbed away from the window. We didn't care—being lost in the endless sarcastic miasma of anecdotal journalistic hypocrisy. Edge related tales of an entire dynastic lineage of hack editors. Milt threw in tales of covered-up crime from the city desk, most often committed by the reporters themselves in pursuit of the unachieved. During one long near socially responsible diatribe against gay-bashing, I realized that Tatty was in fact gay, and I was repulsed to think that he was possessed of any sexuality at all.

Happy Boy came in with several bony followers in shirtsleeves and Eager Stooge darting about him like a nervous pilot fish. "Let's have a few rounds while the clerks finish up putting the old girl to bed," he announced to no one in particular.

"Sloppy seconds!" joked Eager Stooge Steve, "The Very Experienced Copy Editor," wanly. Several other high-strung boymen in shirtsleeves emulating Crane guffawed right along.

By then, as the sun was setting, the Roisterer had crowded up mostly with lone older male reporters slamming down beers, a few assorted conspiring duos comparing sports scores, and Crane and his cronies giving an air of gentility, drinking the hard stuff and watching the boys of summer become the boys of autumn on a TV hung too high to watch comfortably. By then I was catching such remarks from Crane's end of the bar as "murderer," "lying scumbag" and "faggot."

My face flushed, but I let it go.

At first, I had falsely comforted myself that he didn't see me when I saw him. It began to dawn on me that maybe his being here was no accident. After all, where would be the perfect place for one to go to celebrate having peed on the offending editor's rug but the Roisterer? And since I was news of a kind, there might yet be something Happy Boy could wring out of me.

Was it paranoia to believe I had walked into another setup? Was it egotism to believe I in fact mattered that much at all?

It must have been.

I drank and ignored it.

Edge leaned into me with sodden breath and whispered, "I think Happy Boy still has it in for you. He's talking about *you*." He stuck his finger into my breast bone to punctuate the point. "Yes, he seems to want you to overhear him insult you so you can start a brawl. A crude plan, but not without merit, as he's done it before. Watch out for his sucker punch, it's deadly."

"Yes," drawled Milt, "Happy boy likes to start with the upper hand and work his way down from there."

I was warm enough by then anyway and, for the most part, all the pain had fled. Time to go.

I glowed with the artificial health and vibrancy of drunkenness. "Well, I'm not buying," I said. "Edge was buying, I think, but my drinking tapped him."

"One more round?" Milt asked. "If you stick, I can tell you all about Dickie-bird and the hooker in the composing room last Christmas."

I stood and the world swayed gently. "It's tempting, but I have to head back."

"Head back? To what?" Milt countered somewhat annoyed. "She left you, didn't she, Ms. Right? You have no deadlines for this or any other paper that I know about."

I ignored that, grunted something and headed for the exit through clouds of smoke and wisps of conversation. Something stopped me. A beefy hand on my chest and then a shove. My balance was easily upset and I stumbled but did not fall.

Happy Boy.

"Did you like beating that little cunt to death?"

"Out of the way, Crane. I finished with you long ago."

Edge and Milt stood up and back. Milt left the table and approached Crane's band of emulators who were busily pretending that what was happening wasn't happening. He seemed to be hiding amongst them. Edge stood and watched, fascinated, out of harm's way.

I found myself staggering backwards again, and again was able to right myself before crashing.

"Let's see how good you are with a man's man, instead of a bitch's bitch."

I addressed myself to where Milt was now standing. Everyone else, including the frowzy youngish barmaid pulling drafts, affected oblivion to my existence, though I could swear I saw one or two of the solitary beer-swilling newsmen smirk. Her eyes kept darting towards me, or perhaps Crane, then fled back to the surface of the bar.

Edge watched with horrified interest as I spoke up good and loud: "I wonder if it's still considered news when an editor at a major daily threatens a former employee suspected—but not charged—with murder."

"It isn't news if nobody sees it!" piped Eager Stooge from behind Milt, who tried not to watch but failed.

"See what?" asked another voice facetiously through the smoke. Jagged laughter.

"Is it news if I kick your pussy ass?" Happy Boy bleated.

"Maybe," I said. "But you won't. I'm not playing your asinine little game. Go work for some glory, instead of trying to get some by pestering me." I stepped aside neatly and nearly fell over a chair. Happy Boy stood fuming, his thick fists clenched by the pleats of his pants. His chubby, boyish face looked haggard. He hadn't the excuse of a run-in with Miltown's finest, a concussion, or the weight of loss to give him that look, just the tedious frustration of making an impossible push toward having all his early promise kept and redeemed. He had failed upward as high as he was going to go. Next came failing sideways, then down. Even then, as far as I was concerned, it was all too easy for him. I wasn't letting him have his skirmish. I made my way back to Edge to finish the last little bit that remained of my drink (or any drink still on the table, for that matter, not being picky at the moment), motioned for Milt to rejoin us and sat down. My hands clenched around the heavy shot glass of bourbon and I sipped, getting the precise and warming tingle I expected and so needed.

"Now that I'm finished with you, *Happy Boy*, why don't you rejoin your little friends. Today you don't get your way."

Suddenly Milt came racing over, having pushed his way out from Crane's coterie I looked toward him and noticed he was about to say something. I didn't catch it.

Instead, I caught something to the side of my chin.

The sucker punch!

I moved with it, but another one caught me in the eye and then the gut as I rose then fell, the table upset next to me in a silent uproar, the drinks spilled, Edge having fled to the men's room. Milt stood alone in the center of the bar, his mouth open. The shot glass, now empty, was clenched in my fingers.

I tasted blood, mine of course.

I squinted my painful eyes, gauging the damage. I closed them, opened them, focused. There was Happy Boy standing over me, laughing. Edge was paralyzed, as was Milt, who was now faced with the dilemma of whether to interfere with the concrete wrongdoing of his direct superior in the hierarchy of news, or to allow it to continue while still risking everything. My career was finished at the *Register*, but his could go either way. He stood in his tracks, looking away, while still catching glimpses of me.

I noted, in a detached fashion, that this was my lowest moment. I *must* have struck bottom.

This was it and there nothing coming from it but pain, overwhelming pain, unintellectual pain, unrevelatory pain that led nowhere.

Unaccountably, perversely, I felt the beginnings of a smirk at the corners of my mouth where the blood still trickled. I had noticed as Happy Boy continued laughing, surveying his safe wreckage in yet another ambush of choice, that all the hurt, the immense feeling of injury was not really eating me at all. No.

I had known this feeling all my life, known it and mastered it. I was doing what I had done under the hands of all my mistresses. I was eating the pain.

My mind came back. And I realized that while I was casually assessing the situation, I had in fact turned it.

I was *dominating* it.

I had passed through it into peace and clarity lying there on the sticky, splintered barroom floor. Imperceptibly, the balance had changed. Facts clicked through my head as I lay there, seeming stuporous, but actually gathering strength. This was Crane's place, the *Register's* watering hole: no one was going to intervene. The little crowd of Happy Boy wannabes would only watch and say nothing. Milt would turn away and say nothing. The barmaid obviously had been paid not to pick up that phone and dial 911.

None of the solo or duet reporters came to my aid, much less to Crane's.

He had made the game simply between him and me in a place where he knew he had a clear advantage. This was sport for Happy Boy—but more importantly, it was a means of endearing himself to the icy and feckless Dickie Gunn. It was the favor he could call in to continue his failing spiral upward: "I kicked the ass of the ingrate murder suspect former freelancer who peed on your rug when you gave him first crack to tell his side of the story."

Another fact: Crane couldn't leave well enough alone. He had to have the last word, the final say, the punctuation of his authority which he likely suspected all along was weak. I watched him laugh, then begin to turn back to his cronies and where Milt stood like a deer in the headlights.

"Is that all you got, pussy?" I slurred it, sounding brain damaged.

"What did you say, *mook?*"

"I said you're a pussy." I made it sound as bad as I could. Maybe he couldn't make out what I was saying?

Happy Boy snickered. "Shut up, Patetick, and just lie there like the loser you are."

No. He got it. One more time. "Just walk away, pussy."

Crane never made it back to his cronies. He turned on his heels and paced back to where I lay propped against the wall. He crouched down, poured his beer into the neck of my shirt, further compromising my ruined suit. Everybody watched, nobody saw. I lolled and moaned.

"Let me teach you what a pussy is," he said, low, but loud and clear. "You obviously need to learn."

I could hear the cheery baseball score announced as all the other voices were silent.

Happy Boy jackhammered a blow right to my face. His knuckles scraped my cheek and knocked the wall. I had seen it and shifted just enough so that the sucker-punch would fail. His weight was off now, perched as he was on the balls of his feet, crouched down. He had to recover to land the next punch. It all seemed so slow in unfolding.

Without a thought, I brought my hand up and smashed the hardest part of the shot glass into the sensitive dent of his left front temple, just where his thick brow began arching out. It wasn't an expert punch—I was never very good at punching—but it carried the weight of the glass and that of my slackened drunken body as well. This worked to great effect. To my surprise, the glass didn't break, so I did it again, knocking Crane's large but now somewhat feeble hand aside, then kicked up both ankles between his legs and sent him over backward. It took a moment, but I was able to stand shakily to survey Crane more fully.

Apparently, I had hurt his head, as he was holding it with both hands, squirming and moaning on the floor.

Still no one came over.

I dropped the glass to the floor and approached Happy Boy. "Here, Crane. I'm a sport. No hard feelings. Let me help you up."

He extended his hand without thinking and I grabbed it, yanking him up just high enough to knee him squarely in the face.

"What have I done?" I exclaimed, suppressing the urge to vomit.

Now I knew they saw as well as watched.

I "helped" Crane up several times, yanking him up and kicking him back down, each time trying to do my best to comfort him, expressing my concern with such phrases as "I'm sorry," "How could I let this happen?" and "Take my hand—damn! That was clumsy. Here, let me help you up again."

No one came over. No one stopped me. Perhaps it was that— for a drunk—I was moving pretty fast and deliberately. There's also the fact that, despite claims to the contrary, most newsmen have a fear of physical involvement. I gave Happy Boy what I thought would be one last hard swift kick to the ribs, which I hoped would break upon impact, but was unsure about it, owing to inexperience.

I let him take his time getting up to swing at me, then gave him a clumsy ill-placed but enthusiastic roundhouse to his turgid jaw that nearly broke my fingers but which landed him back down on the floor hard.

Still, no one did anything, though the barmaid kept looking at the phone.

"I think we should be calling the police!" This was from Eager Stooge, of course.

Crane's cronies made a cautious collective approach. The rest of the reporters watched and didn't bother to pretend not to.

I stood breathing far harder than I realized, pain boiling back fast to my brain. I felt dead tired, achy, demoralized, but it seemed my brain was working at its most crisp and sober. I would take in some air, make sure Happy Boy stayed down, then leave.

Happy Boy was exactly the type to smash a bottle over your head from behind when you least expected it. That would be about the best he could do at the given moment.

"Kick his ass!" I heard Crane sob, so I nonchalantly kicked him in the head, bereft of any guilt for hurting him as I knew I must have. He gave out with a long liquid sob: *"Kickhisassssssss!"*

Milt spun about uncertainly and faced the cronies. "I think you're right!" he shouted.

I understood. Milt still had a career. And most of that was currently up to Happy Boy. I hated him, but I understood about hard decisions one had to make to continue surviving in the tricky, duplicitous realm of the news.

"Perry should *definitely* press charges. You saw it all—everyone here."

"Saw what?" said the Stooge. The others began deciding on the best course. "There was nothing to see."

Milt interrupted: "Either you all saw what happened or nothing happened. Either way, I WILL be a witness as to Perry's self-defense. You—behind the bar! Go make the call!" He snapped his fingers.

Edge overcame his fascinated paralysis, waddled over and slapped down a bill on the bar. "A hundred says you don't make the call, dear."

She grabbed the bill and went in the back.

"Steve's right," said Milt. "Nothing happened."

The cronies milled their assent.

"But if it did, I'll be right there to help Perry claim self-defense."

"You mean it wasn't self-defense?" Edge called out tremulously. "It seemed p-pretty clear to me that it was."

Stooge and the gaggle went to help Crane up. The Stooge stared directly into my eyes with contempt. I responded by spitting accurately into his weasely face.

"Perfect, Patetick!" he seethed, wiping it off with a handkerchief. "Just *perfect!*"

"I thought so," I wheezed and began making my way out.

Happy Boy was speaking, but I couldn't hear what he was saying. Lights flashed before my eyes, both inside my head and out. Cars whizzed by with disturbing headlights adding to my visual confusion. The Roisterer sign flickered. I began noticing a pleasant scent beneath the taint of diesel. The air. It was as sweet as I was uneasy, as sure as I was unsteady on my feet. Fall was here already, wasn't it?

Odd that the smoky early autumn odor could delight someone in my state.

I breathed in heavily to swallow darkness whole.

My arm was grabbed yet again. My only reaction was a headache.

Milt.

"You need a ride home."

"I'm fine," I burbled.

"It's not a question. I said you need a ride. I'm parked just inside

the fence." Milt held my arm securely. I walked with him and fumbled a bit. "Don't take any bigger steps than necessary," he said,
smirking at his own double meaning.

"Bloodied, but unbowed," I told him, grimacing for a smile.

"No," he replied. "Just bloodied."

NINETEEN

The horror of loss is not that you have to live with it like any-thing, it's that's you have to live with it like nothing. Every day, every hour, every minute—nothing, nothing, nothing. Nothing haunts you with memories of everything. Hope waves goodbye con-tinually in your mind's eye like the last fond look at a lover. Except there was no goodbye in my case, no final parting, just dead-ended promises, everything stopped in the middle for no apparent reason like the last frame of a jammed reel of film before it bursts into flame and melts away.

But certainly for a reason.

The murder served somebody.

And if the police were right, then I had even less of nothing than I imagined.

Regardless, nothing was what stayed with me, dogging every breath and every step.

I was still officially a suspect. The only suspect. And I remained unindicted and unarraigned but for heroin possession.

Conversely, my shaky legal status made me even more attractive bait for the strippers. I was proving to be far darker, sinister and more dangerous than given credit for, yet, for all that, soft and cud-dly, polite and mannered. They were lining up and taking numbers, implants all atwitter.

I steered clear of them and their entire after-hours club scene and setting, not because I had no need for sex. No, that had never left me, just like the ghost of Karenina had never left me. I stayed away to avoid future heroin plants, or some stripper using me to get out of a bust, swearing up and down that I confessed to her all the gory details of how I did what everyone assumed I did but was getting away with due to some failure of justice or the success of powerful friends.

At the time, however, I had no friends.

Nevertheless, my public defender assured me of a slam-dunk dismissal, which to my surprise happened fairly early in the game at the pretrial conference when both the arresting homicide detectives failed to show to testify. My emaciated, pinch-faced and pockmarked public defender in her bizarrely dowdy pink power suit handed me the business card of an attorney who would help me sue the Miltown cops for their abuses.

It turned out to be Herod's card. I laughed with life and tossed it away.

Autumn came down upon me, heavy, clear and chilly. I made the cliché effort to fill as many of the nothing hours with work as possible in a desperately failed attempt to drown out Boot's relentless television and his campaign to get state assistance to help him with his part of the rent. Boot and I occupied our separate rooms and common spaces in unspoken tension and animus. With as much work as I did, I was never able to get out of the hole I had dug with my employer, Chattels and Pelf, invariably penalized for this minor error or that, or for work just presumed to be erroneous and challenged by implication to prove otherwise. This would have entailed an office visit and maybe some supervised work in the actual physical plant of the company to redeem my "merit pay." I elected to leave my nothingness unpeopled and take the correspondingly lower rate of pay.

I did the wire dumps at the same rate of pay as any unskilled laborer and worked to reach the constantly irritating flatline of making as much as I needed to have slightly less than enough to get by.

So, for a time, I dwelled in my nothingness alone but for Bootlicker and the drone of his TV.

No newsman beat a path to my door, certainly no editor.

My phone didn't ring but for wrong numbers and solicitations.

With autumn I allowed the icy wind to blow full and unimpeded over the whole of my life as the world went on with its business and the main of life went on as unaffected as if I were dead.

In a sense I was dead.

I died with Karenina on the rack, or so I thought at the time.

I did quite a bit of thinking then, all of it leading nowhere but to resolve its darkest aspects in my dreams.

So, I stopped dreaming altogether, though I continued waking up at night, my heart racing.

When I could no longer stand the dumbness of my dumb terminal, I practiced with an unprecedented degree of focus using my little bullwhip, idly cracking it to drive Boot out of his mind, learning to aim and hit straight and square. I shredded some pillows with it, took divots out of the plaster walls with it, wrecked my bed with it.

It was a potent little item which served to remind me of the impotence that had cracked down upon me with the end of Karenina, the end of love and the sustained continuum of D/s no matter where I went or what I did.

As could have been predicted, without my participation events took place.

Just after my arrest and subsequent release, Action Team News ran a story several days later about the murder. Jack Tawdry and Jill Crowner were appropriately grim and ran comments delivered with teary stoicism by the huz, Bennie Poshlust-Middler It was a tribute to his long-suffering "regular-salt-of-the-earth-type-of-guy" status that he was at all times referred to as "Bennie." Nothing was said about D/s or the existence of any local community. The term S&M was bandied about as an adjective for the category of murder, as if this were a well-known and all-too usual means of dispatching a victim. The huz was focused on as a beleaguered spokesman for marital fidelity, keeping the family together at all costs and for the inherent dangers of the Internet. His angle was their angle, as they gave him full play on all three of our local affiliates saying the same thing:

"Communication and openness at all times is essential to keep from happening to all of yez what's happened to me and my children," Bennie said, looking clear-eyed and remorseful into the camera, his face taking up most of the screen. "If we had talked more if we had had a complete dialogue, if she wasn't keeping things fro me, then this terrible crime would of been prevented because— this is the most important thing-*she–would–not–have–strayed–fr marriage!* I cannot say this enough. When she strayed is when she put me and my children—her children—at risk! At risk of sickness and death! I plead with all a yez at home with the slightest doubt, with any spouse typing away across the Internet to some scum with a good line like the guy that killed my wife, get into that computer and find out exactly what's going on. Look over their shoulder, pry, ask, insist—*anything.* Don't let 'em have secrets from you! Don't let 'em!" He smashed his palm into his fist to emphasize his message and the camera went in tight: "It may save somebody's *life.*"

Cut back to the anchor desk.

"Safety on the Internet is becoming more of an issue every day, isn't it, Jill?" Jack oozed somberly.

"Indeed-it-is Jack," Jill said with a soft, sad smile. "It's a good idea for you to know just who you're talking to before you enter any Internet chat rooms. And also why. Incidentally Jack, Bennie informed us just after the interview that he plans on legally changing his last name from Poshlust-Middler, the name he shared with his late wife, to Poshlust, his wife's maiden name, as a tribute to her memory."

Jack shifted both expressions and gears. "And on a related story, "How to Stop Spousal Abuse Before It Starts—Know the Signs" from Wellness Editor Marva Miff—just after this."

"So stay tuned," chirped Jill with a wink.

I didn't.

They missed the connection entirely, somehow, between the rant of the huz and the murder of Karenina. The good news is I wasn't even mentioned. Bennie, they called him. *Bennie.* Not a shred of formality at all, like he was a neighborhood Joe exalted for affable common-ness in a human-interest piece, an institution of sorts. And if he wasn't, he was rapidly becoming one.

After that viewing, I began to notice that Bennie had become the story and the unsolved murder was secondary. How he handled his loss and sent his much-needed message of warning against abuse of the Internet, marital infidelity and any lifestyle alternative to sub-ban baby making and baby raising seemed to be unavoidable either he local affiliates or even in the *Register,* who ran supplements and began accepting op-ed pieces from him on the subject almost routinely (obviously heavily rewritten, and even then stiff and clumsy).

It became clear that the horrific murder of his wife was making him a local favorite: an ordinary, decent, hard-working guy overwhelmed by a perverse tragedy that was emblematic of our twisted times.

S&M, "The Internet," Alternative Lifestyles—he cited all of them as bearing a share of the responsibility for his wife's murder.

He was becoming the Miltown poster boy for parochial xenophobia.

You would think this would have given me more impetus to drink, while in fact it killed my desire altogether. It no longer could do the job of warming me up enough to form a semblance of functioning, so instead I faced the cold, accepted it, embraced it. The drinking ended for me without ceremony, without symbolic gesture but hand in hand with the sickness of loss as I detoxed alone while fitfully trying to work pulling news from the jumble of textual muck that kept on collecting despite my absence or indifference. E-mail screamed its dissatisfaction with me, my performance, my very electronic connectedness with every message I opened. I stopped reading my e-mail after finding myself penalized yet again for erroneous edits of the wire dump stories.

Not to whine, but concentration is at a premium and tough to sustain when the systemic need for a drink is quashed, replaced by the accompanying dizziness, nausea and vomiting caused by the simple, harsh refusal to look away.

And I was looking straight into the cold.

I was looking straight into the face of Bennie Poshlust-Middler who had ejected his old self from the hyphenate in favor of a new one—carrying on for his late wife. Taking over for his late wife. Benefiting like never before from his late wife.

I began to sweat everything back out in the gym, made a conscientious effort to eat well, even resorting to the preparation of meals in Bootlicker's debased, fetid and grain-moth infested kitchen. There was no more demoralizing or doomed effort than that of cleaning it, unless you counted journalism.

Time dragged on in this fashion—but not a lot of it.

There was at last the phone.

The first call was from Ms. Right. Her new man was moving in. Moving in where I once lived, taking my place entirely, from my private study to the most cherished affections of Ms. Right herself. You know, the precious affections I tossed away for life and hope somewhere else that ended in a bloody, disjunct dead end. I had made the worst of trades, a bad gamble, a romantic risk that was against all conventional wisdom to take. All of us wish to believe we are above or exempt from conventional wisdom, but of course we aren't. And as conventions go, I'm afraid that, for whatever the exceptional reason, I proved to be no exception. I owned the error and all its consequences.

There was no room for breakdown now or remorse. No room for it because the cold brutal facts stated that there was room for almost nothing else.

I determined that it was desperate for my survival that it be completely disallowed. I was like a man with nothing but reasons to drink refusing to do so. Hell, I wasn't like that man—I *was* that man.

"You have books, magazines and papers that need to be gotten, Perry," she said with brightness in her voice that stabbed me with an anguish I had never known before. "I don't want to throw them out. I don't think I can."

"Burn them then," I gulped.

"You don't mean that."

"Sure I do."

"Perry—stop!" She regrouped. "Should I just drop the stuff off?"

A small mercy. I wouldn't have to see what was happening now to my once-upon-a-time home. I'd take it.

"Yes. That would be okay. I could do that."

She let out a long sigh audible in its every detail over the phone. "I thought that might be better for you." Her tone was absolutely void of emotion, which meant every word must have been choked with it.

"Better for you too, not to have me back where I once was anymore."

"I see your point," she sniffed. Her tone brightened quickly. "There's only a couple of boxes, nothing very heavy. Just one trip up. We can have a drink first. Might make things easier."

"It might," I said. "But I don't drink anymore."

She giggled musically. "That's very good, Perry. Neither do I."

We agreed to meet on short notice at Eliot's off Divinity, a non-smoking fern bar as anachronistic in its upscale ambience as the Roisterer was in its downmarket dilapidation. We ordered sparkling mineral waters from the willowy Trinity University student waitress and left them untouched. She looked heart-wrenchingly better than I remembered. She was giving off waves of sexual attractiveness like never before: her lips were fuller, as was her figure. Her complexion shone eerily, as smooth as the surface of some untroubled lake. I thought it might ripple if I touched it. Her brilliant, copper-red hair had never seemed more lustrous, her eyes never danced with more brilliance, her voice was never as warm and soothing as it was just then.

I suppressed the trembling of my hands with all my might.

"So how's your new place shaping up?"

"Great—if I could get the other half to pick up his discarded sandwiches and underwear up off the floor every once in a while."

"You always were a bit of a slob," she observed. "I can't imagine it's all Mossman."

"Compared to you, the pope was a slob," I countered.

She looked away. "I know. I'm just a bit compulsive."

I reared back and laughed alone. "Just a bit?"

"Well, you know how it is about secret behaviors, Perry."

"Or those not so secret."

"Whatever, Perry. I don't want to talk about that now."

"Too late not to talk about it."

"Don't do it, Perry. I don't want to know anymore. It isn't running through my mind. I don't have to make myself go through it anymore."

"I wish I could do that."

"Are you sure you don't want a drink? You sound surly."

"I *am* surly. Yes, I want a drink, and no, I won't have one. It's bad for me. I'm trying to do things that aren't bad for me anymore. Failing miserably, but trying."

"Good," Ms. Right assented. "You'll get the hang of it eventually. I guess that goes for both of us."

"It does? Why?"

"I'm pregnant, Perry—finally, blissfully, incontrovertibly pregnant."

"Well, maybe we should be drinking then! No, just kidding. Really, I'm happy for you and . . ."

"Bill."

"Bill," I repeated, then laughed alone again. "It would have to be a regular guy, wouldn't it? One of the many Mikes, Bobs, Robs, Joes. One of the nine-to-five guys. One of the unsophisticated vanillas—a wearer of one those turned-around baseball caps, but only on Saturdays. One of the *booboisie*."

"Yes," she answered stiffly. "*Bill*. You know, he may not have sophistication, but at least he can afford to buy some. Mrs. Tsumashedshy accepted an offer we made on the house. No sense in paying two rents while making a down payment."

Visions of Karenina and our once-upon-a-time house drained away.

"So in he moves," I croaked, then swallowed hard. "Ouch. You got me. Am I bleeding?"

"No. Not this time," she sighed. "He's bright enough. Not as bright as you Perry, but bright enough."

"Contractor?"

"No—he's in systems, taking night-school courses in programming."

"Sounds like he won't be around much for living in close quarters."

"No. And he travels."

"You forgot to add, "Thank god.""

A smirk, then a nervous giggle. She suppressed it, then laughed.

"Yes. Thank god."

The tension broke for a moment.

"We're not over it at all, are we?" I said void of any happiness or satisfaction but welcoming a crawling numbness that was too slow in coming.

"No. I'll never get over it. I can't stand it. I can't deal with it—so I don't."

"What do we do?" I asked, genuinely lost.

"Nothing! I don't have to tell you it's too late. It's way beyond too late. Life goes on whether you want it to or not."

"There's always suicide."

"There is—but you're too mean for suicide, Perry. Besides, even after suicide, life goes on because that's the act that matters least."

"It does, doesn't it? For some, it's the pause that refreshes. For others, just the empty can."

"It's that way for everyone."

"It's just my turn. Again."

"I'll never have what I had with you with anyone."

"How do you get over it?"

"You don't get over it. I'll never have what I had with you with anyone. I don't even know if I want to. I don't know who can stand that kind of closeness. That's why I love Bill so much."

"Love."

"I am never going to get over it and I don't want to talk about it, think about it, deal with it, whatever. If I ignore it, I know it will go away. If I don't feed it, it will starve to death and rot away. Let it rot for what it did to my life!"

"It. Love. The demon Love."

"No. I love Bill."

"It. What is "it" anyway?"

"Nothing, Perry. And if that's what it isn't, that's what it's going to be."

"So we both wind up with nothing."

"No. I get a house and a baby. What do you get, Perry?"

"Nothing of course. Not even the check."

"Not even," she said and laid out her credit card.

I THOUGHT IT WAS MS. RIGHT CALLING TO CHANGE MY LIFE, BUT IT was only Dwight DeSeigneur. I was lolling in bed, struggling to banish the effects of not drinking from my mind and heart. I mumbled into it and the gravelly response was swift and sure.

"You've been too busy to pick up the phone, I see."

"The opposite, Dwight."

"Did I catch you napping?"

"Sure, Dwight. The rest of the world has. Why not you?"

"It's inevitable that I would. I haven't seen your sorry ass since you took up with the *rebbetzen*."

"The late *rebbetzen*, you mean," I said without bitterness, bitter as that fact was.

"I suppose I do. I couldn't help but hear. Have you stopped doing those dangerous drugs?"

I was supposed to laugh, but I had lost most of even the token sense of humor I had remaining.

"Yes—but I wish I hadn't."

"Well, get me some, if you start up again."

I sat up and rubbed my head as if that would make it clear. "Are you asking for drugs, Dwight? You don't even drink. I had to do that *for* you. Now you want to get high. You're joking."

"Well, yes and no. Mostly no."

"You know my drug bust was a sham. You must know."

"All the same, I think pain relief is becoming more an issue for me than it must be for you, taking note of how things must have turned out for you. I'm sorry about the *rebbetzen*, really. But it was an illicit affair, and you know how these things end, why—"

"Dwight, don't go on about it. I don't think I can stand to hear any relevant anecdotes involving the Weyerhauser wood-pulp heiress just now."

He cackled, then went on a miniliquid coughing jag. "And I don't think I could stand to relate one."

"We'll have to get together and talk about it sometime. My schedule's fairly open these days, as I almost have a job—when I can bring myself to do it."

"I don't think you want to see me."

"Why. Did you grow a beard?"

"No. But I don't look the same. You probably won't want to drop by."

"Why wouldn't I?"

"There isn't any time."

I laughed an empty, insincere laugh. What game was Dwight on now? Was he looking for some guilt string to pluck? Too late. Mine had snapped through clean and broken. "C'mon, Dwight. I have nothing *but* time. You can at least pencil me in."

"You could come anytime. But why would you want to?"

"So you could gloat about how right you were about the *rebbetzen?*"

He cackle-laughed which soon mutated into a cankerous, abominable cough.

"Oh yes, we can't leave that task undone, can we?" He gave his patrician old-style Miltown accent extra emphasis. "You'd better hurry on by then so we can tie up a few loose ends."

"Loose ends?"

"Yes," Dwight said, clearing his throat with an obnoxious gurgle. "My oncologist and internist collectively informed me I have six months to live, but I'm guessing I have about four at the outside."

WHEN HE ANSWERED THE DOOR, A QUICK, UNSENTIMENTAL LOOK TOLD me he had maybe four weeks, not four months. He was a stooped shuffling skeleton in a baseball cap and warm up jacket. His skin had the appearance of unfinished *papier-mâché* and his breathing produced a subtle but audible groan. He ushered me in and we sat in reversed position, I behind his desk of austere bronze and electronic toys in his hard-backed swivel, and he in the far more generously padded interview chair, sitting slumped and somewhat caved into himself, making an obvious strained effort to keep his head erect.

"Don't get all soppy on me because you're facing a dead man. Say something."

I knew what he wanted from me. And as unprepared as I was, I was going to give it. "I never thought I'd say this to you, Dwight, but you look positively ugly."

"Hell, I should look like death with all the radiation and chemo that did nothing but kill me by degrees. But that's a cliché, isn't it?"

"Like most truths," I said.

His body creaked and trembled with laughter.

Life laughed too, as did death.

When he stopped, there was silence.

"You really don't know what to say to a dead man, do you?"

"Sure I do. I talk to myself continually." His ancient Teutonic clock chimed four.

"Oh, you're far from dead, pal. Don't you believe it."

"Contrary to appearances, that's how it is."

The skeletal frame was racked with coughing. I knew better than to move forward, offer help or even acknowledge it as Dwight reached for a glass of some clear, greasy-looking fluid and a hand-kerchief. I waited. "Things went badly for you, I know that. You lost the Menace, the *rebbetzen*, the column, but that's just ebb and flow. Right now I'm all ebb. Right to the end."

"You'll beat it, Dwight, don't worry. The bastards go on forever."

He laughed and the fluid in his glass sloshed but didn't spill.

"You'd think, wouldn't you? God's plan is a screwed up little system, isn't it?"

"If that," I replied. "I just want to get it out the way right now before anything else happens. If there's anything I can do, Dwight, including what we talked about earlier on the phone, just ask. That's all. I'm only going to say it once."

"Thank you. Once is once too many goddamn times. Did you bring the porn like I asked?

I handed him the packet of slick S/M, leg fetish and assorted smut magazines I had picked up on the way.

"Good." He nodded approvingly, a smile rupturing the sticky seal of his lips. "It'll be a challenge masturbating to these, but I think I can handle it." I didn't react. It seemed he was talking more to himself than me at the moment. After tearing open the oversized envelope and briskly perusing its contents with unsteady hands, he looked straight at me, his eyes glistening and watery, then asked, "Was she worth it? The *rebbetzen*?"

I would not let silence overtake me. "Let me count the ways," I said, my throat clenched and threatening to choke.

"No one's stopping you," he said, spreading out his wizened palms. His eyes turned icy and his jaw was set.

"All right."

"Not yet, though. Something's missing. Something very crucial."

"What?"

"A cigarette. I need one badly, I think. And you know what little goody-two-shoes has done, don't you? Flushed every last blessed one down the toilet. Matches too. I especially *need* matches."

"Are you nuts?"

"Like it's going to kill me?"

I stood up and Dwight thrust his hands in his pockets. His legs quavered with the beginnings of the effort to stand.

"Save it for the cost of a coffin, Dwight. I'll provide the nails."

He snickered, no coughing. "About time you acted like a man."

That's what it was. Acting.

He named his brand, then added, "Make it the 'lites.' I always liked the lites the best. Not too heavy on the lungs."

I saw myself out and stepped from the townhouse vestibule into the cold, gray face of the day. I remember it as a long walk to the dingy corner store with the perpetually grated windows opaque with dust and soot. It was the Miltown weather that would linger for months, sunless and angry with an uncaring despair. Hopeless weather, certain weather. Ironies like only being able to help a friend by aiding and abetting in inevitable destruction lacked humor and cascaded over my mind with a cheerless spite.

I was underdressed for the cold.

I rubbed my ungloved hands together for warmth as Dwight buzzed me in to the building.

He had left the entry door to his townhouse unlocked to avoid getting up from the chair. Even in the warmth and firelight from his den bleeding into the office, I felt the chill. In my mind there was the chill, growing steadily worse.

Even seeing Dwight's expression light up after lighting up his cigarette did little for me. He was like a child at Christmas tearing away the wrapper, tamping the pack with a palm slap, lighting the match and inhaling the first fresh puff with prep-school ease. A puff or two more and he was his old self—despite the lingering skeletal veneer of impending death.

"I warned you about leaving the menace for the rebbetzen. But you scholarship boys always know better, don't you?"

"You were more right than you know."

"Well, I'd rather be alive than right, because it isn't better than nothing. It just *is* nothing." His gaping mouth devoured smoke. When his head reared back with pleasure, his baseball cap hit the floor. Little tufts of pathetic grayish white hair atop a carbuncled scalp were all that remained of Dwight's ruddy salt-and-pepper mane. "So tell me why it was worth it—it couldn't have been all pain and suffering, could it?"

"It could have been and it was."

I explained. I did more than explain, I regaled. I gave him every morsel of the things we had done, with embellishment, with flourish and with the sort of telltale lies that Dwight yearned for and appreciated so much. I told him how we went to some gala in the Catskills run by a fetish shop called Dressing For Pleasure, where Karenina and I, having stolen away from our respective spouses, proceeded to steal as much from our stolen moments as man and god would forbid. I told him all about participating in a fashion show, playing at spanking, anal insertion and straitjacket suspension even as we capered about through choreographed paces on the runway, while ringer professional dancers bussed in from New York City made everything look far more graceful than in truth it might have been with all their slick, extreme and ultimately meaningless movement.

I told him all about the stranger play, being submissive of the minute for any and every jazzed-up dominant wannabe Karenina saw fit to have me do the dance of D/s with. And it was a dance, not a waltz into darkness or light, but a waltz into oblivion, deadly in the progression of every step to the sweet ends of release and eternal return. Always return—but one that was altered forever once you realized you had come back, so there was always the incessant planning to get away again.

Even now I was planning for release.

I relived all that sweet sublime D/s relating it all to Dwight as

he chainsmoked cigarettes like placing nails in his own coffin, with
a sort of raffish care. He cackled commentary, nodded approvingly,
drained his tall glass of greasy fluid—which he explained was some
kind of saline cocktail to keep his throat lubricated so it wouldn't
crack or stick—and overtly hungered for more.

I left everything out of the story but the sex.

At the end of my exaggerated delectation—or at least by the end
of my recounted last best scene—he looked up from the smoldering
filter of his then spent cigarette and croaked "You done good, Perry.
You done real good."

Affectionate affected malapropism by way of Trinity University.
You done good.

"What's the difference between good and evil, Perry?" Dwight
asked with the suddenness I expected from the clearing of his throat,
not from speaking.

"You're asking me? As if I would know."

"Who does? There are those who commit acts of apparent evil
to do good. There are others who commit apparent acts of good to
do evil. There's always the hidden method and agenda in both. In
that they are exactly the same."

I gave Dwight what I rightly assumed he wanted, real responses,
not sympathy, not kowtowing to opinions in the face of death.
"There some yin in the yang up the yin-yang and vice versa. So?"

"So this!" Dwight tossed a folded newspaper into my lap produced from under his chair. The *Register*, of course. Nothing stood
out from the page it was folded over to show. I began to unfold it
and hunt. "Don't do that! Just look at the bottom right-hand corner.

I saw it. It was a mall article, hardly a squib.

"Victim Becomes Victor" was the head.

"Your boy Bennie's been a busy little bee."

"So I see. How do you know about it."

"Well, he is the little *rebbetzen*'s husband, isn't he? The huz?"

"He was. The huz."

"How could I miss him? How could anyone have missed those
grand and teary-eyed speeches he leveled at us all over the Jack and
Jill show?"

"She used to comment how she believed he was mentally challenged, rather dull and slow. I suppose he doesn't seem to be that now, does he?"

"I wouldn't know. What I *do* know is he's now selectman for the town of Swansea. And it seems for him to be just the beginning. If you read further in the article, it shows that he's throwing a Family Safety Rally on Saturday—a call for spouses to patch up their differences for the sake of their families, to prevent unsafe elements from breaching the already rather loose seal of the familial enclosure."

"You think he did it."

"One has to wonder."

"The police don't."

"They don't wonder about anything but pension plans, special details and contracts."

The smoke was fogging my vision and making my eyes sting as Dwight lit up yet again. "He has witnesses, an alibi and I'm part of it."

"Part of what? His *alibi?*"

I explained how the dowager of real estate called Bennie on my behalf when Karenina didn't show. "It's also the reason I'm not in jail. They'd love to get me for it."

"Quite a joke on them. They'd love to get you, but that might make Bennie a suspect, they'd hate that. Bennie is their fair-haired boy."

"You'd go that far?"

Despite his smile and insistent dragging on his cigarette, Dwight was beginning to look wan. "He's a cop wannabe."

"How would you know?"

"I know the type—hell, I'm one myself."

"Now there's news."

"A snob like me can afford ambitions of any kind. Or could."

"It only means I look good for the crime, and he doesn't. Just on the surface."

"Well I caught the license photo on *Inside Affairs*. You do look like a ruthless maniac, and perfect for the part of murderer, I might add. Straight from central casting."

Quaint, obsolete and accurate. All the same, I didn't need to hear it from him just then. Or felt I didn't. I contained my temper, watching Dwight glory in his pack of cigarettes. "I know. I'm a stereotype. A false one. In America, we prefer appearances whether they lie or not."

"Yes. We do. But I don't think you did it."

"What a relief."

"You don't have the guts."

"Just because you're a dying man, doesn't mean I have to take your insults."

"No, you took them well enough before I was a dying man."

"Okay. This is all leading up to some dying man's advice?"

"I have no advice."

"None? Really?"

"No—you're well and truly screwed."

"I did the screwing, though."

"No, you were a noble idiot. You were aiming for something that had nothing to do with money and self-aggrandizement. You were going for the romance of it all. You should have known romance is basically just a tool to close a sale. I used to hear the salesmen say it all the time amongst the thieves when I was working for that rag-trade rag back in New York· 'You have to romance 'em to get 'em to buy.' So, you bought. And bought and bought and bought."

"I'm not buying anymore."

"Really? Then you're going to lie down and take it? What about that editor, Crane, whatsisname?"

"Happy Boy?"

"You didn't lie down for him, did you?"

Dwight wasn't supposed to know. Now, he was positively beaming amid the smoke. "I have a few friends down at the *Register,* remember. Oh, and I just *loved* the pissing on the rug bit. The perfect way of getting out of an untenable situation."

"It was hopelessly juvenile and unproductive."

"Not necessarily. They tried to mark you as their territory, you marked them back. You walked out on your own terms and made a statement they were forced to—forgive my choice of words here—

absorb. Had they any intention of giving you the promised column
and of running your side of the story? We're talking about journalism
here, for Christ's sake!"

"We are. I see your point."

"Do I have to be more blunt?" Now color was actually coming
back to the desiccated, deflated, blanched cheeks. "Don't be as dull
as the *rebbetzen* said the huz was. You're a goddamn journalist! Go
out and do some goddamn journalism before this cocksucker winds
up in the senate!"

"Why? Would it matter much if another murderer and sociopath
wound up there? What's one more criminal down in Washington,
more or less?"

He reared back and chuckled, coughed, discreetly drooled. "I
doubt it would matter much at all, Perry. Except maybe as a personal
matter."

"A personal matter."

"Yes. To you. Make it a personal matter—after all, isn't everything?"

"I have come to realize that again and again while choosing to
believe otherwise."

"This is no exception then."

"No."

"There's nothing more personal than the murder of the love of
your life, is there? Of course not." He lit yet another match. "Never
mind having you branded you the eternal, unproven suspect for the
crime. No career left for you in Miltown. After all, everybody *knows*
you did it. The only way it could have gone better for the huz would
have been if he made the arrest stick. He gets the house, the money,
the kids—and a political career to boot, it seems. Not bad for an
hour's work, or less." Dwight glared at me. Humor and death had
left him for the moment. There was only judgment.

My throat closed up. It could have been the smoke. It could
have been emotion.

"I have no way of knowing the truth," I choked out from my
vocal chords.

"No way but to run down some facts. No way but to find out."

"I'll be arrested for stalking."

"And you'll deserve to be if you aren't smarter than that."
Dwight coughed again and slumped back in his chair, his face a
tortured amalgam of a wince and a squint. He knocked over his glass
of lubricant, which made a slowly creeping puddle on the hardwood
floor.

I stood, knowing it was over for now.

"I'm tired," he whispered as loud as he could. "Very tired."

I motioned toward the glass. He waved his shriveled arm loosely.
"Leave it! Goody-two-shoes'll take care of it."

"Okay, Dwight. I can see myself out."

He motioned for me and I came closer. He breathed and I caught
the scent of a profound personal decay that made me shudder. "Take
the pack of cigarettes and the matches with you—we can't have
goody-two-shoes finding the evidence."

I didn't want to bring up the fact that the smoke would tell the
tale on him as effectively as anything else, so I complied, grabbed
the matches and the pack and left him a few on the arm of his chair,
which made his eyes brighten. I looked back at him from the doorway. He was hardly the Dwight I knew anymore, of course—a skeletal *papier-mâché* Mexican celebration of decay. I could see what
remained of the man I knew fading further and further away into
blackness. "Good-bye, Dwight—for now I mean."

I felt like I was shouting to a distant figure drafting away on a
hunk of Arctic ice.

Before I closed the door, Dwight looked up at me, blinked and
cracked a strained smile. "You done good, Perry," he gurgled
through the last of his fluid. "Really. You done good."

I closed the door to the building and left, managing to feel nothing but the cold as I stepped from the vestibule into the ashen dusk
heading down from the highest slope of Breed's Hill.

It echoed.

You done good.

What had I done?

TWENTY

Kitty O' Shea was icily friendly and offhandedly smug as the camera went tight on her face, showing a reasonable and human degree of imperfection one could attribute to seasoning or weathering or whatever professional euphemism for aging was then in currency. "Just at the finish of last week's broadcast of the 'Suburban S and M slaying' down in Miltown, we received this phone call from chief suspect Perry Patetick. The beeping you hear means Mr. Patetick was aware that he was being recorded."

Cut to the driver's license photo.

Overlay captioning in clarification of the poor transmission quality of the taped conversation.

There, over my lunatic face, in big white type, was the conversation I had with Kitty, in a way I had never had it, delivered as I expected it to be delivered. It offered me no surprises, as I lay awake at 3 am to to avoid cigarette-smoke–befogged nightmares. The conversation boomed with exaggerated bass crackle and breathy distortion, no longer tinny thanks to digital enhancement. They left the electronic humming in for effect. Maybe they even put it in.

"WHAT DO YOU MEAN BY, 'YOU DID HER?' "
"DID I SAY THAT?"
"I HAVE IT ON TAPE."
"I LOVED HER, I NEVER HURT HER, I DIDN'T KILL HER AND THE PERSON WHO DID IS GETTING AWAY WITH IT."
"HAVE YOU BEEN DRINKING, MR. PATETICK?"
"HAVE YOU BEEN WHORING, MS. O'SHEA?"
"THE POLICE WON'T CHARGE ME—WANNA KNOW *WHY?* I SET MYSELF UP."

"WHY, MR. PATETICK?"

"THERE'S YOUR ANGLE, THE FACTS ARE THERE! GO AF-
TER THEM!"

"I THINK WE HAVE ALL WE NEED HERE, MR. PATETICK,
BUT THANK YOU."

Her dubbed-in voice was calm, professionally detached, reasonable. Mine, however, was a cross between that of a heavy-breathing
telephone-sex caller and a drunken maniac.

I swallowed hard hearing it.

Back to a more distant shot of Kitty at her desk, my badly
photographed face blue-screened behind her. "A more bizarre call
we couldn't have hoped for in this twisted crime of the murder of a
young Miltown housewife. An obviously inebriated Perry Patetick,
chief suspect in the slaying who, as of this broadcast, is still at large,
made the call. Local authorities tell us that they are very close to
making an arrest. They also told us that Patetick is still the chief
and only suspect in their ongoing investigation. We'll keep you up-
to-date on this crime and its alleged perpetrator but meanwhile, we
understand that down Texas way there's a certain farmer who's getting more than his fair share—"

She dazzled us with her smile, then continued.

"—of attention. For looking like a pig. Stay with us, won't you?"

I tried to oblige her, but fell back to dreams of the dying Dwight,
the dead Karenina, the long gone Ms. Right.

Dreams came baying like wolves.

I had a nightmare about getting to Karenina before it was too
late, trying to contact her, call her, see her, all to no avail. Her
cellular phone was my only hope. I kept trying the line, but it was
busy—a solid electronic wall of bitter pulsing. When at last I heard
the more hopeful sound of a ring, there was no answer, but I persisted—

Until Bennie answered.

Then I woke to the alarm and the capering cartoon characters
on my television set.

I shut them both off.

It was early for a Saturday, a little after eight before I could rub the fog away from my head, toddle off into the kitchen, make coffee and brood about the coming day. From the furthest end of the apartment, I could hear Mossman's throaty snore. He was good for that until noon. I put on some music to drown him out. There was nothing to drown out the catastrophic mess that Mossman had left for me, overflowing from kitchen to bathroom. I actually quavered at the thought of going into the den. I didn't want to know what mountain of refuse Boot had managed to assemble there since my last stilted effort at cleaning.

I carried my coffee into the one oasis of order in the place that was my room, shut the door and turned up the music.

My mind was as disordered in waking as the apartment was with Mossman's refuse. It was all over the place: dreams, regrets, beginnings, ends, long dusty middles void of light and hope.

There was something about that last nightmare, the short one about the phone that disturbed me. I didn't know what.

I had an inspiration and reached for the phone.

I dialed the number for dowager of realty. As expected, she was still in her office getting the paperwork ready on the houses she would be showing later that morning. She was far from delighted to find me at the other end of the line instead of a prospect, but suppressed her unease with practiced sales technique.

"I'm sorry to hear about what's been happening—the whole thing's a terrible tragedy. Poor Karen, poor you—"

"Poor Bennie?"

"Yes. Poor Bennie. And the children. What can I do for you, Perry? I have a couple coming in about twenty minutes to look at a property so I can't chat long."

I stretched the receiver over to my desk, removed my pocket reporter's tape recorder from the top drawer and pressed play to check the batteries. The thing grunted. I shut it.

"I won't keep you. I just have one or two quick questions."

"You know I didn't keep anything from the police. I answered every question they asked."

I stuck the suction cup of my phone patch to the back of the

receiver's ear piece on the flat, smooth plastic, plugged in the jack
and thumbed down the record and play buttons until the capstans
spun and the telltale red light went on. "Are you there?" she asked
with no little impatience.

"Oh, I'm here."

"Well, what do you want to know?"

"That day—the one where I waited for her and she never came.
To make the offer on the house?"

"The day it happened."

"Yes. When you called her number and got Bennie. Which number did you call?"

Her breathing told me she was exasperated. I didn't care. "I told
the police all that—and you too, come to think of it. I called her
home phone."

"And Bennie answered?"

"Yes. You know all that. Look, Perry, I'm sorry but—"

I suddenly began to feel desperate. "Just a couple of more
minutes, please."

"Just that, okay? I'm really busy." She drawled "really."

"When you made the call, was there anything wrong with the
connection?"

"Why would there be?"

"Was there anything like a fading in and out?"

"Let me think."

I was clenching the receiver in my hand. "It took a long time
for him to pick up. There were a lot of rings, weren't there?"

'Yes. There were. I was about to guess no one was home and
hang up when he picked up."

"How many rings?"

"I can't tell you that."

"Over four?"

"At least."

Karenina had an answering machine with a four-ring pick-up.
If after four rings, I heard some electronic pause or no one answered,
I'd click off.

"Five? Seven? Nine?"

"Maybe ten. Come to think of it, I thought I dialed the wrong number for a second, because if no one were home, her machine would pick up pretty quick. But those things occasionally malfunction. So it wasn't worth mentioning."

Hardly worth it at all. Of course. "Was the connection any good?"

"Clear as a bell." She sounded irritated. I didn't care. "What of it?"

"No interruptions or dead air at all? Like with maybe a cellular phone?"

"No, nothing but the call waiting. You know how those beeps sound on the other end—like a skip in the watchamacallit?"

"Transmission."

"Yes. Bennie told me to hold on, answered another call, then came right back. It was just call waiting."

"Okay. Thanks. That explains a lot." A drop of sweat fell from my forehead and splashed on the plastic case of the minirecorder.

"Glad I could help," the dowager recited rigidly. "And now I have to go."

"Thank you," I said. She hung up before I could even think of doing so. I shut off the tape recorder, rewound and played back a bit of what she said.

"No, nothing but the call waiting. You know how those beeps sound on the other end—like a skip in the watchamacallit?"

I clicked it off, drank my coffee with both hands, drowning for a moment in the warmth as I downed it.

Karenina had no call waiting on her line. It was for one simple reason:

The huz hated it.

I WAS OUT AT SWANSEA HIGH SCHOOL'S OLMSTEAD FIELD BY 10 AM. When I got there, the Family Safety Rally was in full swing. There were at least two hundred people, not counting children, who were there in abundance. There was a bake-sale table presided over by the usual prematurely dowdy matrons, many of whom were themselves pie-shaped. There was a rostrum, decked out with festoons of red,

white and blue striped crêpe paper. There were long tables of pump-
kins and gourds, with a fold-out cardboard Tom Turkey centerpiece
and a plastic cornucopia that bore the dust of previous years. There
was a lemonade stand, a portable sound system blaring frat rock
tunes, a lot of parent-child cacophony as they apparently waited for
the great man to speak.

It was one of those heartbreakingly golden autumn mornings.
The sky was a perfect cerulean blue whose imperfection of clouds
fit just the prevailing idea of what a sky should be. The air was crisp
and sweet as a freshly plucked apple. Even the applause crackled
with benevolent possibility as the huz took the podium and spoke.

There was the inevitable joke about the sound check followed
by requisite polite suburban chuckling. He rapped the mike with a
knuckle, asking whether it was on. More subdued chuckling. The
crowd tightened in on the podium. Then he went into the soft-soap
spiel about safety. I heard nothing about the Safety Club—his presumably aborted attempt to start a franchise of strip-mall shops
specializing in toned-down survivalist paranoia outfitting--window
boobytraps, pocket canisters of pepper spray and such. He was a
hesitant, drawling speaker with a circuitous delivery. He spoke from
the heart, not the head. Because he was obviously overwhelmed by
nerves, he seemed to be speaking from his head, which made him
seem stupid. Oddly enough, this apparent stupidity must have been
endearing. The crowd liked him and was giving him more than a
chance. It was as if his fumbling rambling stupidity elicited something protective in them.

Of course!

He was still the aggrieved widower.

Bennie rambled and eased into a series of platitudes about the
sacrosanct family and the forces of evil at hand working—as if with
no other purpose—to destroy it. He outlined with crudity and in-
accuracy how the family was the cornerstone of all civilization and
that "our civilization" was endangered by the electronic *"busy-goths"*
at the walls of the city. He pleaded for a return of the "busybody."
The busybody, he claimed, was even better than the police. Busy-
bodies were neighbors getting involved in the lives of their neighbors,
the way they should be, so that government could then butt out.

Buttons were being distributed amongst the audience by volunteers from little straw picnic baskets. "I am a busybody. I CARE," they read. I took one and pinned it on.

The applause, which was hit or miss before, was strong on that one.

As they drew nearer, I noticed it was easy to get close to where he spoke.

So, I got close. Good and close. Close enough to see the flecks of sweat under the ill-trimmed brush of his mustache.

I didn't look like myself. My hair was back in a ponytail and I wore an uncharacteristic sports jacket to ward off the morning chill. Cheap wraparound shades that I had picked up at a drugstore on the way hid my eyes, toned down the gleaming sunlight. I began nosing around the rostrum as he spoke, watching the watchers. I smelled the stench of cigar smoke and jerked around. There were quite a few deplorable, coprophagic spit-drenched stogies in evidence dangling from the slackened mouths of the hefty aging suburbanite men.

I was sure Bennie would have been smoking one had he thought of it.

There was no sign of the man I thought might be dogging me— the fat creep with the air of a policeman and the gracious aspect of a strip-club manager. He was nowhere in sight, although there were a number of dumpy, badly dressed, sallow-complected men who could have been him.

I moved on, spotting a few people standing to the side of the podium with an air of involvement. One of them was stooped in his posture, mole-ish and balding, squinting in the sun. I made him for a Bennie type. He looked like he was trying to find something useful and technical to do that would set him aside from being part of the crowd and failing. I sidled up next to him for a little chat. He gestured desperately, as if a technician, that he couldn't hear because of the concert speaker booming Bennie's voice next to us, so I motioned in kind that we both step off. He lit a cigarette, offered me one. I took it, lit it puffed on it, though I don't smoke.

"Great speech," I lied.

"Bennie? Yeah. He always should of gone into politics. It's what he's like."

"You know him then?"

"Sure. We go back a long ways. To his old neighborhood even." He said with hidden pride and overt cool.

"Where was that?"

"A few miles down the road. East Trinity."

"He's gone far for such a short distance."

"Yup. Up to the top of the hills of Swansea. But not without a terrible price." His remark was offhand, which made me add even more into the terrible price of my own. "Don't you want to hear the speech?"

"Oh, I do. But it looks like he'll be going on for a while."

His mole eyes brightened. "You know him?"

"I'd like to. I'm with the *Register*. Reporter. Might be nice to get an interview."

"Oh, sure. That's great. Bennie'll wanna meet you when he's done. And you're right—he has lots to say. That guy can really bend your ear. You won't miss nothin' with him, because if you haven't already heard it, he'll tell you. Or even if you have."

"You'll introduce me then?"

"He'll kill me if I don't."

I laughed. "Isn't that always the way with politicians."

"Oh yeah. He is one of them. *Definitely*. You watch—he'll be up at the State House in no time."

"So, were you one of the guys with him when it happened? The thing?"

His voice dropped to a whisper and his head bowed slightly. "That was a terrible thing, the thing. Yeah. I was with him. Sure. We all were."

"All?"

"The boys from the Rumpot Rats. You know us?"

"Oh, yes. I heard," I lied again to keep it going. "Old-time street-gang?"

"Nah." He waved his hand. "East Trinity motorcycle club. Sort of, I mean. You see, we were too poor to have bikes. I think we all

GARY S. KADET

had like one bike between us that worked. Bikies, they called us—
bikers without bikes."

"Cops must have questioned you hard and heavy."

"Hey, you're a reporter. You know what cops are like. You give
'em what they need and they go away. So we all did and they left.
No biggie. We're off the record here, I hope."

"Everything's off the record till I say it isn't. I have a hunch
Bennie's going to be big news. If I blow it with this, no more interviews for me."

"You got that right. Anyways, we were all there, Dukie, Fuzzy,
me, No-Legs, Spoon and the Governor."

"Governor?"

"Bennie's lawyer now. We all thought he'd wind up governor.
That's why we call him the Governor. Looks like Bennie's gonna be
filling *that* job now, though." He chuckled.

"Bennie's lawyer."

"Yuh. Markie. Mark Straddle. Looks like we're getting to the exciting part of the speech. Bennie'll let loose here." He eyed me coldly
and his expression changed." What did you say your name was?"

"Dwight DeSeigneur."

His face relaxed. "Oh yeah. I think I seen your stuff in the paper
before—"Man Among Men," isn't it? Lotsa family in that, tear-
jerkin' stuff. Bennie will like that. Funny, I thought you were older."

"I am," I said and he laughed, clutching the stomach that lurked
out from underneath his windbreaker.

"Manny here. Manny Brassbrad."

"So, just out of curiosity, when Bennie got that call, was it on
the cellular phone?"

"Cell phone? No. Karen had a cell, but I never even seen Bennie
use it. He doesn't like new-fangled stuff."

"I don't either. Gives you cancer," I said with a smile. "Let me
ask you something else."

"Sure. Bennie will make the better interview though." His
chuckle was insincere and nervous.

"Okay. Who was on the other line when the realtor called
Bennie?"

"What other line?"

"He had call waiting. Someone called when he took the call. Who was it that called?"

Manny's face was set. "No one called."

"That's not what the realtor said."

"Well, pali-boy, if that's what she told you, she's a liar."

"The telephone logs don't lie."

"Maybe not, but you do, if you're saying that's what they say."

"I'm saying so."

"Well, check again. And if you looked at those logs, you'd *know* they never had call waiting, all right? Bennie *or* Karen. Bennie doesn't like to be interrupted when he talks."

"That's obvious." I didn't have to indicate the ranting litany that had become the aural backdrop to our conversation. "So, when you heard Bennie say he had another call coming in, what did you think he meant?"

"He never said that."

"Ah, but what if he did? What if you never heard it? What if you weren't there?"

His face went as red as Bennie's, though Bennie's had become a grimace of squints as he spoke while Manny's stayed smooth and childlike. "If you're here to hang Bennie, you're barking up the wrong tree. We were *all* there when he got the call. He was with us most of the day and the cops already know that—cold."

"But there is that call-waiting thing. The realtor has no reason to lie and I bet the cops never asked her about it. But I asked, didn't I?"

"Yuh. You asked. You aren't doing no interview, are you?"

"Oh, I will. You can be assured that I will. But not today."

Bennie's repetitive incantatory ranting had become passionate and loud, buzzing out the speakers. The suburbanites were rapt, their children fidgety and unruly. Bennie evangelized about Internet scum—sex fiends and predators, homosexuals, lesbians and perverts who preyed on the family like burglars sneaking in through any window they could. That window happened to be the family computer.

"You're just another reporter scumbag trying to hunt up something dirty—you ain't interested in Bennie's busybody campaign," he sneered.

His vocal tone was the message that the gloves were off.

"No. I'm not. But believe me: if I asked, someone else will ask. Better have a better answer ready next time it happens. As for Bennie, well, he and I are going to have our one-on-one interview. You can count on it." I removed my glasses and glared at him hard in the golden light just askance of Bennie's gesticulating shadow.

Manny was a patsy. A lying patsy with my love's blood all over his face as far as I could see.

Fuck him. I let my hair down from the ponytail and grinned.

He looked back at me, crumbled, pointed. "You—you're the guy!" he said. "The suspect!"

"For now," I said, turned and walked away. I clicked the mini-tape recorder off in my shirt pocket with an audible "snap." "Only for now," I told him again. "Things change."

"Hey! Get back here you lying son-of-a-bitch!" Manny shouted almost loud enough to be heard over the ranting Bennie. Almost, but not quite, so no one, not even Bennie noticed as I stepped quickly away.

I smiled a cold smile, waiting for him to give chase, which he didn't.

I knew he wouldn't—not without Bennie's approval, not at risk to Bennie's big moment.

If I didn't know before, I knew then. By Monday there would be no question. By Monday there would be proof.

How would I prove it?

Why, with a phone call of course.

I RETURNED HOME—AND IT GALLED ME TO SAY THAT IT WAS MY HOME—armed with all the cleaning supplies I could carry. Maybe it was the golden perfection of the day, maybe it was the sense that I was beginning to turn circumstances around—to what I was unsure—or maybe it was the simple bolstered hope that hidden evil might be both exposed and stopped. Justice for Karenina, though I hated saying it, suddenly clarified things.

I spent several hours doing what felt like a futile number on the place, but when I stood back, dust-smeared and sweat-drenched, I had made noticeable progress in herding back and in some cases altogether expunging the permafilth Mossman had accumulated about the apartment. It was around three and the beams of mellow golden sunlight streamed in through newly washed windows on freshly mopped hardwood floors. As I was admiring my handiwork, Bootlicker burst out of his room, nude all but for his homemade harness. He posed and modeled for himself before the full-length mirror on the inside of the hall closet door.

"Bootlicker!" I exclaimed.

"Propertius," he retorted. "I see you've been cleaning. You have a long way to go, I think." He stomped into the bathroom and I stood where I was, looking at the sunlight and shadow, fatigued and incredulous, he shouted as he stood peeing: "The way you have things organized in here won't do. Bottles and containers go not just by size, but by category. You can't be putting bath salts with facial scrub and shampoo, you know."

Believe it or not, at the absurdity of this, I laughed.

"Disorder is *not* a laughing matter," said Mossman as he stomped haughtily past me.

I held my anger and went with the reporter in me instead, as Dwight would have liked.

"Fixing the harness, are we?" I asked just as he was closing his door.

"Yes. It needs some adjusting, I think."

"Why? There's nothing on for tonight in the scene that I know of."

"Well," he said pausing to think and then continuing, "I don't see how you would know what was going on in the scene and what wasn't, being that you're out of it."

He had me there. I had in fact been out of it. I was too busy riding out my tailspin to play, never mind to make even a passing effort at it. I was too engrossed with the strippers and then, erring on the side of caution, with nothing at all but the abstracts of my secret crimes and vengeance. "I suppose you're right. I have been out of it."

"That's good. I think you should stay out of it. The scene neither wants nor needs you. You can make yourself useful tonight by staying in and finishing the cleaning."

I nodded. "I could. But I won't. So tell me, Boot. Or I'll find out on-line."

"Do you think you can?" He asked, scratching his slack and drooping balls.

"Sure. It might take time away from further cleaning, but I can. If it's private, I'll whisper 'round the BBS till I find someone talkative. If it isn't, then it'll be posted somewhere in the SIG forums. If that doesn't work, I'll buzz over to my net server and hit the newsgroups."

He sighed and shook his head. "Tutor is having another party for the board. Same as usual. You are *not* invited."

"Au contraire," I said. "Being that I'm a paid-up BBS member, I *am* invited. How do you think people will feel about such discrimination?"

"Pretty good, I think, being that *you're* the one who's being discriminated against."

"Really?" I asked, arching my eyebrow. "Let's put that to the test, shall we?"

"No. I don't think so." He began closing the door. I threw the mop into the crack to prevent him from doing so. He jumped back as I knew he would.

"And if you want some cleaning done, I suggest you start where I left off or go back to your nest of permafilth. Meanwhile, I think I'm going to spend a little time getting ready for the party."

"I—I should punch your face," Boot stammered.

"You should. But you won't. Why don't you just face facts and do some cleaning?"

Mossman looked at me, his face contorted, made something like a grunt—or was it a growl?—then slammed the door so that the vibrations it caused made furniture tremble.

I laughed to myself when I noticed that the loathsome, permafilth–saturated floor mop was still in his room.

I went to my desk and logged on to Dreams-Come-True.

.....................Tutor Welcomes you to ....
ÚÄÄ
ÄÄÄ¿ 18+ Years Only.

[3] DREAMS-COME-TRUE[3]
ÀÄÄ
ÄÄÄÚ
ßßÄÄ¿
ÀÄÄ
ÄÄÄÙ
Time: 14:15:38
ßß¿
Date: 14-NOV

[3] Pansexual Educational, & Support Organization.[3]
ÀÄÄ
ÄÄÄÄÙ
Caution!
ßß¿
Players At Play!

[3] Dedicated to the BDSM/Leather Community......... ....[3]
ÀÄÄ
ÄÄÄÄÙ
Sysop: "O"
Located in Beautiful Miltown!
BBS: 555-520-PERV telnet: dreamscumtrue.com
VOICE: 555-5051
Thanksgiving party is 11/18! This will also be a Dreams-Cum-True-
fundraiser as well!! Now is the time to donate those toys and fetish
items that you are no longer using to a very good cause .. TUTOR!!
<grin>
If you are already a pervster on this
system, type in your handle and press RETURN
Otherwise type "new": propertius
Password:######
PAIDTOP (PAIDTOP)
Make your selection (T,H,O,S,E,Q,F,V,R,A,P,C,G,J,D,B,? for help, or X
to exit):

You are in the Main public Room!
Type "LIST" to see a list of available Rooms.

"O", DickseyChick, MooseCock, TechnoSlaver and Auntie Maim are here with you.
Just enter "?" if you need any assistance . . .
From "O": It's Propertius!
From MooseCock: So you have all the rooms of the house done up as dungeons again?
TechnoSlaver is paging you from the Perv-Curve: How have you been—are you going tonight? Could be a good turnout for once.
/p tech I haven't decided yet. It's at the flatulent fraud's joint?
Paging TechnoSlaver
From "O": We were ALL sorry to hear about Karenina, Prop.
From MooseCock: We were—especially since you did it, you fag bastard!
From DickseyChick: I want a fag bastard!
TechnoSlaver is paging you from the Perv-Curve: Yeah. Usual time, usual players—but it's something to do.
/p tech You have a point.
Paging TechnoSlaver
Maybe I'll see you all tonight. We can chat about it.
—message sent—
From "O": You'll have to be put on the guest list, Prop. And I think it's full up.
From MooseCock: Who the hell would want you?
***Muffy has entered the Perv-Curve**
From Muffy: I'm surprised Propertius still has an account here after what he did.
TechnoSlaver is paging you from the Perv-Curve: Friend—I think support for you here is precious little.
/p tech No kidding.
Paging TechnoSlaver
Perhaps we'll discuss it like the intellectual thrill seekers we are—face to face.
—message sent—

From MooseCock: If you can make it through the door, scumbag!
From "O": You'll have to get permission from Tutor.

x

Exit

PAIDTOP (PAIDTOP)

Make your selection (T,H,O,S,E,Q,F,V,R,A,P,C,G,J,D,B,? for help, or X to exit):

x

You are about to log off the Dreams-Come-True BBS. Press (y) to terminate your connection, (n) to return to the TOP menu, or (1) to re-log.

y

***

I got to the modestly dilapidated sprawling Edwardian house by St. Anselm's Mercy that Tutor and "O" called home around ten, dressed in my best fetish covered by my now–threadbare cashmere overcoat. Cars overran the small side street that the house was on and filled the broad driveway, edging past the curb. I carried my little black travel carry-on bag packed to the brim with every toy I owned that would fit. Once again, crudely made signs marked "Thataway" or "Thisaway" greeted me before I had the chance to ring the bell.

I opened the door and walked in, knowing it wouldn't be locked until after 11 pm, and waltzed into the firelit den where once again the lounging, scantily clad *grand guignol* of ugliness played before me. When they noticed me come in alone, the dulcet conversations stopped.

"What's *he* doing here?" asked Noelle, a four-hundred–pound dominatrix in black spandex and a hairnet.

"Looking for more subs to beat to death?" said some aged, white-haired newbie male in a workmanlike outfit of boots and jeans and biker wallet-on-a-chain, whose salient feature was the black leather vest, possibly casting himself in the image of the party's host. He reclined superciliously on the divan with his hands behind his head. I presumed from his typical Geppetto outfit that he was yet another self-appointed man-dom who I had never met before. I didn't want to meet him now.

"No," I told the Geppetto, "I'm thinking of switching to aging male dominant wannabes. Interested?"

Techno-slaver waved tentatively from the doorway, but remained quiet.

"Nobody invited you," said Noelle.

"I'm a paid up member of the board. Isn't that invitation enough?"

"You have to RSVP!"

"I wonder how many here did? Shall I spend some time polling?"

"You're different—you're a problem," Noelle huffed.

"And that's because the police suspect me of a crime they can't prove? That's because uninformed people like you make up their minds the way they're told to? To fit into the prevailing set of opinions so as not to risk dislike or a minor loss in popularity from people doing exactly the same? Listen, save your nonsense for one of the desperate lemmings. I don't have time for your stupidity."

She tried to get up fast and wave her finger at me, but failed, doing it instead from where she sat. "I'll have you know I'm *very* bright! And I know an asshole when I see one!"

"That must be it! When you see an asshole you get to know it by acting as much like one as possible."

"I would never act like you," she mumbled into one of her chins and I moved on.

I thought for a moment that this was not helping the cause of my popularity.

Then the thought also occurred: Fuck popularity.

I came to play, I decided, and made my way to Tutor's office to hang up my coat, stow my bag and change. "O" barred my passage, wearing her white muslin Egyptian slave outfit, replete with silver necklace-chained headdress. Too much of her flabby withered flesh was in view and the sight of it halted me in my tracks. She flattened her palm against my harnessed chest under the open coat nonetheless—as if that was what was stopping me.

"I told you, you needed permission."

"It's your house, why don't you give it to me?"

"It's Tutor's party."

"And he'll cry if he wants to?"

"You had to RSVP. You didn't."

"Do I have to ask how many people here RSVP'd, or is it just that I'm a special case?"

Auntie Maim flung herself between us and smothered me with kisses. "You've always been a bit special, dear."

I noticed a few others—late arrivals like me—drifting in at the door in a commotion of coats and valises. I smooched Auntie back primly and asked: "Did you RSVP, Auntie?"

"Now why would I do that, darling?"

I could sense the pinched, frowning visage of the gray eminence behind me. I turned and gave it a smile.

"Why would she, Tutor?"

"Everybody follows the rules here, Prop." He failed at sounding affable.

I looked over to the door where the new arrivals were being screened informally by the lounging leaden sybarites, smoking and repositioning their generous bodies deep into the cushions of the overstuffed chairs and imposing divan: "Hey, Baron," I called over to the porcine, pockmarked, crudely tattooed geriatric at the door I had made out among the arrivals as Dreams-Come-True member Baron Land (described in his online profile as "devastatingly handsome and cruel"). "Tell me, Baron Land—did you RSVP?"

"What was that?" he called.

"Did you RSVP?" I shouted again.

Suddenly I was getting once again what Tutor considered to be his share of attention. His face darkened with red.

"No—I just took it for granted any board member was welcome."

"Me too," I shouted back.

The clique surrounding Baron Land at the door entered a querulous frenzy over the right to attend Tutor's little S&M mixer. I decided to help them, being as I stood toe-to-toe with Tutor. "Anybody here *not* RSVP'd please raise your hand?" I shouted. Tutor made a motion to touch my hand, but stopped himself.

"Okay, Prop. That's enough!"

"I just wanted to make sure I wasn't being unfairly singled out."

"Nobody has to raise their hands," Tutor announced quickly. "There's no problem about RSVPs!" he whined at a pitch above the hubbub. "No problem—just go back to having fun please!"

"Any board member can stay!" I shouted, then put my face up close to Tutor's adding: "Want proof of membership, Toots?"

"Not necessary," he mumbled. "I know you."

"I guess that goes for "O" too."

"I don't know." He shook his head gravely. "It's her party."

I burst out laughing; Auntie smacked me on the cheek for my inattention and moved on. Tutor glowered at me. "I can't speak for her, you know," he said.

"Oh. I thought you were the dominant, the one in charge. No matter. I can. She told me it was *your* party, so I guess it's okay." I pushed past Tutor and made it to his cluttered closet of an office. Before I could remove my pants, I was crowded in with several others who were throwing off their coats and changing with hurried clumsiness into their fetish. I joined them and noticed Tutor looming at the doorway. He glared at me. I smiled back and finished slipping into my harness.

Tutor stepped into the room, sidled up next to me. "You made a mistake in coming here."

"I make lots of mistakes. And I'm not the only one."

While trying to ignore him and finish dressing, I suddenly found myself alone with him. The three others who had occupied the room with me left before they were quite finished, shying away from controversy of any kind, anything that might taint their appearance of being willing to go along with anything or anybody as long as they were a group—the public scene shield to cover and protect their private scene lust.

"Teach me my mistakes, O Tutor."

"The scene has no place for you, Prop. We don't need a public witch-hunt. Having you around makes us prone to one and you tend to disrupt the pack."

The pack! So that's what it was! "I do? And I thought you wanted a cause to rally round, Toots. Why not me?"

"You know why—you're just another straight white guy. Nobody cares, least of all me."

"That's blunt of you. Bi white guy, by the way."

"Even worse. If you were a bi woman, maybe, but as it is, you don't count. No one can hear this but you anyway. That's the way it is."

"Is it?"

"Things are changing. I don't want to have to take *my* scene underground, but that's where we're headed. You're too much trouble. People follow you around, pay attention to you—for all the wrong reasons. You should cut your losses and run."

"No, I think I'll be staying, Toots. I'm a member. This party is for members. Try and stop me, why don't you?"

He danced about me nervously, thrashing his hands in the air, sizing me up—perhaps looking for a place to grab—but shifting his weight away, too, apparently afraid to do anything. "Your account is cancelled as of now!" he sputtered. "You're no longer a member and have no right to be here."

"Okay. I'll enjoy myself till you get around to deleting the membership and then leave. Unless you're going to physically throw me out while I'm still technically a member?"

"I will!"

"How do you think—*if* you think—that that will make you look? Throwing a fit at a club can be spun all sorts of ways, but throwing one here? Throwing me out, with a number of my friends in evidence? I don't think so."

"You have no friends!"

"Care to put that to the test? What if I do? What if they surprise you by who they are when they object? What if they even intervene? What if word gets out about it? How will the liberal, pansexual, scene-supporting, tolerant-of-everything-but-abuse Tutor defend his physical attack on a perhaps wrongly accused member of the scene? It's already bad enough you're a known homophobe."

"I am not—they have a right to the scene just as we do."

"Uh-huh."

He rubbed his face, spun around, turned back. "You may have a point."

"Worse than being a politician, isn't it? Besides, how would it look if I kicked your sorry ass in the process?"

"You couldn't." His knuckles whitened and his face was clenched like that of a comical gnome—the ones in my head that gave me a headache!

I bowed. "The opening move is yours."

Tutor backed away, opened the door. He smiled his most insincere, spastic smile and let the door glide open fully to prying eyes, intrusive ears and intrigued faces of his party guests. "Stay as long as you like!" he boomed. "We treat all our members the same!"

"You're so fair, Toots."

"Who's Toots?" I heard some voice ask. We had caused the crowd around the food at the social table to peer in the closet-office door. There was an explanation and some laughter.

He had to do something, so this was what he came up with: "I don't think promoting you as a cause is a very good idea, Propertius. Right now, I am taking the scene out of the public eye—not drawing attention to it by making someone like you a *cause celebre*." It was an announcement he made more to the room than to me.

"No," I replied just as loudly, "that would only work if we could somehow make *you a cause celebre*."

"We don't need negative attention. We don't need attention at all—I'm playing it low key!"

"You make it sound like *you're* the scene."

"Haven't you heard? *I'm* the one building a community here."

I waved my hand, moved through the doorway past him, making him suck in his gut. "No, not really. You're just exploiting one."

He sputtered something about leadership. It was hard to hear as I was walking away. I could hear him soft-shoe smoothly into his self-promotional song and dance routine and I plainly made out the word "sad."

I interposed, my face close to his and said it loud: "You've got it all wrong, Toots. What's sad is that the community around here thinks that it's exploiting *you*."

I had their attention after that remark, but nobody stopped me as I pushed past a table of men spanking, fisting and genitally torturing a blindfolded woman with a knife. Nobody stopped me as I ascended the stairs.

Nobody stopped me as I went for the dungeons.

TWENTY-ONE

I reached awareness strung up from my wrists high off the damaged hardwood floor, my feet in black plastic stirrups. The flogger was long and heavy, smacking my back with a sweet, pain-heightening thud. I could look behind me and see Widow's Pique laughing maniacally while at the same time grunting and groaning with effort. Auntie Maim was caressing my erect cock with the spinning spikes of two Wartenberg wheels, one in each hand, riding my helpless flesh from tip to shaft.

She licked occasionally in between strokes to keep me erect and desensitized with frustrated arousal.

I had played all night with as many as would have me, which meant that I was the extra hand or add-on in any newly emerging domme's scene, helping to facilitate that essential—and so fleeting—first big social splash. I had been a human spanking bench, an equipment bearer and even a demo model for a timorous but eager new submissive's mistress so as to demonstrate just what was expected of him. I was an extra sex toy for the old efforts of the newly arrived to announce their arrival.

I lived up to my name—I was a *prop.*

I was sluttish, outrageous, against decorum and yet perfectly within my rights to offer myself to be used by others as I saw fit. Just as life and love had sought to do and had so easily done.

Funny how they were not—to my inner ear at least—laughing now.

I was doing the laughing.

Finally, Widow's Pique and Auntie Maim had decided it was time for me to get my just desserts. Each had reached a level of anxious frustration over long romantic affairs that had no hope of working out, pursued with the ruthless ardor of a programming analyst in search of a bug. Since they had no satisfaction on any other sexual front, making a scapegoat of a scapegrace like myself proved nearly irresistible. Would I refuse, as the toad-like toadies and obese coquettish bisexual harridans made clumsy come-on gestures to the femme fatales in turn luring me to pain and release?

I had come to the party in the spirit of acceptance, not to be accepted.

I was there in honesty for myself and not to make pretenses toward any collective agenda, benign, malignant or indifferent.

I brought them close to me to bring me the fruits of their own desperate, impassioned longing and despair.

They had been working on me for over two hours as the party began thinning out. After I inadvertently splashed Auntie in the face with my unruly ejaculate, she excused herself for a cigarette, which left only Widow's Pique to torture me. Auntie went laughing all the way in disbelief out of the room. I laughed and shouted: "I'm not done yet! Not done!"

Widow's Pique stepped it up with the flogger and I braced for the blows.

When my head cleared, I was back in the nest—the little pillowed and screened-off area of seemingly so long ago—and Karenina was working on me, inserting a well-lubed plug in my behind as I moaned disconnectedly. I startled and the pain increased. It was Widow's Pique, of course, wielding the plug and stroking me, feeling the electric shimmering of my surrender even as the image of Karenina flitted away like an unwanted fly.

I moaned again. She set the plug and smiled.

"I'm going to fuck you just a little bit with it now."

"No, you won't," enunciated a violent wheeze.

Tutor.

"Something wrong—Toots?" asked Widow's Pique, grinning.

I scrunched my eyes shut, and fought back stinging pain for a bit of clear consciousness.

"Cardinal sin, Toots, breaking someone's space like that," I said.

"Has he no manners, Prop?"

"Obviously not." I grunted.

"This is *my* space, not yours," Tutor fumed. "And I want you out of it."

I kicked out and the screen fell over, causing Tutor to jump back.

Several other couples looked up from various intimate sloweddown scenes positioned about the bondage bed and rug of the room to see who had caused such commotion. "Asking *them* to leave too?"

"Eventually," said Tutor. "But I want you out now. I told you before, there's no place for you here."

I stretched out on the pillows languidly ignoring the butt plug and said: "Just me, Toots, or should I take a few with me when I go?"

"You can stay awhile if you want, Widow's. I may be cooking up some early-morning scenes if you want to participate." His put-on menacing laugh fooled no one.

"No thanks." She smiled her most alluring smile, standing up and getting close to Tutor. "I think I'll head off with Prop."

Tutor glowered down at me.

"Or, in a word: fuck you, Cousins, you lecherous hypocrite!" I turned to Widow's Pique. "Now, if you take that plug out of my ass, darling, we can leave the dirty old man to his wretched space and have a little fun."

She obliged and I screamed involuntarily.

Tutor walked away, but not before shooting a hateful and somewhat pathetic glance backward.

Widow's Pique bit my ear. Her scent was as thick around me as a fog.

"*My place,*" she ordered.

IT WAS A GOOD, LONG NOURISHING FUCK, A D/s FUCK, AN ALL-night, liquid, lascivious fuck—the unapologetic to any god, Judeo-Christian, pagan or otherwise kind of fuck. It was the kind of fuck one enters the scene—any scene—thinking about, hoping about, urgent about. Widow's Pique ground me down to the very center, as I lay bound and spread across her bed. We were both inspired to make this a fuck for the ages, perhaps because we had no interest or caring to make it such a fuck at all.

We fucked without love, we fucked without regard for anything but the fuck itself.

Loveless gratuitous sex, brute, rote meat stimulation crowned by a thorny aureole of D/s invested with each personality completed by and complete within each role, each place, each position.

We fucked long, hard and well.

I submitted, she extracted. I gave, she took.

Then she graced me with her sex straight and long on my face and I did so until her bucking ceased.

As a reward I was beaten, bruised, bitten, whipped and brought up the dawn with an impossibly long bare-handed spanking that was so thorough and protracted I thought my butt was bloodied by its end.

But it turned out that, despite the severity, it was barely bruised.

The Widow and I spent a lazy, languid Sunday together before I packed off to my apartment by dusk.

We exchanged anecdotes, not troth, but humor and lust, no passion or longing.

We did everything without love, shooed love from the room, banished it and all the other demonic comedians. I knew it was a struggle for her not to discuss her failing romance with the neo-psychedelic rock musician/record-store clerk, as it was a struggle for me not to bring up Karenina. We persevered in the struggle by fucking at a hectic, thumping stride or with an extended gyrating glide, nerve to nerve and flesh to flesh, as it felt in the liquid orgasmic rush that it was meant to be.

She slid from my face, untied me, wiped my chin and we hung out in bed in the cave-like splendor of her apartment. She had *papier-mâché* stalagmites and bas-relief stone concavities vainly changing the aspect of the dingy box in which she lived. She had red brick hastily painted for a dungeon wall that remained incomplete, along with the usual squalor that went with struggling youth in the city supported by checks from home.

She lit a light cigarette—one of Dwight's kind—and said, her robe falling open, her belly lustrous in the shadows:

"I'm sorry about Karenina. Really everyone is—they put you in the same category with Ally. Remorseless abuser."

"But I'm a bottom!"

"Since when did logic enter into it?"

"Or truth. Well, I'm sorry about it too."

"Lousy thing. I wonder how everyone else took it." She posed with her cigarette, uncrossing her legs on the bed and exposing her pretty glistening twat.

"Everyone else?"

"You know she played with other people."

"Haven't we all?"

"She used to like to get involved—very emotional."

I didn't like where this was going. "Play without emotion is usually a dud."

"Most play is—most public play anyway. But Karenina was looking for surrender of an emotional kind. It was her kink, her submission needed tears and frustration, bondage as romance."

"We were in love."

"Weren't we all?" said Widow's Pique. She moistened her finger with her sex, smeared it across her lips, dragged on the light.

"No—it was a different thing, I think. It was the meeting of soulmates, true lovers."

"Folk history is riddled with false true lovers, you know."

"This isn't folk history—this is life!"

"I'm just saying she was involved with other men—don't get tense. You were involved with other women, you know."

"Well, if it was like it was with me, then it was fine. We wanted that for each other."

"That's probably what it was."

"Yes—I'm *sure* that it was." She grabbed me by the hair and forced me to go down on her by dragging my face down between her legs. I did so thoroughly, enthusiastically, without protest. I tried to say, "Everyone always thinks it's cheating, but to avoid it is only to cheat yourself," but my mouth was full of her fluid flesh so all I could do was emit eloquent muffled groans.

It didn't matter. She knew. She was a player. Karenina.

She was sex, she was hope, she was life.

I buried myself in the act rather than let those thoughts go on.

"Lick me, damn you, till I can't think anymore!" she shrieked. "Lick me now!"

There was no humor in her voice, no lightness, no social irony, just a raw plea unaltered from the core of its origin. I tongued, laved and sucked as passionately as I had ever kissed anyone, ever laid my lips on anyone. Ever.

I washed that man right out of her hair, so to speak—or, to be more accurate, I *licked* him out.

Either way, at the point of her own release was when she finally released me.

At its finish, I showered, gave her still musky lips a prim kiss goodbye and went home untroubled.

It was just play, after all. Everybody knew it was play, all involved knew it was play. Only play.

I felt sure of it, going up the steps of my apartment clearheaded and alone in the cold November night.

Play.

"NEIGHBORLY NETWORKS, WHAT CAN I DO FOR YOU TODAY?"

"Yes. I'd like check the status of my account?"

"Number please?"

I gave it to the bright young man at the end of the line. I guessed his suit was stiff, new, cheap and uncomfortable. He was thin and nervous with hopeful youth. As yet unbroken. Was I ever that way?

"Okay, Mr. Poshlust-Middler, what information would you like?"

"How's my call waiting?"

"From what I have on the screen you've never had that service on this line. If you'd like to order that service, I can do it for you now."

"How far back do your records go?"

"At least five years. You've been with us a long time, Mr. Poshlust-Middler, so yours go back even further. Would you like me to make that change for you?"

"No. That's all right. Let's keep that as it is."

Key clicks—I could hear them. I was attuned to them.

"Do I have any special features at all?"

"Just a moment."

Key clicks.

"Just making sure I have everything."

"Take your time." I could afford to be magnanimous.

"You ordered call forwarding last March."

"I knew I had something on the line. Do you know the last number I had my calls forwarded to? Can you look that up?"

"Let me punch up the history."

"Sure." I was sweating again; my heart was beating between my teeth.

"I have a short list here. Do you want them all?"

"Sure."

He read them all off and I copied them down.

"Seems you did most of the forwarding to a cellular line—I can tell from the exchange."

So could I. I could no longer feel the phone in my hand. I cleared my throat.

"Those are dated?"

"Yes, they are. And it seems you haven't used the service for quite a while. Do you want to continue with it?"

"Of course. Can you tell me the date of the last forwarding?"

"Sure. That was to your cellular line."

He recited the date and time. My chest was heaving. I grappled for control as my focus on the room zoomed out.

No surprise, but it affected me just as if it were one: the forwarding was made when the dowager called. The interrupted signal? The bastard was in his car—coming or going from the scene.

The scene.

"Can I help you with anything else today?"

I croaked a wild sound.

"Can I help you with anything else?" He was trying not to sound impatient, but his irritation was growing.

I coughed. "Do I have anything else on the line?"

"No, just the contiguous metropolitan calling plan. I can make some updates and upgrades, if you like. Show you how to save money on your monthly bill."

"Not right now. But as is, I have no other features on my line?"

"No—except for the forwarding, it's plain vanilla."

"DO YOU HAVE AN APPOINTMENT SCHEDULED FOR TODAY?"

I smiled my best dress smile upon the receptionist. She was a desperate cheapie, one of the big-haired girls in a knock-off power suit suppressing the urge to snap the gum she indecorously chewed.

"He wants to see me."

"He's booked all day and in court at the moment. Leave me your business card and I'll have him call you."

I went for the door, she stood up and barred my way. "Excuse me!" she hissed.

"You're excused," I said and pushed past her. The door was locked. I began kicking at it. The cheap receptionist moved back, bewildered as to what to do. She picked up the receiver. I could see she was dialing 911.

The door opened away from me and the slouched though towering figure of the attorney loomed before me. He had the same thick, razor-trimmed and bushy-edged mustache that Bennie had.

"What the hell do you think yaw doin'?"

"Getting in to see you, *Governor.*"

"You've seen me. Now get out."

"I don't think so," I said, standing pat and staring straight into his tie. He was very tall, thickly built, raw-boned and ham-handed, but for all that weak in his expression and his practiced attorney's slouch. I looked up into his face. "Going to spend a few minutes with me talking about your future, *Governor?*"

"What future?"

"Exactly," I said with a smile.

He focused his scowl on his red-lipped, big-haired, power-suited receptionist, and his body language suggested a street thug ready to fight for every inch of petty turf if there was the slightest question that any of it was his. And this small, low-rent office was all his. "You get the cops yet, Jeannie, aw *what?*"

She shrugged and made a fey gesture with her glitter-spotted fingernails, each one alternately blue and pink. "They just put me on hold."

"Hang up the phone."

"You can't tell me what to do, buddy," she snarled. "You're nobody."

"True. But I can tell *the Governor* here what to do, can't I, Gov?"

He swallowed hard and didn't move an inch. "No."

"No? You don't think so? Can you guess why I call you that— *Governor?*"

"Do I know you?" Dark spots were appearing under his arms, making his robin's-egg—blue shirt look drab and soiled.

"No, but I know you, and some of your buddies from East Trinity. You know, the official Bennie Poshlust fanclub? The club that's yet to have a meeting—Bennie included?"

"I have them on the line, Mark."

Straddle took a small step backward into his office, rubbed his face with his hand. "Hang up, Jeannie."

"But I'm giving them the information now—"

"I said hang up!" he bellowed and Jeannie fumbled the receiver until it fell to her open-toe–shod feet. She sank awkwardly down to the floor to retrieve it.

Straddle should have moved back into his office, but instead stood the ground that was left him. He was still doing his street-corner real-estate dance of respect, where every inch lost cost him his standing.

He couldn't grasp the simple fact that he had no standing with me—and that I was determined to cost him. "Shall we dance, *Governor?*"

He sneered. "You think you're some sort of tough guy?"

"No. But compared to you, there's no question."

Nobody would dare say such things to him now—he had out-grown them, moved on to consolidate his street-corner, urban-neighborhood, lower-class respect into professional success. He didn't have to take this.

But, as far I was concerned, he *did* have to take it. In fact, he'd not only take it, but I was quite prepared to ram it down his throat.

Straddle's face darkened to the color of fresh liver. I pushed him back by suddenly grabbing the door handle and shutting it firmly with a crisp slam. "I could toss you out of here physically, you know," he warned weakly.

"Okay. So let's add assault to the obstruction of justice, interference with a police investigation and accessory after the fact to premeditated murder charges I'll be filing against you then. What's one more felony between friends? That's a concept you understand fully, isn't it, *Gov?* Friendship?" I approached him again, touched the toes of his shoes with my own. I flashed him a smile. "So, go ahead, Governor. Please. I *beg* you: Go ahead and assault me. Take your best shot. When you do, I'll be within my rights to defend myself and then I can rip that mustache right off your fucking face in good conscience." I flashed him a smile.

He shook his head, sighed and sat behind his desk. "I don't have time for this."

"Then make time, Governor, because I'm staying put until I get some answers."

"Maybe if I ignore you, you'll go away?"

"Oh, only one of us is going to go away, Governor, and it isn't going to be me."

He shook his head again, as much in exasperation as in resignation.

"You don't listen very well, Gov. I said I'm staying here until I get some answers.

"About what?"

"Why about our mutual friend Bennie, of course."

"He's my client. Anything I could tell you would be breaking attorney/client privilege."

"Fuck privilege, Straddle. You *will* answer my questions."

"Fuck you, whoever you are. I'm not telling you *nothin'!*" He slammed both fists on his desk like a toddler.

"You really think that, don't you, you pathetic, stupid son of a bitch? Cool. Let me give you a quick demonstration of just what an idiot you are and why you'll be telling me everything I want to know."

His liver complexion darkened. No one spoke to him like this. His hands balled into fists and he snorted short hot little breaths out his nostrils, struggling for composure, not quite sure what I had or didn't have to hurt him.

He was about to find out.

I pulled up a chair, sat and placed my reporter's mini-tape recorder on his desk and gave him a blast:

"SEEMS YOU DID MOST OF THE FORWARDING TO A CEL-
LULAR LINE—I CAN TELL FROM THE EXCHANGE."
"THOSE ARE DATED?"
"YES, THEY ARE. AND IT SEEMS YOU HAVEN'T USED THE
SERVICE FOR QUITE A WHILE. DO YOU WANT TO CON-
TINUE WITH IT?"
"OF COURSE. CAN YOU TELL ME THE DATE OF THE LAST
FORWARDING?"
"SURE. THAT WAS TO YOUR CELLULAR LINE."

I snapped it off after he recited the date.

Straddle's liver complexion was replaced by one considerably lighter, if not outright blanched.

"Gonna throw me out now, *Governor?* Gonna call the police on me?" I reached for the receiver, picked it up and tossed it to him. He caught it without effort and slammed it back down on the cradle. He pressed the intercom and Jeannie's voice yawped a response both distorted and fuzzy.

"No calls." He announced.

"You want I should 911 this guy?"

"Just take messages!" he barked, then snapped off the intercom.

"So when Bennie asked you to cover for him, to lie for him, why did he tell you he did it?"

Straddle sat back and laughed. "I know who you are! The suspect. That Patetick guy!" He laughed again. "Lotsa luck, Patetick. They'll hang you eventually."

"Okay, lawyer. Maybe my luck's run out, but yours is going to be quick to follow. This tape proves you lied to police officers during an investigation."

"So what? Everybody lies. I made a mistake. Bennie used the cellular instead of a land line. Big whoop."

"Think so?"

"I do."

"Think again." I clicked play on the tape again."

"SO, WHEN YOU HEARD BENNIE SAY HE HAD ANOTHER CALL COMING IN, WHAT DID YOU THINK HE MEANT?"

"HE NEVER SAID THAT."

"AH, BUT WHAT IF HE DID? WHAT IF YOU NEVER HEARD IT. WHAT IF YOU WEREN'T THERE?"

Straddle looked at his watch. "This is boring. I have appointments to make and you're not the only one who can file criminal charges, Pathetic."

I played him some of the dowager's part:

. . . "NO INTERRUPTIONS OR DEAD AIR AT ALL? LIKE WITH MAYBE A CELLULAR PHONE?"

"NO, NOTHING BUT THE CALL WAITING. YOU KNOW HOW THOSE BEEPS SOUND ON THE OTHER END—LIKE A SKIP IN THE WATCHAMACALLIT?"

"TRANSMISSION."

"YES. BENNIE TOLD ME TO HOLD ON, ANSWERED AN-OTHER CALL THEN CAME RIGHT BACK. IT WAS JUST CALL WAITING."

I stopped it. "Do you get it, Governor? Or shall I explain?"

"You got nothin'."

"No. I got a break in Bennie's alibi. I got a circle of old-time friends caught on record lying to save the ass of their buddy. Because they love him? Because they were *bikies* together? Maybe. Why don't you tell me why?"

Straddle gave me frowning silence and the liver complexion again.

I upended his desk and he nearly jumped backwards out the window trying to get out of the way when it fell. He was breathing hard, all but ready to hit me.

"What did you do that for," he asked with an angry whine.

I laughed. "Don't be an idiot, Straddle. You can walk away clean from this—*if* you think it through. Remember what they said about me on *Inside Affairs*? I'm a freelance journalist—or used to be. It won't take much investigative reporting to prove your vouching for Bennie was an outright lie. You made too many mistakes, used too many witnesses. I have enough to start the ball rolling to end your career, Straddle. If I push hard enough, the cops will follow along. Your life can go right down the drain along with Bennie's. It's your choice."

Straddle rushed toward me and I jerked away. He grabbed the desk and heaved it back to its original position. He sank down to the floor on hands and knees gathering papers and pens, righting the telephone.

Jeannie knocked on the door, but we ignored her and she went away.

"He was desperate," said Straddle. "He needed my help."

I held the recorder in front of him.

"Turn that thing off, or I stop talking now," he bellowed.

I wanted to kick him, but I restrained myself. "No—you'll talk anyway. You have no choice. Don't worry, Governor. I don't care about you, just Bennie. I want Bennie, and you're going to serve him up for me, like it or not. Now. *Go on!*"

"He was never very good at keeping up with our old mutual associates—"

"Your fellow Rumpot Rats."

"Yes." He continued fixing his desk. The intercom buzzed, he pressed it and screamed "Leave me the hell alone!"

"So you arranged a story."

"Yes."

"Say it."

"I got them all to agree to cover for that feckless son-of-a-bitch."

"It wasn't just loyalty, was it?"

"No. Money may have been involved."

"It *was* involved. Sing for me, counselor, or sing for the DA. Make up your tiny fucking mind!"

"We paid them all!" he blurted. "Loyalty and money are a good mix!"

"Did he tell you why he murdered her?"

"He didn't . . . murder her. It'll be manslaughter, max. Heat of passion. Bennie was very passionate about *Karenina.*"

I wasn't going to show him how much that last remark hurt me. "You, know, it takes a lot to beat someone to death in the heat of passion, then convey her somewhere and strap her to a piece of bondage equipment—while she was still breathing! He could have taken her to the hospital, he could have gotten help. He had a choice. But he was more concerned with covering up and letting her die. How bright an ADA do you think it will take to make the case for first degree? Hell, even *you* could make that case."

Straddle was sweating. His hands were shaking, so he thrust them in his pants pockets and sat back behind the desk. "Bennie lied, I guess. He swore it was an accident, one where he lost his temper and went too far. Bennie has a temper. It's always been his greatest failing."

"Willful murder is his greatest failing. You know I know you were Bennie's campaign manager in addition to being his attorney?"

"A matter of record," he coughed.

"Getting him into politics was your idea, wasn't it? Your career wasn't happening, so you saw an opportunity for you to jump start it by kicking off Bennie's. It was perfect. An aggrieved righteous regular guy with a cause. The memorized speech recited for Action Team News, the bid for selectman, the "busybody" campaign—all of if it pure Mark Straddle."

"That's no crime. It just shows you what a guy like me can do with half a chance."

The tape was still running.

"Yes—it does. It shows me how you can aid and abet a murderer, suborn false testimony, obstruct justice and benefit from the crime. It shows me you might have a future in politics."

"I do," he said, rocking back, calming down, feeling he had a handle on the situation at last.

"And you may continue that future, if I get what I want."

"Aha!" Straddle boomed. "At last the wheel spins in my direction." Straddle leaned forward, smiled a salacious smile. "How much?"

I was derailed. "How much?"

"Money," he laughed. "This is a shakedown, isn't it? Okay. Fine. I'll pay. So will Bennie. Pay good too, by god. You deserve something for being the fall guy—and the best part is you won't serve a day for it. The cops know they have no case against you what with that realtor's alibi thing on the record. So what's the harm? The dead aren't going to rise again over this, you know."

Karenina would have said take the money, go and live.

"I'm thinking," I said.

"You're not as stupid as I was told. A guy like you who's burned himself out in this town while standing on his last bridge, who's wasted himself and his life chasing after married pussy. Well, we all need cash to go on, bro. And you're at the end of your rope. Just name your price—and make it reasonable—and everybody wins. You can leave me the tape too. We'll get your other copies when we get the money together and make the exchange."

"Bennie's a murderer."

"You've convinced me. I'll remind him of that with every political step he takes, make sure he does the right thing." The fucker winked at me.

"You'd be running him with these tapes."

"I would. I do anyway." He looked at the recorder. "You can shut the damn thing off anytime you like."

"Yes. I can."

"I admit Bennie's a shit for killing her, but I can understand how he felt."

"You can?"

"Sure. We're men of the world, after all, you and me. She deserved it anyway, the little bitch. She took Bennie's manhood away from him. Treated him like some dull-witted, mangy dog. Tolerated him and flaunted all her affairs in his face till he was ready to explode."

"Ka-boom," I said.

"What else can I tell you?"

"Nothing."

"Now—I really do have appointments coming up. Can we talk numbers?"

I clicked of the recorder and pocketed it. I approached the desk, smiled at him, nodding approval. He pulled in his chair and jotted down a figure.

If there was a gun in his top drawer, this would have been as good a time as any to reach for it. Even if I were unarmed—and I was—who would question an attorney protecting his office from a psychopath and accused killer? It was too cliché, too pat. I watched his fingers.

I studied the piece of paper he slid over to me. I folded it up and slid it back, nodding. He chuckled.

I leveled the best and surest punch of my life straight into his face.

His head wrenched back loose like a dummy's, but looked all the more human bloodied and astonished as it was. His knees jutted up and slammed hard into the heavy wood bottom of his desk. Before he could get up, I smacked him down again, threw my weight into it.

I felt like I had broken my hand—it was numb and tingling. Straddle's blood mixed with my own, as my knuckles were cut, which made the scrapes seem to sting even more.

He moaned and I grabbed him by the shoulders.

"You're on notice, Straddle: If I ever find out you put your rat bastard friend Bennie up to this, gave him the idea, I swear by Christ I'll come back and kill your ass wherever I find it. You understand?"

I wanted to choke him dead.

"She deserved it anyway, the little bitch."

He made a noise that said he understood.

"Now, counselor, you go file your charges and I'll go file mine."

I WAS OUT OF BREATH WHEN I LEFT, FEELING LIKE A FUGITIVE, EVEN though I was sure I had nothing to run from. What could he do?

The answer was easy: Call Bennie.

But that was exactly as I expected. The bribe was a surprise, but was it real? Perhaps the exchange of tapes and notes and computer files for cash would just be another routine set-up. If I were them, I wouldn't give me money, I'd get rid of me. I was a proven loose cannon, someone who constitutionally refused to go along, to cooperate, to play on the team if indeed to play at all.

Such a subversion it was of the term "play."

As far as they were concerned, I didn't. Play.

Play, however was exactly what I had in mind.

I took the orange line straight to downtown Miltown, reading an abandoned *Register* I found on one of the seats to kill time.

Bennie had another "Busybody" editorial—they were called that now—running on repetitiously and solecistically about the evils of pornography, unrestricted Internet freedom and the insidious destructive nature of alternative lifestyles. Today's editorial was "Cyber Chic or Compu-Poison?" I laughed.

It was obvious just who was writing for the subliterate Bennie. It was the Governor, campaigning to ride Bennie's coat-tails into office. I noticed a small squib about Bennie in the Register's new 'Burbs' section: " 'Victorious Victim' Sets Sights on State Rep Seat."

The piece mentioned the grass-roots appeal of the new "Busybody Movement," and how it was picking up steam. Bennie was getting fan mail from benighted bedroom communities across the nation cheering him on in his efforts "to limit choices so as to increase responsibility" and his call for "a return to shame."

I flung the paper across the subway car.

My intended stop was several blocks away from an army surplus store. They had just the item I needed, just what I had been combing the city for by phone. It would break me to buy it, but that hardly mattered, even though Straddle was more right about my need for cash than he knew.

I wasn't expecting much for myself after Thanksgiving.

And on Thanksgiving, I was going to be well prepared to give good and proper thanks.

TWENTY-TWO

"A PLACE WHEREIN GATHERS
THE OLDEST AND MOST BOON OF FRIENDS
BE WARNED AND MARK THIS WELL WITH CARE:
WHAT'S SAID AND DONE BEHIND THESE VENERABLE WALLS
NOW AND FOREVER—REMAINS THERE."

It was a small piece of calligraphied doggerel illustrated by a carefree, happy gaggle of drunks framed and covered with dusty glass I stopped and examined after stepping into the unwelcoming bar with the offputting name of Rat's Palace. I wiped it clean, read it twice, straightened the frame and sat at the long deserted bar waiting for god knows what. Service? An ambush? Something. It was a dive, unapologetically unkempt, dusty and dank, deliberately dark, unadorned and spare with a surprising lack of early drinkers and barflies on the stools. The jukebox was filled with Irish and Italian favorites, Sinatra and antique heavy metal that must have sounded like Sinatra to contemporary youth, just as gutless, droning and cliché. I knew the place wasn't as deserted as it looked. Some idiot had selected "Shaving Cream" off the box, playing at a mercifully low volume. "Anybody home?" I asked loudly, sitting at the bar, resting my elbows on the drab formica surface, my face in my hands.

Some forty-something thug sat down next to me. Big, thick, rumpled, dressed in soiled contractor's clothes, he thundered onto the stool and faced me. He had the filthy smell of honest work about him, good honest sweat work that fertilizes fields of dishonesty and profit like rich dung. He breathed on me and spoke low.

"Guy like you comes into a place like this could get his face broken."

"He could," I agreed, staring at him coldly. "You going to do the breaking?"

Another figure moved into the glowing dimness. The bartender? I went with my guess.

"About time," I hailed. "Get my friend here a bottle of whatever. Draft looks like a risk to me, as clean as those taps likely are. And I wouldn't want my pal here to get sick."

The man I thought was the bartender went past the cases and taps, out from behind the bar and bolted the door, not even bothering with the "Closed" sign.

"You're in trouble, pali-boy," the thug next to me breathed.

"Nice place," I said, ignoring him. "Which came first, the street gang or the dive?"

Another figure emerged from behind the bar.

"He's a funny guy," said the thug.

"Wicked funny," said Manny Brassbrad.

"Nothing funny yet," another voice disagreed. A stooped, more-elderly figure came out from that same back room to the right behind the bar.

I turned to the thug, gave him an accounting. "Well, there's Manny. The Governor's off somewhere getting his nose fixed. Which one are you? Dukie, Fuzzy, No-Legs, Spoon? Sneezy, Dopey, Grumpy, Doc? What? Maybe you should all get name tags?"

"He's funny," said one of them. "I thought you said he wasn't funny."

"Let's make him laugh," said the more elder of them.

"You already are," I said, then I stood up and bellowed forth laughter to back that up.

It was cut short by the thug who sat in the stool next to me. He got up, loomed over me—being both bigger and taller—and slammed an uppercut into my abdomen. I crumbled to the floor doubled over, wheezing and gasping for lost breath.

"Shaving Cream" kept on playing—was it quarters they had wasted or was it set up as some sort of sinister interrogation technique?

"I'm Fuzzy," said the thug.

Me too, I thought, stupid with pain and hypoxia.

"No–Legs," said the elder.

"Me, you know," said Manny kicking me.

Fuzzy knelt down, put his face close to mine to speak.

I spat in it. He punched at my face, but I rolled away just in time. His fist smacked the floor, but he himself didn't make a sound as he drove his hand into splintering wood.

They all three lifted me off the floor onto the bar with little incident despite my wiggling about.

I forced air into my lungs as they held me down to keep me from struggling. I tried to speak and failed. No–Legs held a rag as if he were about to stuff it in my mouth. Manny was playing with a good sized pen-knife. A well-sharpened three-inch blade could still do significant damage, pen knife or not. "You guys are stupid!" I managed to blurt with authority. I knew they couldn't let me have the last word.

"Really?" asked Fuzzy. "You're the one on the bar about to be reamed."

"Better be quick about it then," I panted. "The two detectives tailing me should be coming in for a beer anytime now."

"Shit!" said Manny, letting go of my leg and punching the bar. It rang true to him.

"He's a lying-ass faggot!" No–Legs added.

"Hey, you guys can lie for a friend, I can lie for myself—except what makes me dangerous is that I'm telling the truth! That's why I'm on the bar!" They backed off for a moment of deliberation and I sat up. Fuzzy looked like he was about to punch me again, so I kicked him tidily in the balls. "An old jock like you ought to re-member to wear a cup there, Fuzz." The toe of my shoe carried precise impact.

Fuzzy danced about the room, fighting the impulse to buckle to his knees. "The bastard's a liar!"

"Big sin among you East Trinity homeboys—you *bikies*—lying. But the thing is," I said rubbing my jaw, "I'm still the chief suspect in a murder. *I'm* the one being investigated. Granted the cops don't care if I live or die, but if it happens when they're tailing me? How can you be sure some detective won't actually do his job? Especially if a real crime is practically waved in his face?"

"I say we off him," said Manny.

"I say no," said No-Legs, pondering in the half-light, his craggy unshaven face conjuring up long lines of convenience-store clerks I had ignored throughout my life.

"Off me. What a good plan." I said with a joyous handclap. "We'll all go together then!"

"You think you have brass balls, Patetick. I'd like to see if it's true."

"You can inspect them later, Fuzz, to see what real ones look like. In the meantime, though, I just need some answers to some questions."

"You need to get out of here before you can't," No-Legs announced.

"They call you No-Legs because you have no legs to stand on?"

"Better than having no dick to fuck with," he growled.

"Well, well, well—my, my. When punks get older, they just get embarrassing, don't they? What's next? Playing keepaway with my beanie?" I hopped off the bar. "Look. I'll be brief, boys. I know you lied for Bennie, lied to the cops, alibied him up. I don't even need you to admit it—I already got all of that from Manny there."

"Shaving Cream" droned on and on.

"I just want to know what happened."

"Cops coming in soon?" Fuzzy asked snidely, his face tightening, the color rising up in his cheeks.

"Maybe not. But I think you have more to worry about killing me than letting me walk out of here. I don't care about you. Your being accessories after the fact speaks volumes about how dreary and sad you do-nothing-say-nothing-know-nothings are. I just want Bennie. Straddle's scared I'll screw up his future career by screwing up Bennie. That's why we're all here today. But fuck Straddle—he'll fuck you if he gets half a chance to make sure you can't fuck him."

"We're on the line too, ya know," Manny whined, void of anything but rage as he hung in the shadows.

"Oh. I forgot about all your fellow Rats' promises: State jobs and fat pensions for all should he get in. *Should.* But he won't."

"We can stop you from stopping him," reasoned No-Legs.

"But you won't. If you do, then you'll be really stuck with one another. Forever. You'll all be wide open to blackmail from Straddle and Bennie both—it'll cancel out whatever hold you have on them. No more payoffs, no more possible state graft. You might wind up being the ones making the payoffs while Straddle and Bennie reap the rewards, laughing all the way to the bank."

"Shit!" screamed Manny, as if wounded.

"They're loyal," sneered Fuzzy.

"Bennie was married. Took a vow. Killed his wife. Is the rule you only fuck the ones you sleep with? Tell me, "bikies," do the Rumpot Rats have an oath?"

Fuzzy swallowed hard. "We do."

"Loyalty. They have that in marriage too, I hear."

"The cunt was *dis*loyal. She fucked *you*," No-Legs offered with no small degree of indignation.

"Bennie's fucking me too. What of it?"

"He's in the right!" shouted No-Legs.

"One oath goes, the other follows. Look, I'm not standing around here arguing. I just want to know what I want to know and then I'll leave you guys to work out the arithmetic on your own. I charge too heavy a fee to do that for you."

"He's right. I'm not putting my life in the hands of a lawyer—and Straddle was always the biggest pussy among us." This from Fuzzy.

"You'll get nothin' from me!" Manny shouted nervously.

"I guess not," I said and approached the bar. "Mind if I draw some beer?" Fuzzy grunted, but otherwise, there was no objection. I got myself a glass, filled it, then walked over near Manny and sipped it. "Tastes about as bad as I thought."

"Drink it and screw while you can," said No-Legs. They were all wondering what to do. I decided to help them. I poured the beer over Manny's head, he threw a punch and missed and as he was off balance anyway, I kicked his legs out from under him. Then, after he hit the floor, I kicked his head a few times for good measure. Before they could get close enough to interrupt, I knelt down, got a choke hold across Manny's neck, then fought him for the knife.

The fucker cut me, but I got the blade away from him—drew

a long shallow mark across his throat with it. "So," I said firmly, "let's see some of that loyalty!" I waited two beats. *"Now!"*

No-Legs and Fuzzy stood together, aghast as Manny struggled, squirmed and bled slightly from his neck (though I admit it looked like more owing to the bigger wound across my palm, which bled freely). They were dumbstruck that I would go so far, despite what Straddle must have told them. How could one of the soft boys from Trinity University, one of the journalist scum with a soft job and a soft life dare to play their oldtime hardscrabble neighborhood game?

Manny's tortured squint drove the point home.

I asked them slowly and carefully, hammerlocking Manny's arm to just the point of a discontinuous creaking sound that meant it was near to breaking. The blood asked my question again for me, and slowly and carefully they answered.

Getting out was easier than getting in. I walked home in the sunlight and fresh air, sheltered by a perfect, calming cerulean sky, my bloodied hand thrust tightly in my pocket and decorating my pants with a growing stain. My steps were as light and jaunty as they could be in the face of pain. I had a broad, near-narcotized smile on my face.

I knew. And knowing was all of it.

So I thought.

THANKSGIVING.

A murky Thursday.

Just another day for me, just another long relentless day. A solitary day.

A day that took forever until the dying of the light.

I took it slow, drawing everything out as if it were all practice and procedure of some great, painstaking methodology. I went to the gym, did a light, leisurely workout, stretching my muscles at every point and turn that I could, exaggerating every range of motion to its fullest conclusion of energy and expense. I was unhurried, despite the fact the gym shut down at noon. The holiday of universal familial insularity had no place in it for the odd man out, and the odd man out had no place for such holidays. Just like the scene had no place for individualism—or Tutor's scene anyway—neither did the straight world. Disconnection was its own reward, never its own punishment. It just kept leading to other punishments, other denials, other rejections and rigidly modifying limits.

No place for the man who has nothing.

I laughed at that. No. There *was* a place. I had just the place in mind. I left the gym refreshed, in a good mood.

There was no Thanksgiving Day feast, just a fast.

I starved to get an edge.

Despairing of Bootlicker's apartment and glorying in his absence, I spent a good part of the day organizing my papers, reading over the medical information I had cadged off the wire dumps pertaining to a certain procedure of insertion and removal. I wanted to make sure I had it right, had as many of the likelihoods and contingencies covered that I had only begun reading about weeks ago.

How it could go wrong, how I could make classic mistakes.

It seemed the worst mistake was a failure of nerve.

I was fighting not to make it.

There was no parade but the long, incessant parade of days that led me to this point, this silence, this practice, this room.

This reflection.

I liked the way Fuzzy put it: *"The problem is, nobody's directin' Bennie's traffic but Bennie. He and Straddle are at each other's throats— it's a wonder they get anything done."*

"Directing his traffic?"

"Telling him what to do!" he said as if I were the one with the knife at my throat.

"It was all Bennie's idea?"

"No—Straddle's."

"Everything? Karen too?"

"No. Bennie had to do that himself. It was a matter of honor. He couldn't let her go on with the way she was doing. Straddle just made the best of a bad business. He had to bring us in on it, thinking he was so much better, throwing us a few bucks here and there. We'd have done it for nothing."

"You would have," said No-Legs.

I ignored Manny's overstated choking as I cut a bit into his throat for emphasis.

Directing his traffic. I clicked off the tape recorder.

I would stop his traffic.

Traffic. *Red light*—a favorite safeword. I laughed at the thought, heard Karenina say it softly and then pushed her out of my mind.

This scene would have no safeword.

I went over very little else as I waited for the grim, tortuous autumn day to die its mellow, flaming death.

I watched it from my windows, the dying afternoon, smoky, ruddy and crespusculate with a burning light that grew more distant until the hard fall of darkness swallowed it all—everything—and lingered in its place. I walked out to watch it end, skirting the highway and main roads by my apartment building as I headed toward the river. I shivered at the blast of arriving cold, breathing in the darkness as it fell heavily and suddenly, recoiling at the scent of staid riparian rot. I shuddered continually when it was fully dark, which happened early now that we had sunk back into the wintry, preparatory mire of Eastern Standard Time, a hope-fraught turning-back that only seemed to push out further at the edges of a diminishing hope. I walked back, cold, stiff—clear minded.

I showered and taped up the surprisingly neat little wound on my left palm. It stung and throbbed with a life all its own as I dressed it. I reveled in the renewed pain.

I put on a pair of black jeans, black shirt, thick black sweater and boots.

I took my little three-foot bullwhip, the signal whip, coiled it, carefully slipped it into the back pocket of my jeans where it fit handily, the pommel easily grabbed from behind.

The tape recorder went into my shirt pocket.

I unwrapped and slid my new, precious little item into my left motorcycle boot. It made it no less easy to walk, which was good.

I would be walking some distance.

I put on my motorcycle jacket and pocketed a pair of Peerless serial-numbered nickel-plated handcuffs for luck.

For luck and Karenina.

I didn't want her with me. I could bear it, as I much as couldn't bear being without her. Knowing her as I thought I did, I suspected that despite what she might say, she would want to be there. This scene would be her meat.

Denying her only brought her closer.

I gave up, kissed the cuffs, brought her with me.

Somehow her memory only made me feel colder all along the nine-mile walk to Swansea.

Taking the back roads and tributary streets, travelling all the ill-lit routes I could, I hid from sight. Not that there was much more than the occasional car to pass me by the time I had made it out. Just as the boys at Rat's Palace had said it would be, it was dark at the house when I got there. Bennie was too cheap even to leave an outside light on for himself. I checked my watch. It was still early. All I had to do was get in.

Bennie would be with them, after all, his buddies, his fellow Rumpot Rats. Not because no one else would have him, which used to be true, but to keep tabs on those who might destroy him, checking to see who was in line and who was not, who was naughty, who was nice. Perhaps they were discussing what was to be done about me. No one would have any idea. No one would say.

I was a problem Bennie would have to take care of himself.

The kids were with grandma—the Snuffleupagus in Long Island—as they were most years—safely away from the huz. "The Snuff" loathed the huz.

I used the basement entrance to the side of the garage door at the level of the recessed driveway. I popped the old doorknob lock with Manny's pocket knife, a technique Karenina had shown me in case it froze, which it sometimes did, and punched in the alarm code she also had shown me. Or started to.

I stopped.

I waited for my heart rate to come down and meet my breathing. Something was off. The alarm—it had not been set!

It was off altogether.

Stepping lightly in time to my breathing, I padded through the house I had once known so well in total darkness. Little had changed, down to the kids' toys strewn as key obstacles to be avoided in the hallway by the stairs, which I failed to do. As my eyes adjusted, I noticed that framed photographs, gew-gaws and bits of tawdry *objets d'art* all had vanished, replaced by brand new mass produced bits of kitsch recently acquired from a local Miltown tourist clip joint with "Historic Miltown" decalled all over them. Likely they were more of the free junk Bennie prized, collecting for the price of a pick-up.

As darkness adjusted enough to hold dimension, I made my way over to the leather recliner, sat back and waited, ratcheting one handcuff through over and over again in my jacket pocket with peculiar calm and dissociation.

The sense of time having passed within a single liquid moment in the shadows was finally marked and quickly broken by the sound of keys inserted and hanging from the lock of the front door.

The huz.

HE DIDN'T STARTLE AT ALL.

"I'm gonna call the cops! Who do you think you ah, breakin' into *my* house?!" Bennie sneered, settling into an angry slouch offset by the airy pocket of his open, flowing windbreaker that was clasped at the bottom.

I started to speak, but my throat fought the idea and made a rumbling sound instead. I cleared it, tried again. "It used to be Karen's before you killed her."

He went for the phone. "Yaw ass is goin' to jail, pal. Breaking and entering, assault, attempted murder."

"You should have been an attorney, Bennie."

"You can call me Mistah Poshlust."

"That's what they called you before you killed Karen. Now I guess everyone can say that to your face."

"You don't know shit about me."

"I know you won't call, Bennie." I produced my tape recorder, played him a few bars of my favorite tune:

"NO. BENNIE HAD TO DO THAT HIMSELF. IT WAS A MATTER OF HONOR. HE COULDN'T LET HER GO ON WITH THE WAY SHE WAS DOING. STRADDLE JUST MADE THE BEST

OF A BAD BUSINESS. HE HAD TO BRING US IN ON IT, THINKING HE WAS SO MUCH BETTER, THROWING US A FEW BUCKS HERE AND THERE. WE'D HAVE DONE IT FOR NOTHING."

"What's the matter, Bennie? Your memory *fuzzy?*"

"It's just jealousy and talkin' trash. Proves nothing. Yaw the one breakin' the law here and I'm gonna fix ya for it."

"Call, Bennie. Let's do it the legal way. I wouldn't want to ruin your new career with any impropriety. I think you and me should go with the cops and put our heads together—maybe we could solve Karen's murder. Wouldn't you like that?"

He hung up the phone.

"No?"

"I need a drink," he said and stepped away to the sideboard, drew out some cheap bourbon, poured it out and gulped. Karen told me Bennie never drank, as his father died of cirrhosis and his mother never made it though detox. He shuddered, put the glass down, then turned to face me. "You get out of here."

"I will. I just want your confession. On the record."

"I didn't do it, you lying prick!" He raised his voice without conviction. "Everyone knows you did it! You beat my wife to death with yaw sick, sadistic games, yaw roleplay! You *scened* her to death! It went too far and you covered it up. I should beat you to death, myself. I'd be within my rights to, protecting my home and my children and what not!"

"They're in Long island, Bennie, the children. It's just you and me here." I stood up, drew the blinds.

"I gut friends outside! They'll be in in a minute."

I made sure the door was locked. "Have another drink, Bennie. It'll calm you down."

"I don't drink."

"I didn't see anyone outside, Bennie. You sure they came with you? I thought your fellow Rats were going to have you meet me unaccompanied."

"They don't know yaw here."

"Don't they? They never mentioned me?"

"My attorney said you're violent and crazy. I should protect myself."

"With a gun? You want to go upstairs and get it? I'll wait."

"I don't need no gun. I'll just yell for my friends."

"Yell away. No one will hear it for two reasons. Reason one: there's no one there. The Rats were going to let you take care of anything that might be here—meaning me—alone. I know. I saw them this afternoon. Why Bennie, you look surprised!"

"They would nevah—"

"Reason two: The house is scream-proof. Karen was always talking about the improvements she made to her beloved house, her historic Tudor, all the things she did to make subtle improvements. You probably didn't pay attention, as you had her do most of the work anyway. She had it all insulated with an ear toward noise absorption. We tested it. She tested it—made her scream and scream right there on that sofa. So, please. Go scream your head off. Maybe you'll feel better." I smiled.

"That's a lie—we split the work 50/50. Half of everything was mine." His body was rigid with unfocused rage. He could hardly move, but his head was visibly squirming.

"*Was* is right. You know, Karen and me had a joke. We used to call you the huz."

"I know she called me that. It wasn't you."

"Then we called you "The Was." Because, to her, you were over and done. And just before the end. Before you killed her, we called you "The Scuzz. The Scuzz." You lived up to it, didn't you?"

"Yaw the trespasser here, buddy, not me. I belong in this house. Yaw just a speck a dirt on my marriage." He took his windbreaker off and threw it on the sofa. Then paced about changing the lighting. "Too bright in here." He mumbled.

"So how did it go, Bennie?" I picked up the recorder, pressed Record, walked over to the sideboard and set it down by the bourbon with a brisk tap on the wood.

He shut off the front light he had turned on after entering. The den where we stood was now softly lit, the halogens also having been cut, the glow of the two replica Tiffany lamps making the dimness of the room easy and pleasant on the eye. "It didn't go. Now *you* go."

He loomed over me, taller by a head at least even as he slouched. His little eyes darted about the room and fixed on me. At last, he was sizing things up. "I think I'll stay until I'm finished."

He chuckled. "You may be more right than you know."

I snapped my fingers. "I have it. This is what happened: Karen told you she was leaving and taking whatever she brought into the marriage with her. You said you'd give her a bloody divorce—what was it you said? 'Spend you both down to the last dime?' But you couldn't do that, really. That would have been a fate worse than death, losing all the money and whatever social position you thought you had gained. It wasn't the infidelity that freaked you out, it was the loss of the lie of the marriage. Without Karen and the money, her business-sense, real-estate connections and trust fund, you'd be back to the Rumpot Rats in no time. Naturally, she would take the kids, bring them up her way. You didn't care about the D/s—hell, that was just the sales pitch, a courting technique. The affairs didn't bother you as long as they went nowhere. This one was going somewhere. It had to stop. *She* had to stop."

"She broke my heart. I was the victim! So were the kids." His fists hung by his side, balled, unballed, repeated.

"You smacked her during an argument that morning about where she was going, who she was meeting—an accident. Then it was decision time. Move out, stay and get the restraining order slapped on you, or—"

"That's bullshit!"

"Or call your attorney. Maybe smack her again to buy some time. Straddle and you hashed it out. He made a few suggestions."

"Straddle takes orders from me, not the other way around. Nobody directs my traffic but me. He—" Bennie caught himself.

"Bravo. You knew the cross was hidden all folded up in the basement. You knew. So you helped Karen to the car, exiting through the basement, took her for a spin, the cross in the trunk. Maybe they were *both* in the trunk. The sunken driveway makes it hard to see what happens by the garage door or basement entry— unless one watches straight on. You waited till no one was. You took the cell to have a line to Straddle. Karen had it with her anyway, as she usually did. When it rang, you were sure it was him. Imagine your surprise at hearing the realtor on the other end! You realized that Karen must have had the calls forwarded." I laughed. "So she wouldn't miss hearing from me. Just in case!"

"Enough with that crap! She said you were a writer. And that's all yaw saying is—fiction."

"Journalism. And I'm going to prove it."

Bennie smiled and shook his head. "This scream-proof thing works two ways, you know." He went to the kitchen and I followed. He bolted the back door. "Just locking up—for security."

"Afraid I'll leave?"

"You should have when you could. Now you won't."

"I won't."

"Exactly. "He went back to the den, plopped down on the sofa. He gestured me to follow. I did and his eyes never left me. I could see his mind working.

Bennie didn't understand that this was my scene, not his. He didn't understand that everything in it was controlled and accounted for. Everything.

"I have a nice gun," he said smiling. "Wanna see?"

"The Sig-Sauer upstairs? You still know how to use it, big ex-infantry grunt like you? Isn't that too much gun for you anyway?"

"You could find out."

"I already know. You won't shoot me. I'm unarmed and smaller than you. Not much of a threat. Your Rumpot Rats might get nervous and cluck. I bet even Straddle would balk at a second murder. And it would look like that, wouldn't it: murder? No real evidence of self-defense. Maybe the police would reconsider you for chief suspect when I'm out of the picture. Hell; I'm your best friend alive. *I'm* the one they want for the Karen. While they waste their time with me, you're free to turn your outrage into political aspirations and media contracts. Maybe you can guest-host *America's Most Wanted?* Show my picture to America?"

"Funny. No, I won't shoot you. I don't have to." He stood.

I moved in front of him, took measured steps backwards.

"Guys like you that come from places like this don't understand nothing. I sweated hard to get here, to get a woman like Karen, to have nice kids and a clean life up from the gutta! First she tried to take everything away, then you. Well, I ain't going to let ya." He moved toward me. "And f'the record, I would nevah, evah lay a hand on my wife! I was the one that loved her, and she loved me. Simple as that. Alla *you* guys were the problem, *you* were the threat. Sure, she made mistakes, had lapses in judgment. But I took her back anyway 'cause that's the type of guy *I* am—and she wanted to stay. She was going to tell you to take a hike, but you got spiteful, gave her a last scene and *ba-da-bing-ba-da-boom*—"

"Instant political career. Such a persevering regular Joe you are."

He advanced. I retreated. Then he went over to the tape recorder and clicked it off. "These little things are amazing! I remember when one like this cost a mint. Now, the minis go for what? Ten bucks?"

I shrugged.

"Well, I think that's enough, don't you?"

"Yes," I agreed.

"I could nevah beat her to death. You on the other hand are going to be pretty easy."

"Really?"

He strode over with near-comic rage contorting his face and rammed his fist into my midsection, sending me to the floor. It was so direct and leisurely a move, I was unsure—owing to my inexperience—that that was what he was actually going to do. I misjudged, and thought he was only getting ready. Not that it mattered. I gave him a well-earned groan.

"I'm just protecting myself and my home from a known felon who broke in. I'm the victim here! I'm protecting my home from you! By the way," he said out of the side of his mouth slyly, "I hope you fight back a little. I'm going to need a few bruises to corroborate my story after I pound you down to grease." His cheek twitched.

I groaned again. Bennie laughed, stepped back, allowing me to get up. I no doubt looked unsteady on my feet, dizzy, a perfect target for rage.

Bennie joined both hands into a club, swung back, took one step toward me. His face was creased with joy, his teeth flashing. He was set and ready to swing.

Crack!

An explosion.

Bennie staggered back. Covered his face with his hands, blinded for a moment.

The three-foot signal whip danced energetically in my hand.

"You just took a 750-mile an hour blow to the face, Bennie. How's it feel?"

Blood seeped out from between his fingers in answer. "Your endorphins coming up yet?"

It had been an easy reach for the pommel of the whip in my back pocket. In a single, practiced motion after grasping it, I had extended, uncoiled and cracked. My stance had changed from one of affected dizziness to one of command. He went for me again, and I cracked it square and full into his chest, tearing both shirt and flesh.

His face was a mask of bloodied shock.

He actually waved a finger at me, one eye swollen closed. "You! You can't do that! Karen —! You! She told me. You're a submissive! *You're just a little submissive nothing fuck!* You're just *supposed* to take it!"

"I did," I agreed.

I smiled, stroked the whip.

"But I forgot to tell you something, Bennie."

He lunged into another step and I fired off four stiff, swift overhand cracks directly into his side, spun about a bit then backwhipped an extravagant crack to his chest. His hands flew about uselessly. He let out a yowl. Then I straight-arm punched his face with my left for fun.

"I switch."

He backed off, started to play it smart, get me talking again as he looked for an opening. "C'mon!" he said. "C'mon, you faggot!" I felt I was growing immune to sucker moves. I judged my distance, aimed for the damaged eye, released and struck.

It was a hit.

The whip came back to me moist and slick with gore. He fell.

"You don't get it, Bennie. You see: We're not here to play your scene. We're here to play *mine*. It's a scene for Karenina, a memorial scene. I want you to enjoy it as much as she enjoyed yours. You know, *appreciate* the play."

"Play?" Bennie rasped stupidly. He managed to stand, half-blind. His left eye was closed and oozing black. His breathing was fast and jagged.

I projected the whip out to him teasingly in what must have seemed a premature gesture, and he grabbed the tail with both bloodied hands and chuckled. His good eye twinkled.

"That's right—*play!*"

It was easy. One hard yank and the whip was mine again, back and ready for cracking, as I knew it would be, burning both Bennie's hands like a poker, which I intended. He screamed a surprised scream, thrust his arms up by his head until I whipcracked them savagely down, going for his hands, each finger, each wrist until he was forced to bring them down. Then, with a sob of anger, he went down too as each rending lick of the end of the whip bit through his clothes and into his flesh.

"I'm going to play with you to death."

As he struggled to his knees, I whipped him steadily overhand until he cowered back down to the floor. I was grateful for Karenina's insistence on owning a house with twelve-foot ceilings.

"Did you enjoy it when you beat Karenina, dragged her to the cross, strapped her in and beat her again?" I screamed. "Was it fun? Did she cry, scream and beg, pleading for the sake of her children? Did she offer you a way out? Did you offer her one?"

He made for my legs from the floor.

As a reward, I gave him my beautifully mastered repeating overhand crack as hard as I could. I opened the scalp in the back of his head. Ripped his shirt and the flesh under it to shreds. He began to cry.

"Fuck you!" he squealed through mucus and tears.

I strode over to the sideboard and found a cloth napkin, which I used to wipe down the whip, which was already growing stiff with Bennie's blood and aqueous humor.

"I want you to take every blow as if Karenina were here watching, savoring every moment. I want you to taste the fear as if she were here to appreciate it."

"My children—!"

"Will be much better off without the influence of a the man who murdered their mother. Don't you agree?"

"But-I-did-not—" Bennie heaved.

"Then neither did I." I answered him with another crack of the whip to his back.

It wasn't as hard as I thought to crack him in the face in his prone position on the floor. He kicked his legs uselessly and positioned himself to get up.

"You didn't even have the guts to kill her, did you? You just left her there to die."

"Didn't!" he gasped throwing himself at me from the floor with a grunt and missing.

Standing over him, I laid open his back. Not good enough. I poured bourbon on the napkin and wiped down the whip again. I knew the alcohol was bad for it. But the blood was worse, and I had taken great pains to keep it supple, limber, ready.

"I'm not a coward like you, Bennie. I'm ready to do it to the end. Can you get up? I want you standing."

"No," he whimpered.

"Yes." I insisted.

He was a mess, bloodied, damaged, badly torn.

I felt less for him than I would for road kill; I couldn't even bring up mild nausea for him. In fact, to tell you the truth, the sight of him this way made me happy. It seemed to light a faint spark of hope within me.

This was the man who beat the love of my life to death with his bare hands. Lied, connived and gloated over making it his ticket to politics and public sympathy. This was the parasite who had ruined it all, killed our one mutual life, Karenina's and mine, left me to take the fall, made his immoral act the platform for trying to dictate and control moral conduct. No, as shameful, evil, repugnant as it was—and nothing any reader of what I am writing now could ever feel or understand—the sight of Bennie maimed, beaten and bloodied was a comfort to me. It was a relief.

Of course, I knew it wasn't going to bring Karenina back.

It was going to bring *me* back.

And it sure as hell was going to stop Bennie from going forward.

Here was the emperor of convention, the demonizer of all things alternative, sexual and aberrant in his full glory—the rank animal beneath true to himself at last. He was reduced to his most basic identity: a desperate, self-serving beast. He made for me with his full weight.

I struck out at him again. He stupidly headed into the crack, trying to fight it directly, instead of recoiling, which might have bought him some time. As it was he sped things up, met it and fell back. He was no match for what I was doing.

I estimated he might be good for a half hour or more of such play.

Decisions had to be made.

Blood splashed onto my face, warm, salty.

I shuddered with revulsion. I was trying to do this clean and it was getting all over me.

Crawling like a crab and cringing into the floor, Bennie tried for irrational escape.

I kicked him over and methodically whipped him, flinging away blood-soaked tatters of his shirt, saturating the whip and the cushions of the couch that he had yanked off and hugged for futile protection.

I gave him some more, stopping to wipe down the whip with a fresh napkin from under the sideboard. He put up his hands, I whip-cracked each finger, aimed hard and with satisfying accuracy at his knuckles. He kicked up his thick legs, and I whipped them down, making my right arm ache brutally at the shoulder with the force of each crack.

I stopped when I saw him quiet, lying bloodily there wheezing.

I was drenched in sweat and blood as was he—he simply wore more of both.

We looked at one another breathing. I knew he could see me out of his one good eye.

With a comic snort, he flipped over onto his belly and made a surprise rush for the door. I slammed my boot into his face to give him pause, flipped him back over, dragged him back to the sofa. He flipped his arms and legs in token protest and I punched him still until my fist was numb.

In the quiet of his feeble breathing, I knelt close to him, feeling almost intimate with him, as he lay now so overcome with weakness and pain. He was completely in my care now—it was totally up to me how I shepherded his life to its end.

I had become another person during his beating, calm, responsible, directed, purposeful and clear.

I knew Karenina was watching. This was for her.

I went to the sideboard, cleaned the whip with another napkin and more bourbon. I wiped my hands, checked the dressing on my wounded palm, grabbed my recorder. Bennie just lay there breathing. I knelt down to him in a crouch, rocking back on my boots. I withdrew the item, unwrapped it.

I gave his torn cheek a gentle slap. "Know what this is, Bennie? I got it just for you."

He grunted.

I let it gleam by his good eye. "This is a miniature Korean version of a K-Bar military knife—barbed and serrated. Goes in beautiful and smooth. Goes out tearing up your insides and making a wound that won't close. Very illegal, very expensive. Care to try it?"

"No." He waved his crippled hand.

"Oops—too late." I slid it in, biasing the blade slightly to the side, just between the second and third ribs, careful to miss the right lung, skirting any major arteries, up close to the heart, but hopefully not even nicking it. There was hardly any blood at all. I waited for the flow I had seen in so many movies gushing freely from a villain's gaping maw. I got barely a trickle from Bennie. He lay there trembling, but was mindful enough now to hold still. He suppressed his whimpering.

I held the handle of the knife and whispered: "Every scene should have a safeword—you know. A word to end it, to keep things from getting out of hand. As you know, nonconsensual scenes can be deadly. We know Karenina didn't get a safeword, but being that you're the victim—and for once, Bennie you're right: you *are* the victim—I'm going to give you one. Your safeword is: *confession.* Just say it into the tape recorder, and you know what?"

"What?" he rasped, his good eye alive.

"Aren't you glad I studied, Bennie? It took a lot of work not to hit the heart and the lungs. Maybe I missed my calling? Anyway, after you say your safeword, I call an ambulance, the EMTs stabilize the knife, you have it surgically removed at the hospital and survive. Even after you go to prison—and you will go—you can still get visits from your kids. You can even be some type of father after they parole you."

"No."

"Fuck with me, Bennie, and I yank out the knife. Know what happens next?"

"No."

"I rip up your guts, you bleed out and *die,* motherfucker. So which is it?" I clicked on the recorder. "You're on Bennie."

He whispered and creaked: "I wanna live. Kids."

I touched the lacquer handle of the knife. "Talk."

He heaved, which upset his body and made me nervous. Flecks of bloody saliva hit the recorder, which I held up to his lips. "I did it. Beat her. Like you said. No accident. I couldn't stand it. Beat her in the middle of the night till morning. She wanted pain? I gave her pain. Her and her men. Laughing at me. No 'spect f' me. Bitch. Put her and her toy in the trunk, cunt. Drove her to the lofts, to one I knew was empty. Carried her up in a sack. She didn't struggle. She was asleep. I set it up, beat her some more, left her. She wasn't dead. I didn't kill her."

"Who did?"

"You did. You made it all happen. You and the other guy. The one she was in love with."

"That was me."

"No. She wasn't gonna leave. I kept her. Me. So fuck you."

"You were on the way when the realtor called."

"Yeah." His throat began gagging slightly. He fought it. "On the way home. She was sleeping on the cross. Had to think quick." Small relief. There was no interrupting by then what had already been done—no remote chance as there might have been had she been in the trunk at the time.

"Not your specialty, was it, thinking quick? Now, say you did it, Bennie, and that you're very sorry. I want it on tape."

I felt his brutalized neck. His pulse was uneven. I made him kiss the condenser mic'.

"I did it. Killed Karen. I'm very sorry."

I grabbed the knife at the hilt. His eye widened.

"You gotta call! Get me to—hospital!"

"I'm very sorry too, Bennie."

"No! You said—safeword!"

"I did, didn't I? I guess if you believe in safewords, Bennie, you shouldn't get involved in nonconsenual scenes."

I pulled the knife out slowly, methodically tooth by tooth. He tried screaming which only made it worse. "No-no-no-no," he huffed like a child forced to accept a much-feared medical procedure. Then, as I gradually eased out the blade and his good eye bugged and watched with what I guessed was terror, he sniveled and cried. "My kids!" he coughed, then slumped, as I tore it out all at once with a final jerk and his chest immediately pumped thick gore. He spasmed, vomited blood, passed out.

The gagging came—death rattle.

I knelt and held him, cradled him in my arms and held him close to feel him die in my arms. My hatred for him was as tender as a love in the intimacy of my waiting for him to bleed out his life.

I stood, unmoved.

"My kids!" His last words. They caught in his throat, nearly silent.

"Not anymore," I said, looking down on the mess of ruined meat he'd become. "All you have now is Karenina to meet you wherever you're going. And I hope wherever it is, they gave her toys." I stepped toward the sideboard, but my feet went out from under me. I slipped and fell in Bennie's blood. I laughed.

I started to get up, but collapsed back down.

I closed my eyes, burrowed my head in my arm and laughed till I cried. Then, despite some feeble effort toward sense, I cried and cried again, more like vomiting than weeping—a violent crying. I came back to myself, mixed tears with blood and was repulsed, felt my body buck and give. I could not vomit, though I tried. I lay a long time crying, not for Bennie, not even for Karenina. My life, I knew, was also done. Whoever I was had died twice, once for each of them. I had lost myself irrevocably. Perhaps I had died the very moment I resolved to leave Ms. Right, when I cast my lot with the doomed Karenina. Perhaps it was when the palpable realization of every hope concluded with a policeman's fist in my mouth.

I lay numb and beyond thought, away from the world even as I lay facedown in the very blood of it. The darkness behind my eyes blew out into white light.

Someone kicked me in the head.

Couldn't be. I was alone with a dead man.

I was kicked in the head again and the I heard a voice say, loud and clear:

"You're stupid!"

I opened my eyes, rubbed my head. When I focussed, I saw him, plump and irritable in the returning light. I smelled his cigar, his aging sebum scent, his perspiration. "Not you," I groaned.

"Never me," he said.

"I am hallucinating."

"Poor choice of hallucination, if that's the case. Couldn't you at least come up with some dancing girls? Maybe bondage cheerleaders?"

"Do I look like I could?"

"You look only slightly less a bloody mess than Prince Charming over there."

My head throbbed, I stood, nearly slipped. The paunchy, portly man grabbed my arm to steady me. "Christ! Don't get me bloody while you're at it."

"I am unconscious."

"You only wish you were."

It dawned on me. Of course. My body became a lump it was almost impossible to stand erect. "You're a cop!"

He laughed a bitter sham of a laugh. "No. Once maybe. Not now."

"Who the fuck are you? You must be even more fucked up than I am to be standing in a mess like this."

"I've seen worse. Which isn't to say you didn't make a pretty impressive, colossal mess of things. How did you expect to get out?"

"I didn't."

"Atoning for your sins?"

"What of it?"

"It's a waste. It's no sin at all to undo a maggot like that one."

"How do you know?"

"I'm here, aren't I? In fact, I was here for the whole thing."

My heart pounded and my brain ached. Blood oozed down from my nose. "You—you turned off the alarm."

"Well, you're not exactly god's gift to breaking and entering, you know?"

"You were there at the beginning—"

"And I'm here at the end. So what?"

"So who the fuck are you?"

"I'm the fuck who's going to get you out of this, so pay attention."

"What?

He walked over to me, grabbed my jacket, smacked my face. "I said pay attention. This is a gift, Patetick, so listen carefully. You are getting your life back, so you will hear me, take it and go. Or I'll have to play Indian giver."

He revealed a long gun from the inside pocket of his overcoat.

"Nice piece," I said, not knowing what the hell it was. "What's that long thing at the end of the barrel."

"Suppressor," he said tightly, adding, "Shhhhh," his finger to his lip."

"Oh."

"Now, you'll go get as much of that blood off of you as you can, sponge down your jacket and boots and get lost, preferably same the way you found your way here. Don't get seen by anyone for at least an hour. Then get arrested. Get into a fight. Cause a public commotion. Anything. Just do it. An hour or so after you leave."

"It's at least a two-hour walk."

"Run then."

"Kill me then. I'm not going till I know."

"We don't have a lot of time, *Propertius*, but I guess a journalist just has to know. It's physiological, isn't it?"

I nodded.

"Fine. I'm an investigator hired by some guy in DC you know

and don't want to know. He and Karenina met each other some weekend at a party. You know what kind of party. She was all hot to run away with him. He was rich, dominant and had a thing for real estate. They even went house hunting in Virginia together. Sound familiar?"

"Not true!" I yelped, even as I recalled all the times I could not reach her. I was cold again, but didn't head for the bourbon.

"True! He was all set to go, having just cleared up a divorce, but our guy here's a pretty good businessman. He felt that if Karenina would cheat on her husband, why wouldn't she cheat on him? Personally I felt she was a bad risk. She was clean though—until you came along."

I could almost hear the laughter. "And you helped me along, right from the start, didn't you?"

"*Bang-o*—or is that Bingo? I kind of steered her in your direction. I wanted to protect his interests—not that she didn't seem all too happy to oblige. I just didn't realize how bad that maggot really was. But here's something for you: we'll never really know if he killed her over you or the other guy, my boss. So let's call it a draw. Anyways, I was hired because I'm sort of in the scene. And when he heard about the murder, well, once again for protection, he wanted some loose ends tied up."

"Like any connection he may have had to her? Pretty," I sniffled.

"And I got to say, I had a hard time watching you get the shaft, even when I didn't know she was going to wind up busted up on a cross to get buried under all the mud they'd throw at the scene. I tried to warn you, but you were too smart to listen. I did try."

"Too stupid."

"Yes and no. I'm a former cop, Prop. I know some of these guys down here in Miltown. They know you didn't do it. They just don't care. They thought Benny was one of them, did some lousy work on his case. Deep down, they were just like him in a way, so maybe they were right that he was one of them. They felt she deserved it."

"But you didn't."

"I'm one of those in the scene who believes we take care of our own. We have to. Self-preservation."

"Who are you."

"Call me Tinker. I like to mess around."

"Not your real name?"

"Why would it be?"

"Why didn't you kill the fucker?"

"I didn't need to. You, however, did. I don't think I could have done any worse than you, though. You know, I think these Miltown dicks have it in their minds now that he did it, though they don't like it. They'll be breathing a big sigh of relief when I'm done, don't worry. I think it was best for everybody that you bid a final goodnight to Prince Charming there."

"What about me?"

"I told you what to do, so do it—scrub up, leave the knife and the whip, and get the fuck out of here." He spat tobacco juice into blood and added as an afterthought. "Go out the way you came in."

"Like a lamb—to the slaughter?"

He laughed hard and gave me a push to go. "Hey, Prop," he said.

I looked at him over my shoulder, opening the door to the stairs that led to the basement.

"I *switch* too."

He crushed my tape recorder and the tape with an emphatic slamming of his heavy shoe.

EPILOGUE

Life is ridiculous.

This is a simple truth as obvious to adolescence as it is to old age—it's the in-between age that can't accept it, know it for what it is, relinquish laughter and despair and just gape in awe at it, in the witless surprise that pushes aside the remotest chance of ever preventing it from becoming exactly what it must always be to our civilized eye: ridiculous, absurd, horrifyingly comical. That's how I must have appeared to anyone but god who might have seen me on the back trails and furze-covered heaths and marshy moors between Swansea and Trinity.

There I was, in my leather jacket and boots, madly, desperately racing the ticks of time, riding a blue child's bike lacking the top middle bar on the frame—a girl's bike. It had belonged to Karenina. There was no other way to cover the distance and get done in an hour what was given to me to do in an hour. He had said an hour, Tinker, and I believed him. I had no choice not to—either he was giving me something back or everything would be gone.

It wasn't mine to give or take anymore. He could do with it what he would.

I knew then and know now the one truth we all fight to know— the one that does us absolutely no good at all: Everything is D/s. Everything. Dominance and submission.

Anything that lies between is the unresolved struggle for supremacy—

For dominance.

For submission.

I thrust up the never-locked garage door—one of the many points of Bennie's world not included in his Safety Club—scrambled through the tangled wreckage of pipes, bike frames, chicken wire and extruded rubber and yanked the thing out, bloodying my hands some more. I kicked up the stand, threw myself onto the seat and out the door, and sped down the hill, waving my too-long legs up and down for balance like there was no tomorrow.

There might in fact have been no tomorrow.

I took the bike-wheel width Distillery Bicycle Trail (named for the bygone depression bootleggers who had once used the narrow path as a road) that connected several parks and outlying Miltown communities, racing painfully and clumsily in the darkness on a bicycle that had never been made to hold me. I managed to fall into mushy clay and rushes only once. Somewhere, far off, some unidentifiable bird was crying.

At the trail's end, I tossed the damned bike into a roiling portion of swamp and ran back along the river to the apartment. It was too ill-lit for me to be seen by the path to my building. I staked out the entrance by the hedges. It was clean of people. Everyone had gone to their respective enclaves. Bloody, muddy and demoralized as I was, I was determined not to be seen.

Sweat streaked with blood ran down my face.

Time was fighting against me. It would win the war, but I needed to win the battle. I bolted down the path, into the vestibule then up the stairs. I began tearing off my clothes even as I made to it to the door to my place, oddly not drawing the slightest glance from the unemployed educational-radio consultant who lived next door to me as I flung myself past her through the doorway and slammed the door shut. She had kept her back turned toward me at all times, singing to herself full-throated, using the stairwell as an echo chamber.

I showered fast, dressed my wounds, dressed wet in clean clothes then headed out, after bagging my incriminatingly filthy clothes up tight. My jacket had been sponged clean of blood. I passed my neighbor again and she was still singing.

The hour was just about up. I hailed a cab off Divinity and made it to where I was going with few minutes to spare.

I had to laugh. My brain was working funny—the ride had so depleted me, blood was no longer carrying adequate amounts of oxygen to my brain. I had a flickering thought before I went inside.

The thought made me stop to buy some coffee in the shop at the lobby—two cups—then at the front desk. I asked to see Detective Ellroy, slurring my speech and wavering in my stance. Ellroy emerged with daunting speed, sat down with me on a bench amid the quiet hubbub of police headquarters at holiday time and told me to get lost. I told him I wanted to confess. He smiled broadly and said that was a different story. He would listen.

I offered him a cup of coffee. He said sure.

I threw the thing in his face, drenched him good.

To my amusement he shrieked like a baby, even though I had thoughtfully added cream.

When he punched me with a wild though seasoned punch which caught me this time in the shoulder, I snapped out my right arm and punched him back, square on the bridge of the nose. He yowled. In short order, I was cuffed, cuffed about, then tossed into the drunk tank—not arrested but slammed into protective custody. After all, there were just too many gray areas about the incident to press charges. I was obviously drunk and slipped, it was a mistake. I wasn't under arrest, yet he hit me when he could have arrested me. On and on.

They booted me out at 6 am, bloodied and unkempt again.

I went home ignored, tossed my bag of clothes into the incinerator and slept the sleep of the wretched and depleted.

Before I did, I went down to the basement to watch them burn.

I learned from Action Team News that "Everybody's Favorite Busybody," as Bennie had come to be known, had been pronounced dead late on Thanksgiving, the victim of a fire. Arson was suspected and being investigated. I later learned that the "deadly blaze" was the result of a furnace that had gone years without having been properly inspected. I was shocked by Karenina's lack of thoroughness there. Or had Bennie lied about it to save money?

There was quite a bit of news about Bennie, grieving friends and relatives trickling tears and trembling lips on television. I watched none of it.

The *Register* published a memorial edition.

Goody-two-shoes called me the next Monday to let me know details about Dwight's funeral—where and when. He went quickly, she said, surrounded by loved ones. I had been a good friend to the last. She knew he wanted me to be there. I went, wearing a new gray mourning suit bought with the last of my savings. There was a crowd of urban grandees, lawyers, and several recognizable lesser Forrestals in attendance and—true to Dwight's specifications—no eulogy. I suppose in all the wonderful lies he told, Dwight had nothing but impatience for fulsome and substandard product being laid about his casket like cheesy garlands of plastic flowers. I sat in my place on the church pew, alone, cursing him for being right about my wearing a suit to his funeral, cursing him for making me live further outside the means of my inadequate checks from Chattels and Pelf than I might have if I had kept true to my principles.

And then I had to laugh along with life at that.

I kept calling him a bastard all through the service, sitting alone as the mourners, sycophants and socialites commended his spirit to god. I knew he was there all the time, hoping to hear all the dirt, lurid content emphasized, and to the devil with the god to whom we were giving him up. I gave him all the details, and people near me moved away, justifiably thinking I was crazy. Dwight left me with an approving chuckle.

"You done good."

When it was time to go, I folded the program and crammed it into one of the formerly stitched-up pockets of the suit's jacket and skirted the long receiving line that had formed to condole Goody-two-shoes, her son and several of Dwight's other children from his previous marriages. I was tapped on the shoulder by a weedy man wearing hornrims, a patently more expensive suit than mine under his open mourning coat and a sadly bedraggled expression. He introduced himself as a partner in the law firm of Hawking, Weaver and Dun. He was Hawking. I believed him, as he looked about ninety, with wattles and jowls that wagged at the floor. He suggested I visit his office as soon as it was convenient. When I asked him why I should, he pressed one of his business cards into the palm of my hand with near violence then had to steady himself on his cane.

"Because *I* am the executor of the late Mr. DeSeigneur's will."

I stood there staring at the card as Dickie Gunn stopped in front of me, shot me an angry glance, then shunned my response as he made his way out of the Miltown Church of the Advent. By then Hawking had hobbled off and was gone.

You can guess that I was eagerly present at Hawking's office the next morning. Despite the firm's occupying the twelve most choice floors of Miltown's Furtum Building, it took very little time for me to get to see Hawking, Weaver and Dun's remaining founding partner. Upon my entering, he tossed me a thick envelope as soon as I could get near enough to his desk in the cavernous glass-walled aquarium that passed for his office.

"News clippings. That's what it says he left you," Hawking said testily.

I started to open it; but he cautioned me not to. Hawking explained that he was bound to make sure all appropriate state and federal inheritance taxes were paid upon bequests of certain monetary value—this pertained *especially* to cash bequests. News clippings—which the will stipulated he had left me—had no such value and were therefore exempt. If that's indeed what was in the envelope. Hawking was sure that's what it was, read the section of the will whereby I was to receive the corpus of Dwight's journalistic "dirty work" to inspire me. And there had been a lot of it. He shot me a remorseless stare and practically snarled that I was free to open the envelope anywhere I chose. *Anywhere.* I said thank you and left.

I later opened it lying idly on my bed, suppressing a headache and playing music to drown out Bootlicker's incessant TV. A note from Dwight was the first item to be removed, taped as it was to the lip of the envelope.

"*Look,* Kiddo," it read.

"By this time, I'm dead and you're seriously in the shit. I knew it would happen, because I know you scholarship boys by heart—always destroying yourselves by trying to act like goddamn gentlemen. Whatever happened, I'm convinced you've either nuked whatever career you had left in this sorry jerkwater city by bucking our fellow newsies' love for Bennie and by royally screwing him up somehow. Maybe even getting him arrested, if not yourself. Anyway, I know you've botched things up so brilliantly by now that *no one* is going to do a thing for you. No one. Not that anyone would have anyway, seeing that you're such a social nonentity in this very social world. So, this is my way of saying thanks for the smokes, Kiddo.

"One last thing: I know you never listen to me, but I suggest that this time you do. Get out of town while you can, if you can.

"Another last thing: I think I enjoyed your kinky romp a whole hell of a lot more than you did!

"I'll be looking for a hot spot in Hell to keep us both occupied for when you get here—you know we bore easy.

"You done good, Kiddo!

"Unregenerately,

"Dwight DeSeigneur"

I counted out an even $50,000, in big bills, the smallest being hundreds.

It didn't take long to leave.

Which brings us here, to where we are now, to the city of restless rain and grim warmth. It brings us to this room and our mutual pursuit- -or my pursuit, as your fulfillment lies over there somewhere in my bag, in my checkbook. This is agreeable to me. We are here for me, only for me. I know this city has a scene: another bar, private club, support group, Internet chat society formed out of some typographic chat room available on whatever America's favorite on-line comicbook is winning the market this month. I know I don't have to pay for it. I know I can't afford the price of not paying for it. You know I can't. You've seen it before. It's why I called you.

It's how we agreed on a price.

Now you're not so sure after hearing all that.

You think I have violent fantasies—that I might snap back, switch and hurt you.

Don't you understand? *You're* the one here to do the hurting.

Don't you understand? My submission is assured. I have always been submissive. Always. I will always be, even should I switch, should I betray my soul and take what is never given, take what's mine.

Mine.

I know how you want me. Let me undress, climb into the stirrups suspended from steel chains hung in parallel from the ceiling.

They look like they'll hold. Yes, my body is good. I need it to be.
We're falling into it, aren't we? You know I know how it will play,
how we will play. Go ahead. Lay the stroke, bring me up strong and
solid to your best apogee of impact and will.

Go ahead.

You feel me there. You feel it with every good strike that brings
my body up and chivvies down my mind to a moan. You feel it. I
know you're smiling. I know it.

You might walk past me at the airport, sit next to me on the
subway, do business with me some other way. We could have a
pleasant chat as between strangers. You could trust me as a confidant.
You could fear me as a competitor in the office. Notice me chatting
idly in a pack of drab-looking friends.

There are so many of us all around you.

And you might know me from this pursuit alone.

The strikes are getting better, harsher, biting with more directness. You feel the rightness of it, see my blood is up. What?

You want to know what I think of it all, what I'll carry away
with me as a remembrance?

What I will treasure?

Let me tell you:

I think of the pain.

I think of the pain.

I think of the *pain*.